THE POWER AND PERIL OF THE CROWN . . .

Surrounded by deadly, sword-wielding attackers, I had no choice but to don the crown I had sworn never to wear again. The sensation of remoteness, of endless power, flowed through me, exactly as of old. My arm and hand were sticky with my own blood, but I scarcely felt the wound as I called to the enemy spearmen: "Turn, you lice, and look upon your destroyer!"

At my mental gesture, a cold white light began to flow from the Crown, and the faces of my opponents turned blank with horror and dismay. Triumph was within my grasp until I made the mistake of saying, I alone am in charge here."

Suddenly, a grip of numbing power closed around my brow. I leaped up; my scalp felt aflame. The doors of my head were being closed up, imprisoning me within. "Who is in charge?" the Crown echoed my words nastily. Then, stripped of all sensation, I floated in nothingness. Even the pounding of my heart in my chest was gone. Surely from here the only portal was to the Deadlands. . . .

THE NAME OF THE SUN

B.W. Clough

DAW BOOKS, INC.
DONALD A. WOLLHEIM, PUBLISHER

1633 Broadway, New York, NY 10019

First Printing, June 1988

1 2 3 4 5 6 7 8 9

PRINTED IN THE U.S.A.

To Diana,
who left her mark on the manuscript.

THE
KNOWN WORLD
AS MAPPED BY
XALAN MASTER MAGUS

50 LEAGUES
130 MILES

CITY
ENNELITH-RAL
MISHBIL
OORSEVESH
E-BASU
COLB
UWUNA
RRIPHIRRIZĒ

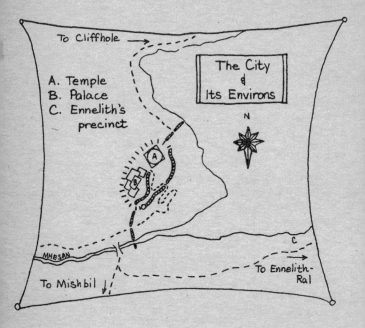

To Cliffhole →

A. Temple
B. Palace
C. Ennelith's
   precinct

The City
&
Its Environs

N

MHESAN

To Mishbil ↓

C

To Ennelith-Ral

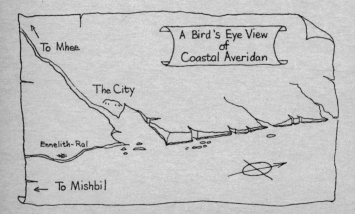

To Mhee ↖

The City

A Bird's Eye View
of
Coastal Averidan

Ennelith-Ral

← To Mishbil

What has gone before

Liras-ven Tsormelezok, a young nobleman, is surprised when he suddenly becomes Shan King. The monarch of Averidan is selected by a mysterious process from all Viridese of royal descent. Since that class includes nearly everyone in the realm, Liras justifiably feels ill-used. His reluctance turns into horror when he dons the Crystal Crown and finds it is far more than the insignia of an absolute monarch. The Crown confers peculiar powers upon its wearer and exacts a price for them. His nerve cracks, and Liras leaves town, taking with him a young magus named Xalan.

Their hasty escape ends in disaster after the two are robbed in the desert. They are rescued by one Sandcomber, a foreigner of a race never seen before in Averidan. Exhorted and braced by Sandcomber's advice, Liras returns to the City and achieves his first uneasy mastery over the Crown.

A state marriage is contracted for Liras with Melayne, a princess of the neighboring country of Cayd. In return for her hand Liras leads an army to the west to help the Cayds battle the renegade magus Xerlanthor. After several fights they defeat him. Liras returns home and discovers his Caydish in-laws plan to murder him and take over the country. With the Crystal Crown's help he foils these plans.

Two years later the Cayds return in force and conquer much of western Averidan. They attack the City and after a bitter siege it falls. The Crystal Crown betrays Liras, battling him for possession of his own body. The Cayds capture him and take the Crown. Abandoned by the Sun, his tutelary deity, Liras forswears religion and resigns himself to death.

The pregnant Melayne defies her brothers Mor and Musenor to rescue Liras. She spirits him to the coast, where his mother is organizing a resistance movement. Liras and Xalan trick the Crystal Crown away from the usurper King Mor. But in token of his breach from traditional Shan belief, and from pure cowardice, Liras does not dare to wear the Crown again.

Xalan accompanies Liras, Melayne, and the new baby in their escape up the coast. The Cayds track them relentlessly. Just when all seems lost they see Sandcomber on a ship, making ready to sail back to his distant home. They invite themselves aboard and join the expedition.

The greatest thing a human soul ever does in this world is to see something. Hundreds of people can talk for one who thinks, but thousands can think for one who can see. To see clearly is poetry, prophecy and religion all in one.

—John Ruskin, *Modern Painters*, Vol. III

Flora sighed. It was curious that persons who lived what the novelists called a rich emotional life always seemed to be a bit slow on the uptake.

—Stella Gibbons, *Cold Comfort Farm*

CHAPTER 1

An Undignified Escape

My fundamental mental error centered upon all the stories and plaiv. Like every Viridese my head was stuffed full of them, epics crammed with incredible coincidence and romantic revelations of unsuspected kinship. In them the Shan King of Averidan always wins. Alas, the adventures of Liras-ven Tsormelezok, Shan King, did not tend that way. First the war went against us. Now, hounded from my realm, I found myself escaping to sea. It was unreasonable to feel deprived of my just due, but I did. "There is no such thing as an exiled Viridese monarch," I tried to explain to Sandcomber.

Being a foreigner, our rescuer naturally did not understand. "Why should you not be the first, Liras, my friend? You have the Crystal Crown, do you not? And there is no other requisite for rule, in your unusual country."

This was not the moment to explain that I could no longer don the terrible Crown. Xalan called to us from up on the high poop deck. We ran to the ladder and I swarmed up first, leaving Sandcomber to hoist his white-clad bulk up more slowly.

Our ship, the *Kingfisher*, had swung far out to sea, to elude pursuers and dodge shoals. Now from the deck we watched a number of ships coming to meet us from various directions, as we angled back toward land. "Those *could*, of course, be a messenger craft and its escort." Sandcomber's oddly-accented Viridese

12

freighted the words with hope. "Perhaps in your brief absence your folk have thrown down the Cayds, their conquerors, and with pomp and joy now restore you to the lordship of Averidan."

"Perhaps ducks will grow teeth and refuse to be roasted any more," I said, more crossly than was strictly regal. The Cayds' anxiety to despatch me was in downright poor taste.

"Now, the ducks in my country do indeed have teeth." An equable smile spread over Sandcomber's dark-skinned face, fringed all around by fluffy white hair and a rim of equally fluffy beard. "But we roast them anyway."

A high gray sky, featureless and bland as the back of a shield, arched overhead. The cold damp wind set from the southwest. Though spring had begun, the day was more reminiscent of late winter. Wisps of vapor blew over the surface of the lead-colored ocean. Most of the vessels in the distance were fishing boats and shrimp trawlers—hostile, I expected. With his magic mirror Xalan confirmed this. "Their sailors are Shan, but Cayds walk among them with bared axes and long knives," he reported, leaning elbows on red-clad knees to gaze into his glass. "They must have planned this, in case you fled south. Can we fight so many?"

"We'll have to." The only real sea battle in Averidan had been fought many hundreds of years ago, but I spoke as firmly as possible so that no one would remember this. "But what about that big ship there, to the south? That's no fishing boat."

Obediently Xalan shifted his scry. "Oh, ho! Hooray! We're saved! They're friends!" He rocked back on his rump, uncrossing his legs and expertly untangling them from his long red robe before jumping to his feet. "It's the lady Zaryas!"

Xalan and I dashed to the poop rail, waving and yelling like idiots. Sandcomber went aft to tell the pilot to swing the *Kingfisher* around. I had fought so long almost alone, that I nearly forgot my strongest

ally. During the siege Zaryas, viceroy of Mishbil in the
south, had sent a fleet on an abortive rescue attempt.
This vessel, looming bigger and more cheering every
moment, must be one of its survivors. And, sure
enough, there was the princess herself on the fighting
deck, her gray hair covered by a helmet.

"She's a phenomenon," Xalan said with pride, for
his family hails from Mishbil. "How many ladies of
seventy could build and command a battle fleet?"

"I was sure she died when the ships were burned
and scuttled."

"The lady Zaryas can survive anything. You should
ask my grandfather, sometime, about the Mishbil
flood."

Soon we could make out the name of the ship, *Lily
of the South*, neatly lettered in red Viridese characters
along the rail. The princess wore a very sour expression, and even from this distance her dark, keen eyes
flashed. Cupping her hands round her mouth she called,
"Look in your mirror!"

The hiss of the waves and the steady wind made me
doubt I had heard right. "What did she say?" I asked
Xalan.

"Your *mirror!*" she yelled.

"She must mean this," Xalan said, puzzled. He
drew his thick round mirror from the case strung around
his neck, and glanced dubiously into it. "Oh! There's
Xeel, one of the magi of Mishbil. He's, yes, on board
with the princess."

"I see him!" I could just glimpse a head and red-
clad back through the *Lily*'s rail, crouched close beside Lady Zaryas. The *Lily* had evidently been com-
missioned as a coastal trader and only recently converted
to a war ship. Her reworked hull rode the waves much
less smoothly than our solid *Kingfisher*, sliding up and
down in a way that must have made everyone aboard
queasy. The hapless Xeel plainly did not dare to stand
upright on the bucking deck, and risk losing his precious mirror overside. "What does he say?"

"Uh—" Xalan hesitated a moment. "He says that

she says to put about instantly, and sail farther out to sea. The Cayds are almost upon us."

"Viris!" His words were like a bucket of cold water. I had completely forgotten about our pursuers. I ran aft to tell the steersman, tripping over my own feet in my haste.

Xalan trotted close behind, rapidly reciting, "He says that she says the *Lily* will follow. We should have been communicating by mirror all this time, she says. She says you should never have let the Order of Magi be split, some to support the invaders and some faithful to you."

"I didn't plan it that way," I said indignantly. The steersman had his own little booth at the very stern. "Head her to the east, quickly!" I commanded him.

I dashed across the deck to the forward rail and shouted to Sandcomber on the main deck below, to have the crew raise more sail. At my elbow, Xalan said, "He says that she says your advisors should all be lapidated, unless King Mor has done us the favor of beheading them. He says she says that your new Master Magus—" Here Xalan faltered a bit, for he himself actually held that office now. "Well, she says I'm as feckless as a day-fly and have no more sense than a two-year-old child."

"Why don't you spare me the 'he says she says,' " I suggested.

A look of alarm spread over Xalan's long face, and his thin, sunburned cheeks flushed redder. "The Lady Zaryas didn't want there to be any mistake, about whose opinions these are. She was very firm to Xeel about that."

"I'll wager she was." As I climbed down the ladder past the luridly painted poop to the deck, I could just make out the unceasing movements of my redoubtable viceroy's lips. I felt deeply grateful for the water that separated us.

The *Kingfisher*'s head came slowly around, and more glazed-linen sails were hoisted. The *Lily* cut past behind us. I realized that the gallant princess intended to hold off our pursuers until I, her King, could flee. This torrent of naggery and advice was being hastily sent in case she did not survive to deliver it in person. I swallowed the sudden lump in my throat and said, "What else does she say?"

Xalan shot me a glance of exaggerated surprise. "You want more? Well, he says she says that after we break away, we should cut back east to Ennelith-Ral. That's where the *Lily* took refuge, after the harbor battle . . ."

The wind was not particularly favorable to our new course. Our smaller, faster enemies evaded the *Lily* and swarmed around both ships like wasps, trying to cut us off. I hailed Sandcomber, whose long white robes fluttered like banners as he paced back and forth. "Archers—do you have any bowmen aboard?"

"The *Kingfisher* is a merchanter, not a warship," Sandcomber said. In his own language, he tallied men and weapons. "With only half a dozen crew we have few to spare from handling the ship. There are javelins and bows prepared against the day we shall need to hunt our own meals. What of the Lady Melayne? Is she not an excellent bowman?"

My wife was indeed, having learned the art in her native Cayd. Unfortunately, her landlocked heritage had left her acutely subject to seasickness. When I explained this to Sandcomber, he sighed deeply. "Then two bowmen are all I may offer you. Will they suffice?"

"They must," I said. It was plain that Sandcomber had fought even fewer battles than I. Posting the two archers amidships, I ordered them not to waste arrows on distant foes, but to shoot when the vessels came close. They could dart between the port and starboard rails, as targets offered.

There was nothing more to do now but wait. I became aware of Xalan's voice again, which all this time had continued to repeat Zaryas' sound advice and tart criticisms. "You don't want to be in the battle, do you?" I interrupted him.

"To be truthful, no," Xalan admitted. "But shouldn't I be nearby in case you, ah—"

"I won't die today, I promise." Thus reassured, Xalan retreated to the foredeck. Already one boat was close enough to see into; the deck of the little pinnace was crammed with fair-haired foreign warriors. I drew my sword and watched the boat edge closer.

The two vessels skimmed side by side for only an instant. But several Cayds dared to jump the gap, and I thought we were lost. Then our steersman veered the *Kingfisher* away, and to my stupefaction I saw that no lines or grappling hooks had been fastened. If we had little practical knowledge of sea-battle, the Cayds had even less. These few warriors had sundered themselves from their friends. The knowledge seemed to bother them not at all. Seeing me, they raised their axes and yelled barbaric battle cries.

I fingered the razor edge of my sword and drew a deep breath. After years of pursuing courage, I had finally stumbled on the trick of it. There is a realm that underlies our own, nearer than the palm of a hand, yet foreign as the back of one's head: the mythic country of plaiv and legend. I stepped over the unseen divide into that country, and nothing changed to the eye. But now I too was more than real, briefly borrowing the inexhaustible power and uncanny luck of the Shan heroes. To duck under the sweeping axe stroke of an approaching Cayd was simplicity itself, and no fear oppressed me as I hacked at his throat. Hot blood spattered my face, and renewed the stains on my yellow tunic. I elbowed my dying opponent into the path of the second Cayd, and as he dodged cut at the third. His leather helm could not turn my blade; bits of skull and brain flew in a grisly spray across the deck.

The last, seeing himself alone, took a stand with his back to the central mast. I paused. As the dancers are confident the flutes will chime in at a certain point, so I was sure that some happenstance would distract him. Sure enough, the *Kingfisher* turned again, into the wind, and the sail above us snapped like a wet towel against its rigging. As the Cayd's eyes flicked upward, I lunged. My knee took him hard in the stomach, and he crumpled with a wheeze and a gasp.

I like to think of myself as a clement person. My personal inclination now was to spare my helpless opponent—or at most toss him overside to take his chances with Ennelith Sea Queen. But I was no longer myself, and the person I became on the other side did not hesitate. My foot flicked out to nudge the Cayd onto his back. His blue eyes bulged, and the fair beard split as he cried out either defiance or fear. He tried to writhe out of the way, but too slowly. With deliberate precision my sword curved down and across, gutting him like a pig in a butcher's yard. But at least the subdivided pigs are dead. The life lingered yet in the dead man. He clawed at his scattered intestines and glared up at me with an absurd outrage. I kicked the hand aside, and trod on the shining pink loops.

A haze seemed to lift. With an almost palpable thump I fell back into reality. The *Kingfisher*'s twisting evasions had brought her very near the *Lily* again. That vessel, better prepared than we, slung a firepot onto one trawler. Its Shan crew had instantly abandoned ship, leaving their Caydish oppressors to splash sea water on the flame. A few of the Cayds' vessels turned to help them, but the rest continued to harass us. Some tried to close and board, while the faster skiffs cut across our course to slow our escape.

The riven corpse still fixed me with a reproachful blue-eyed glare. A butchery litter of organs, limbs, and miscellaneous fluids fouled the deck. My hands, my sword, my clothes, even my face, all were sticky and red—a souvenir of what the realm beneath was like. A deadly nausea gripped me. With the last of my strength I tottered to the port rail. I vomited as if my body revolted against its very soul.

Such undignified ailments do not afflict heroes in stories. Fortunately, no one aboard had time to notice me. Up on the foredeck Xalan shouted innovative suggestions to the Cayds, a waste of energy since they spoke no Viridese. As a geomant, a student of earth magics, Xalan's usefulness at sea was limited. The sailors busily aimed their arrows off to starboard. On the poop Sandcomber shouted frantic instructions at the sailors in the rigging, who persisted in pausing at their work to watch the fight. Another boat edged close to our port side. I leaned exhausted on the rail and watched without interest as Caydish bowmen fired across the gap. The swaying decks and blowing mist made archery chancy at best. Bronze-headed arrows clattered and thudded along the planking around me.

Other Cayds crowded onto the rail, ready to jump as soon as the ships were close enough. They brandished their axes and yelled imprecations in their own tongue: "Witch-King!" "Monster!" I stared across the gap with a vague envy. How pleasant it must be, to live in so simple a world.

Closer yet, and closer—I could make out the bright curling hairs on the bare forearms of the foe. The archers gave over firing and poised for the leap. But just then their ship swerved sharply away. The sudden course change jerked most of them off the rail and into the sea. Weighted by their bronze-sewn armor, the Cayds had to thrash to stay afloat. And as the ship veered off, I saw its steersman—a Viridese, of course, since the Cayds cannot sail. Discreetly, behind the screen of his cloak, he waved at me. Even through the gathering fog, I was sure I saw him wink.

My horror lifted, and I sat down on the deck and laughed like a fool. The Shan are rather soft and unwarlike, but it seemed a leaven of strength still lingered. The remaining Cayds howled their frustration, and more arrows fell whistling around me. But I did not stir until Xalan hurried down to drag me under cover.

"You aren't proof against arrow-shot, we've seen that before," he scolded when we were safe behind some rolled sail.

I ignored him and peered through the rail. We were

startled to see the *Lily* crowding very near. Her wooden flank seemed close enough to touch, and for the first time direct conversation was possible. "Halloo, Xeel!" Xalan called. "Are you a good sailor?"

"No!" the other magus yelled, and indeed his face was white and shiny with sweat. "Greetings, Your Majesty," he added, seeing me. Clammy threads of mist swirled thinly between us.

"Where is the lady Zaryas?" I demanded, but even as I spoke I saw her, staggering forward against the lurch of the ship with a large burlap-wrapped bundle in her arms.

"Here, you," she unceremoniously commanded Xalan. "Unclip that boathook above your head and drag this over." Xalan hurried to obey. To me she said in a stern level tone, "The priestesses of Ennelith did the best they could with this. There are finger-sized slips of gold sewn into the wadding below the shoulders, front and back. And there's a small pearl quilted into every one of the lower squares. Don't you dare let it drop overside," she admonished Xalan.

"The lower squares of what?" I asked, bewildered.

"It's a significant fraction of the Treasury of the Goddess," she said, passing over my question. "You might say the priestesses are betting the holy money—on you." She scowled at me from under her helmet brim, a hardened gambler inspecting badly loaded dice.

With a grunt of effort Xalan hauled the bundle over our rail. When I helped him to unhook it from the pole, I nearly dropped it, it was so heavy. "Haven't had a chance to tell you," Xalan panted. "He said she said that Ennelith-Ral will fall."

I understood. This pathetic bundle was all that could be spirited out of the holy city to me before its sack. The fog curdled between the two ships, which were edging a little farther apart. A fine misty rain began to fall. I stared across at Zaryas of Mishbil, yearning to somehow tap her experience and intelligence. Once, the Crystal Crown could let me do that, I remembered wistfully. This war had always been beyond me.

A more or less steady racket of battle surrounded us, sails flapping, steering cables groaning, Cayds yelling in their own language, and we Shan calling comments and encouragement. Suddenly the noise increased tremendously. Xeel and Zaryas were jerked off their feet by some impact. Leaning over the rail to look, Xalan reported, "Incredible! The *Lily* has actually run over a sailboat!"

"Accidentally, I hope. I suppose their pilot will blame the fog." We were on the whole rather impressed with the *Lily*'s little victory—too ignorant to know that ships must be specially built for ramming. When the *Lily* began to list, we could only gape in astonishment. "Will you put that bundle away safe?" was Zaryas' only concern. "And don't fall overboard while wearing it! The weight would drag you to the Deadlands before your time."

"Right away," I called back, still not really alarmed. With some difficulty we hoisted the burlap parcel into the nearest locker, among the extra ropes and bronze pulleys. "We can drag it up to the cabin later—" I began.

Xalan broke in with a wordless yell. I whirled. The *Lily* was turning turtle, wallowing over onto her port side as the top-heavy mast dragged her over. A tangle of spars and sails stooped over our heads like bats, drooping lower and lower.

"You, Xeel!" I shouted. "Lift the princess here, to safety!" For magi can use their arts to walk on air, a very useful trick.

But to my surprise Zaryas seemed to be countermanding my order. With an apologetic gesture Xeel rose slowly up into the white-veiled sky, empty-handed. "No," Xalan said. "He's got a knife, can you see?" The magus began to hack at the ropes, and I suddenly knew. The *Lily*'s rigging was fouling our own. If the masts and ropes were not cut free, she would drag us down as she sank. Xalan, far quicker than I, had already seized an axe and soared up to chop at the spars. Already one could sense, whenever the *Kingfisher* rolled starboard, that she did not roll quite back again. The *Lily*'s weight was pressing us dangerously.

The sailors scurried to help, swinging from mast to mast like monkeys. Sandcomber yelled incomprehensibly at me. Not until the gray-faced pilot dashed down to pluck at my sleeve did I remember the danger from falling spars and tackle. I followed him up to the poop. From its height we could just make out the *Lily*'s plight through the mist. Like vultures, the smaller Caydish craft circled the wreck, and to our horror we saw they were killing the swimming survivors, prodding with javelins or hacking with axes in a splash of red water. "Barbarians!" the pilot said, making an avert sign. "Ennelith will be furious." He glanced worriedly up at the raveling streamers of fog.

"So am I." The Caydish blood-thirst made my stomach turn, and impotent fury made my voice shake. I was numbly glad that the roiling sea mist hid most of the carnage, and then ashamed of my gladness. "Dive!" I yelled into the milky void. "Swim and dive! Hide in the fog!" The pursuing boats seemed to be losing interest, and I thought my advice was sound.

Then Sandcomber grabbed my arm. "What is that?"

We stared into the blank bright wall of fog until our eyes ached. All I heard was a rhythm of shouts. The Cayds were yelling, cheering someone on. With my smattering of Caydish I was able to translate, "They say, 'go! go!' But who are they, and where do they go?"

The pilot pointed aft. The breeze shifted slightly, clearing a brief opening in the mist. Directly down the wind came a trawler. Propelled by sail and oar, it slid faster and faster at us. "They're not going to board," I cried. "They mean to ram!"

At my warning everyone clutched the rails and benches as if we were already drowning. Egged on by their fellows, the Cayds seemed intoxicated by excitement. With terrific speed the trawler hit the helpless *Kingfisher* on one side of her stern. Its momentum was so great that the trawler drove part way up the stern before crashing back down again. The vessel broke into several pieces and almost instantly sank beneath the surface. "May the starfish gnaw them!" the pilot groaned.

The impact might have flung more overboard if we had not had an instant's warning. As it was, one sailor was jerked loose from the rigging and fell with a wailing cry into the sea, where the Cayds waited. We clung, staring at one another, for a long moment. But our brave *Kingfisher* showed no signs of sinking. There was still hope. If we could cut ourselves free from the wreckage of the *Lily*, the fog would be our friend. Under its cold shield we might slip away to sea.

With feverish haste we hurried to break away. It was a cruelly difficult job to do by guess and touch, for by this time the masts and riggings might have been wrapped in wool. Down at sea level the miasma was a little less, and we saw the shapes of our enemies, dark against the darker water, moving back and forth as they trolled for swimmers. I trailed one length of line over the side, hoping that a survivor of the *Lily* would find it and climb up. But none did, and I did not dare to drop another rope elsewhere, lest some Cayd find it. As it was I had to ceaselessly patrol the middeck, in case they dared to storm us.

An eternity later we were able to begin easing the *Kingfisher* away from the wreck of the *Lily*. It was not possible to do this silently, as we shoved with poles and dragged at tangled spars and ropes and hissed urgent commands at one another. The Cayds must have known we were up to something. "But we shall slip away yet," Sandcomber vowed. He rubbed his broad dark hands together. "As soon as we are clear, sail shall be very quietly raised, and we can rest. Would you mind, my friend, bringing up some oil? Some of these pulleys are too noisy."

From the white curds above Xalan said, "That's not a proper task for His Majesty."

"That's right," Xeel agreed.

"Whisper if you have to talk!" I hissed back, acutely

conscious of listening enemies. "Of course it's a proper task, while the Cayds are busy elsewhere. And you, Xeel—since we're nearly free, lift over to the *Lily* and see if anyone is alive. The lady Zaryas' fate weighs on my mind."

It was impossible for me to see whether Xeel obeyed, but I was sure he would. I made my way to the deck hatch. At the foot of the ladder I groped about for the clay lamp and tinderbox. They were where Sandcomber had said they would be, and after I fumbled inexpertly with the flints the little wick caught.

Viridese merchant ships are built of several watertight compartments. The little wooden chamber I stood in was a sort of lobby with doors all around and a trap in the floor, that let one into the various holds. The ghosts of every cargo the *Kingfisher* had ever carried lingered here—the stink of raw oxhide, a vinegary tang of cheap wine, the harsh smell of dye. I began jerking open doors, leaning in with the lamp to look for the ship's stores. When my light flickered and reflected off rising pools of water in the rear hold, I could hardly take it in for a moment. Then I blew out the lamp and tore back up the ladder.

"They're just getting ready to raise some sail," Xalan greeted me in a low voice. "Where's the oil, was it too heavy to carry?"

"No," I whispered back. "Sandcomber, we're leaking!"

A strangled panic began to infect us all at this fresh calamity. In an undertone Sandcomber mourned his ruined cargo of souvenirs. The steersman ran to test the response of the crushed rudder, and Xalan, obeying my muttered directions, swooped through the air to inspect the damage to the outside of the hull. The sailors, torn between two urgencies, darted back and forth, first forming a brief bucket line to bail out the hold, then swerving to attack the sails and drag at ropes.

Xalan returned to report, "The rudder is hanging loose. And there's a hole the size of a dog through the

stern planks." One sailor began to moan out prayers
to the sea goddess. Sandcomber raised his white halo
of beard to the sky and joined in with zest. "After all
my journeyings, through deplorable conditions of every description, to be holed by musclebound barbarians, and drowned like a runt in a bad year! The world
is cruel, the sea unjust!"

"Oh, hush!" Xalan exclaimed. "All isn't lost yet—at
the very worst I can lift His Majesty to safety."

Sandcomber poured scorn on this reassurance, en-
tering thoroughly into the situation. "What of your
beloved wife?" he reminded me. "Your newborn daughter? No, no, they must not perish! Better far, that you
move now to rescue us all. Are you not rightful King
of the Shan? Do you not possess the Crystal Crown,
abode of a fell and arcane power from the dawn of
your race? Save us, Lord of the Shan!"

Apparently our friend was capable of enjoying even
the most imminent peril. But the crew took his melo-
dramatic plea completely at face value, and what remained of their courage collapsed. To a man they
prostrated themselves on the deck, howling for me to
intervene with our patron deity the Sun. Their noise
roused our foes; the Cayds, who had boarded the *Lily*,
began to yell threats and clash their weapons. The
racket was meant to be intimidating, and in spite of
myself I felt it. It was hard not to think of baying wolf
packs, or hungry sea drakes gnashing their teeth. My
voice, when I spoke, sounded feeble in comparison: "I
no longer use the Crown to do miracles."

"Tripe!" Sandcomber dismissed cheerily. "Why not?"

With a sinking heart I realized that Sandcomber was
not being argumentative but really wanted to know. I
was at a loss, but Xalan supplied a sensible answer. "If
he could, how should we have lost the war?"

"The point has sorely taxed my curiosity," Sandcomber admitted. "How could a wealthy and populous realm, defended by strong magics and infected by
no discontent, be so easily overthrown?"

"The answer is twofold," I said harshly. "The Shan

were unbelieving and ill-prepared. But that would not have destroyed us, had not the god given us out of his hand."

It was almost a relief, to say aloud the terrible secret I had nursed alone for so long. But immediately I realized my mistake. The sailors wailed even louder. Xalan seemed stunned. I had just publicly abjured the foundation of our beliefs. And Sandcomber grinned so broadly his face was perfectly circled by its fluffy white beard and close-curled hair. "You must tell me all about it," he said. "My liver has been troubled all these years, on account of the Crystal Crown—my people hold that the liver is the seat of the intellectual appetites. The customs and superstitions of simpler cultures have fascinated me since youth."

I bridled at this condescending description. "In the first place, Averidan is not a simpler culture," I began crossly.

Beneath us the deck gave a slight lurch. It now had a definite list to port. The other holds would probably keep the *Kingfisher* afloat for a while, but in her crippled state the Cayds would have no difficulty overrunning her as soon as the fog lifted. Xalan broke in, "Suppose we argue later, eh?"

Emboldened by his example, the pilot crawled forward and hugged my feet. "Oh, Your Majesty, have pity on us. If you've fallen out with the Sun Temple, you could still intercede for us with Ennelith. It's her hand we're in now, anyway."

I was startled at the idea. "Surely she would never hear *me!*" The Shan King is the Son of the Sun; Ennelith has her own heirophants. But after all she is the first goddess of Averidan. More importantly, she had bet a substantial bundle of treasure on me through her priestesses and might well want the bet to pay off. Lastly, we were rapidly running out of options. A chilling noise of gurgling water came from below, and the deck sagged another handspan or so beneath us.

"Ennelith, Ennelith!" the sailors cried. "Pray to her, please, lord of the Shan!"

"Do, please," Sandcomber urged eagerly, as one might urge another helping onto a dinner guest.

Xalan rolled his eyes. "Maybe you'd better at least try," he agreed. "What have you to offer?"

For all the deities have their proper offering. The Sun accepts organic but nonvital presents, while river spirits are very partial to food and sweetmeats. Ennelith, as the quintessential female, is always offered jewels or clothing. With some regret I drew my sword again. Its hilt was carven into two ivory fishes reaching for a berry of sardonyx. I pried out this sardonyx bead with my dagger while Xalan steadied the bronze sword blade against a bulkhead. "If Ennelith doesn't regard this gift with favor, and if we ever come out of this, my mother will have something to say to you all," I threatened. "She gave me this sword, you know."

It took some nerve to stagger down the moisture-slickened slope of the deck to the lower rail. I hung on tight and leaned over the sea, which gleamed gray through the fog. "What if the gem falls onto a Caydish boat? I refuse to throw a gift to these barbarians."

"Just hurry and do it," Xalan said, floating in mid-air beside me. "After it fails, we'll think what else to do."

I let the bead fall and prayed aloud, "Ennelith Sea Queen, please rescue us, your loyal subjects."

"Is that *all?*" Sandcomber called, disappointed.

"I don't know any rites, or the ritual language." I carefully hauled myself back up the slanting deck, very tired. I hadn't slept last night, and had been fighting since dawn. Now that petitioning the goddess had failed, my duty was to escape. Xalan's offer would be the final resort; at this point the ship's boat was the most convenient way to safety. But my spirit quite failed at the thought of packing Melayne and the baby into the dinghy and trying to give the Cayds the slip on the open sea. Though time was short, I reclined on the planking with closed eyes and groaned at the burdens of being a hero.

"You must not collapse now," Sandcomber said

with repellent cheer "Xalan shall patch the hull from
without, while we bail . . ." His voice trailed off.

"Patch? What with?" Then Xalan gave a sort of
hiccup, and tugged at my foot. "Liras? Your Majesty,
wake up!"

"I'm not asleep." I sat up and rubbed my aching
legs. "What is it now?"

Sandcomber pointed wordlessly over the rail. I craned
my neck to look. A bluish phosphorescence was gathering on the surface of the water, a short distance
away. The veils of fog obscured it less and less as it
grew stronger. "It *could*, of course, be a natural phenomenon," Sandcomber said faintly. "Like the cold
fire one may see on tropical waters at night. I have
never seen it on a foggy day, but why should it not
occur then as well as at any other time?" But he did
not sound as if he believed it.

The blob of light spread, attaching long trailers and
glowing strings to itself. The central area was perhaps
a bowshot across. It looked like an enormous flat
octopus, with many long spidery legs, or a huge flat
flower. The weird soft illumination cut through the fog
like sunshine. "It *is* Ennelith," Xalan said, nervously
twiddling his long black wand. "Is it safe, what they're
doing?"

For the crew was edging down to crouch at the rail
and peek through the bars at the wonder. Apprehension had quite purged me of exhaustion. "I wish I had
never let you crowd me into this," I said. "I've had
bad luck, dealing with deities."

Abruptly the center of the glowing flower rose up.
The rounded peak went up and up, rail high, then
mast high, then higher yet. And suddenly we were
looking up at a gigantic woman with long phosphores-
cent green-blue hair. The shining wet upper slopes of
her enormous pale breasts just cleared the surface,
and she flung back a dripping tress of light with a
smooth arm about as big around as the *Kingfisher*'s
midsection. She surveyed us, cowering just below her
chin, without much favor. "Well, Shan King?"

Her voice was very deep, utterly wild and untamed. For an instant of sheer terror I thought my mouth was too dry to speak. Hoarsely I stuttered, "I, we are assailed by enemies. They've crippled our ship."

"I've been advised to save you," Ennelith said grudgingly. "'So I will bring you safe to your destination. Where do you go?"

No words would come, and desperately I kicked Xalan's ankle. He was pale as milk himself, but quickly asked Sandcomber, "Where *are* we going?"

Sandcomber was staring with bulging dark eyes at the goddess, clinging to the mast as if his legs would fail him. "Rriphirrizē," he managed to say.

I had never heard of the place, but never expected to—no one like Sandcomber had ever visited Averidan before. More surprisingly, the name was new to Ennelith too. But omniscience is not one of her attributes. "Is that on the sea?" she demanded.

No one said anything. The Sea Queen is notoriously capricious, with a very short attention span. In fact, the brevity of the worship services is one of the main foundations of her cult's popularity. Already I saw that the goddess was no longer looking at us. In a moment she would be gone, her favor forgotten, if we hesitated. "Sandcomber!" I barked. "Where is the nearest seaport to your homeland?"

"I shipped from Uwuna," he said weakly.

"We go to Uwuna," I shouted up at the goddess. She turned away, sinking back into the waves, and everyone moaned with despair. But the waves raised by Ennelith's body did not subside. Of their own accord they rocked bigger and bigger, as if stirred by a hurricane that we mortals could not feel. The total absence of wind, the still foggy air, made the experience doubly eerie. For a moment I could not shake the impression that we were on a *toy* boat, bobbing in the steamy confines of a bathtub while some gigantic bather absently scrubbed at his back.

The waves waxed so high the *Kingfisher* almost foundered. Suddenly, a huge glassy one arched roaring right up over us. Yelling, we grabbed at the rigging and rails, expecting to be washed overboard in an instant. It was a sad anticlimax when the wave never broke. Confused, I rolled over and looked up. The curve of the wave soared right over the mast and down the other side. I crawled over to the starboard rail and looked down. The arch of flowing water continued right down to the water line. The *Kingfisher* was cupped in a tunnel of endlessly rushing water that swirled continuously around her, safe as a bug in a bottle. Even the air had an echoing enclosed feeling, as if we were shut in a very large cave.

I dragged myself upright and almost fainted as the blood rushed to my feet. "We're safe," I announced, reeling. "Ennelith has us in her hand. I'm going to sleep now, and Viris help anyone who stops me!"

CHAPTER 2

An Unprecedented Voyage

For many days now I had not slept in a proper bed. Melayne took up almost all the space in the wide bunk in our cabin, and the baby slept in a nest of quilts in the protective curve of her arm. I slept on the floor rather than disturb them. In my exhaustion it felt comfortable as a down mattress.

Sometime that afternoon I woke briefly when the baby cried. Melayne put her to the breast and said, "You poor darling! Come sleep on the bed, Liras. I'm getting up."

Only half-awake, I crawled up into the bunk and blissfully snuggled under the covers into the warm spot Melayne had left. With a pillow jammed over my head I scarcely heard her cooing to little Tarys-yan: "Didn't my honey pot sleep well! Mother did too, once that dreadful tempest passed over. Now the ship isn't twisting or rolling, Mother feels good—no more seasickness! Perhaps we'll go down, after your lunch, and find some food for Mother too . . ."

Being only a few weeks old, Tarys' reply to this was a belch. The little smacking noises of her nursing and Melayne's inane motherly chatter soothed me into sleep again, and I did not hear Melayne go out. When she whirled back in and slammed the door behind her, it was a severe shock.

I clawed the pillow off and sat up, mumbling. Melayne snatched it from me and cried, "What is going on, on this terrible boat? What are we doing in the *water?*"

"Boats are always in the water," I said, lying down again and trying to gather my wits.

Melayne stamped her foot and dragged the quilts off before I could draw them up. "Answer me, Liras! The boat has *sunk* in the storm, is that it? Have we drowned? WHAT WILL HAPPEN TO THE BABY?"

Sensing her mother's emotion, Tarys began to wail. There was no hope of any more sleep, and I sat up again. My eyes felt swollen and grainy from lack of rest, and my limbs ached from fighting. Melayne shifted the baby to her shoulder and leaned on the pillows beside me. Her long red-brown plaits hung in a thick twisted rope down her back, and a no-nonsense light glinted in her eye. I tried to remember where it had all begun. "Actually, dearest, it's been relatively calm. But there was a sea battle. Your kinsmen tried to capture us, and forced us away from port."

With a jerk Melayne sat up, tense with fury. "I'm never going to forgive Mor for this!" she cried.

I nodded, infinitely preferring Melayne to be angry with her brother rather than me. "Yes, and they rammed a big hole into the *Kingfisher*, and we did begin to sink." When I explained about Ennelith Sea-Queen, though, her mouth began to sag open. By the time I concluded, "And she's very kindly transporting the entire ship to Uwuna," Melayne had edged away to the farthest corner of the bunk.

"First that Crown, and now this! You must be a witch, Liras!"

She used the Caydish word our enemies disparage me with, and I felt rather hurt until I realized she was not serious.

The *Kingfisher* did not move very far beneath the surface. During daylight hours we could see the Sun describe its course across the quivery flat circle that the horizon had become, a short distance above the rotating arch of water. Ennelith could apparently haul our ship and its accompanying bubble of air at a supernatural speed through the depths. Beyond the glassy arching walls we could see occasional schools of fish, always sliding back and being left behind at an amazing rate. At this rate we should get to Uwuna in no time.

Sandcomber's state was truly pitiable. Even his well-fleshed face seemed to sag. For the first day or two he haunted the common room, refusing to step on deck except to scurry to his cabin. When he had to go out, he would often start violently and whirl, glaring at the endlessly moving wall of water as if he expected to see Ennelith's gigantic face pressed against it, watching us.

"It's just that I have never had dealings with a goddess," he explained, with some embarrassment. "You see I have never believed in their existence at all. You Shan are more accustomed, I am sure."

'We are not," Xalan said. "Last night I dreamed that a large pin pricked our bubble." He shuddered. We were in the common room, which took up most of the poop's lower level, the cabins being located above. Our meal was dried meat, barley porridge, pickled cabbage, dried fruit, and bread. From the square cabin window we could see the water flowing down in a solid wall about two feet away from the glass. It would have been like being under a waterfall, except for the eerie silence; the ceaselessly circling water made only a slight rippling noise. The view from Sandcomber's cabin window was worse—on that side the water flowed *upward*, a very unsettling sight indeed.

I saw that Sandcomber had scarcely touched a morsel. To be unable to enjoy your food is deplorable to Shan thinking, and I resolved to cheer my friend up. "How can you not believe in gods?" I rallied him. "When you've spent so many months in a country founded by one?"

"There are no genuine ones where I come from." Sandcomber raised his bowed head and glanced at me in his old skeptical way. "As to the founding of

Averidan, I seriously doubt the tale. Why should a deity, even if he exists, desire a mortal woman? Like mates with like."

Of course Sandcomber is very wise, and I had known he would have an unanswerable retort. All the same I felt uncommonly silly. Xalan, however, grinned at him. "I don't think anyone in your current situation, Sandcomber, can dare to disbelieve."

Sandcomber's face filled with apprehension again, and I frowned reprovingly at Xalan. "I only wish we had been more sensible about our request," I said. "The lady Zaryas was right, Xalan. Why don't you advise me better? We should have asked the goddess to take us to Mishbil."

"You did the talking," Xalan defended. "But I see what you mean. It will take us a year, now, to sail *back.*"

I carefully didn't look, but I could feel Melayne's compelling gaze like a sharp nail on the side of my head. "I suppose we could try to attract Ennelith's attention somehow," I mused. "We could say we changed our minds."

"No, let's not!" Xalan said hastily. "I'd sooner travel for a year!"

And Sandcomber begged, "Indeed, let us not impose on her good nature again! She looks a most tempery lady, to my inexperienced eye!"

"And there's something to be said, for taking a holiday," Xalan pointed out. "It will do the Cayds a world of good, to waste time and energy looking for us. So long as you're gone, without explanation and without trace, King Mor will never consolidate his rule. He could search the sea for a year, I'll wager, and never find a clue."

The picture was an attractive one. My incredible vanishment would vastly bolster a reputation for miracle working that already kept King Mor uneasy on his stolen throne. "I wonder if he still sleeps with ten warriors on guard inside his bedchamber, in case I walk through the walls," I said reminiscently, and everyone chuckled.

"*I* wonder how his women like that," Melayne added, and even Sandcomber joined in the laughter.

"You have altered greatly, Liras," Sandcomber said, reviving somewhat. "More than I would have thought possible, when you vowed to change. Admit it—such a situation would have prostrated you a mere four years ago."

"That's true," I said, much struck. Four years ago I had yearned to become a hero. And behold! I had done it. Then I recalled how foreign the realm beneath was, and wondered if I really enjoyed it.

Sandcomber popped a bit of dried apple into his mouth. "Once I said I had never met any purveyor of bravery," he reminded me. "Can your transformation be distilled into a regimen? Or better yet, into a cordial—tincture of courage. Does the voice you hear when you wear the Crystal Crown instruct you?"

Xalan goggled at me, and Melayne paused with a spoonful of porridge halfway to her mouth. "Hearing voices is a sign of madness," she remarked.

I was holding the baby while Melayne ate her meal, and now I laid her in my lap to free one hand. "Pass me some of those," I asked Sandcomber. "Do you know, that was supposed to be a secret?"

"You Viridese have too many secrets," Sandcomber retorted. "It's tripe, and purposeless to boot. Besides, is not young Xalan here to be Master Magus, whenever Averidan settles down under your benificent rule again? And is not the lady Melayne your faithful wife? And am I not perishing of curiosity?"

It had not occurred to me before, that these ritual secrecies worked against all the Kings of the Shan. "That which inhabits the Crown has taught me courage," I said slowly. "But not the way I'd like. The last time I wore it, it tried to push me out of my own head."

"In truth?" Sandcomber's round dark face glowed

with excitement. "The way a hermit crab will steal a shell from some other creature?"

Having never seen a hermit crab at work, I could not say. Melayne set down her spoon. "I have always believed that servants should know their place, dearest. If that Crown is encroaching, you should discipline it—sternly."

"It doesn't work like that," I said irritably, jiggling the baby on my knee.

Xalan poured himself some tea, and topped off my mug too. "Is that why we lost the war, then? Because you and the Crystal Crown were at odds?"

His voice was entirely nonjudgmental, but I could not help wincing anyway. "I try not to think so. The root of our difficulty, I will always believe, is with the Sun god, who abandoned us in the hour of need. But I will never forgive myself for losing Averidan."

I bowed my head, fixing my eyes on Tarys' tiny back and swallowing sudden tears. There was a brief uncomfortable silence, which Sandcomber broke. "I don't suppose I could see the artifact again," he suggested. "I have never touched it."

Xalan and I looked at each other. No one but a Viridese ever has, I began to say, but then remembered that the Cayds had held the Crown for some time before we tricked it away from them again. I nodded, and Xalan went to fetch it.

He returned with a small cubical hand-trunk of cheap wood riveted with copper. The Crown had once resided in an elegant casket adorned with gold, but in our escape that box had been lost. Now I opened this humbler casing and drew the Crown out.

Its crystal was always cool to the touch, the mysterious many-faceted white substance the most rare and precious element known. While Xalan explained this at length, Sandcomber reached a tentative hand to feel, glancing at me first for permission. "Not glass," he noted. "Was it cast in this form, as windowpanes are, I wonder, or carven like gemstones from a bigger block?"

No one knew. "What a silly way to run a government," Melayne said. "Now that Mor has seized the country, perhaps no one will care that the Crown is gone."

But both Xalan and I were firm about this. "How can he rule, except by the Crystal Crown?" Xalan asked. "He isn't Shan King, unless he wears it."

"Yes," I agreed. "Some countries are ruled by families, like Cayd. And I hear that Colb is run by a council, can you believe it?"

"They must get nothing done," Xalan said.

"And no one could say those countries are better run than Averidan. It's so much more consistent, to have a Crown."

"What would happen," Sandcomber interrupted, "if *I* put it on?"

Startled, I exclaimed, "Only I can do that."

"Or, after Liras' reign, another Shan," Xalan added.

I found that my hands had instinctively returned the Crown to its box. "The system allows for very little in the way of independent experiment," Sandcomber remarked, resigned.

"It's not supposed to," said Xalan.

"Then my only advice is to wear it once again," Sandcomber said to me. "One can't make a final judgment based on a single experience, however unpleasant. In prudence you might choose your time—allow us to be at hand, for example, that we may rescue or revive as needed. Or, if your concern is 'losing' yourself, some word or act of recognition could be arranged before the attempt."

Such measures, rational and sensible as they were, struck me as slightly irrelevant. Supremely native to that other realm, the Crown could never be trapped in simple and sane nets like these. But at this point Tarys, whom I had almost forgotten, became tired of hanging over my knee and began to whimper. Melayne set down her spoon to hold her, and I began my belated meal with relief.

*   *   *

The wan green light filtering through the waves gave
our journey an unsettling, unearthly quality. There was
no strength or warmth to it. Since we did not dare to
light fires except to cook, we suffered somewhat from
cold. When he purchased the *Kingfisher,* Sandcomber
had begun to repaint it in the fashion of his country,
wherever that was. Luckily he had not progressed past
the upper poop. There, curly green stripes wrestled
with red and bright blue bars, and no two railings on
the half-landing were alike. Our cabin door was painted
in concentric brown and white ovals. The sight would
have made the stoutest sailor queasy. Melane swore
that she would as lief have sunshine, and be seasick,
than this uncanny smooth glide through twilight.

We found, by experimenting with the slop buckets,
that anything liquid flung at our enclosure was swiftly
drawn in to the rushing water. From there it was left
floating behind as we skimmed on past. Secure in this
knowledge, we spent five days unloading and bailing
out the flooded hold. When the last bucketful was
hauled up, I could stand in the dim hold and reach
through the jagged hole to touch the silvery skin of the
sea. It slid by upward and did not leak in a drop.
Whatever held the watery wall in its place extended
right down to the keel and up around to the other
side. It gave everyone a queer sensation to look and
feel through the hole, but at least repairing it was a far
simpler task than it otherwise would have been.

Fortunately, Sandcomber waited until the hole was
patched before trying his grand experiment. His inquiring spirits recovered rapidly, and he now burned
with curiosity about how Ennelith maintained our undersea bubble. "We know that fluids are drawn through
to become one with the sea beyond," he said. "But
what of solids?"

He flung a scrap of wood over the rail. It hit the
wall of water and fell rattling into the narrow space
between the hull and the skin. "I beg you, lord foreigner," the pilot groaned. "Do not enrage the
goddess!"

"My good Forlen! She will scarcely heed such a minor sensation! Now, suppose I push with this stick?"

He leaned over the rail with a stick of kindling, and poked it like a nail into the water-wall. The rushing water snatched it down from his grasp, and we saw it whirling back and away into the dim blue depths. "Ah! But is the water moving so swiftly all around us?"

Armed with a bundle of twigs Sandcomber circled the decks, jabbing the curving skin of water at different points. With an unwilling fascination we followed him. To inquire methodically into anything is foreign to the Viridese mind. But Xalan was quick enough to grasp some of the advantages of method. "Do you realize how much more the Order of Magi could accomplish, if we studied our Arts in any organized way? As things stand now, apprentices learn tricks by rote, and full magi simply repeat them. New applications of power are discovered only by chance. And whoever discovers them sits on them, like a hen on one egg."

"My brothers always said that you called up ghosts and spirits to help you," Melayne volunteered. "And you rob graves."

Master Magus Xalan was justly appalled. "We do not!"

"Burying the dead in the ground is unsanitary, anyway," I said. "Uses up good farm land. Proper funerals are held at sea."

Melayne grimaced, looking up at the arch of ocean above us. We were on the foredeck, where Sandcomber was poking about near the prow, and the sheet of water curved down close around us. "How I wish we were out of here!"

"As a matter of fact," Xalan pursued, "in the stories and plaiv every new discovery, of anything, is always revealed by a deity or spirit. Each new idea for fishing tackle is always Ennelith's gift, and every innovation in geomancy or herognomy is sent by the Sun."

"And they were wrong," I said. "The gods care

nothing for us." I was carrying the baby again, and when I looked down into her tiny face, innocent and yet wise, my heart misgave me. But I did not retreat.

"Now I vow you are becoming wise," Sandcomber said, turning briefly from his poking. "The stories our good Magus cites are doubtless figures, a representation of inspiration or intellect or some such." And he thrust a long stick into the water-wall at its most forward point. The curve of the wall was quite sharp, rather like the small end of an egg, here where it bent around the bowsprit. The stick was not pushed up or down at all, and Sandcomber crowed in triumph. Then, as he pulled it out, a stream of water shot out of the spot at tremendous speed, and hit him in the face.

Xalan, whose sense of humor is very well-developed for a magus, began to laugh. But I was horrified. Suppose the leak widened, to flood our refuge? We would drown like trapped rats. Worse yet, suppose Ennelith detected our meddling with her transport? Already at outs with one deity, I could well imagine what Ennelith would say and do.

The stream showed no signs of abating. A pool of salt water rapidly spread on the foredeck. Melayne grew alarmed too. "Let's bring the boat up to the air," she begged, seizing my arm. "Liras, arrange it!"

"I don't think I can, dear. Sandcomber, let's use that board and hold it over the leak." Sputtering, he helped me pick up a short board. We tried to force it over the leak. Water sprayed high over all of us, and the board was drummed from our grasp.

"What you need is a heavier shield, and some way of bracing it," Xalan suggested. "We don't need to plug the leak, just divert the water over the rail. Now, if we hauled up one of those long wooden lockers, and stood it on end, and lashed it to the rails . . ."

Until we unclamped the chosen locker, I had quite forgotten about the lady Zaryas' bundle. I let the others drag out the ropes and tackle, and untied the burlap wrapping. Inside was a handsome long vest of green silk, embroidered and padded and quilted in the southern style. When I put it on, its unusual weight pressed comfortingly on my shoulders like two lean hands. The treasures sewn within made it hang stiff and heavy as armor. I rubbed the soft yet rigid hem between my hands and sighed. "She's lost, you know," I said to Xalan. "Xeel never came back. I expect when Ennelith snatched up our ship, the *Lily* foundered in the back-wash."

"Don't despair," Xalan replied. "I tell you, the princess is a phenomenon. She survives everything."

"Liras! Xalan!" Sandcomber called, from the fore-deck. "We'll need every man aboard to lend a hand!"

To haul the locker up onto the foredeck involved running a hawser up to a pulley on the mast. The locker we slung in a crude rope cradle. If the castle had been two stories, like the poop, the task would have been utterly beyond us.

Melayne held the baby and leaned on the rail to give us advice. It was her idea, when the locker had been manhandled up, to stabilize it further with some ballast stones. The thought was a good one and we acted on it, but wrestling the weighted upended locker along the deck into position almost killed us. Muscles cracking and backs breaking, we forced it against the powerful thrust of the water stream.

When the locker was roped into place, we lay on the wet deck panting like dogs. Melayne surveyed the leak, which now hit the locker with a rattle like hail and then sprayed over the side. "A job well done, boys. It relieves my mind, to know we won't suffer the consequences of Sandcomber's stupidity."

Sandcomber sat up, groaning with the effort. "Dear lady, even if I put you and yours at risk, it was in the cause of knowledge!"

Melayne sniffed scornfully. But before she could make any more cutting comments, the most heart-breaking sound imaginable came to our ears. It was the gradual lessening hammer of water on wood. For-getting my stiffness, I leaped up and ran to the rail. Sure enough, the spurting leak was slowing. Like a

water clock running dry, the stream was very gradually
weakening. As one we turned to glare at Xalan, and
Forlen the pilot voiced everyone's sentiments. "You
and your grand ideas, magus!" he snarled.

Embarrassed, Xalan picked up his red lappeted cap,
which he had laid aside while pushing the locker, and
bowed. "Perhaps I was a little hasty," he apologized.

Sandcomber began to laugh. "I only hope that
Ennelith, wherever she is, saw us!"

CHAPTER 3

An Insalubrious Sojourn

The next day I was roused very early by Xalan pounding on our cabin door. "Your Majesty!" he yelled. "We've arrived!"

Even in the bunk I could feel that the eerie smooth motion of the ship had changed. The *Kingfisher* now rolled and rocked slowly back and forth, as a proper vessel at sea should. I flung on some clothes and hurried out onto the narrow landing.

What a wonder it was, to see the sky again! The *Kingfisher* floated on a blue tropical sea, quite different from the foggy green waters we had sailed in Averidan. A steep mountainous country stood sharp and black against a glorious sunrise that flushed all the eastern sky into rose and gold. Sea birds piped and called as they circled lazily around the masts to inspect us, and the salt wind lifted my hair. I laughed with pure joy. How easy it was to forget the breadth and size of the world! "Come out, Melayne!" I called. "It's going to be a beautiful day!"

My only answer was a moan. I went back inside and was only just in time to hand Melayne a chamber pot. "I'm going to die," she whimpered. "Tell your white-haired friend to get us to land, instantly!"

I tiptoed out, a prey to sobering thoughts. Up on the poopdeck Xalan was gazing into his mirror. After staring for some time he sighed. "My schooling was right, then. Once you leave Averidan, scrying works poorly, unless there are other mirrors to talk to. I can't even descry Uwuna."

"A marvel! It isn't perhaps your skill at fault?" Sandcomber suggested, as he hurried by to the rudder. "Or no, better yet if the country ceased to exist the moment we sailed over the horizon—like a scroll curling up as you read along."

Before Xalan could reply to these innovative speculations, I interrupted to ask, "What day is it?"

Xalan thought for a moment. "The nineteenth day of the spring season. We left Averidan a mere two weeks ago yesterday. When we get back, I'm going to make a really fine present to Ennelith."

It will take us months to sail back," I reminded him. "And Melayne gets seasick."

"Oh! well—perhaps she'll become accustomed to the motion?"

"If we don't come to Uwuna soon, she'll bite all our heads off."

Xalan shook his head ruefully. "Thank Viris magi don't marry! The mirror shows me nothing, but I think the town must be near those headlands there. And the sails are going up, so we won't be long."

After all these days undersea with nothing but dim diffused bottle-green light, the sunshine seemed inordinately strong. It warmed my skin like a hundred massaging hands. In all the turmoil of departure I had lost my straw sunhat, and was now sure I would miss it. We squinted and shaded our eyes with our hands, trying to make out the shore better. All the coast seemed to be big tumbled gray rocks right down to the water, not very suitable for settlement. Uwuna proper was still not in sight.

All of a sudden my eyes adjusted. What I had taken to be a small mountain was a city. Thousands of buildings of gray stone marched down the gentle slope. The shoreline was fringed with handsome stone quays that spread east and west out of sight. On the crest of the ridge sprawled a huge gray castle complex, with many square towers. Uwuna was enormous, the biggest city I had ever seen. It seemed unfair, that so huge a city should exist and we Shan know nothing of it. My own capital was a village compared to this. Beside me

Xalan gasped too, as he finally saw what his eyes had been looking at.

One by one the sails were raised, and as the *Kingfisher* foamed closer in we could make out some details. The broad paved avenues were arched over at intervals with freestanding bridgelike monuments. Adorned with statues and friezes, the buildings looked as if their masters had never had to consider construction costs. And my heart warmed when I saw that the people seemed to love gardens. Everywhere were vines trained up walls, or riotous flower plots.

It was a shock, to notice that many of the grand buildings were roofless. Then, as we entered the harbor, I saw the true Uwuna. The fine buildings were mostly rubble, their windows dark and blank or filled with sky. In the angles of fallen walls were lean-tos and miserable huts. Many dwellings were obviously converted from larger and grander quarters, as one may cut down a big cloak into two or three children's garments. The vines and flowers were not tamed guests in the city, but insolent invaders from the wild.

"What happened to the town?" I asked Sandcomber as he bustled by again. "Was it sacked?" For a dread had come over me, that someday my own City would look like this.

"Not at all! It is simply antique. Uwuna is one of the former seats of the Uorvish Isles of old. Most of that country is drowned now—" He waved his white-draped arm north and west. "What you see here are the remnants of the Uorvish town, inhabited by lesser men. Have you ever visited Oorsevesh in the north?"

We shook our heads; most Shan rarely leave Averidan. It was depressing to reflect that I was the best traveled Shan King in generations. "If you had, you would recognize the stamp of the old realm there too. But come with me, while I dress appropriately for our landfall."

His words reminded me to consider what kind of appearance we would make in Uwuna. None of the pomp and trappings of the Shan King had survived the

wreck of my fortunes. The vest with its hidden treasure was very plain, by my viceroy's express order, I
was sure. And I could scarcely enter town in the
Crystal Crown. The yellow linen outfit I stood in had
been scrubbed and soaked, but the bloodstains were
still palely visible. Xalan changed his plain traveling
suit for his long robes of magian red. He carried his
wand, mirror, and the box that held the Crown.

A factor neither of us had considered was the heat.
Uwuna is far to the south and west of home. Where
Averidan is warm, Uwuna was hot. Already, so early
in the day, the heat shimmered ferociously over the
broken cobbles of the streets. A thick humidity like
sodden quilts hung in the air. Xalan and I waited on
the garish little landing between the cabin doors, and
sweated in this strange climate that seemed as hot and
close as the inside of a teakettle.

Then Sandcomber emerged. For an instant I thought
he had exchanged his flowing white draperies for a
bright woven suit. But no—his very skin was patterned
in the dazzling colors and designs he loved: wavy strips
and zigzags in red and blue and green. They were not
merely painted on, but somehow marked indelibly
into the skin of legs, torso and arms. Even when he
wetted them, the patterns remained clear and true. "I
can see why you had to wear long robes," Xalan said,
impressed. Our friend's only real garment was a waist-
cloth, but one scarcely noticed his undress. The luridly
colorful poopdeck could not hold a candle to his glory.
For a time thereafter I could not help goggling every
time my glance struck him.

In a suspenseful frame of mind we watched the
Kingfisher ease into a quay. The harbor was full of
shipping—from dugouts, to strange barges made of
reed bundles lashed together, to true ships made like
ours out of wood. The *Kingfisher* was the only Viridese
ship; I had expected that, since Uwuna had never
been heard of before.

In our part of the world peaceful travelers are not
encouraged to carry weapons. But Sandcomber begged
me to bring my sword. While I fetched it, Melayne

came out. She was a sad sight as she emerged into the sunshine. Her tangled red-brown braids hung past her waist, and there were haggard purple smudges under her eyes. The baby wailed dismally on her shoulder. I took her so that Melayne could safely totter down the poop ladder to the deck. Tarys immediately took the opportunity to spit up. With my free hand I scrubbed at my yellow tunic front, in vain. My clothing, already stiff with bloodstains, now reeked of old milk.

"And this is the first visit of a Shan King to Uwuna!" I could not help exclaiming. "They'll think we're a nation of oafs!"

"Never mind your vanity," my wife snarled, "just hurry!"

"The residents of Uwuna are hardly in a position to cast aspersions," Sandcomber said with a chuckle. "You'll see." Tarys screamed in my ear, tiny fists flailing. Melayne drooped beside me like an unwatered sapling. With my worn, soiled clothing I knew I looked like a beggar. Gathering up the last shreds of my dignity, I took my wife's arm and marched down the gangplank.

We stepped onto the quay and were instantly surrounded by people. Most of them yelled their wares or services at us in Uwunan, which only Sandcomber spoke. Due to the heat the fashions of the city are minimal—for men a kilt of supple beaten tree-bark which left their brown upper bodies and limbs quite bare. For a while until I got used to it, I scarcely knew where to look. Even more startling were some women in the same garb, though others wore slightly more decent long, sleeveless gowns. In Averidan even swimmers wear shirts, and women bare their bosoms only in the marriage bed. "I suppose if they don't blush, we need not do it for them," Xalan said at my elbow, but all the same his thin cheek was pink. The noise and strange sights brought home as never before, that we were exiles in a foreign land.

Sandcomber pushed past, impressive in his garish body markings, and dispelled the crowd with a few sharp phrases of fluent Uwunan. His well-fleshed bulk breasted through the press like a keel through brown water, and we followed behind. The paving stones were dangerously worn underfoot, and many were missing. I held the screaming baby carefully as we edged past the crumbling stone verge of an ancient dock. A handsome bridge arched over a ditch or small inlet, but the central section was fallen. The gap had been filled with timbers and rough matting. When we crossed, the reek of raw sewage rose from the water below.

On the other side stood some sort of cook-house. Reed awnings were strung between three or four ruined walls. In this shade tables and crude benches were set. Sandcomber sat down in an inconspicuous corner and gestured for us to join him. The whiff of sewage came distinctly when the breeze veered, and I said, "There must be some more savory place to dine. If it's a question of money, I have—"

"Hush!" Though surely no one in earshot understood Viridese, Sandcomber glanced around. "I hope to find a harbormaster here, to take my bribes. While we wait, allow me to explain the workings of Uwuna to you."

My dignity only slightly appeased, I sat down. Melayne took the sobbing baby and quieted her by offering a modestly-draped breast. Xalan wedged the casket of the Crown carefully between us. I smelled at the cane beaker of clear yellow-white fluid Sandcomber poured me. It had no aroma of beer, and certainly did not look like wine. "Atye," he named it. "Very poor, of course."

I took a sip, and the harsh powerful spirit made me gasp. "Ugh! Give me plum brandy any day!"

"One might say the root of evil in Uwuna was the collapse of the Uorvish queens' rule," Sandcomber began. He spoke so glibly that I was not surprised, much later, to learn that he had made this speech before. "The loss of their authority, oh, many generations ago it was, has led to the city's current decay.

Uwuna is now divided amongst four or five powerful barons, or perhaps six depending on who has been murdered since last I was here."

As a professional ruler, I was appalled. "How does anything get *done?*"

"Nothing is." Sandcomber shook his tight-curled head. "Uwuna is without law, a jungle more wild than any forest beyond its borders. I warn you to walk carefully, speak softly if at all, and keep your valuables about you." I saw him glance at the casket my elbow rested on.

Melayne hugged the baby nervously. "I'm hungry," she announced.

"You feel better!" I was delighted. "Will they serve us food here, Sandcomber?"

"Of course—and, while we speak of food, let me caution you about eating anything raw . . ."

Without thinking about it, many Viridese assume that Averidan is the only genuinely habitable country in the world. Though we trade with Colb and Oorsevish, no one really wants to visit there. I had seen enough now to know this assumption was naive. But for Uwuna I felt the old prejudice was completely justified. No one could possibly want to live here.

I became certain of this when the food came—oddly-flavored marrow balls, flat hard bread, and flat brown leaves of something that a nibble revealed to be a meat, very tough but sliced thin as parchment. Everything was piping-hot, and we tasted things cautiously, like explorers testing a quagmire. Or rather Xalan and I did. Melayne buckled down to her trencher like a starving woman. Making up for lost time, she heaped her plate twice, and had Sandcomber send for more bread.

Sandcomber himself scarcely took a bite. All this time he had been surveying the tables, as patrons came and went. At last he said, "I must stroll along the harbor a bit and see if the harbormaster is about. Without the proper seals, you see, we will not be permitted to use our quay. Wait here, and I shall return soon."

I held the baby while Melayne scraped the platters, and idly watched the passersby. There were folk of every race, nut-brown Uwunans, paler travelers from Oorsevish in the north, even some natives of Colb, who looked rather sallow in contrast. No one present had a particularly savory look, but I had met one or two traders from Colb and now their white tunics and shapeless white cloth hats looked friendly and familiar. There were groups of slight dark men in loincloths, and once, in the distance, a man of Sandcomber's rich ebony color. He wore long sleeves and hems, so we could not tell if he was tattooed. "Rriphirrizē, wherever it is, must be yet a journey from here," I remarked.

With a wetted finger Xalan traced a crude map on the table top. "Sandcomber told me that Uwuna is here," he said. "Averidan is north and then west, like this. While Rriphirrizē is south and west, many leagues inland. One goes up a river, I understand."

"We're not going on a river, are we?" Melanye asked with horror. "Aren't we going to stay here a while?"

"I don't know." Our dilemma was awkward to say the least. I did not fancy lingering in Uwuna, where we could speak to nobody. Nor was the prospect of joining Sandcomber on the journey to Rriphirrizē appealing. "Ideally," I said slowly, "we could sail the *Kingfisher* back to Averidan, and then reconquer the realm."

Xalan sighed. "Just like that, eh?"

"I'm quite aware we were miserably defeated before! I said ideally."

Melayne scowled, "I won't sail anywhere, I won't!" Her voice, never soft anyway, quite dominated the shop.

Remembering Sandcomber's warning, we hushed her quickly. But a number of patrons had turned to stare at us. Our long, full-sleeved Shan dress made us conspicuously foreign. Their glances looked threatening, their comments sounded coarse. Suddenly I knew my reactions were being colored by Shan insularity. When a man in Colbic dress rose and approached, Xalan reached for his staff. I elbowed him and hissed, "Relax!"

In the most atrocious Viridese imaginable the fellow said, "You from Averidan, yah?"

I nodded, and gave Melayne's ankle a little kick beneath the table so that she would stop glowering. the Colb was obviously a sailor of the lowest sort, and Xalan muttered, "Let's just get up and leave."

"We have no local coin to pay for our meal," I whispered back. "Just calm down. We'll talk to him, and Sandcomber will come back soon."

The Colb grinned, displaying broken and discolored teeth. "At home we hear of Averidan, of the king, and his foreign wife, and his magician friend. You are he, yah?"

The thought of my legend spreading even to such outlands as Colb touched me. Such is the power of the realm beneath that tales of its users spread no one knows how. In Averidan our plaiv, the oral legends of our people, bend and sway like reeds in its flow. In the face of this testimony a sense of *chun-hei*, of crazy honorableness, drove me to tell the truth: "Yes, I am the Shan King."

"Oh, Viris!" Xalan muttered, in a tone of disbelief.

"It's quite true," I defended. "So long as I hold the Crystal Crown—"

A stunning blow whistled past my head. Melayne screamed, and Xalan jerked me back. The other Colbic seamen gathered loosely around us, cutting off escape. The other customers hardly bothered to look up, and I realized how common such affrays must be.

Melayne shielded the baby in her arm and very wisely shrank into the angle of the rough walls. I drew my sword, and when our foes hesitated at the sight of it ducked under the table. With a heave I flung the table-top over at the sailors, knocking two of them down. "Come on now, we can run for it!" I panted.

Unfortunately one sailor fell onto the next table and shoved his elbow full into another diner's meal. This person stood up and shouted at him, pulling a knife. "I don't understand why fighting is so *complicated* with you, Liras," Melayne criticized. "Why didn't you just cut off his head and have done with him?" The truth was, I hoped to avoid two equally terrifying stratagems. I dared not put on the Crystal Crown, and I devoutly hoped not to have to step into the realm beneath. My battles were indeed cruelly complicated by my own denials. And though I was not believing in the god any more, I resented the way every supernatural advantage I happened upon instantly melted my hand.

Xalan held his black stone wand poised in one hand. "Shall we find out what's behind this stone wall?" he suggested.

"Yes, let's." Someone tripped into an awning support and so ensured the brawl would spread. Above us the matting swayed perilously, shedding clouds of insects and dust. I hacked at the pole on our side. Slowly, majestically, the awning sagged down, to a chorus of screams and yells of rage.

Xalan finished muttering at the wall, and beckoned to it with his wand. The great gray stones trembled and jerked. Several small ones fell off the top. A horizontal slit gaped between the courses of stonework at waist level. Xalan's geomancy had wrenched open a temporary door, the way a potter may thrust a hole through clay. "Quick, now!" he gasped, and I gave Melayne a boost through. After I passed her the baby, Xalan wriggled through. I followed, my sword in one hand and the Crystal Crown in its box under my arm. Xalan pointed commandingly at the opening, and it snapped shut like a trap.

"Very nicely done," I commended Xalan, before I saw where he had brought us. We had climbed right out of the cook-house, and stood on a narrow path that ended at the sewage ditch. The litter of trodden egg shells, fruit rinds and vegetable parings showed that the kitchen staff dumped offal and cooking debris there. In one wall that bordered the path was the kitchen door. And there stood a group of thugs in crude armor, just bits of leather strapped onto their bare limbs. Only their spears were uniform, doubtless issued by their baron. The cook standing in the doorway waved a dishclout and shrieked, pointing. Lowering their spears the men began to approach, grinning with confidence.

Now that events had turned serious, I was very calm. The ditch was too wide for anyone but Xalan to jump. "Can you lift Melayne over? And the baby?"

"Not together," Xalan said, eying the distance.

"Melayne first, then." I set down the Crown and she reluctantly let me take the child. Mercifully, Tarys had fallen into the sleep of repletion. Xalan seized Melayne's hand and rose slowly into the air. The spearmen shouted in wonder, and pointed. We had forgotten, that magery is almost unheard of outside Averidan. I was grimly glad of it; to hold off spears with a sword is just about impossible anyway, without the further handicap of a sleeping baby.

Xalan bounded back like a goat and took the baby. "Fight them off for just one minute," he said, panting.

Even as he soared away, they charged. On the narrow path hemmed by walls there was no room to dodge. I threw myself forward, under the spearpoints, and cut at the first one's shins. Most eyes were following Xalan's red floating figure, so I escaped being stuck like a pig for an instant. With annoyance I saw from the corner of one eye that instead of prudently retreating out of throwing range Melayne stood on the farther side of the ditch, nearly dancing with impatience as she waited for the baby. I rolled, kicking with my heavy boots at bare legs and slashing with my sword. A spear is awkward at very close quarters, and my foes tripped each other, or jammed their spearbutts against the walls, or nearly impaled themselves trying to poke me.

All of a sudden I froze, as one may on the verge of a high cliff. Unthinkingly I had come very near the realm beneath. Cold sweat started on my brow, and I recoiled. The momentary loss of concentration was fatal. Spears stabbed down around me into the filthy earth. I squirmed past the shafts like a snake, but too late—my wide tunic sleeve was pinned. As I tore it free, another bronze spearpoint pierced my right shoulder.

I yelped. The pain and shock made my head swim. The spearmen fell back a little, relaxing and chattering in their own tongue. Now I was wounded, they plainly felt I could be dispatched at leisure. Xalan, hovering high in the sky, was a more immediate threat, and many of them craned their necks to watch him.

Gasping, I hauled myself up to sit against the wall. Blood seeped horridly into my tunic sleeve. Someone kicked my sword out of my powerless hand and picked it up. From above Xalan yelled thinly, "Liras! What should I do?"

I could not spare the breath to say so, but he was doing very well as he was—distracting my foes. They pointed and jabbered, and someone threw a spear which came well short and fell back into the ditch. I had one more resort at hand. The Crystal Crown in its box was at my knee, and no one had kicked it away— yet. Of course, I had sworn never to use it again. But in this crisis I felt it was time to reconsider. Nothing the Crown could do to me now would be much worse than being speared through and then rolled into the sewer. Awkwardly I clawed open the latch with my left hand, and dipping my head slipped the Crown on.

For what seemed like a dangerously long time nothing whatever happened, no altered perceptions or special awareness of my surroundings. I had plenty of time to consider whether the Crown's indwelling intelligence was snubbing me. Or had the Cayds somehow damaged it in their attempts to smash it? The spearmen who were not watching Xalan had begun to quarrel, hissing comments at each other. When I finally realized that one accused another of stealing the gem out of the empty socket on my sword, I sighed with relief. For the Crown's power is such that the rightful wearer may brush aside minor impediments to understanding like language, and peer into men's hearts. The sensation of remoteness, of endless power, flowed through me exactly as of old, so heady that my throne and kingdom might have been my own again, and all the Uwunans at the bottom of the sea. My arm and hand were sticky with my own blood, but I scarcely felt the wound as I called to the spearmen: "Turn, you lice, and look upon your destroyer!"

At that moment the Crown spoke within my skull. "Where have you been? What has been happening? Months have gone by!"

Startled, I said, "Oh, not months. Just six weeks or so perhaps." Never had that voice, usually so sweet and cool, sounded so distraught. The mere knowledge of its mortality—acquired when the Cayds had planned to smash it—must have disturbed the eternal governing presence greatly. The Crown would just have to live with it, I decided. "A great deal has happened, but we can gossip later."

Of course I had said all this aloud, and now was irritated to see the expressions on the Uwunans' faces. Surprise had given way to an amused contempt. They thought I was raving. I had forgotten that outside Averidan the Crystal Crown has no significance whatever. And meanwhile the Crown was arguing. I could hardly believe my ears, if ears were what I used in these internal dialogues; it never used to stoop to argument. "I want to know, now! Is it safe for me? Are the Cayds gone?"

"Not precisely," I said to it. "Will you wait a moment?" The situation was getting out of hand, and I decided to resort to fear. At my mental gesture a cold white light began to flow from the Crown, leaching the gray from the ancient stones and picking out every scrap of eggshell ground into the dirt. The unshaven faces of my opponents were blank with horror and dismay. As impressively as I could I said, "For laying hands upon my royal person the penalty is death. Of my mercy, though, I am inclined to overlook your ignorance and sacrilege."

Since they could understand me while I wore the
Crown, the effect of this was all I could wish for. The
spears fell from their hands, and the men nearest the
kitchen were beginning to back away up the path.
Triumph was within my grasp, when I incautiously
added, "I alone am in charge here."

Under the circumstances it was not a wise thing to
say. A grip of numbing power closed around my brow.
I leaped up; my scalp felt aflame, but when I thrust
my left hand under the Crown to wrench it off the
crystal was still cool under my fingers. Sweat made my
hands slip; the thing might have been clinging to my
hair, it was seated so firm. "Wait, let go!" I gasped,
before my tongue turned flaccid.

One of the spearmen laughed jeeringly. A fragment
of my power loitered long enough for me to hear
another say, "What a batch of new-laid grasshoppers
you are, to be frightened by the sun shining off a
piece of glass." The deep voice ceased abruptly, as if
a door had slammed on it.

Indeed that was no more than the sober truth. The
doors of my head were being closed up, imprisoning
me within. "Who is in charge?" the perfidious Crown
echoed me nastily. I tried to suck in the air for a final
wordless shout, and found I was gasping at nothing.
The gray stone wall swam into view, edged at the top
with the brown startled faces of nosy cook-shop customers. Before the sight blurred I realized, irrelevantly, that my body had fallen onto its back. Then,
stripped of all sensation, I floated in nothingness. Even
the pounding of my heart in my chest was gone. Surely
from here the only portal was to the Deadlands.

CHAPTER 4

A Shattering Fracture

After a time that had neither length nor width I fell back into my head again. Not the slightest transition warned me, it was as sudden as stepping off a roof. When I reached up to explore my skull, I found an aching and tender lump on the back of it that made me wince. The Crystal Crown was gone. I wanted to leap up and search for it, as Melayne might search for the baby. But when I made to rise, my shoulder gave a tremendous throb and fire swam before my eyes. I lay back gasping, and decided to survey my situation first.

My clothes were grimed and torn, as if I had been dragged along the streets in my interval of mental absence. My boots and belt and jewels were gone; I was weakly grateful I had left my money-vest on board ship. A number of scrapes and bruises were new. Very gingerly I explored the wound. My arm had not been pierced right through, as I had first thought. A nasty deep gouge was torn through the flesh just below the point of my shoulder. I spat on a rag from my sleeve and tried to clean off some of the clots, without much success.

When I came to examine my prison, I was much heartened. The split canes of the woven roof were black with rot, completely missing at the farther end of the square room so that a flood of hot yellow sunshine poured in. The gray stone walls were crumbled and only partially complete. My captors had underestimated me seriously; they must believe I was completely mentally deficient. Of course, my disturbing adventure with the Crown made that conclusion only reasonable. The recollection cast me down for a moment. Then I pulled myself together. At least escape would be simple. I scrambled to my feet and skipped to the biggest gap.

The glaring light dazzled me, and I actually stepped onto the broken wall before I saw. The world fell away beyond it. The wall dropped sheer for several stories, ending in a narrow strip of tile roof. Beyond, a hill sloped steeply down. Below that were more ruined walls and seedy roofs. My prison was in a tower.

I threw myself back from the verge. One big stone shifted under my foot and toppled out. I hugged the dirty plank floor and listened for its fall. It must have cleared the strip of roof directly below, for I heard no clatter of smashing tile. Instead there came a heavy thud, and a few rolling, crunching sounds as the stone tumbled into the brush. I wiped the sweat from my face and realized I had always loathed high places. It was unfair—I dreaded being buried too. Things seemed deliberately contrived for my maximum discomfort.

Gloomily I explored the rest of the room. On all sides but one the walls felt sheer. From the terrain I had seen I realized I must be in the high castle on the ridge. However, the side where the tower connected to the rest of the building was different. The drop here was only twelve or fifteen feet, to a flagged area edged by the remains of low parapets. Beyond it was another crumbling tower. I realized that the flags were the flat top of the castle wall. Once, the defenders of the place could have run from that tower to this along those flags, and fired their arrows from the gaps in the parapets.

It would be easy to shin down the rough old stones to the courtyard. But by now I had less contempt for the Uwunans. I waited and watched and, sure enough, from the chamber directly below strolled my jailer. It was a leopard, bigger than the silver-pelted sand leopards of Averidan. The creature noticed me immediately and we looked at each other.

The creature's spots were black and white on the dark gold fur, very striking, and it wore a red leather collar. No one keeps leopards in Averidan; the cats are prized only for their pelts. But this leopard was well-trained in its business. When I sat on the edge of the wall and dangled my legs over, it made a running leap at them. I snatched my feet back up and heard the terrible claws scrabble on the stone. When I ventured to peer over again, the leopard was still leaning its front paws on the wall. It looked up into my face hungrily, and licked black lips with a pink leathery tongue.

So I was trapped, like a mouse in its hole. Restlessly I prowled around the room again, but I had seen everything already. There was nothing to eat or drink; I was nettled to observe the leopard lapping from a stone trough of water below. There was a bowl of meat scraps too. A ladder lying on the flags showed how I had been brought in. The tower beyond was even more overgrown and ruined than my own. Only birds looked out of its gaping window-holes, and as the shadows lengthened brown bats fluttered out of the upper crevices. The baron in charge of this ruin must maintain himself and his troops on the other side of the building.

It was the loneliness of my prison that gave me an idea. There were plenty of loose blocks in the walls. Suppose I could kill the leopard by throwing one? If no one stopped me, I might well be able to slip away as night fell.

Immediately I set about gathering suitable stones. The day was burning to death; if I left it too late the darkness would force me to postpone the attempt. And I seriously doubted that I would be left so long. There were not as many useful blocks as I would have liked. Some, loose in their places, I could not pry out with my bare hands. Others were too small. Painfully I hauled over all the likely ones and laid them ready to hand. Then I sat again in the gap over the courtyard. It hurt to pick up the biggest rock but I persevered, sweating, until it was balanced on my left hand and shoulder. Then I lowered one foot over again. The leopard pretended to be busy washing its face. But I knew house cats, and could tell by the twitch of its black-tipped tail that it saw me. Very slowly, I dangled the other foot over too. With a nonchalant air the leopard rose and ambled over, as if it were thinking hard about some abstract matter. Then suddenly it lunged. I swung my feet up so quickly the rock slipped backward out of my grasp.

Fortunately it did not fall outward, and so warn the cat. Gritting my teeth, I heaved it up in my arms like a bundle. It was just within my strength to do so, and my hurt shoulder ached fiercely under the strain. But when I peered down the cat was directly below. I let the rock fall.

The leopard was almost too quick for me, twisting away from under the descending block. One back paw was partially pinned; the creature shrieked its rage and pain until my heart almost stopped. Hastily I clawed at the other rocks, blindly shoving them over as fast as I could. Only a few were left by the time I dared to look.

My missiles had crushed the leopard's ribs and broken its legs. Dark blood was seeping out from under the stones. The creature was helpless, but still its yellow eyes glared hotly up at me, and its snarl made my hair rise. I picked up a final rock, and stood up to make the blow a sure one. I hurled it down as hard as I could at the leopard's head.

My knees felt suddenly weak. I had to sit and rest a bit, sucking at the raw scrapes on my hands. Then I slid down the wall. The rough stones stabbed my bare toes when I felt for footholds, and my hands trembled so that I feared their grip would fail. But in a few moments I stood in the courtyard. It was in a shadow now, but the sun still lit the tops of the towers.

My first goal was the big cat's water trough. A week ago I would never have believed an animal's water would taste so good. When my day-long thirst was quenched, I washed my face and dabbed carefully at the hole in my arm. It was bleeding a little from all my exertions.

The body of the leopard still twitched a little as I stepped past it to explore the lower level of my tower. It was much the same as the floor above, except for a wooden trap door very noticeable in its newness against the ancient plank floor. It did not move when I tried it—bolted from below, I guessed. It would not have been prudent, anyway, to go through portions of the building that were in use. I only prayed—obscurely, to no particular god—that the cat's death-yells had attracted no notice.

My prospects looked much more promising from the side parapet of the courtyard. The strip of tile roof ran around my tower and extended along the wall about ten feet below me. Once there I could creep along the tiles until I reached an overhanging tree. The twilight deepened with amazing speed, a phenomenon that I later learned was entirely usual in this clime. I had to be on solid ground before full darkness descended, and scaling walls and climbing trees became too difficult.

I rolled onto my stomach and eased myself down the wall. The years had spared this face better. My groping toes found little purchase even when I hung by my hands. As my bare feet scrabbled desperately for a crack, I could feel my grip slowly weakening; with the hole in my shoulder and the old scars on my left hand I should have known better. At last I lost hold completely.

I fell with a thump that made the entire roof quiver. The tiles seemed far steeper than I had first thought. My hands got no grip on the moss-slick weatherworn surface, and I slithered feet first in a rattling shower of loosened clay tiles toward the verge. The noise was tremendous. At the very last moment I stopped myself by catching my toes in the gutter. I lay unmoving, digging my nails into the moss, so scared I felt white to the core.

My descent had scraped off many tiles. Without

moving my head I could look through one of the gaps. Below, a startled woman's brown face was upturned to mine. She had been bathing a child, who sat roaring with fear in a basin. The woman scooped up the dripping child and backed out of the room, screaming for help.

The tile gutter was rickety, entirely missing in sections. I bellied along the roof as fast as I could, my heart in my mouth, until I came to the nearest tree. When I tried to make out its way of growth, I realized how dark it had become. The tree was rather far away for my taste. Only one long flat bough extended my way, like a languid but beckoning hand. But a tremendous hue and cry had started inside, and I could see flecks of lantern light on the wall above. There was no time for niceties. I coiled my legs beneath me and sprang straight out into space, clawing.

The tree was needles after all, and not leaves. As the flexible branch sagged and cracked under my weight I swarmed up its length, striving to reach the main trunk before it broke. I couldn't do it. The bough snapped where it joined on, and fell in an arc to smack me against the rough scaly bark of its parent stem. I was not too stunned to quickly transfer my grasp before the branch could quite tear away. As I shinned down to the ground, I had ample opportunity to gather splinters and itchy bits of bark. My ragged clothes offered no protection at all.

By now the sky was totally dark, spangled with stars that were not entirely familiar. I scurried into the underbrush, tearing my skin on brambles and tripping over unseen stones. I had not taken careful note of my direction, and in any case did not know the ways. But when I came to a paved lane, I followed it downhill; if I kept going down, I should eventually reach the sea.

It took me almost all night to walk back to the quays. My bare feet soon grew very sore, and every time I stubbed my toe I cursed the local road repair crew. For a while gangs of noisy men roamed the roads searching, I assumed, for me. Whenever I heard them, I hid in the ruins. Uwuna is a gift to fugitives—the mazes of broken walls and crumbling buildings could have hidden a regiment. My pursuers seemed feckless and disorganized, far more so than any armed men I had ever met. And I became lost several times, which doubtless threw them further off my trail.

Still heavy with moisture, the night air was no hardship to walk in. My only present trouble was hunger, which I could do nothing about until I reached the *Kingfisher*. I had plenty of time to mull over events. Losing the Crystal Crown was not the calamity it had been in Averidan. These barbarians (I told myself) had no notion of its value or powers. True, whoever held it could claim the rulership of all the Shan. But even if that unknown baron had heard of this—very unlikely in itself—it was beyond the realm of possibility that he would take ship north to Averidan to do so. I would have plenty of time to buy, trick or, if necessary, steal the Crown back.

Far more worrying was the Crown's rebellion. I knew now what I had been unconsciously dreading all these years. The teetering balance between Shan King and Crown had finally come down against me. Or was I wrong to draw back? Perhaps there had never been more than one ruler of Averidan? Now that the Crown was lost, perhaps I should seize the opportunity, free our race from the burden of this accursed artifact. The Uwunans could deal with it, as they did the leftovers from other kingdoms.

Unlike the rest of town the quays were well-lighted, what with the lamps hung from ships and the fires of watchmen. Sensible captains post guards on their vessels when they dock in Uwuna. I remembered exactly where the *Kingfisher* was berthed—past the fountain house, and half left. It was all I could do not to run there, but though there seemed to be no search and no watch on the harbor, I did not wish to be conspicuous.

Nonchalantly, I strolled around the final corner. I got halfway down the quay before I noticed the people trooping off the gangplank: a trio of bare-chested women carrying a door painted in jagged colors, some men with ropes and tackle, a gang hauling a sail-locker between them, a lady holding four squawking chickens by the feet. The *Kingfisher* was being stripped of everything movable. None of my friends could be seen anywhere.

Now I nearly did despair. I sat down on a mossy bollard and choked down desolate tears. Possibly the crew had been imprisoned too, on my account. It would not have been hard to learn which ship the troublemakers had come on. My family and friends might even be dead. Sandcomber particularly would never otherwise have permitted the ship to be looted.

I had to find out. But the thought of the enterprise's difficulties made me sick. My various hurts ached abominably, and I was starving. Without so much as a copper piece, I should have to steal my food. I could not even speak the language; my very face and form marked me as foreign. My only weapons were my fingernails, encrusted with dirt.

Obeying a dreary sense of duty I rose and went back to the fountain house, where I scrubbed my hands clean in the overflow basin. The cold touch of the water was so comforting I splashed my face as well, and drank deeply. Dawn blushed along the seaward horizon like a ripened peach, and the square bustled with those who came to draw their morning water. I turned too abruptly and jostled someone who was just lifting a full bucket. The resulting splash wet his feet and my own. "Sorry," I said in Viridese, and then could have bitten my tongue.

"Sorry!" He grabbed my arm. "Liras, is that you?"

"Xalan!" I never would have recognized him, in his unfamiliar garments. They were of thin white cloth, light and loose, with a shapeless hat to match. In my relief I threw my arms around him.

"We can't talk here," he said. "Come along this way." Hefting the half-spilled bucket he hurried me down another street. When it was plain no one was paying us attention, he added, "What an exhibition you make, in those rags! No wonder I didn't know you."

"Well, if it comes to that, where did you get that outfit? I'll wager it's not of Viridese tailoring."

"Do you admire it?" He adjusted the floppy white hat, grinning. "It's Sandcomber's old white robes, cut up and resewn. We tried to make it resemble a Colbic tunic, but you have to use your imagination. It might be dangerous, to be seen in the clothes we had that fight in."

"And where is everyone? Is Melayne safe?"

"Both she and the baby are blooming." There was a note of exactness in his voice that immediately alerted me. Something was not right. Plainly, though, we could not talk here in the street. I swallowed my questions and trotted along behind Xalan as fast as I could.

Dawn broke almost directly before us, since Xalan was heading east along the docks. From every patch of jungle wedged among the buildings rose flocks of birds. Green and scarlet and black, they swirled up into the first light with whistles and shrieks of joy. A smoky white mist rolled off the rather dirty water to our left, modestly hiding the floating trash that bobbed against the quays. Gangs of little boys raced past whooping, brown as nuts and naked except for a twist of fabric at the loins, and dived in with hardly a splash. Their task, I later learned, was to scavenge amongst the tide-borne jetsam for scraps of food, salvageable wood, or anything of remote value—a hard and perilous life. But now in my ignorance I only thought how much fun it would be, to swim in the dawn with such light-heartedness. For a dread was beginning to gather in my chest, a fear of something still nameless but soon to be born.

Suddenly Xalan turned and ran up some worn cracked steps to a long, low, windowless building. It was in fairly good repair, a warehouse still in use and so kept up. Xalan went around to the back, where a high wooden fence enclosed a loading yard. The double-door gates were big enough to let a span of oxen and a wagon pass. In one gate was a little postern. Xalan rapped upon it. The postern cracked open, and then swung wide to admit us.

As soon as I got inside, I was smothered in Melayne's frantic embrace. "Oh! you poor darling, you escaped! Oh, you're hurt! You should have hacked them to pieces!"

"Will you hush that noise!" Xalan urged in a low voice, gesturing around at the surrounding ruins that peered eyelessly over the board fence. "At the least, come inside!"

Inside it was so cool and dark my eyes were dazzled for a moment. It was indeed a warehouse, a big empty space heaped with bales and boxes. Sandcomber had evidently saved our baggage and cargo. In one corner were some bedrolls and sleeping mats, and in another a table and some benches. Sandcomber started from his seat, beaming all over his dark face. "My poor friend, however did you escape? We thought you lost. And I'm afraid I must break some very bad news to you, Liras—"

"No, no!" Xalan broke in. "Not on an empty stomach!"

"That's right, dearest—I'm sure you haven't eaten in an age." With a sweep of her arm Melayne pushed the maps and records off the table to the floor, ignoring Sandcomber's yelp of protest. "Sit and I'll bring some food—"

I cut off their protests with a gesture. "I can't eat a bite until you tell me."

The three glanced at each other, looking more guilty than handkerchief snatchers caught in their crimes. "Sit, darling, please! Oh, Liras, promise not to be upset!"

She dragged at my hurt arm and, when I winced, burst into tears of remorse. To calm her I sat down. "Xalan—can you explain, clearly and simply?"

I was surprised to see my faithful magus genuinely shaken, all the self-possession and humor fled from his face. "I don't know how to say it, Liras—the ultimate calamity."

"Oh! you mean the *Kingfisher*." I almost laughed at the anticlimax. "When I went by, the Uwunans were stripping her bare. What did we lose?"

Sandcomber gave a snort of humorless laughter, and Xalan said, "I wish it were so minor! Look!"

He reached under the table and bringing out a croker sack emptied it out. Three large white chunks of ice tumbled out. A cold hand seemed to squeeze my chest, and I leaned back against the wall. "The Crown?"

"I saw you stand up amongst those spearmen," Xalan recounted unsteadily. "You were shouting something I couldn't understand. Then you fell back. Your head hit a loose rock. And it shattered!"

"No one struck at you, or it either," Melayne contributed. "I'm sure of that."

Xalan continued as if it were vital to complete his tale. "When you didn't stir, they dragged you off. The last one picked up the pieces and put them in the sack. I dove down to snatch it away."

"This is impossible." My lungs refused to work right, so that I had to gasp the words. "King Mor deliberately tried to smash it up, and found he couldn't. He must have tried sledgehammers and saws . . ."

"Maybe he weakened it," Melayne suggested. "Like the first crack in a wine bottle."

I turned the pieces over on the tabletop, a sense of nightmare unreality grinding at me. The fractures were clean, and the chunks of crystal fit together perfectly. I ran my thumbs down one of the breaks and remembered when I had the power to unite the shattered. But that power itself was shattered now.

Still hoping to offer comfort, Melayne said, "We could try some beaten egg white. That's what cooks use on smashed crockery."

"This isn't a plate or cup," Xalan said. "Perhaps there's some magus I haven't heard of yet, with the gift—"

I shook my head. The knowledge of the Crown's

making has been lost for eons. The only modern-day
magus who might have succeeded was Xerlanthor, and
I had helped kill him myself. "It can't ever be repaired," I said at last. I felt as if I pronounced the
death of the love of my heart.

"Well, what shall we do?" Melayne asked.

Xalan almost wrung his hands. "Does this mean
Averidan is lost forever?"

Sandcomber, who had been watching all this with
intense interest, now spoke up. "I fail to see how it
can mean any such thing. Every political reality tends
to accumulate supportive artifacts. Do not your own
elaborate and largely fictional genealogies prove it?
Whoever is selected to be Shan King is always of
impeccable royal descent. In the same way, should our
friend Liras return in power and seize the throne again,
in time no one would ever notice that he has no
Crystal Crown. Of course," he added, as if suddenly
struck by the notion, "if the Cayds should prevail, the
genealogies will doubtless be adjusted to prove their
unblemished Viridese blood."

Xalan stamped with frustration. "You don't understand! The Crown is all that makes Averidan. Every
monarch for ten thousand years has worn it. What
other continuity have we—plaiv, as changeable as
weather? the chronicles, that anyone with the bribe
can have altered? And after all these ages of being
kept in reverence, the Crown passes to Liras here—"

"—and I break it," I finished for him. I buried my
head in my arms to shut out the sight of the shattered
crystal pieces before me.

"Now, you promised you wouldn't get upset,"
Melayne lied valiantly. "I don't care a copper piece
about the politics. What are *we* going to do, today?"

But it was beyond me to answer her. Slumped on
the bench I felt as gray and wrung out as an old
washcloth. After a bit she turned her gray-green gaze
upon Xalan and Sandcomber, who looked at each
other. "Well, we can't stay here," Xalan said at last.

No one disagreed with this. "We are safely hidden

for the moment," Sandcomber said. "This is a different sector of Uwuna, run by a crusty overlord. But in due time Liras' captors will prevail upon him, to search us out."

"And we can't go back to Averidan," Xalan reasoned further. "Even without this disaster. We brought the crew and all the cargo here, but the *Kingfisher* is seized. Unless—how much does it cost to buy passage on some other ship? More than Liras has in his vest?"

"Probably so," Sandcomber said. "Remember, you must transport Melayne and the babe as well as yourselves, for a half-year journey."

"I suppose Liras and I could *work* our passage," Xalan said doubtfully, and with good reason, since neither he nor I had ever done a real day's work in our lives.

"I will not sail anywhere," Melayne said with great firmness.

Xalan glared at her. "We have to go by sea somehow, to get home at all!"

"We could walk along the beach!"

"For a thousand leagues?"

Before they could fly at each other, Sandcomber intervened. "Have you considered the possibility of returning to Averidan by an inland route?"

"No," Xalan said. "Is there one?"

"Surely." Sandcomber retrieved one of the fallen maps and spread it out. In the southern style it was embroidered onto a piece of coarse cloth. "Rriphirrizē is up the river, here. And here, far to the north and west in this blank area, is a lake. The local people have their own name for it. But in Averidan I understand it is called the Tiyalene Sea."

Melayne, who in spite of much tutoring is only vaguely literate, brightened at the sound of the familiar name. "Tiyalor is near Cayd!"

"So it is, and we know the way home from there."

"And Rriphirrizē is well worth seeing in its own right," Sandcomber said, spreading out his broad dark hands persuasively. "My home is rather remote, and we see few visitors. You would be honored guests there."

Again Xalan looked to me for a decision. But I could say nothing, and after an embarrassed pause he said. "Let us do so, then."

"And thank you, Sandcomber," Melayne put in. "You have been a true friend." She used the Caydish word, which (unlike the Viridese) connotes a battle-brother, someone who guards your back in the fray.

Sandcomber ducked his head modestly and said, "Oh, do not praise me, dear lady, I beg. The pleasure is mine."

The warehouse had never been intended for a residence. We had to cook in the yard, haul our own water from the distant fountain house, and carry nightsoil away. The *Kingfisher*'s sailors soon wearied of camping in such discomfort. With no ship to tend they were as lost as fish in trees. Also the prospect of traveling upriver daunted them. A few days after my escape the best sailor nervously announced he had joined the crew of an Oorsevin trader making for its home port. "The mate is Colbic, so I can make shift to be understood," he said, addressing a point midway between Sandcomer and me.

The other men murmured in envy. Sandcomber said, "Alas for my hopes, that you would accompany His Majesty to Rriphirrizē! But I quite comprehend your inclination to hew to your trade."

These kindly words seemed to open a sluice. The other sailors made their excuses too, and begged the first to put in a word for them with his new employer. Only Forlen the pilot came forward to say, "There's no call for my knowledge in these waters, Your Majesty, since my home waters are around the mouth of the Mhesan. So I'd be happy to go home the long way, with you."

Sunk in black depression, I scarcely heard him. Xalan had to make suitable thanks.

Though at the time it was a matter of indifference

to me, I later learned that my abrupt decline was a subject of hot debate among my friends. After administering without success the Viridese home remedy for ailments—some plum brandy—Xalan suggested consulting an Uwunan healer, the city having once had some reknown in the art. My shoulder could be inspected at the same time, though the gouge was healing well. But this Melayne absolutely refused to countenance. After the attack in the cook-shop she had concluded foreigners were not to be trusted. "This is silly, you're Caydish," Xalan complained, with some reason. Only among our insular people are such attitudes common. But Melayne stood firm.

For his part Sandcomber was anxious to push on, and not only for reasons of safety. "Our journey will be far easier if we leave soon, during the season of easy travel," he declared. "Besides, our friend's affliction will, I am certain, pass off."

"How can you be so sure?" Xalan demanded.

"Consider the upsets of these past few years." Sandcomber tallied them off on his thick fingers. "Liras has in the past three years become Shan King, gotten married, become a parent, fought a war, lost two sieges, and been abruptly deprived of throne, Crown, and many kinfolk."

"It does sound mournful when you put it that way," Xalan admitted.

"I don't think getting married, and having this beautiful baby, should count as upsetting," Melayne said crossly. "Are you saying he'll always be fragile of mind?"

"Not at all! I simply point out that one can only force a donkey to pull so far, before it must rest. In time he will be himself again. That is," Sandcomber added, "if the difficulty revolves around his accumulated burdens. If the cause is rooted in his sudden and final severance from the Crystal Crown, then no one can say what his fate will be. In that case he may well decline away totally."

But this prospect was so distressing Melayne forbade

all discussion of it. In the end Sandcomber agreed to begin making discreet arrangements for our departure, enlisting the help of a few countrymen who might join us for the trip inland.

As soon as night fell he slipped out to begin this. Forlen dragged his pallet out into the yard, to watch the gate against his return. We kept within doors during the day to escape notice. But now Xalan and I sat outside too, to enjoy the night air and give the baby a chance to fall asleep at the breast. The lights of the wharves gave our warehouse a pale halo against the sky, and Xalan pointed out the young sickle moon hanging low in the west. "The same moon shines upon Averidan, and the City," he said. "You mustn't give up all hope, Liras. You'll make yourself ill."

"I am ill," I said morosely.

"No you're not, or not yet," Xalan unexpectedly retorted. "Shattering the Crown didn't make you sick. Otherwise you would have been ill before we told you about it. What's really eating you up?"

I roused a little, enough to glare at him; Xalan is far quicker than I. But in the faint moonlight his long face showed only sympathetic concern. Since before my accession Xalan has backed me, even in my follies, and now I found myself speaking almost as freely to him as I might to my own heart. "This catastrophe is the end. The god is through with us now, forever. The Crystal Crown was our only link with him, you know."

But Xalan has never worried about supernatural affairs before in his life; magi seldom do. So he was able to hear my words dispassionately. "What about the Temple of the Sun?"

"Sacked and pillaged, remember?" I said bitterly. "No—he's cast us off for good. We're alone now."

"Well, I don't quite see why you're so upset." Xalan spoke in the soothing tone one might use to question a frightened child. "You weren't on speaking terms before anyway, isn't that so?"

He was peeling an orange, his long clever fingers

prying the rind away in one large connected piece. He offered a bit to me, but I waved the fruit off. His question was beyond my answering. I knew my sense of crushing hurt was completely without foundation. The severance had been made long ago. And yet I felt forsaken and lost, like a fledgling thrown from the nest.

Xalan chewed meditatively without speaking for a while. At last he said, "I'll wager you're wrong—about the god throwing us off, I mean."

"Done," I said instinctively, and then thought to ask, "How can you be so certain?"

"Because of Ennelith," he returned. "Remember what she said—'I've been advised to save you'? You know as well as I, that her priestesses would never presume to *advise* the goddess about anything. So it must have been the Sun."

I did not give this wonderfully original idea the weight it perhaps deserved. "What shall we stake?"

He thought about it. "If I win, don't make me Master Magus."

Startled, I sat up so suddenly my shoulder gave a painful tweak. "But don't you wish to rule your Order?"

"I've never much fancied it," he admitted blithely. "A lot of work and responsibility, and not as much fun as being a plain ordinary geomant."

I leaned back again with a grunt of disgust, unsure of how serious he really was. It would be just like Xalan, to try and lighten my gloom by pretending to kick over the traces. "Your late uncle would tear his mustaches out in fury, if he heard you. If you win, I agree only to allow you to consider it again."

"Good." He crammed the last piece into his mouth.

I had been fidgeting with the orange peel, shaping it back into a sphere again. Without the fruit inside to support it the rind collapsed. I threw it down and muttered, "I've even lost my sword."

"Your mother will understand that it wasn't any of your doing," Xalan said patiently.

At that moment we heard Sandcomber calling and

knocking at the postern. Forlen only rolled over, yawning, so Xalan ran to open it. Sandcomber brushed past him, in a great state of excitement. "Alas, that we let the sailors go! Now we must hire Uwunan porters, who will surely betray us to their countrymen!"

Xalan shut the postern and said, "What, have the authorities traced us?"

"No, but they soon will! The baron Liras escaped from has made agreement with his compeers. Soon there shall be nowhere for us to hide!" He wrung his hands, with a spice of enjoyment in the gesture. "Something must be done! We cannot leave Uwuna for several days yet!" He looked at me.

Though I did not know it at the time, Xalan's attempts at distraction had done me some good. "I fail to see what use porters would be," I said slowly. "Dragging all our goods to some other hidey-hole is a waste of energy, if the net is spread throughout Uwuna."

Sandcomber looked as if he would have liked to groan at my obtuseness, but restrained himself lest I be disheartened again. Instead he flung his well-muscled arms around me, dragging my head down onto his broad chest. "Fear not, my friend! We shall find some diversion, some sop to fling to the searchers!"

I wriggled free with some difficulty, and adjusted my rumpled tunic. "I wish you wouldn't fling yourself into these situations this way," I said bitterly. "Anyone would think being hounded out of town by five or six barbaric despots was a rare treat."

"It is exciting, is it not?" Sandcomber smiled broadly. "You should learn to savor the unexpected, dear Liras. It is, after all, so common!"

The warehouse door opened and Melayne tiptoed out with a big basket under her arm. "She's asleep," she announced. "Why don't you come to the fountain and help me wash some things, husband? Xalan can listen for Tarys."

Sandcomber clutched his head with horror. "You must not do any such thing, dear lady! The baron has exact descriptions of all three of you! And you in particular are too striking—the only red head in Uwuna!"

"I could wear my hat," Melayne countered.

But I broke in. "We will fetch as much water as you need, so you can wash here. You can lend me your hat for a disguise, and Xalan can wear those white clothes. What would happen to the baby, if you were lost?"

The mere thought of this made Melayne pale, and she gave way instantly. "I've carried enough water in my time anyway, in Cayd," she said. "But where is Xalan?"

We all stared around. He was nowhere in sight. I even looked inside the dark warehouse. Sandcomber stepped over the snoring Forlen to try the postern, and found it off the latch. "He must have stepped out," he said, puzzled. "I hope he hasn't been hounded down already, in those long red robes and his tall hat!"

A further search, however, showed that the white tunic and cloth hat were gone too. With them, and his magian powers, Xalan was not likely to come to grief. Or so we earnestly tried to assure each other. But it was all rather a failure. Toward dawn Sandcomber grew too uneasy to hide it, and rousing poor Forlen commanded, "The Lady requires water—let us fetch some." To us he added, "I shall keep my eyes and ears open for our friend as we go."

"Bring him back, and I'll give him a piece of my mind." Melayne promised.

I agreed with her. "Viris alone knows what silly stunt he's pulling off."

Though it was nearly time to hide inside again, I felt too anxious to do so. Nor could I retreat into my former torpor. Instead I helped Melayne sort and soak the laundry, a task I had never set hand to before. Except for the diapers it was not difficult, and I boasted, "Wait until Siril-ven hears, she'll be envious."

"Your sister probably discards every garment when she's done with it," Melayne said.

Then Forlen entered, alone, staggering under the

weight of two full buckets. "The foreigner ran off," he reported, wiping the sweat from his weathered face. "Said to tell you there's something happening up atop."

"Atop what?" I demanded.

But Forlen shook his head. "He gibble-gabbled with some of the locals, and then dashed off. Leaving this water for me to haul back," he added sadly. "I'm hoping, my lady, that'll be all?"

"No, I need more water for rinsing," Melayne said. "Liras, you go help carry."

Forlen rolled his eyes, but I was philosophical. "At least I'll be able to look about too. Let me have your hat, dearest."

The thick humid heat of the day was almost completely gone. Under my bare soles the worn pavements felt deliciously cool, and the paling eastern sky gave enough colorless light so that one did not often trip into middens or potholes. There were people about, but nothing like the crowd that thronged during the day. The fountain house was grandiose, a portico of carven pillars supporting the usual half-rotted roof. Inside, the water piped in from the hills gushed from chipped stone fish-mouths into deep basins upheld by coiled serpents. It was a pleasure to have some mindless physical work to hand. If tribulation befell at home, I instinctively went out to dig over my garden.

The pleasure was lessened, after we filled our buckets. Made out of a big light gourd, my empty bucket had weighed like a big bubble. Full, it was almost too heavy to lift. I shifted the rattan sling-handle from my weakened left hand to my right, with the hole in the shoulder, vainly seeking a comfortable hold. I ended up clasping the bucket in my arms against my chest. When I tried to walk down the steps, the water slopped down my front. I had left my distinctively Shan tunic behind, and the water dripped down my bare chest to soak the front of my pants. "Perhaps Your Majesty should let me tote it," Forlen said, taking pity on me.

"Sandcomber warned us about speaking Viridese in public," I rebuked him ungratefully, and clutched the

bucket closer. Outside the first pale sunshine had just
warmed the sky into blueness. The crumbling road
back to the warehouse seemed about ten leagues long.
And Melayne had carried water regularly, in girlhood!
I knew people did live without servants, but had never
considered the drudgery that entailed.

We had scarcely staggered into the street when I
had to step abruptly back. A troop of armed men
came jogging down the street, urged on by the yap-
ping commands of their leader. Suddenly grateful for
the bucket which hid my face and form I peered around
it, to see the cause of the turmoil. There was certainly
something going on up on the ridge. The troop leader
pointed there, and yelled in Uwunan. "Wouldn't it be
handy, if the castle were on fire," I said to Forlen.

But he only stared, his mouth open. The men had
gone by, so I set down the bucket and stared too.
High above the castle, against the blue morning sky, a
tiny red speck showed. "Oh no!" I cried. "It's Xalan!"

Abandoning the water, I began to run up the street
after the troop. But immediately more sensible thoughts
prevailed. I had no idea what Xalan was doing. Nor
was there any way of finding out, short of climbing up
to the castle's towers and then shouting. Without weapons or language I could neither talk nor fight my way
into the stronghold. I turned, seething with frustration,
and trudged back to the fountain house. "What soup-
headed trick does he think he's at?" I growled to
Forlen, who wisely made no answer.

There was nothing for it but to haul our buckets
back to the warehouse, and wait for tidings there. My
temper was not improved when Melayne greeted us
with more work. "What took you so long? Find some
string or rope, Forlen, and rig me a clothesline. And
you, dear, change the baby's diaper and bring it out
here—I'll do it with this batch."

Time seemed to pass very slowly. I loitered around
the gate, listening for Sandcomber's knock, and scanned
the sky for a floating red figure. The citadel could not
be seen from our yard, but I looked anyway.

It was nearly noon before I heard Sandcomber's heavy tread outside. I flung open the postern. "Where's Xalan?"

"A moment, Liras, a moment! I am famished and dry. I hope your good wife has not put suds in all the water!" Sandcomber handed Forlen a large basket of food. I waited impatiently while he drank and splashed his face. Not until we were inside sitting down to our meal did he ask me, "Did you lay any command upon our young friend? I quite understand that the Shan King is an absolute monarch, by the most ancient custom, but some tasks are inherently impossible—"

"I don't know what you're talking about!"

Melayne stared at me over her cup. "But that would be a truly clever idea—to command someone to sacrifice himself to save the rest of us. Except that Xalan is very useful. You might have done better to use Forlen here." The pilot gave Melayne an aggrieved look.

"I wouldn't have done anything like that," I said heatedly. "Especially to a friend. It must be Xalan's own idea. We must rescue him, Sandcomber! Somehow, we must shield him from the consequences of his own *chun-hei*!"

Sandcomber brightened. "His what?"

I was sorry I mentioned it. "It's the quality of unreasonable and romantic high-mindedness," I explained impatiently.

"And why it's admired I can't tell you," Melayne put in. "Now we Cayds value common sense instead."

This was completely untrue, but I was too anxious to argue about it. "I'm sure that's why Xalan is up there," I said. "But what exactly is he doing?"

Sandcomber sliced a dark hand sideways through the air. "Just sailing about, above the citadel. I understand from the Uwunans that he actually skipped in and out of some windows at first. The women and servants were terrified. The baron evacuated everyone, and called upon all his peers for help. Every roof and terrace in that district is bristling with armed men."

"Well, at least he looked to be well out of arrow-shot," I said, relieved. "Although I don't know what good scaring all the barons will *do*."

Melayne helped herself to more parchment-thin meat. "But how long can a magus walk on air?" she asked. "Not forever, surely?"

"Indeed—and if he should falter or fail, they'll be on him in a trice." Sandcomber's dusky forehead wrinkled in a worried frown.

My appetite was quite fled, and I pushed away the leaf trencher before me. "We must do something— distract these soldiers, or attack them—anything, to give Xalan a chance to escape them." And, though no one could think of a way to accomplish this, I insisted that Sandcomber and I should at least go up to the ridge to see how matters stood.

For the first time in my experience here the towns-people were not thronging the roads. Everyone takes naps in the middle of the day. Hotter than a bake oven, the streets of Uwuna shimmered in the after-noon sunshine. I had to hop over the scorching paving stones. "I must buy some footgear," I panted, wincing.

Sandcomber smiled at me. "You feel better, I deduce. Yesterday you did not care whether you were shod or not."

Our walk was shorter than my own trek had been because Sandcomber knew the ways and we could safely use the main byways. Still, Uwuna is so large the afternoon was well advanced before we came near the citadel. The Uwunan vendors, refreshed by their midday naps, surged around us crying their wares. Sweating and thirsty, we sat down on a bit of wall. Sandcomber bought some slices of melon from a wom-an's tray and then casually questioned her. I sucked at the cool pink fruit and tried to look as if I understood their chat. In Melayne's big hat I did not much resem-ble the bold foreign swordsman the barons sought, but I eyed passersby nervously anyway. The burning sky above the castle was blue and empty, and there were no armed men about. I feared the worst.

Then Sandcomber sat heavily down beside me, and

buried his face in a wedge of melon. "Well?" I whispered.

"The populace has been in a tizzy," he said quietly. "After fluttering above the ridge for some hours our friend began to drift off to the south. The barons and their men followed him, of course, along the ground."

I would have wrung my hands, except that it might be noticed. "He must feel himself tiring. Let's hurry and see if we can catch up!"

"A moment," Sandcomber groaned. "My feet hurt. I wonder if it would cool them, to rub them with the melon rinds? Please, Liras, consider again! South of town is cliff and jungle—even if we could follow, we would be most obvious!"

"We can hide behind the trees." In my resolution I forgot to speak quietly. Several folk turned to look curiously at us, and to my alarm a stout Colb detached himself from a cluster of bystanders and approached. No longer prey to feelings of tolerance, I felt instinctively at my waist where my sword used to hang. "Sandcomber, talk to him!"

Sandcomber was wary too, though he did not show it. "Oh, he can't be very effectively belligerent, with that big bundle of kindling." Slipping into his fluent Uwunan, Sandcomber hailed the newcomer. When there was no answer, I carefully set down my last slice of fruit on a stone and gripped the hilt of my knife. We were not to be caught that way twice.

Balancing his billet of wood on one shoulder, the Colb lifted the floppy brim of his hat. And Xalan's thin face grinned out at me! Luckily, I was too stupefied to say anything indiscreet. Sandcomber, who is rarely at a loss for words, continued with his chatter, and pretended to examine Xalan's bundle of brushwood with a view to buying some. Casually we drifted back down the hill.

As soon as we sidled round a corner Xalan muttered, "Can I have that last piece? I'm starving!"

I handed him my slice of melon and said, "I'm very

cross with you, Xalan—slipping off to indulge in point-
less derring-do!"

Xalan slurped a messy bite. "You said yourself that
we had to distract the Uwunans. And I did. All those
thugs are floundering though the brush back there,
craning their necks to see where I'm flying to. With
luck they won't come back for days. I just tucked up
my robes and put this tunic on over, before I slipped
back."

"So you did!" Sandcomber patted his well-clothed
back. "You must be poaching like a crayfish in there."

"I am. Now we're out of sight, you can help tote
this."

Sandcomber took the bundle of brushwood while
Xalan devoted himself to gnawing the melon right
down to the rind. "I'll hold it," I volunteered. "Find
another vendor, Sandcomber, and buy him something else to eat."

"May Ennelith bless you with full nets and heavy
crops," Xalan said, so enthusiastically that Sandcomber
hastened to wave over a man selling fried dough. The
piping-hot squares were so beautifully golden brown
that I could not resist filching a bite. Disappointingly,
the crisp tender dough had a repellent taste, imparted
by the strange fat the Uwunans use in cooking. But
Xalan was so hungry he ignored the undertaste and
crammed his mouth full.

"You've been undeniably helpful with your magian
tricks," Sandcomber said to him. "Without your red
robes no Uwunan will recognize you. I daresay we can
roam the town in peace now, while the barons scour
the southern wilderness for traces of your lair. That will
make our departure far easier."

The bundle of twigs, tied with a rag, was awkward
and heavy. "Let's leave this," I suggested. "You don't
need it to explain your presence in the woods any
more."

"No, wait! that's my surprise!" Xalan glanced cautiously around and, seeing the street still busy with

evening traffic, ducked into a crude privy behind an old wall. "Look what I picked up!"

He dusted oily crumbs from his hands, and fumbled at one end of the bundle. From the middle of the brushwood he drew a long bronze sword with an ivory handle. "My sword!" I cried.

"Yes, I rescued it!" Xalan spoke with justifiable pride. "I was diving in and out of windows up there, to annoy people and attract attention, and I saw this on a rack of other weapons. It's the first time I've ever stolen anything," he added.

Eschewing common passions, magi are certainly supposed to be above theft. "Tripe," Sandcomber said. "You were just reclaiming it."

"I agree," I said, moved almost to tears. "And I'll see to it that no one will forget this feat, Xalan. "When we come back to Averidan I'll tell the rhetors to make a plaiv of it."

"But Xalan himself has derided their stories as cheap and easy," Sandcomber objected, as we hid the blade inside the bundle again.

"No, that is the proper accolade," I said, and Xalan endorsed it.

"Shallow they may be, but plaiv are real too, in a different way."

"They depict the realm beneath," I said, suddenly grasping what I had only looked at before. But my insight was forgotten when several men came in to use the facility.

CHAPTER 5

An Energetic Embarkation

Very early the morning of our departure we went to meet Sandcomber's countrymen at an agreed-upon quay. Tart and yellow as boiling lemon juice, the first sunshine preluded another hot day. All our cargo had been hauled out and stacked on the dock. Melayne sat on a bale and said sharply, "I warn you, Sandcomber, I won't sail far. And it had better be a trusty ship!"

"I trust you will approve our choice," Sandcomber said, quite undisturbed. In the harsh morning glare his skin patterns shone in rainbow glory, like an intricate mosaic floor.

After more than a week in the dark warehouse, it was a holiday to hear the seagulls mewing overhead, and see the sunshine dancing on the turquoise water. My depression had cleared, though the loss of the Crystal Crown would never heal over. I felt as if, having been lapidated under a hundred heavy rocks, my flattened corpse still held some life in it, however humble—nourishment for worms and roots, perhaps. One could live around the gaping empty hole of its loss.

And in its raffish, ramshackle way there is no place more alive and alert than the quays of Uwuna. Or rather, there is no other place where alertness and a lively look-out are so vital. Our goods were carefully sequestered at the farthest end of the rickety pier. At the shoreward side Sandcomber sat behind a barricade of bales and brushed off an endless caravan of vendors, pimps, and salesmen, whose wares ranged from sweetmeats, to rugs, to dead blue lizards strung on reeds, to each other. Nor was his watchfulness unnecessary. An urchin on a floating log skittered up like a water bug from the seaward side, and nearly made off with a bag.

The noise was terrific, the bustle of ships and sea overlaid by the shrill cries of vendors and the squawks of animals and birds. A more foreign racket could hardly be imagined, and I sat on a barrel behind Sandcomber to look over the peddlers' wares.

The instant they noticed my interest the shills' efforts redoubled. Cloth was shaken out so cunningly that the entire breadth was displayed without once touching the filthy quay. A man with a felted black rug embroidered in red and yellow wrapped it around his body to better worm toward the front. A whore wearing almost nothing except a quantity of clattering shell necklaces winked at me; I glanced nervously back at Melayne to see if she would take umbrage. Then Sandcomber pointed and called to a shoemaker who held up a dozen shoes and boots dangling by their heels or laces from a long pole. "There's what you need, my friend!" he said in Viridese. "Stout footwear!"

Grudgingly the crowd made way for the shoemaker. With Sandcomber's help I chose a pair of knee-high boots with thick soles, stitched out of some stiff hide I did not recognize. The soles were studded with short pointed spikes of hard wood. My feet felt hot and heavy as I stamped them to test the fit. "In this weather wouldn't sandals, like those, be better?"

"No, no! Trust me, dear Liras—these are, in fact, not as sturdy and high as I would like to see."

He set about dickering for them while I fetched my purse. Melayne had taken charge of it, lest I be robbed in a moment of absentmindedness. She perched on our heaped luggage like a small watchdog who momentarily expects thieves. The baby cooed in her lap, her fuzzy dark head shielded from the Sun by a cloth.

"You look so much better, husband," she greeted me. "Are you going to buy me a present?"

"Of course." It had not, in fact, occurred to me to do so until this moment, but all of a sudden I was ashamed. Melayne had left everything she knew and owned to follow me into perilous exile. And in the baby she had had excellent excuse to stay. Yet uncertainty and hardship had not quenched her spirit as they had mine. I took the money-bag and returned to Sandcomber resolved to shop some more.

After paying for the boots—Sandcomber could not grind the shoemaker down to less than an entire Viridese pearl, a scandalous price—I surveyed the other offerings. A felt rug was not useful in this hot weather. Food was too transient, and only a newborn babe would have trusted the honesty of the jewelers and silversmiths. When I confided in Sandcomber, he was very encouraging, doubtless looking upon my reviving interest as a further sign of recovery. "What your lady wife will assuredly require in the weeks to come is a traveling cushion. See, there's a ventilated leather one."

"Too unromantic. No, I see exactly what she will like!" An old lady displayed a brace of leopard cubs in a large wicker cage. Remembering the intelligence and valor of the one that had guarded me, I was instantly fired with the desire for one. Using a stick, the old lady pinned a cub to grab it by the scruff. I carefully imitated her grasp as she passed it to me, since the little creature was not tame. The baby mouth opened in a silent snarl, and the needle-tipped paws paddled helplessly in the air. It was a female, her velvety pelt speckled with small black spots that had not yet developed their striking white ring. Enchanted, I said, "Is she weaned?"

"She says she's been feeding it on scraped meat and asses' milk," Sandcomber translated. "Liras, you have no conception of the rigors of the journey before us. I feel certain you will find such a pet burdensome."

"Nonsense, why should it?" After some bargaining I bought the cub, and its wicker cage as well. Without

ceremony the old lady took off her blouse, startling
me very much, and rolled the unsold cub into it.
Leaving Sandcomber to secure some leopard food I
carried my prize back to Melayne. "For you, dear," I
said proudly, displaying the cage and its inhabitant.

Melayne stared at the little leopard, which lay with
claws dug into the floor matting against the motion of
the cage, yowling for its sibling. "How do you cook
it?" she said at last.

Xalan, who sat watching everything, shouted with
laughter, saying, "That's a very *Shan* comment!" I
opened my mouth to correct her, and left it open from
pure surprise. Three men had pushed through to the
front of the crowd. Sandcomber embraced them with
joy. In Averidan Sandcomber had been utterly unique,
and this I suppose accounted for my assumption that
he was truly one of a kind. These, however, were
obviously his countrymen the Rria—tall solid fellows
in vivid body patterns. All three were apparently of
mature years since their close-curled hair was as white
as Sandcomber's. Close to, the variety and brilliance
of their body colors dazzled the eye. The most rotund
fellow had yellow and green spiraling around his body
from one ankle up to his neck; the other leg and his
arms were tastefully scattered with triangles in puce.
The brief loincloth girdled beneath the broad belly
was hardly needed; the tattoos clothed better than any
garment.

We stood by as the four Rria clattered away in their
own language, like children watching a game and hoping to be asked to join in. Belatedly Sandcomber
noticed us, and said in Viridese, "You will forgive me,
will you not, if I make proper introductions later?
Greenleg here says our si'avs are almost in sight, and
soon there will be much to do."

"What are si'avs?" Melayne demanded, but Sandcomber had already begun to apportion the cargo.

Forlen spoke up gloomily. As the sole sailor among
us, he had accompanied Sandcomber when the arrangements were made. "They're boats, my lady," he

said, with the dour disapproval only a Shan seaman can profess for unusual vessels. "You won't like them." He nodded toward the southeast.

On the prevailing wind came a fleet of boats so odd I could not at first take them in. Headed directly toward us, they looked like jug-eared, skinny old men balancing trays on one hand, while wading through the water with their canes held out at arm's length in the other. As they scudded nearer, I blinked and stared again. The canes, I saw, were really outriggers; the lopsided look came about because each craft had only one, off the starboard side. The resemblance to skinny old men resulted from two long stout planks balanced edgewise onto the gunwales of each boat's dugout base. Only the trays were really trays, rectangular raised platforms set on top of the planks. On closer inspection the jug ears turned out to be two ridiculous little sails, inadequately flapping like laundry from two raking masts. And worst of all, when I saw the two sailors manning each craft I realized how small they were—scarcely the size of a dinghy.

"You must be joking," I said. "A washtub is more seaworthy than these toys."

"Don't let the owners hear you insult their boats," Sandcomber cautioned. "They are exactly suited to our needs: swift to sail in open water, and small and light to ascend the rapids."

Melayne scowled. "What rapids?" But almost soundlessly the twenty little cockleshells darted up to the dock. The Rria hastened to load the cargo, a few bales onto the tray of each boat.

"We Rria are more ponderous and ought to ride singly," Sandcomber said. "But you are slight enough to go easily two and two, at least for a while."

"I don't like the look of this, Liras," Melayne grumbled. She held on tightly to my arm while she climbed over the tray's flimsy rail. Then I handed in the baby. When I stepped in, the entire unlikely structure rocked, and I quickly sat down. The rectangular platform was not much larger than a big table, and the rail was

distinctly rickety. On the solid carved bows and stern
of the dugout perched our two boatmen—lean men
who were brown-skinned as all of the folk of these
parts were, though not as dusky as the Rria. Their
long fuzzy dark hair was coiled round their long skulls,
and long-handled paddles with wide blades were laid
out ready in the narrow dugout space between the
upright planks.

"They can't be comfortable balanced like that," I
called across to Sandcomber. "Is it safe? Suppose they
fall?"

"Worry not," he shouted back. "The rivermen of
the Iwa basin always sail so." And we were off, as the
absurd matting sails spread to catch the wind. Uwuna
dropped behind as we rocked with eerie speed north
and west along the coast.

To us the si'av was a completely new way of travel.
At first we did not dare to move about lest the boat
upset. But when we saw our two crewmen lounging on
the dugout prow just below, picking their teeth and
yawning, we took heart. Even when I joined Melayne
on one side, we did not turn turtle. The outrigger
stabilized the entire topheavy craft, and unless a foolishness like climbing a mast was tried, the si'av was
steady enough.

After some tense minutes Melayne realized she was
not becoming seasick. We rode so high above the
waves the motion was like flying, skimming the waves
as the seagulls did. And like a flock the fleet maintained no particular order. One and then another
si'av would forge ahead on a lively gust, and then fall
back. Because of the outriggers the little vessels could
not pass very close to each other. But on one near
transit I saw Sandcomber, enthroned on his platform
like a satisfied and unnaturally-variegated frog on its
lily pad, and yelled across to him, "This is fun!"

From the map I knew the main shore would swing
east to form a tremendous bay, choked with rocky
islands, and after noon we began to watch for them.
But the first herald of this new country came on the

wind. A stray breeze from the northwest brought the humid smell of swampy vegetation, thick with leaf-rot and wet jungle. The odor was not unpleasant in so brief a dose, but its strength, so far out to sea, staggered the imagination.

Then the greenery on the coast began to change. As Sandcomber told us later, the myriad islands were once the peaks of a mountain range, and no doubt had then been barren enough. But the land had sunk. For ages now the ocean had washed round their flanks, sundering one peak from another. And as if each island mourned its solitary state their forests waded out to sea. Masses of snaky bare brown roots curved up out of the salt water to support huge twisted trunks, and the thick tan boughs stretched across as if their many leafy hands yearned to touch those of their neighbors once again. Lianas thick as my waist drooped from islet to islet and let down seines of tough white roots to sip the brine and choke up the straits. And where the water was too deep for the wading tees, other undersea growths reared up blobby or stringy heads of sickly pale green or slimy brown—the sea's vegetable army invading the land. In Averidan we give Ennelith Sea-Queen the credit for filling earth and sea with life; I had never fully appreciated her inventiveness before seeing what Sandcomber termed the seaboske.

"It must be like trying to navigate through a good chowder," I said.

"And we have to go *through* this mess," Melayne said. "What if it's like this all the way to Rriphirrizē?"

"One can see why it took Sandcomber a year to reach Averidan," I said.

The bare contorted branches and roots of the trees showed black against the sun as he dropped slow and red behind them. Supper and sleep began to loom large in my mind, but I said nothing to Melayne. She hated above all dining at sea, and it was hard to imagine where we might halt. The shore was utterly invisible, solidly cloaked in seaboske. Any streams or rivers were masked or drunk up by the plants. But at last we came upon a sign of human habitation: a crude tunnel hacked and dredged out of the living saltwater jungle. Tied to a branch a faded strip of orange rag further marked the entrance.

The si'avs clustered around the opening like the bats of Uwuna flocking to enter their lair. Inside, the close hot tunnel of leaves would have been dim at high noon. In the abrupt tropical dusk we could see hardly anything. A mash of chopped leaves and stalks obscured the surface of the water; we seemed to glide across a roughly-scythed lawn. The crude passageway was barely high enough to clear the masts, and just wide enough to accommodate the boatmen's paddles. It curved this way and that to avoid shallow water or particularly stubborn trees. Since the shores had once been mountainsides, they were steep and uneven.

Every now and then a boat became immovably entangled in the tough stems and sinewy tubes. The boatmen hacked at the stuff with billhooks and light hatchets. I borrowed a hook to haul some of the weeds to the platform. Melayne scowled and drew her skirts aside, but I was fascinated. The plants were alive. The thick tubelike stems and leathery wet leaves slowly writhed and curled in the air. And as the plants twitched in their death-throes a host of minute life tried to escape. Little shrimps, shiny as glass, scuttled for the drying puddles, and hairlike sea worms coiled themselves into complicated knots. To see better in the twilight I bent near the tangled growths and prodded them with my bare foot. I almost shouted with surprise. The tubes and leaves stung my toe like nettles.

"For Viris' love, shovel that trash overside!" Melayne scolded. "Suppose the baby should get stung?" I quickly obeyed her, and then rooted through our baggage for my new boots. They were evidently going to prove well worth the money.

The boske became less attractive the farther in we got. The bare, bent knees of the wading trees trapped and withheld the rotting vegetation from the cleansing tides, so that the water became turbid. Huge glittering insects shrilled around us, and fat drops of sticky tree sap occasionally plopped out of the dark leaf canopy onto our heads. When a paddle lifted, sometimes a bubble of stinking swamp gas would follow, making us gag and choke. We sweated in the close hot air, scraped gummy sap out of our hair, and exerted the utmost care not to fall overboard.

Suddenly we turned a corner, and arrived. A tiny hidden harbor, green as jade, lapped a narrow earthen shore. A leaf-thatched reed hut perched on short legs out over the water—a guest-hostel for travelers. The wiry-thin man who ran it welcomed us with sour beer in cane beakers. Much heartened, we gathered on the porch around a meal of starchy baked roots and frog-leg gravy. The hib-roots, as Sandcomber named them, were a staple in this part of the world. To us they tasted tough and dry, savorless as boiled sawdust. "And what about tomorrow?" Xalan asked. "On up the coast?"

Sandcomber drained his beaker and sighed hugely. "Tomorrow we go there." He pointed due west. Through the green twilight I could just make out where he indicated. Solid as a brick wall, the nightmare plants seemed to grin back at us, confident and impenetrable.

We neophytes shivered at the idea. But despite the unpleasant prospect ahead, our meal that night was convivial. We became better acquainted with our three Rria fellows. The one who had been first to hug Sandcomber called himself Greenleg, from his tattooing. Similarly, the other two were in translation Four Circles and Spine of Red, who sported a startling hair style of white braids which stuck straight out from his head. Apparently names—or, more accurately, nick-names—in Rriat described either physical attributes or some notable function. Sandcomber's appellation was of this last sort. Beneath the vivid body patterns they were all very like him, ranging from solidly fleshed to downright stout. Despite their white hairs, they did not act or move like old men. We're anxious to learn Rriat," I told them over supper.

Melayne, who had not been consulted, sighed. "It was so hard to learn Viridese," she said plaintively.

But Xalan supported me. "It wasn't worth the trouble to pick up Uwunan, but Sandcomber is the only Rria who speaks Viridese. We can't ask him to translate for us forever—that is, if we stay in Rriphirrizē for any time," he added, with a sudden doubt.

Vaguely I said, "Surely, for a while anyway."

"You must stay for a very long time," Sandcomber said with grand hospitality. "And if you are anxious to learn Rriat, we are equally anxious to teach you." He translated my announcement to his friends. Greenleg took it as a compliment, and began to name objects around the thatched porch we were dining in.

Xalan, as possessor of the only writing tools, began to note down sounds. His stylus and travel-grimed waxen tablet interested the Rria greatly, as did Shan writing. Four Circles—the tallest Rria, with the four circles of his name limned in blue on a deep broad chest—produced a hand-sized wooden case that held strange reed pens and purple ink. He traced Rriat characters for us on the tabletop until the hostel's proprietor interfered.

We made no proper embarkation next morning. Rather, we waded our way around the swampy perimeter of the little clearing to its westernmost point. Here and there a zealous eye could just discern the traces of previous passages—the hacked bark on a tree trunk, now nearly mildewed over, or an infinitesimal thinning of the undergrowth where the trailing lianas had not laced themselves quite solidly together yet. Whether beyond it was land or water was impossible to say.

The slimy green-brown water squelched under our feet as we approached, burdened with knives, hatchets, and billhooks. I discovered my new boots were watertight, and it was just as well. Apart from stinging nettles and bad-tempered turtles, any solid patch or tree bole could easily house a snake or lizard. Xalan stepped on what looked like a mottled, half-submerged root, and it writhed away under his foot. He would have fallen backward in surprise, but Greenleg caught him. "What was that?" he cried, shaken, but no one could say.

To clear a channel for a proper ship would have been, I now admitted, impossible. As it was, it took all morning to scrape out a narrow, low tunnel. The pointed solid prows of the dugouts could almost always glide over the tangle of roots and weeds below the surface, so we did not need to dredge much. But it was still grueling, filthy work. We took turns to balance precariously on thick arched roots or submerged networks of growth, and hack at the vines. The bigger branches and main trunks were not worth sawing through, so our passage wound crazily about, deeper and deeper into the seaboske. Mysteriously, the trees sometimes of themselves left lanes and pools open— the aquatic equivalent of a forest glade. Then most of all Sandcomber carefully watched the green-filtered light of the Sun, and kept us more or less heading west; our relief at the short holiday might otherwise mislead us.

The first time I tripped and dropped my billhook, I bent and groped beneath the surface for it. The turbid water there came up well past my ankles, so that the footing was invisible. The tool could not sink far into the tangle of underwater roots and I soon recovered it. Bits of vegetation, both newly-chopped and long-rotted, clung to my bare arm. I brushed most of them off, but one would not move. When I plucked at it, the thing stretched out long and gray, like a fragment of old string, but the end remained firmly attached. I splashed forward and with my free hand tugged at Sandcomber's arm.

"A leech," he said absently, wrenching with all his weight at a tangle of slick vines. "Don't pull at it."

"And why not?" I asked, and did. Astoundingly, it hurt like pincers. The leech broke in two, a disgusting gray hinder half between my fingernails but the majority, including the head, still tightly stuck on my arm. A large red drop formed at the broken end, and I exclaimed in horror.

"I told you," Sandcomber said. "A whole leech would drink until it was full. Yours will now drip continuously—with your blood—until removed." He wiped the sweat from his broad brow with his forearm.

"How? When?"

"Later." Sandcomber sighed. "These waters are infested with them; we'll remove everybody's at once." I learned later that the intelligent way to retrieve a dropped tool was to scuffle for it with booted feet, and kick it above the surface.

At midday, tired out, we went back. I had slightly cut my good hand on a razor-sharp leaf, a falling branch had hit Forlen on the shoulder, and Four Circles had stepped into a pothole and fallen flat with a mighty splash. Everyone had at least one leech fastened onto arm or leg. We were muddy, wet, and insect-bitten nearly all over, and frantic for an opportunity to wash and empty out our boots.

Meanwhile, the rivermen had not been idle. The outrigger had been removed from each si'av, and the component bits stored under each riding-platform. There also went the two masts and the sails, tightly rolled. The entire fleet had been converted from sail to paddle by noon.

The Rria showed us how to remove the leeches, which otherwise would cling forever, blushing from gray to pink with their hosts' blood. One wet them thoroughly with atye, and touched them off with a coal or flame; the heat was intense enough to cook the creature but so brief the skin was not burnt. A little round sore remained on the unbroken skin; the leech sucked so fiercely it did not need teeth. Melayne turned pale at the sight, and cried, "Be sure you're clean, or I won't let you into bed!"

After lunch we set off at a good speed over the water we had cleared so slowly. The rivermen now wielded their paddles, which were shaped like shells fastened to long handles. Quite soon we came to the end of the passage. But now we sat in relative ease while the rivermen took their turn at attacking the jungle. Leaves and sap flew. From years of practice they were rather more efficient than we, and soon were tunneling beyond view.

The pleasure of sitting still passed. The hot, close tunnel of leaves lowered right over our heads. A juicy rustle of leaves soon submerged the thrash and splashing of excavation, and it was difficult to keep from glancing up to see if the balked vines were not reaching down to grab us. Watery sap from the cut ends pattered down on us to mingle with our sweat. The tree branches were green in shadow, or, where a beam of sunlight struggled down, mottled in yellow and purple. Now and again a larger sticky drop of tree-sap made a thick hot sound as it hit the platform. A glittering cloud of insects buzzed around his head as Xalan pored over the map. "Perhaps the seaboske doesn't extend very far," he speculated.

"Seventy leagues," Sandcomber said; we were too crushed to say more.

The Rria, however, seemed quite resigned—of course, they had come this way before. With fluid gestures Spine of Red invited me to join him on his si'av. Now the outriggers were put away the boats lay close together, and it was easy to step from platform to platform. My avowals to learn Rriat were taken very seriously. Spine of Red began enunciating slow short sentences in the tongue, indicating their general meaning with gestures. Sandcomber helpfully translated a few into Viridese: "This is a boat." "Those trees are tall." As a matter of fact these translations, though accurate as far as they went, were quite misleading. Compared with declarative Rriat, Viridese is an infinitely tentative tongue, full of subtleties and qualifications: a paintbrush to the Rriat hammer. At this point, though, I knew no better and repeated the strange words happily enough.

The others sat on their si'avs, fanning themselves and swatting at the swarms of flies. It was really too hot to talk. The only sounds were a thousand insect whines and the sullen drip of sap. Then a more substantial squelchy plop came from a farther si'av. Sandcomber shouted a command in Rriat, and the others leaped up to investigate. With a great deal of yelling and lumbering over rickety railings they herded the cause of the trouble along the row of platforms. It was a frog, a huge creature as big as my head and shiny-red as an apple. Now and again it tried to bound between the platforms to safety, but someone always headed it off.

Deftly, Spine of Red brained our visitor with a hook. "What good fortune!" Sandcomber said to us. "The turtles of these waters will eat no other viand." The frog was speedily dismembered, and its component parts baited onto half a dozen fishhooks. Four Circles threw one over the side and without pause began to haul it back again. I thought he had miscast somehow, and was astonished to see that in those few instants submerged the bait had lured a turtle.

The creature was not like the meek brown turtles of the Mhesan. This fellow gnashed a wickedly-hooked green beak, and thrashed wildly as Four Circles lowered him to the matting. The wrinkled head continued to bob and gnash even after Sandcomber cut it off with a hatchet. Carefully, Spine of Red poked it overboard with a stick. The yellow-green shell was the size of a serving platter when we pried it open. After the meat was cut out the thick top shell made an excellent platform for a cooking fire. The little leopard got the bigger bones. As the turtle meat stewed down, some boatmen came back for us; there was one per si'av. The others still labored to carve out our way. In this fashion we made perhaps two leagues that day. A man could walk that far in an hour, on a good road.

Nor, when night fell, did we find much respite. Stewed turtle was a thoroughly uninteresting dish. No cooling wind could reach us. Entombed as we were in the swamp-growth, neither moon nor star was visible. It was far worse than being undersea, for the inky night was alive with lights: glowing animal orbs, reddish snake eyes, and multifaceted insect ones. Our turtle-shell fire kept predators at bay but raised the temperature to roasting. The boatmen took turns to keep watch. Still, I startled out of my uneasy doze every time the boat rocked, fearing some uncouth forest dweller had crept aboard.

Near dawn the cap was put on our discomfort when a brief tropical storm blew up. The fathoms of leaf-canopy above us filtered the rain's fury. But the steady pattering drip wet us through. On another si'av the little leopard in her cage yowled with misery. I hid my face under my arms and tried to ignore the puddle rapidly spreading beneath me.

The itinerary for the second day was no different from the first. Our arms aching from yesterday's efforts, we began the assault again. The tangle of roots and vines under and over the water seemed even more maliciously impregnable and unexpected. Deep spots were a constant annoyance, invariably exposing one to leeches.

By midmorning we had carved our way out of sight of the boats. My current task—chopping the narrow channel wider—kept me at the back of the work party. Then, without warning I stepped into a pothole. The opaque brown water surged past my knees and into my boots. Muttering imprecations, I wallowed out. It was not worth the trouble to pause and shake the water out. The boots should soon fill again, and any leeches had doubtless already begun their meal.

As I took another step though, I felt movement inside my boot near the right ankle. A twitching something wriggled its way past my instep to squirm desperately in the water pooled around my toes. "Disgusting," I grumbled. I sat on an arched root and dragged my boot off, grunting.

A cascade of water poured out of the boot, and with it a tiny emerald-green salamander. The half-suffocated creature landed lightly on a stalk and slithered away. I wriggled my toes with relief, glared at a newly acquired leech, and wedged the boot beside me for safekeeping before reaching down to remove the other.

Then something hit my right leg, hard. Like a swatted fly I fell forward off my perch. Even as I grabbed at the festoons of vines, a solid curve of something caught me around the shoulders and held me suspended. I looked down and gasped to see a flat yellow head clenched tightly on the outside of my thigh just above the knee. Around my chest was a sinewy coil of yellow and purple body. I sucked in a deep breath, the better to yell, "Snake!" But an even thicker bight of its body hooked with terrifying strength round my throat.

Just in time, I got the fingers of my good hand inside the tightening coil. With my left I groped for a weapon. My knife was pinned to my side, and I caught up the boot. But hammering the biting head had no effect whatever. The creature's hug slowly drove my knuckles into my own neck. Through blurring eyes I saw an incredible length of purple-mottled body coiled on a branch above. The snake was easily thirty feet long, big enough through the body to comfortably swallow me whole. Below my embattled torso my legs kicked helplessly, like the mouse's tail twitching convulsively beyond the cat's claw.

The red-tinged haze in my eyes dimmed into roaring blackness, in which a familiar landscape began to coalesce—a rugged mountain range under a lowering midnight sky. As the tide of my life ebbed, the Deadlands emerged from their hidden place beneath the waves.

The road beneath my bare feet was scarcely worthy of the name. I stared up and up, appalled, at the craggy and steep trail lurching between sheer barren cliffs. At the very top of the pass the starless dark was thinned by a dim pale glow—the light from the city of the dead. In our tales the road is less or more hard according to how difficult or easy a person's death is.

But this was preposterous, a path not even for goats, but for eagles.

As sometimes may happen in dreams though, I found myself attempting the ascent despite all common sense. Perhaps it was the knowledge that this hurdle was indeed and forever the last. Or perhaps I could not bear being again riven from this realm beneath, however fatal my stay might be. Digging my fingers and toes into cracks, relying more on touch than sight, I inched my way up in the close cold dark.

Time does not run in the country of the dead, so I cannot say how long the climb took. But at last, muscles aching and toes flayed, I hoisted myself onto a narrow rock ledge. Twenty feet straight above was the head of the pass. I could just see one leafy tip of a branch of the tree there, showing like lace against the faint colorless light.

I turned my attention to the climb again, fumbling in the shadows for a ledge or crack. Suddenly the rock was visible, brown and seamed between my bare dirty feet. The light poured down from above, just as if I wore the Crystal Crown. I leaned my forehead on my hand to remind myself it was gone forever, and then looked up again.

And there at the edge of the cliff stood the most unknowable of the Shan deities, the White Queen herself, ruler of the Deadlands and all its residents. Her pale hands were folded together between her trailing white silk sleeves, and her beautiful pale face was suffused with divine light. She gazed down at me the way one would look at a leech. Xalan had been right—something was going on among the Shan gods. "I am told it is not your time," she said, in a soft voice that nevertheless chilled me. "Go back to the lands of life yet a while."

"That's not the customary greeting!" I could not help exclaiming. "And who is it, my lady, who says that?"

The quality of light that overlaid the goddess changed very slightly as she frowned. "You were more mannerly last time," she said coldly. "Do not be importunate."

But I had been younger, the last time I met the White Queen. Now I reached up for a projecting point of rock and began to scrabble up the cliff. The goddess clicked her tongue with annoyance and stepped back from the verge. I redoubled my efforts, but then saw with a shock why she had done so.

The vertical rock was crumbling, picked away from within. As the stone fell away in little showers of grit, I saw that roots were burrowing through and through the cliff, white and sinewy or thick and muscular. The Tree up above rustled its leaves ominously. Before I could slide back down to my ledge, the entire cliff-face disintegrated into gravel. A roaring wave of dry earth rolled over me. Dust filled my ears and blocked my nose. I could see nothing as the earth dragged me down.

In a panic I scrubbed my hands over my face. The instinctive gesture must have cleared my eyes—all of a sudden I could see again. Trees hung like stalactites from the sky, which flowed with water. I gasped, and found I could breathe. It was announced with joy: "He's breathing again!" My surroundings righted themselves, and I was stupefied to recognize the seaboske, and my friends about me.

"Excellent work!" Sandcomber congratulated everyone.

Xalan, overwrought to the point of tears, continued to choke, "He's breathing!"

I tried to lever myself up from the fallen tree I had been propped on, but Greenleg held me down. "Where's the snake?" I panted, thrashing.

"A very odd thing," Sandcomber explained with the greatest satisfaction. "Usually these reptiles will not relinquish a prey without a fight, which may then prove fatal to the victim. But when we looked back to see your kicking legs dangling from the forest canopy, we each took one to attempt a rescue. And the beast released you at once—so suddenly, in fact, that rescuers and rescued fell into the water. You made an unprecedented escape from a constrictor, only to nearly drown."

"We held you upside down to let the water run out," Xalan explained in unsteady tones. "Now, if you just survive the snakebite—"

For the first time I noticed the narrow copper knife Sandcomber was holding. "I'll be perfectly fine," I hastily insisted. "Let me stand and I'll show you."

The strong dark hands that held me did not relax. "Now don't get excited and stir your blood about," Sandcomber warned. "That will spread the venom." He passed the blade to Four Circles, who began to whet it. "You do not, I presume, recall whether the snake had dull purple angled bars on buff, or the reverse?" he continued, like one offering the best alternative in his power. "The buff-on-purple snakes are said to be harmless, not that we'd risk the test."

Of course I could recall no such thing. If the White Queen of the Deadlands rejected me, I was surely not going to die today. "I know that snake wasn't poisonous!" I shouted, but to no avail.

Four Circles gave a rueful shake of his head, and Sandcomber told Xalan, "That had better not be delirium." With sick fascination I watched as Spine of Red bent over my leg and deftly cut across each puncture. There were ten of them in an irregular oval on the outside of my leg. With tidy efficiency he sucked and spat. The blood ran tickling down my calf to mix with the drying mud that coated my skin.

"We'll rinse it with brandy the moment we get back to the boat," Xalan promised as he knotted a rag over the wounds. It was painful but not very difficult to walk back; neither tendons nor nerve in the leg had been hurt. Melayne wept at the sight of me. I forbade her to watch the rinsing operation lest her milk sour.

"I don't suppose you rescued my boots as well," I said, determined to find fault, but Four Circles had brought them.

By unanimous consent I was forced to lie down and

rest. "There may yet be a drop or two of poison lingering in your veins," Sandcomber said. I was sure there was nothing of the sort, but made only a token resistance. Now I was safe the nearness of my escape came home. The Rria nodded wisely over my sudden shakiness, and Melayne thanked them tearfully for their prompt and effective treatment.

"This dreadful country will be the death of him," she sobbed.

"Melayne, don't cry," I commanded, and sat up to comfort her.

"You go to sleep!" she rounded on me with illogical petulance. So I leaned back on the improvised pillow, and closed my eyes—only to spare her worry, of course.

CHAPTER 6

A Vegetable Impediment

At a steady two or three leagues a day, Xalan reck-oned it took us four full weeks to carve our slow path through the sea-jungle. The speedier progress was made when our route coincided with the occasional open channel. Food and water soon ran short. The si'avs could carry little in the way of provisions, and the racket of our cutting drove away all wildlife during the day, so that Melayne's bow was useless. We drained the last water cask about a week after leaving Uwuna. "Somehow I don't fancy drinking the boske water," Xalan said, gazing thoughtfully over the side at the green opaque surface.

"You could not, even if it were not full of insects and grubs," Sandcomber said. "It's brackish—we are, after all, still very near the sea." He pried off the lid of the water cask. Only a few cupfuls were left. Dip-ping them out, he passed them around. Then he took up a pole-axe and, raising it high above his head, slashed a cable-thick vine. Cut through, one half of the vine instantly retreated up and away into the fo-liage, like a mortally wounded snake. Of course the long stalk was probably weighted beyond, by some fallen branch or upswelling root. But we were discon-certed all the same.

The other half hung forlornly in midair. Green-brown and of a twisting growth, the liana brought to mind not plant life but animal—a navel-string to for-ever connect the si'avs to the humid green womb enclosing us. Sandcomber set the empty cask under the suspended vine. Very slowly a drop of sap collected on the cut end.

"We're going to drink vine-juice?" I exclaimed. "Ugh!"

"It will take weeks to fill the cask at that rate," Melayne made the more practical objection.

"We have no other option," Sandcomber said. "The contributions from several other vines will speed collection. And rather, you should think of this as a new gustatory adventure!"

He chopped through as many vines as he could reach, and put the cut ends in the cask. When a puddle accumulated, I smelled and tasted the fluid. The flavor was strange—leafy and blood-heat warm. "Like water after vegetables have been boiled in it," Xalan pronounced, tipping his cup. "Look, it's even greenish."

"Perhaps in time we'll get used to it," I said, without optimism. One sip vanquished thirst, the juice was so unappetizing.

Decent baths had long been merely a fond memory. Now washing went the same way, except for the baby. Xalan and I gave up our sporadic attempts at shaving; the Rria all wore short beards and the boatmen by nature seemed free of facial hair. The reek of sweat-soaked, sap-drinking people would have been overpowering, except that our noses grew dulled to it.

Melayne suffered considerably under the weight of her long red-brown braids. The suffocating mass was little better than having a fur hat stuck to her head. At last she grew thoroughly disgusted with it. One noon, when we came back from chopping at our passageway, Melayne greeted me with a wave. "Look what I did today!"

My jaw dropped. "What have you done to yourself?" The knee-length braids were all gone. With gleeful grin my wife rumpled hair shorn man-style to shoulder length. "I used my sewing shears. Should I cut it shorter yet?"

"Don't touch it!" I said. "Your hair was so pretty, I liked it the way it was!"

"But it was so hot and dirty," Melayne said, without a particle of repentance. She gave me a consoling peck on the cheek, and broke off to giggle at Xalan's surprise. "It will grow back fast enough."

"It had better!"

As a nursing infant, only little Tarys-yan's life ran as usual. Nearly three months old now, she could start noticing things. She was an attractive baby, plump and sweet-tempered, with a single tuft of fuzzy black hair. She ruled as the undisputed queen of our party. There was never a lack of willing arms to hold her. The softness of her tiny wiggling body between my palms was such a delightful contrast to the feel of billhooks and slimy vines. With their big gentle hands the Rria showed themselves to be excellent nursemaids, and in time Melayne even unbent to let the boatmen play with her. Tarys' only toys were gifts from these lean brown men—a shiny purple hollow seedpod, big as her head and light as an oval bubble, and a clicking rattle made of nuts strung together. In the sticky humidity these nuts quickly grew soggy and lost their attractive click. So every few days the boatmen would gather another handful, and spend hours laboriously drilling and stringing them.

Far less happy was the leopard cub. With his foreign sense of humor Sandcomber named her Fleabite. We contrived a collar and a short leash, so Fleabite could lounge on a platform instead of in her cage. And we fed her what we ate ourselves—turtle and frog, mostly. But she languished anyway. Nor did she grow tame, as I had hoped. We soon learned to isolate her craft at the back of the line. If you chanced to cross her platform, Fleabite would attack your ankles.

I found the boatmen difficult to understand. The barriers were more than language. With the Viridese crew of the *Kingfisher* we had all known exactly who everyone was. As Shan King, monarch supreme over

Averidan, my opinions were solicited and my slightest wishes deferred to.

Now when I woke early, my request for breakfast—I had picked up the local words for meals already—was met with total calm. Only when the Rria had roused, yawning, did the boatmen stoke the turtle-shell fire. Having bitterly protested being named Shan King, I was startled to discover that over the years my self-esteem had expanded to fit the title. I was now not worth lighting the cookfire early for, and felt the loss of respect.

Melayne worried about me, but hid her concern until one morning about a week after my snakebite. She lifted the bandage from the wound and shrieked at the top of her lungs.

All the startled jungle residents answered her cry with screams of their own, and Four Circles leaped up from a sound sleep so abruptly he nearly fell out of his boat. I had been half asleep myself, and this sudden alarm in my ear jerked me awake to glare around for the foe. To my fuddled suprise Melayne, alone and apparently unharmed, leaned weeping against the further rail. "What's wrong?"

"Look at your leg!" she wailed, pointing. I did, and noticed nothing odd. The group of punctures had scabbed over nicely some time ago, and I now did my fair share of chopping and dredging. But when I looked more closely I saw a tiny movement. A white thread was moving under one scab. Torn between fascination and disgust, I picked at the place. When I worried the crust free, the flesh underneath was still raw and red. The white thread stayed behind, squirming; Melayne, who had knelt down to watch, recoiled again. "It's a *maggot!*" she cried.

"Oh, surely not," I said in a shaky voice, carefully averting my eyes. "The place was clean and dry—"

Xalan climbed into the boat, his black hair wildly disordered from sleep. "What's a maggot?" he wanted to know.

"Right there," Melayne quavered. "Oh, look, it's

gone—burrowed in!" She scooped up Tarys and burst into dry sobs.

This reaction struck me as excessive. "If you must cry, let me hold the baby," I said briskly. But when I made to take her, Melayne clutched her and retreated. I hauled myself to my feet. "A few bugs are nothing to cry about; Viris knows we've seen enough of them here. How much will you wager, that Sandcomber will have a cure?"

Luckily for me, Melayne was too upset to take me up. When we consulted him, Sandcomber was unhelpful. "Worms are a common complication of open wounds contracted hereabouts," he assured me. "They're not fatal, I am told, merely debilitating."

"That's comforting," I said with some sarcasm. "What do I do about them?"

"When we come to the rivermen's villages, their wise men vend a cure," said he. "A brisk trade in it has sprung up. At present I can offer you no other encouragement, and only one admonition—don't scratch!" So there was nothing for it but to endure. My parasites were only visible when the bandage was changed; the rest of the time I sternly ignored any aches or fever.

An even worse day began when, over a repellent breakfast of turtle broth, Xalan said, "Where's Forlen?"

A glance around the clustered boats showed he was nowhere near. We all thought hard, trying to recall when he had last been seen. "Sometime during the evening?" Sandcomber hazarded. "But even a call of nature should not keep him all night. We must search the surrounding boske, quickly."

Abandoning our food we floundered through the muck, quartering the jungle between us and shouting as we went. "Suppose we never find him?" I worried. "If he drowned and sank beneath the surface, or was swallowed whole by a snake, we might never know it."

"On the other hand, he might merely have twisted his ankle, or caught his leg in the crotch of a tree-branch." Sandcomber put his entire weight into a mighty tug on his rake. The matted vines refused to budge until I slashed at them with my hatchet.

"The soul of optimism," I remarked.

"At the very least, he cannot have gone far," Sandcomber panted. "No one man can."

From the other side of our little clearing came a faint halloo, the sound almost completely smothered by leaf drip and the rustle of growing stems. When we had floundered across, Four Circles came forward to confer with Sandcomber in Rriat. "What is it?" I said impatiently. "Is Forlen hurt?"

"Forlen appears to be dead," Sandcomber translated. His wide forehead was puckered in a puzzled frown, and Four Circles looked ashen under his dark skin as he led us farther into the boske. Ahead was a small open space. I saw a figure dark and solid against the wall of greenery. If he was dead, Forlen had perished quite peacefully leaning there. But the Rria kept well back, muttering among themselves.

Xalan splashed up to me, his face greenish white in the dimness. "I never used to visit such repulsive places, until I met you," he accused, wiping his forehead. "Viris, I feel sick!"

And when I saw, my gorge rose too. Forlen's body did not lean on the vines. It was sewn there, literally pierced through and through in a thousand places by wiry stalks that insinuated through flesh and clothing. Green leaves unfurled from his eye sockets and sprouted out of his tunic sleeves. His body was being devoured from within, consumed scarcely before he was done with it. The endless rustle of the seaboske was suddenly menacing and hungry. I gulped hard and said, "We must cut him down, give him a proper funeral."

"I agree," Xalan said shakily. "We can't leave him like this."

But Sandcomber begged us to think again. "I have never seen such a plant before, and neither have my companions here. We know nothing of its habits, its weaknesses, its way of predation. Suppose you fall victim to its darts too? We would be unable to help!"

I wavered; the enterprise did seem beset with unknown dangers, and any funeral would necessarily be crude and simple. The seaboske would have Forlen anyway—did it matter how? But Xalan set his chin in a stubborn line. "We can't leave him like this," he insisted. "I'll just wade out and cut him down."

The only precaution I could think of was to hitch one end of a rope to Xalan's waist. If he fell, or if the weight of the body became too much for him, we could haul him back. This done, we let him go. Xalan stepped primly, feeling with foot and rake for sound places to step beneath the surface. The opaque water rippled green and oily brown around his high boots as he shuffled into the little glade. We watched the water and the undergrowth like hawks, in case something, no one knew what, attacked. But the jungle was as unmoving as Forlen himself.

Xalan's steps grew shorter and slower, and at last he stopped, just in front of the corpse but not within reach. "Well, what is it?" I called. "Are you going to be sick?"

But Xalan was looking down at his legs. "My feet feel a little odd," he said, in a tone of puzzled interest. "My toes have fallen asleep."

Sandcomber became violently agitated. "Raise your foot, Xalan my friend!" he urged. "Pick it up, above the surface of the water, that we may look at it!"

"I'm trying to." Xalan bent one knee, without result. "It feels very strange," he added dreamily.

He still did not sound frightened, but when Sandcomber translated, all the Rria grew frantic. "We must haul him back, Liras!" Sandcomber said to me. "Lend a hand with the rope, quickly!"

In a moment we were ready. "Xalan, we're going to pull!" I shouted, but he made no answer. Sandcomber rapped out a sharp command in Rriat and the others gave the rope a mighty tug. Belatedly I added my own strength. Xalan wavered against the drag of the rope as if he were bolted down. Then he slowly toppled backward at the knees, his back hitting the water with a splash.

"His head's gone under!" I cried.

"Don't stop! Pull!" Sandcomber said, and shouted again in Rriat.

As we dragged Xalan's supine form toward us, his feet broke the surface. We all exclaimed in horror. Long tough roots hung from every seam in his boots. We yanked, trying to tear Xalan free, and they hung as stubbornly as weeds. "All together!" I panted, and Sandcomber gave the word.

One by one the wiry strands reluctantly snapped, and in a frenzy of haste we hauled Xalan clear. The Rria seized him by the slack of his faded red tunic, and draped him over a convenient bough to let the water drain out. While Spine of Red stripped off his boots and hose, I peered into Xalan's blank eyes. "He looks stunned!"

"Doubtless the plants exude some stupefying juice or vapor, that their prey may be lulled into surrender," Sandcomber said. "Had we oil or enough good dry wood, I would incinerate this spot—kill the growth outright, and make the way a little safer for travelers to come. This is not my first journey through the seaboske, but I have never met these terrible plants before. So they must not be wide-spread—yet!"

In his drugged trance Xalan had not breathed in much water. His feet and legs were covered with tiny red sores where the roots had begun to dissolve away the skin. We had been only just in time.

We carried him back to the si'avs, and left him in the care of Melayne and the boatmen while we hurried to begin the morning's cutting. No one knew how broadly the plants grew. The sooner this frightful district was left behind the better.

When we returned at midday, Xalan was just waking up. "I'm sick," he groaned, shivering and sweating despite the heat.

"From the poison," Sandcomber nodded wisely.

"And just look at my boots!"

The seams, pierced again and again, hardly held one piece of leather to another. "I can overstitch the seams a little," Melayne offered. "But they'll never be the same."

We swathed Xalan in blankets that no one had used since Ennelith deposited us at Uwuna. I dug out our brandy bottle and with many fretful complaints Xalan accepted a sip. Remembering my own adventure with the snake, I was curious. "What was it like, being drugged by a hungry plant?"

Xalan turned a morose and bloodshot eye upon me. "It was very similar to being beat up by Xerlanthor," he growled, and pulled the blankets over his head. I had to conclude that either the poison was not as deadly as a snake bite, or Xalan was right about the deities' interest in me.

The main consequence of Forlen's unhappy end was a new anxiety, not for myself but for my daughter and wife. We had seen unpleasant lands aplenty, but this country was dangerous. Tarys was just the size of a square snake-meal. And even a slight ailment on Melayne's part would doom the baby as well. The dreadful fragility of the mortal flesh tormented me. Once, when some insect stung the baby, her hand swelled to three times its proper size. Melayne and I watched over her helplessly all night until the inflammation subsided. To Tarys' credit, she took the heat and vermin in stride. When I realized this was because she had never known a better life, I was ashamed.

The rigors of travel did not agree with Melayne either. When we wed she had been pleasantly plump, like a young partridge. But the demands of motherhood, coupled with weeks of indifferent and irregular provisions, had worn her thin. She needed a proper Viridese regimen—four or five luxurious meals a day, leisurely herb-strewn baths, and crews of nurses to watch the baby in the meantime. Or even a slice of her old Caydish life would do—goat cheese, milk, plenty of roasted meat, and cool upland breezes to nip the pink back into her face.

None of these were available, and I had never yet succeeded in persuading my wife to accept an extra share of food. The only hope was in a swift journey to Rriphirrizē. I had not so far considered what our life there would be; the struggle to merely arrive had bulked too large. But now, under the lash of concern for my loved ones, I looked ahead. Sandcomber—my only source of information—assured me all would be well. "Do you recall, when we first met, whether I mentioned my occupation?"

"You said you traveled, and then made a living selling the accounts of your journeys," I remembered. "It isn't something you could do in Averidan. And isn't the copying bill very costly?"

"No, your folk are singularly insular," he agreed. "So, in a different way, are mine. My journals shall be copied out fair for the benefit of our learned men. But the bulk of my trade is with the common people— attending parties and dinners, and so on. You," he added, "will naturally be invited also. Worry not—life will be good there. I may venture to promise that everything shall be planned for your entertainment."

"Thoughtful of you," I said absently. "I love dinners." We were busy attacking our daily accumulation of leeches with atye and fire, a business I would never get used to. The haze from the coals heaped on the turtle shell lowered in the thick, muggy air. We worked in a smother, and our eyes stung and watered. "But we can't accept your hospitality forever."

"Our customs are not as yours," he dismissed my protest. "Do not, I beg, concern yourself in the least." This was all very kind. But it was a comfort to feel the weight of my ragged money-vest, and reflect that here at least was a solution to almost any difficulty that might arise in Rriphirrizē.

Almost a month after we left Uwuna, the seaboske abruptly thinned out. Beyond the last arches of knobbly bare roots was a vast expanse of restless blue-green water. Xalan actually voiced my first dismayed thought:

"We lost our bearings, and cut our way east to the ocean again!"

"No, no!" Sandcomber laughed at him. "This is the Wiladu, the largest inland sea in the world, if one accounts the jungle-choked Uorvish Isles a solid barrier. Here the si'avs shall serve as well." Already the rivermen were busy re-assembling outriggers and stepping the queer slanted masts.

What a relief it was the next morning to climb onto the platforms and let the paddlers take charge! We set off with the sunshine leaning on our backs not yet unbearably hot. Quite soon the prevailing wind picked up, that we had been unable to enjoy while immured in the jungle. The silly rectangular sails caught the breeze, and we skimmed across the waves at a speed that intoxicated us after all the days of crawling through undergrowth.

For most of the first day neither shore was visible. We could have been on the bosom of the true ocean. But the winddrift told the tale—its taste on our lips was much less salty than sea spray, though the water was still too brackish to drink. As our fleet skimmed like waterbugs over the sunny water, the discomforts of the jungle passage faded like a bad dream at morning. We had almost forgotten the world was so wide, so generously proportioned.

As dusk fell we could make out, far ahead to the left, a rolling, forested shore. A single fleck of yellow light gleamed against the smoke-blue evening. "The river-folk's village," I hazarded.

"My thanks to Limaot and Viris!" Melayne exclaimed, with commendable broad-mindedness. "Now we can buy a cure for your leg."

"We'll probably arrive too late," I said. Between the desire to be rid of my repulsive passengers, and the certainty the cure would hurt, there was not much room for an intrepid posture.

After so many days of travel in a small group, it was peculiar to see new faces and hear new voices. The village consisted of a mere dozen long low houses built of reeds matted together. So many slim nut-brown villagers gathered at the common fire to greet us, though, that each building must have housed a whole clan.

We were made welcome with baked fish from the bay and the local atye, a raw virile brew that nearly blew the tops of our skulls off. As I had surmised, it was too late for any cures that evening. No one offered us a house; such an intimate favor is offered to a traveler only if he is dying. But the air was so warm and moist it was no hardship to sleep in the open, and anyway we had done so now for weeks.

We Shan insisted on bathing first in the clear lake water. The locals watched in astonishment as Xalan and I swam well out; Melayne retreated modestly behind some boulders with the baby. Afterward, I derived considerable pleasure from the simple act of shaving. When Xalan's turn with the razor came, though, he spared his upper lip. "I'm about old enough to begin my magian mustache," he said, critically inspecting himself by firelight in his mirror.

The next morning after breakfast Sandcomber found the local healer. He was a wizened toothless man, so old he looked as if he were made of dark sun-dried leather. His horny brown hands lifted the bandage off my leg, and I set my jaw at what its removal bared. The healer shook his head, and in the clicking local tongue told Sandcomber the price. "Eight grains of gold!" our friend translated, in the proper, almost ritually scandalized tone. "Outrageous! We'll go on to the next village."

"No, we'll take it," Melayne cut in quickly. I scowled at her, and Sandcomber heaved a sigh. No Cayd will bargain; they think haggling undignified, and Melayne's deplorable habit of accepting the first price offered had made her very popular among Viridese merchants. "What better use for your hoarded gold," she told me, as her clever fingers picked at the frayed stitching of my vest. I had to content myself with watching sharply as eight grains' worth was pared off and weighed in the village scale.

The healer nodded like a satisfied turtle, and for want of pockets or purse, since he was nearly naked, tucked the fee into the leather bag around his neck. Then one of his assistants dug into the glowing embers of last night's fire, and dragged out a charred but still unburned log. With the air of one demonstrating a grand mystery, the healer pried the log apart. It had been split in two, I saw, and hollowed out, the two halves being rejoined by crude copper hasp-and-pin arrangements which the healer carefully set aside to cool. A gout of pungent steam rose from the center of the log. With a long-handled spoon he scooped out a steaming lump of stuff, and before I could protest dropped it on my leg.

"Yow!" I exclaimed, jerking away. "Is this a cure or a torture?"

"It's what you paid for," Sandcomber said, inexorably leaning on my shoulder. I sat rigid, breathing hard through my nose, while the healer prodded the sodden scalding mass around to cover the entire oval expanse of the wound. The stuff was greenish and fibrous, derived from the chewed leaves and stalks of some secret herb. "It will draw the insects to the surface," Sandcomber predicted.

The healer knocked aside the steaming poultice before I was ready. I was looking straight down into the oval channel the snake-tooth punctures had gradually become, and the sight made me gag—white wormlike threads crawling slowly through the swollen and much-mortified flesh. The healer flourished a pair of ancient copper-tipped tweezers, and began to pick the parasites out one by one. He threw each onto the glowing coals of the fire, where it exploded with a tiny pop.

Xalan, who was hovering about from curiosity and sympathy, turned pale under his mustache and beat a hasty retreat. Having gotten me into this, Melayne also excused herself. "I have to dress the baby, dear." Sandcomber heartlessly sat on a stool to chat with the healer as he worked. I held my breath as the worms began to submerge again, knowing what was to come. Sure enough, the healer spooned up some more hot paste and slapped it on.

After half a dozen applications no more worms appeared. Morosely I said, "Is that the end?" As if in reply, the healer produced a gourd full of atye, and after fortifying himself with a sip splashed it on the wound. It burned worse on my leg than in my stomach, so I did not refuse a substantial sip myself.

"There you are, good as new," Sandcomber translated the healer's words. "Bathe it with atye twice a day till it heals over completely, that will prevent any recurrence. He offers to sell you some atye for the purpose, but I shouldn't advise it. Their price is, at a guess, triple the market value, and you've already been charged high once today."

"Don't remind me," I said resentfully, tottering to my feet. The wound throbbed like a sore tooth, growing so painful I was glad to finish off the gourdful. But as a matter of fact the place healed well, and only a shallow oval trench remained on the side of my leg as a memento of a repellent adventure.

Otherwise our westward progress was calm. In one place the shore on our left curved away south to form an inlet extending almost out of sight. A mighty river emptied into the head of that bay, we were told, but all we could see of it was the change in the waters we skimmed. The bay's liquid sapphire dimmed to green-brown, then slowly grew clear and blue again. Many little boats skimmed by daily, some fitted with platforms for passengers or cargo and others armed with strange cone-shaped nets for fishing. Though the weather continued hot and wet, the breezes helped us endure it better.

The only annoyance during this leg of the trip occurred one evening when I bent to lift Tarys. The sea-stained and sun-whitened linen of my trousers split open all up the back, neat as a baked root. "May the tailor who stitched them lose all his body hair," I swore, while brown river-children screamed with laughter. When I clutched the burst seam together the linen shredded under my pinching fingers. "What happened, did the garment decide to wear out all at once?"

"The heat is to blame," Sandcomber said. "Fabrics and leather can mildew away overnight. It seems you must at last resort to loincloths."

I shot Xalan, who was wiping away tears of mirth, a sour glance. "What about your magian robes?"

Startled, Xalan brought out his bundle. A discouraging smell of rot arose as he untied it. "This isn't decent," he groaned, as he held the long formal overrobe up to the light. Warp and woof had become netlike, clearly visible. The weight of the cloth was enough to tear the garment away from its seams. "And my hat!"

I shook my head over the wreckage. With the stitching decomposed, the hat fell apart into its layers of red cloth and buckram.

More saddening was the sudden and final disintegration of many of the Shan textiles Sandcomber had brought so far. With regret we uncorded the burlap-wrapped bales and unfolded gleaming silks that collapsed at an incautious touch. We could now poke our fingers through cloth that would have lasted for years in Averidan. Their crumbling glory freckled the lake waters with scarlet and topaz, silver and blue. Sandcomber shook out the wrappings and thriftily re-rolled them again. "So all I bring back is Shan burlap," he said, with resigned amusement.

The local weaves held up better, being processed mysteriously from tree fiber. Melayne cut out some kilts from them, and also a loose robe for herself. There remained of the garments we had brought out from Averidan only the long vest the lady Zaryas had given me. The silk shell rotted away and gave the garment a very strange appearance. But the wadding and stout linen backing held it together.

One would have thought that we had seen everything the earth was capable of bearing. But no—we

now traveled through an entirely strange terrain. Beyond
the marshy and reedy shores grew lush forests—of
trees, not seaboskage. The boatmen's villages were
populous but well-separated and inconspicuous; we
might have been explorers probing an uninhabited
land.

We had never seen such forests. Even Melayne,
who does not share my interest in gardens, was struck
by them. They were more like groves of giant grasses
or ferns than trees—tall stalks that plumed out far
above our heads in feathery growth, or thickets of
slim reedy stalks, branchless but nevertheless clothed
in leaves. There were no flowers as we understood the
word, but as if in compensation the animals all flaunted
the most preposterous tints. Everywhere we glimpsed
flashes of scarlet or brilliant blue, skittering through
the undergrowth or gliding and leaping from boughs.
Though one never got a clear glimpse of anything, the
creatures were by no means shy. Night and day they
proclaimed their presence with an incredibly varied
din. Squeals, whistles, toots, and clicks echoed through
the woods.

The fundamental oddity of this realm, though, became plain when one of these creatures fell into our
hands. Fish in plenty could be bought from the
rivermen, but Melayne took up her archery practice
again. One morning, as we were preparing to depart,
she pushed her way out of the rustling reeds, bow in
hand. One look at her face, and I immediately said,
"What's wrong?"

She held out her kill, gingerly, by the arrow that
transfixed it. "Look at this. Is it flesh or fowl?"

"That's a good question," I had to admit. The thing
was the size of a small goose, and wore a coat of either
spiny downless feathers or coarse hair, of the most
vivid purple imaginable. Its long back legs were bare
yellow skin and ended in feet with four toes, each
tipped with a birdy black claw. The front limbs, by
contrast, were almost handlike. The head was also
bare, long-jawed and toothed like a lizard's but tufted

on top with red plumes. A glazing orange eye, beady as a chicken's, stared reproachfully up at us. "I shouldn't eat it," I pronounced. "It's a freak."

"No, it's the first sign of home!" Sandcomber corrected me jubilantly, as he looked over my shoulder.

"Is it a bird or a beast?" Melayne persisted.

"We name animals of this sort boulirr," he replied. He bent and plucked out the arrow. "A bird-lizard, you Shan might say. This one will make a pleasant addition to our breakfast." And when the thing was plucked and cut up, it did resemble a bird. The bones were light and the reddish flesh stewed down firm yet well-flavored, like a duck's.

After this we watched the woods and shore with interest. If there were any true birds or genuinely furred beasts, they were rare. The life we saw was sometimes quite reptilian, and sometimes reminiscent of birds. But every one had some trait that marked it as a boulirr. In the mornings the winged lizards, as green as a bottle, soared down to skim for fish on the water. Their wings showed bare and batlike against the clear sunrise, but any bird might be proud of the long beaks with which they scooped up fish.

And one evening after we camped for the night, a pointed head the length of our boat poked out of the upper boughs. Xalan jumped up and spilled his plate into the fire. "Where's my sword," I gasped.

Sandcomber did not even look up. "It's harmless," he said. "They eat insects and stems."

"How do you know?" Xalan asked, shaken. "Look at its teeth!"

"It's what you would call a wyvern," he said. "A wild one. The Rria are the only race that tames them."

"You can tame wyverns!" I exclaimed, genuinely impressed. "I thought they were fabulous animals only, in plaiv for heroes to fight." But Sandcomber laughed at this idea.

Ten days' sail brought us to the southwesternmost corner of the bay. Here the northern shore bent to meet the southern one. The land was rockier and

higher, and we guessed there would be climbing where
the Iwa flowed into the bay. The mighty river roared
cold and clear into the warm lower waters. It was
perhaps half as wide as the Mhesan, and far swifter.
Even with sail and paddle the current seemed nearly
too much for the rivermen. When I peered upstream,
I could see the water tumbling foamy-white over a
series of rapids.

Our guides, though, were well-prepared. Very slowly
the rivermen coaxed their crafts against the current up
to the north shore. There we landed on a strip of
beaten earth. Up the hill beyond was a notch cut in
the forest—a portage path.

"We're going to have to work again," Xalan proph-
esied, and he was right. In its own fashion the labor of
dragging the si'avs up the Iwa was nearly as great as
getting them through the seaboske.

The first step was to climb the path and clear away
fallen trees and branches. Then we hauled the baggage
bit by bit up past the rapids. This weary work took all
of one day, and that night we made two camps, one
above and one below, lest either boats or cargo come
to grief.

Disassembled, the boats were relatively light but
unwieldy. Though two men could manage a stripped
si'av on the level, it took six of us to pull and push
each one up the steep path.

After so many ascents and descents, the narrow
track grew trampled and slick with red mud. In this
way we lost one of the boats—two of the six haulers
had the bad luck to slip at once, and the dugout broke
from the grasp of the others to career down the hill.
The path curved round the larger trees. As the boat
arrowed straight down toward a huge plumy one everyone winced. It hit the green trunk with a tremendous juicy smash, making the tree shudder from root
to crown. Feathery green frondlets showered down
over a wide area.

When we scrambled down to inspect the dugout, we
found one end and side staved in. The damage was

irreparable, especially as we had no tools. It was not even worth shoving the wrecked boat farther up or down. We levered it off the path into the ferny undergrowth. The two rivermen who had managed it wept as if for the death of a kinsman, and even we Shan were discouraged.

When the final boat was hauled up, it was very late. We were almost too worn out to eat, which is saying a great deal. The next morning we looked forward to a day lounging on a platform, sipping atye; after much encouragement and example from the Rria, Xalan and I had got quite accustomed to the liquor.

There is no pleasure like watching other people work hard. Our progress up the swift green current was slow but steady. But to my disgust we halted, well before sundown, at the foot of yet another set of rapids. "How many portages are there?" Xalan groaned, rubbing his blistered hands.

"Half a dozen worth mentioning," Sandcomber tried to comfort him. "And we can hire help in the carrying later on."

Only by doing so were we able to slowly work our way upriver without killing ourselves. The villages on the lower Iwa had a brisk business in hauling goods and boats up or down the river.

As we climbed ever higher into the heart of the continent, a sensation of distance grew more and more upon me. We had traveled so far, leaving known lands and even familiar plants and animals behind, that I could almost convince myself the writ of old deities did not run here either. One evening, after our meal of strange starchy roots washed down with searing atye, with the weird calls of night-roaming boulirr ringing through the forests beyond, I dug the Crystal Crown out of the bale I had packed it in.

In the ruddy light of the pungent village fire the three chunks of crystal looked utterly foreign, like an oar on a mountaintop. But time, or distance, had perhaps wrought some healing in me. I thought of its white-hot power broken, its indwelling spirit perished or fled, and felt only a calm grief. Something wonderful had died from the world, but one cannot mourn forever; life goes on.

As I put the fragments back into their box again, Sandcomber came up to refill his beaker and noticed what I was about. "If ever you become weary of conveying those bits about, speak," he said. "I should be happy to take them."

I replied without needing to think. "I couldn't do that."

"If you do not return home you shall not need such melancholy souvenirs." Raising the beaker to his lips he sucked the potent spirit down, slowly but steadily. Then, refilling it again from the big gourd, he added, "Your folk are perhaps well rid of it. The Crystal Crown has haunted your race too long, like an over-tenacious house guest. In its absence they will learn to live in the real world."

I did not think so. But rather than argue about it I drained my beaker also, though without Sandcomber's easy air, and let him refill it for me.

CHAPTER 7

An Awaited Arrival

Despite intensive tutoring, our progress in speaking Rriat was not swift. A Shan tongue went round the twisty and complex sounds with difficulty, and the grammar remained opaque. Somewhat easier than speaking Rriat was to hear and understand it. When you say something, you needs must say and know every word; in listening, the ear can skim general meaning from a few important words. In this way, listening to the others talk, we heard Sandcomber using different names for the other four Rria than we did. "Oh, you knew that," Sandcomber explained when I asked about it. "Every person has a quantity of names. No, not epithets, but nicknames, you might say. One is called differently in the mouths of different people because the relationships are different."

When I thought how many names this must involve, my head spun. Such a supremely inconvenient system must have more to it than mere custom. "Your genealogies must grow very cumbersome. Does no one use their real name?"

"A true name expresses what you are," Sandcomber replied. "It is engraved, or being engraved, during the course of your life, on your heart. Only death reveals to you the secret name you wrote for yourself within, in life. It's deemed unwise to try to anticipate that name." So diverting was this philosophy, I quite omitted to ask what the other Rria's names meant.

With great labor we ascended four major rapids and

several minor ones, before passing one of the Iwa's major tributaries. "A hundred of your leagues remain," Spine of Red said to me in slow Rriat, and to my delight I actually understood him. Perhaps we should not always have to rely on translators after all.

The rapids became fewer but far steeper as the river was squeezed between huge buttresses of rock. Little by little as the country rose, the heat and humidity lessened, though the climate never grew as pleasantly dry as Averidan's. The strange forests became more wholesome-looking to the civilized eye. The plumy trees held their ground, waving from the hills like the fringed tails of a thousand dogs, but the weird reedy thickets were taken over by groves of what could almost have been proper trees.

Only those interested in plants, like me, found oddities. Their green trunks, for instance, seemed to be clothed in a rough thick bark like loosely-attached fishscale. By devoting an entire evening to the experiment, though, I found there was no trunk at all underneath the bark. Or rather, the trunk was all bark, as an onion is all layers. I plucked away tier upon interlocked tier of juicy green bark chips, each the size of my palm, without ever coming to any supportive core.

In fact, since my efforts were concentrated on the section of trunk I could reach, I seriously weakened the tree. My botanical reflections were rudely broken into when the thinned trunk teetered under my hand. As I gaped in surprise, it overbalanced with a slow rending crash, sending the lizards and snakes resident in the moplike crown scurrying. Everyone in camp jumped. Startled boulirr rose chattering on leathery wings, or stuck toothy feathered heads out of their dens to curse me. Melayne, whom I had frightened very much, scolded me no less severely: "You could have been killed, if you hadn't the dumb luck to be standing uphill of it!"

"It wasn't luck but wit," I retorted indignantly, but she snorted at the suggestion.

At last, at the close of a long day on the river, we

came to where the forests ceased. A final foamy waterfall marked the transition from forest to tableland. The sloping land was clothed in a short turf of every possible tint between yellow and green. In the distance a range of mountains fenced the western horizon, sharp-cut as a hedge of knives against the sunset. The farther peaks were tipped with white, a marvel in this climate. But the nearest one, which reared up close enough to the Iwa to make it fork, bore no snow. Instead a gray banner of smoke fluttered from the jagged summit. "A fire-mountain!" Xalan gleefully rubbed his hands. "I've read of them, but never seen one. Wait till I tell the other geomants, they'll perish of envy."

At the green foot of this mountain glittered what looked like a gold sequin. "Rriphirrizē!" Sandcomber said softly, his eyes wet, while the others capered, shouting their joy.

In the clean moist air the city looked considerably closer than it really was. We paddled two days against the deep swift current before we came among broad fields of some lush flowering crop I did not recognize. They were tended by Rria of both sexes, whose tattoos fit them quite well into the landscape. We were astonished, when some youths threw down their hoes to wave at us, to see that even the children had white hair. In Rriphirrizē hoary curls are not a badge of age at all. I had to revise downward all my estimates of my companions' age.

Xalan picked up another interesting point. "Where are the villages?" he wanted to know.

"There are none, everyone lives in town," Sandcomber called across from his boat.

"It's a long walk," I said appalled, for at the time—the late afternoon light was silvering the river—we were still ten leagues from the city. A sturdy man might need no more than a day to walk the distance, but very little work would be got out of him at the end of the trek.

Our si'avs had swung apart again, so Sandcomber could respond only by pointing toward shore. He shouted, "They ride!" but surely the noise of the rushing current confused my ear. For want of better occupation though, I did watch the banks as they slid slowly past.

Wide beds of reeds, shiny green as if they were lacquered, fringed the river and were home to wildly-colored boulirr that flocked and honked and preened on the water just like ducks. Only the taloned fingers at the "shoulders" of their wings showed the lizardly blood, and their orange bills full of sharp fishy teeth.

Beyond rolled fields of dark green bushes. Though we saw no flowers, their strong foreign perfume wafted to us whenever the wind veered, and the dark motes of bees swarmed from upriver down toward the fields. The prevailing wind must be laden with scent. My mouth watered at the thought of the honey that might be distilled from the blooms I could not see.

The fantasy was too nostalgic to entertain alone, and I mused aloud to Xalan, "Look at those bees—when was the last time we ate honey?"

Xalan stared. "If those are bees, I don't want anything to do with their hives!"

I looked again, with astonishment. What I had taken to be small insects, not very far away against the setting sun, were really large but distant animals. They looked like bees because they flew not steadily, but up and down—a steep upward soar into the sky, punctuated by a great flapping of stubby wings, and then long serene glides down to the ground. Each creature rose or fell at a different rate, so it was hard to judge how many there were. Perhaps fifty of the things rapidly approached, following the course of a beaten track between the reeds and the fields.

With a mighty racket of wings the flock surged to a gradual halt a little way ahead of us. Like a coopful of nervous chickens they did not stand still, but bobbed up and down, skittering back and forth with piercing hoots of excitement. But in their relative repose it was possible to clearly see the beasts. Right away I recognized the thick pointed beaks. "These must be wyverns," Xalan said, awed. "Sandcomber did say the Rria tame them."

I could still hardly believe it, but for the evidence of the light trappings above each thrashing pair of wings. The wyverns were, of course, boulirr, gaudy and strange. Their short necks were bare as a chicken's in the stewpot. Thick gooselike orange beaks made a clattering noise like mallets pounding a brick wall, and two vestigal fangs peeped down in front. A deep ruff of hairy feathers at the base of the neck clothed the thick shoulders and keel-sharp breast. The wings were also feathered, but were so short and almost armlike it was plain the wyvern was no flyer. Each wing sprouted three clutching bare fingers at the first joint. The two three-toed hind limbs were so huge a wyvern in repose tended to slump forward between them. If I had never seen a boulirr and become used to their lizard-bird look, I should have likened wyverns to the little green mantises that patrolled gardens at home.

At first we saw only one rider, a Rria apparently clinging for dear life to the back of a huge blue and white wyvern. But the workers had put away their tools and now ran to mount also; the beasts were about as tall as a man so only the youngsters needed a boost. As we learned later, intelligence is not a notable wyvern trait, or indeed of boulirr in general. Wild wyverns faithfully follow the patriarch of their flock. In their training the Rria took advantage of that trait. This entire flock had been brought out by one rider on the blue and white leader.

Observing the niceties of wyvern management enthralled me. The proper seat on the beast seemed to be just in front of the wings. Two stout woven bands passed round the beast, one circling what on a horse would be the shoulders, to hold on to, and the other in a sort of noose arrangement round the wyvern's throat.

Now the flock seemed ready to bound back to town. Riderless wyverns leaped up and down, shrieking like pigs in the slaughterhouse, until the leader moved off.

Then they all bounced flapping after him toward the
city again, bearing the Rria with them. In the space of
two breaths the wyvern flock looked no bigger than
bees again. At that tremendous rate the ten-league
journey would take no time.

"And they ride to and fro every day," I marveled,
more than a little envious. "What fun it must be, even
more speedy than a horse—more exciting than walking on air."

"I doubt it," Xalan said, in defense of his craft.

And Melayne added, "If being asea makes a person
seasick, what would riding a wyvern do?"

In spite of these dampening comments, as soon as
we disembarked for the night I demanded of Sandcomber, "Why don't we ride wyverns the rest of the
way, and arrive tonight?"

"Such steeds are not for the uninitiate! Every year
lives are lost when folk fall off. The rivermen must
come to Rriphirrizē anyway, so we may as well ride
along." And with this I had to be content.

Because we passed no outlying villages the impression that Rriphirrizē was a small town became hard to
erase. In Averidan no smallholder would ever consent
to live far from his property, lest in his absence a
neighbor nudge a boundary-stone, divert water from
his canals, or otherwise lapse into chicanery. But the
Rria apparently ran a more trusting society. The next
day when we came in sight of the city, its size and
glory looked foreign and incongruous above the fields.

Rriphirrizē was built on a wide ledge at the foot of
the fire-mountain, which Four Circles identified as
Iphalar. The site gave the inhabitants a fine view of
the tableland and the Iwa valley, but Xalan shook his
head at it. "No geomant would ever build so near the
mountain," he said. "Its internal fires can be dangerous. I hear that volcanoes are filled with rock that's
hot enough to run like water."

Sandcomber, whose si'av happened to be near enough
for him to overhear this, was scandalized. "Rriphirrizē

is safeguarded by sentinels who have shielded us for generations. I beg you not to repeat those sentiments!"

To our dazzled eyes the city looked to be made of gold—not just gilded with sunlight, but cast of solid metal. No building was unduly tall, but all were heavily festooned with porches, balconies, terraces, and verandas, so that their shape was hard to see. I had thought Rriphirrizē would blaze with the gaudy colors the Rria love. This unexpected restraint in adorning the exteriors gave the place a comfortingly well-managed and uniform air.

At the fork we bore left; the other branch looked shallow and rocky. The city gleamed very close above on our right. Behind and higher yet Iphalar bulked green and gray, so high we had to crick our necks to take the entire peak in. Its massive closeness made me giddy. For a moment I had an idea that the mountain and its smudgy banner might topple over on us.

Docks and quays did not appear to be the fashion in Rriphirrizē. Si'avs and other small craft were simply drawn up on the bank, which hereabouts was flat shelves of rock. The home-going farmers must have brought word of our arrival, for many townspeople were come down to meet us. Under their stiff capes or short open jackets every adult fairly blazed with tattoos. Only the children, sleek and lively as black puppies, ran about in mere loincloths; their unpatterned skins made them look bare compared to their elders.

A sense of shyness overwhelmed us. Lean, sunburnt, and clad in rags, we none of us cut very impressive figures. Body colors at least lent dignity. I remembered with regret the hundreds of gorgeous robes of the Shan King; it might have been another existence. "You could comb your hair," I told Xalan, dragging a borrowed one over my own unshorn head. "What a pity all your robes are lost—we look like beggars."

"Well, we're not," he returned, "so long as you have that vest."

"A good thought." After I carefully unwrapped the

fragile garment and put it on, no further improve-
ments came to mind. We composed ourselves to look
calm and important.

Sandcomber's si'av landed first. As he leaped nim-
bly ashore, the townspeople cried out welcomes so
swift I could not understand any words. One needed
no Rriat, though, to recognize the handsome strapping
woman who ran to embrace him. Melayne wiped a
sentimental tear from her cheek. "If I hadn't insisted
on coming with you, we might have been parted as
long."

We were pleased to see that our appearance excited
the Rria greatly. Dark fingers pointed, children wormed
madly through the crowd for vantage points, and the
short stood on tiptoe or hopped to see better. People
pressed down to the water's very edge. "Hold on tight
to the baby," I told Melayne. "We're going to have to
push for a foothold."

But Sandcomber's forethought had extended even
this far. Our paddlers slowed their stroke and allowed
the other Rria to reach shore first. Four Circles waved
at all his kin but did not hesitate to shove them back
to make room. Spine of Red came ashore and scolded
the agile children in voluble Rriat. Gradually a narrow
space, fenced by our friends, was cleared.

"The last stretch of water we'll have to cross!"
Melayne exulted, as our si'av neared the bank. The
others had jumped to land before their boats were
hauled onto the rock. From the space cleared for us,
though we were plainly expected to sit until the craft
was safe ashore. Then I suddenly thought how tame
that would look.

As our carved wooden prow grated onto flat rock I
stood up and threw a leg over the platform rail, ready
to leap. At that moment, however, the riverman pulled
the boat higher with a vigorous tug. The platform
jerked neatly out from under my bare feet, my inside
ankle slipped off the rail, and I fell with a mighty
splash into the water.

The river was unexpectedly swift and deep—the current had cut a deep bed for itself. My surprise was so great that for an instant I did nothing to save myself, and sank right through the clear green depths to the stony bottom, perhaps a fathom down. Instinctively I kicked off again for the surface. But as if some unseen hand grasped my legs, I found myself sinking right back again. The cold water roared in my ear; I had not breathed properly before my plunge. Then with a last vestige of common sense I realized the culprit was my gold-weighted vest. As Zaryas had foretold, its hidden treasure was better than any anchor.

Shrugging off the garment, I let it sink. Right away I was free. One desperate kick, and my head broke the surface. Cheers and yells resounded, and in Viridese Melayne cried, "How can you be so careless!"

A dozen dark hands reached to help me out, and I was dragged safely onto land, mortified and sodden as a soused cat. In the interval Xalan and Melayne had disembarked. Our companions now surrounded us closely to keep the people off—"You're going to get me wet," my wife scolded—and Sandcomber led us away.

In the press it was impossible to see where we were going. We did not however walk very far. After several uphill turns we climbed two steps onto a porch where the crowd did not follow. Our escort stayed there, as Sandcomber conducted us within doors. "My home," he announced. "Do not unpack—you will probably not be staying here. I feel sure the Governor of Rriphirrizē will insist on offering you official hospitality. I must hurry now to apprise him of your arrival." And with this abrupt welcome he darted out again.

But his wife stayed. Her generously-built body was adorned with patterns in red and yellow, and her white hair was pinned on the crown of her head. She did not seem dismayed at having to entertain us, or at the brevity of Sandcomber's stay so far. In slow clear Rriat she asked, "Do you hunger? Thirst?"

"Yes," I said carefully in the same tongue. While she bustled about filling carved wooden cups with the inevitable atye, we sat gingerly on the low wooden stools scattered around the room, and stared. The low broad chamber was open on one side to catch the breezes. The wooden walls were carved with shallow abstract reliefs, painted in the vivid colors of Rriat fashion. The dizzying effect quite made the large room close in, and when our hostess stood still she blended into the walls like a beetle on a leaf.

My kilt and hair had stopped dripping, but I still felt cross and rumpled, and sourly accepted a towel. "You haven't made an impressive entry into town," said Xalan after his first sip of atye.

I was too disheartened to do more than throw the wet towel at him. "To drag that gold so far and then lose it is sickening. What shall we live on now?"

The question does not often concern the Shan King, and I considered myself a paragon of forethought for thinking of it. So my temper was not improved when Xalan dismissed the problem with an airy gesture. "We'll stay with whatever-his-title-was, your equivalent here in Rriphirrizē. If the positions were reversed, you would put him up indefinitely, true? Besides, it's not lost forever, I'm certain they can drag the riverbed."

Before I could retort, Sandcomber returned, barking quick instructions to the others outside and then bursting into the room. "The Governor shall be delighted to meet you right away," he announced. "Do you have any little gift to bring? No, no, your pearls and gold would not be appropriate in any case. A *foreign* gift."

Of course we had almost nothing. When he noticed me eying his bronze mirror Xalan clutched it protectively. "I don't use it now, but when we get back I'll need it!"

"I know—the leopard." I turned to Melayne. "Do you mind giving up Fleabite, dear? She was your present."

"Not at all," Melayne said with great graciousness;

the appeal of a tame leopard had always escaped her.
"You can give me another gift some other time—
something of gold, say, or set with gems."

Meanwhile Sandcomber had thought of something
else. "Have you no Viridese clothing whatever? We
must not idle, but a showy impression could not do the
least harm."

What with the rigors of travel we had lost all our
apparel except for some night robes. "Tarys has some
lovely dresses that still fit," Melayne said helpfully,
and it was true. The tiny regal garments we had brought
out for her from Averidan were not quite outgrown
and still relatively sound. Crammed into a white satin
robe quilted in red thread and embroidered round the
wee sleeves with garnets, Tarys outshone us all.

"I knew this would happen," I said gloomily. "In
comparison we look like the lowest sweepers on her
grandmother's estate."

The crowds outside, not knowing how long we would
stay indoors, had dispersed. So we got some glimpses
of the town. Rriphirrizĕ had looked level from below,
but walking about, we discovered it clung like a wasps'
nest to the sloping mountainside. The streets were
often stepped, so crowded by houses that no wheeled
vehicle could ever pass. In fact we rarely saw a wagon
or cart within the city. They were used mostly in the
fields.

I stared narrowly at the first building we passed. It
was sheathed not in metallic gold, but only a powdery
golden yellow plaster. The stuff shed like pollen on
the shoulders and heads of passersby and sifted down
to sprinkle the gravel-laid streets, setting its mark on
everything. To accommodate the slope, the houses
also stepped terrace-fashion up the hill: a tiny ground
floor was taken up by an entry and a hat table. The
floor above spread rather farther back, and sometimes
sprouted a porch sideways. Additional levels were increasingly more commodious, sometimes branching off
into short towers to allow room for more terraces. The
neighbor farther up the slope did not scruple to build

his terrace scant inches above the roof. The entire
effect was like a cliff where mud-swallows have nested
for years.

Iphalar's shadow lay blue and cool over the streets,
but as we climbed higher, glimpses of the valley, brilliant as enamel-work in the westering light, could be
seen between the golden walls. The different crops
shone in tints of green, each more vivid than the last.
Certain broad fields north across the mist-veiled river
were divided by thorn hedges into large enclaves for
the wyverns. I puzzled briefly over how such lively
steeds could be fenced in.

At the topmost edge of town, where none could
overlook it, perched the Governor's house. "Not palace," Sandcomber emphasized to us. "The Governor
merely represents the real master of Rriphirrizē."

"Who is?"

He shot me a surprised glance. "Iphalar," he said.

I nearly whooped with glee. "Do you mean to say
after all this dissection of our customs, you've been
nursing your own set of superstitions about a mountain?"

"Please do not use the word 'superstition,' " Sandcomber pleaded. "It is, rather, pure practicality and
common sense! Month by month, by our reverences,
we have kept the mountain quiescent these many years."

"This is primitive, no more enlightened than believing the solar orb has congress with mortal ladies!"
Sandcomber made no retort to my unkind raillery but
gripped my arm hard in almost a pinch. Then I saw we
were nearly at the house. The yellow glow from a pair
of oil lamps on the wall showed how dark the street
had become. Between the lamps thick wood double
doors swung open as we approached. Excited dark
faces peeked from behind them as we passed into a
narrow vestibule. I stared back with nervous curiosity
until I came to think that the Governor of Rriphirrizē
would hardly be tending his own door.

We climbed up a broad stair that circled an air shaft
and came to a chamber that took up most of the

second level. In the Rriat style it was low but very large, glowing with teeth-jarring color. Oddly-built furniture cluttered the corners. Our noses tingled with a supremely foreign smell compounded of strange soaps, strange dyes and paints, and the aroma of people who ate nothing but strange foods. We stared dumbly back at the brightly tattooed crowd that filled the room. A most hospitable and amiable spirit animated all. They pressed forward to talk or offer refreshments, and the Rria who could not—the room seemed packed to bursting—had to be content with nodding and waving vehemently. Our only competition seemed to be Fleabite, who had been bodily carried in her cage to one end of the room. With discreet nudges and tugs Sandcomber slowly herded us across to the other side. In a window seat the Governor of Rriphirrizē sat with his feet up on a stool. He was deep in a conversation which Sandcomber did not interrupt, so we had ample opportunity to look him over.

Like most of the countrymen he was tall. But the Governor was a large man in every other respect as well. A long broad nose, large deep eyes, a big chin and a wide mouth all crowded into his face. In the Rriat fashion he wore a loose and stiff white jacket for show only. Yellow, green and light orange body patterns gave an already solid torso the massive quality of a lichened boulder. His big flat feet were thrust into slippers, and his hands were like spades.

I watched them clench and point and make chopping gestures in midair, and strove for patience. Nothing ravels the nerves like the consciousness of need. After our amazing journey to get here, we might at least get a prompt greeting. On this man's favor now hung all our fortunes. When we had left Averidan, I had been a hero-king going out to seek his fortune. The declination into a mendicant in search of a haven mystified me. I shot an impatient frown at the Governor just as he looked up.

In Averidan it is bad manners to glare. Either customs ran differently in Rriphirrizē, or else the Governor was too secure to bridle at minor discourtesies. We received a formal welcome of great cordiality, unfortunately in Rriat too fast to follow, before he turned to Sandcomber. Here I was able to grasp at least a part of what was said, more because I could read Sandcomber's face than anything else. Also, our friend's introduction perforce used many Viridese words. "In the distant land he once ruled this one is called Liras-ven Tsormelezok. And Melayne his wife, and their child. And his wizard and friend, Xalan."

"What is 'wizard'?" Xalan whispered. "Does it mean 'magus'?"

I hushed him with an impatient gesture. The Governor was saying something about wizards too, and Sandcomber nodded. "Plenty of room for inquiry there," he agreed.

The Governor spoke further, and at length; to us Sandcomber said in Viridese, "Of course everyone in Rriphirrizē has a nickname. The Governor wishes to know if any of you already have one?"

After we had gone through so much to get here this final hurdle seemed senseless. I cudgeled my brains in vain for a suitable nickname. My elder brother Zofal had often called me "little brother," but that would hardly do. In my ear Melayne grumbled, "I don't want to be called the 'little one' any more," while in the other Xalan whispered, "This is crack-brained. How can we change our *names?*"

Seeing our confusion the Governor began applying nicknames without further discussion, rattling Rriat words as briskly as beans into a copper bowl. Sandcomber helpfully translated, "You are 'Red Hair,' Melayne. The baby can very properly be the 'Little One.' 'Wizard' shall be our name for Xalan, and Liras is 'Once-King.'" You must make sure to soon learn the sounds of your Rriat names, so that you may answer when folk address you. And now," he added, shifting into Rriat, "I presume my return is in order?"

I must have misunderstood some crucial word here, because in the same tongue the Governor seemed to reply, "Yes, your name is changed back."

As soon as this pronouncement was made, Sandcomber clapped me on the back. "I must depart," he told us, in Viridese again. "My wife and family, you understand, have festivities planned to mark my safe return. I have mentioned to the Governor that you have begun learning Rriat, and can contrive to make your wishes known. Save up your questions, and tomorrow I will return to answer them." And with that he was gone.

With some self-contempt I fought down a surge of loneliness. The clack of a hundred foreign tongues rattled as empty of sense to our ears as the noise of boulirr. The utter strangeness of the situation overwhelmed and oppressed more than I would admit. But there was nothing to be done, but smile at people, sip atye, allow the Governor to shuffle his friends past us for a word, and in general ape a complete congeniality.

"And I thought we Shan had a name for relentless revelry," Xalan groaned as we descended next morning hungry for breakfast. Platters of fruit and poached boulirr eggs were being circulated among a far larger and entirely new crowd. The Governor was nowhere to be seen. The old Shan rule—no substantive talk or activity at meals, lest one's digestion be disrupted— had never seemed so wise. Today my digestion felt quite petulant at the lack of concentration.

Our only comfort was that we spoke so little Rriat no conversation was possible. Other entertainments there were none. But everyone seemed hugely content to stare at us, make comments in incomprehensible speed, repeat our Rriat names, and occasionally venture a surreptitious finger, to see if we were really there.

The artlessness of this last gesture underlined the difference between this crowd and last night's group, for the scanty Rria fashions did not give much scope to sartorial rankings. Compared with this morning party, the people we had met last night seemed more sophisticated, more poised. We had met the Rria equivalent of counselors and landed lords last light; these here now were of a second rank. I was amused to find the Governor used such crude social stratifications. The Shan King's gatherings are arranged with far more subtlety, to keep the perennial Viridese social feuds at a minimum.

It became obvious our hosts' enthusiasm could bubble up undiminished from dawn till dark. So we put an end to the festivities by retreating up into our tower at noon. Our suite of rooms, cool under the thick earth-shielded ceiling, gave onto a tiny peaceful terrace, so high on the side of the house that no one could see us. United in fatigue we collapsed onto the wooden benches. No one said anything. The grilling Sun poured rays like heavy molten gold onto our limp bodies. After a while I said slowly, "There's something odd about all this. They can't celebrate all day, every day. When does any work in Rriphirrizē get done?"

"Well, after all, the Shan King doesn't call every day," Xalan coughed. When he had used up his Rriat, Xalan had chatted in Viridese. The Rria had been so completely delighted at the condescension that Xalan had nearly talked his voice out.

Melayne yawned. "I'm going in to nurse the baby."

No one disturbed us for the rest of the day, for which we were grateful. The transition, from endless travel in a small party to a seemingly perpetual flow of strangers, would take time. After an evening of peace and a full night's sleep, though, I felt better. Curiosity revived green and strong; who knew how long Rriphirrizē would be our home? I climbed carefully out of our strange creaky bed, of flat strips of tight-stretched hide woven on a low frame. Wrapping myself in a kilt I padded barefoot down the cool winding stair for some solitary exploration.

The Governor's house boasted several sets of stairs. I met nobody on ours. Occasional slits cut in the thick plastered wall let golden stripes of sunshine through, and framed vivid slices of the town outside: yellow-gold walls, hot blue sky, narrow graveled streets winding downhill. As I trotted down past a final window-slit, though, the corner of my eye caught sight of greenery and bright colors. I had seen no gardens in town; perhaps the Rria adhered to strictly practical horticulture. So I wedged my head and one arm through the slit to see better out and down.

The angle I glimpsed on the house was a new one. The public entrance to the building was just below, a gateway opening onto a paved courtyard shaded by tall feathery trees in pots. Like the Kings of the Shan, the Governor lived adjacent to his place of business. The bright colors were the tattoos on a teeming crowd of Rria. People filled the courtyard and overflowed out into the street.

I craned my neck to see the big attraction directly below me on the ground floor. But all I could make out was the gold-plastered lintel of a doorway. The white fluffy head of a doorkeeper bobbed in and out, so foreshortened I could not make out what he was doing.

The sunshine was already hot on the sill. I edged farther out into the glare and cast a professional ruler's eye over the crowd. In my estimation they were humble folk—men clad in the coarse white loincloth of field workers, women with bales of leaves balanced on their heads. After seeing so many Rria the differences in their tattooing was becoming clear. These poorer people wore simpler and more crudely brilliant designs. The guests at that first gathering had been adorned with patterns as delicate and complex and richly colored as the Shan silks that take years to embroider.

I watched the cheerful and bustling crowd for a while, musing on what it must be like to wear your status on your hide for all to see. Clothes one may buy anew; if a poor man in Rriphirrizē came suddenly into wealth could he get more elegant tattoos over his old ones? Several exchanges of the copper beads that are the basis of Rriat currency went by before I noticed them. Then I watched narrowly; everyone below pressed toward the door with a copper bead ready to hand. My conclusion was so appalling I had to say it aloud: "They're paying to get in!"

I had not the least doubt that we were the attraction. The simplicity of the whole scheme took my breath away. I struggled free from the window and tore back up the stair.

My dudgeon received a setback when I blurted my discovery out. "That seems quite a fair thing to do," Melayne said, picking up her comb again. "We must be the most exciting visitors here in years. What you ought to do is demand a share of the proceeds."

When I turned, dumbfounded, to Xalan, he grinned. "A typically practical bit of advice. Do you know, if you had ever called on me in Mishbil, my family would have done something very similar. All the important people great-grandfather wanted to impress would be invited to dinner first."

"But you wouldn't have made a crude paying proposition of it!"

From his calmer vantage, however, Xalan was able to put his finger on the sore point. "Sandcomber must have known," he said thoughtfully. "Could he have had this in mind from the beginning?"

"He did say we'd get a hearty welcome," I recalled. "Parties, he promised."

We were interrupted here by a little Rria maid, who with giggles and gestures invited us downstairs. "Think of it as earning your keep," Xalan suggested with humorous resignation. But I declined, preferring to stay and sulk. With mime Melayne persuaded the maid I was ailing, and after they went down, I closed the slatted blinds and pondered. I had been half-aware, and half-resentful, of my slide in status, but thought it temporary. Now I realized—a very tardy discovery for a Shan King—that status equals power. I had concentrated all my energies on paddling, and let someone else direct the expedition. The bed creaked in protest as I lay down on it and remembered the ruined tower-prison of Uwuna. What would happen, if I marched down to the door? Would it be locked against me?

I had not considered that, given the circumstances, seclusion was a course of action certain to produce results. The hot saffron stripes of sunlight had scarcely crept down from wall to floor when a discreet tap on the door-frame gave me a start. A close-shorn white head popped cautiously round the curtain which passes for an interior door in Rriphirrizē. In the low voice suitable to sickroom visits Sandcomber asked, "They say you're ill, Liras—are you really? Where does it hurt?"

The bed's webbing groaned as I sat up and glared at him. "What, did the Governor complain you had sold him defective goods?"

He hooked a foot under a stool, and dragging it over sat down. "It is not what you think, my friend," he said mournfully, "though I completely understand your feelings."

"It appears you've trapped us nicely."

"But you never asked," Sandcomber protested. "Never did you inquire for details about how your life in Rriphirrizē was to be sustained, or what provision I had made. Problems, you may recall my saying once, are functions not of circumstance but of inner flaw."

I remembered. The truth of his words galled me so that the real grievance burst out in a shout: "I trusted you!"

"Gently, gently," Sandcomber said, glancing nervously towards the stair. "I'm inquiring after your health . . . Will you have an explanation of my predicament, and learn how you have been my salvation?" When I ungraciously conceded Sandcomber sighed. "You have borne very patiently with my inquisitiveness all these months," he began. "Did you know that those bad habits first drove me to leave my home?"

"No," I admitted, interested in spite of myself. "How did you come to choose Averidan for your destination?"

"Oh, I refer not to this most recent journey, but my first—to Uwuna, as it happens. At the age of fourteen I pointed out, aloud and in public like a fool, that Iphalar (the god and not the mountain) is probably a superstitious remnant of our unsophisticated past to be outgrown. Like the wyvern contests."

When I looked confused he added, "Once we used to pit our wyvern flocks, one against another, until a champion was found. But it became too wasteful of flock strength . . . Anyway, the Governor was livid. His rage made it expedient for me to join company with some older cousins in shipping a load of ore down to the seaside metalworkers. There I learned the tongue, and with it many legends and tales of the Uorvish realms, for which I found a ready audience when I returned home again. So the pattern of my life was set, and very lucky I was to happen upon it. Though we tolerate no new ways here, or even too zealous questioning—or perhaps even because of these customs, who can say—the Rria have a mighty appetite to hear of strange places and things. Else my periods of exile should have been painful and not profitable."

Out of this curious history I fastened upon one word. "Exile?" I asked. "Lapidation is kinder. And how is it they let you come back?"

"When the Governor names me exile, the appellation sticks for seven years, and he may rescind it at any time," Sandcomber explained with a cheerfulness that I thought inappropriate considering his career to date. "He's quite used now to banishing me and seeing me return with exciting tidbits. My absence this time has been a mere five years. Your company being an irresistible key to the gate, he let me in early. I must see how long I can contrive to keep out of trouble this time."

"So that's why you brought us," I said bitterly. "To barter us into captivity for your entry."

"Oh, not like that!" Sandcomber exclaimed, hurt. "The exchange is not blatantly unfair. You needed somewhere to go, and I needed someone to come. Every time to win my name again I am forced to excel my previous feats, you see—another reason to curb myself. Of course, at this point, before you are fluent in Rriat, there is no profit except in parties, of which today's is surely the last. But you shall be honorably maintained while you learn the tongue, and then most cordially embraced by our learned men. In exchange for your intelligence of the Shan—a race unheard of here, you understand—we offer you a home here, for as long as you care to stay."

"And suppose I don't?" I said. "Suppose I decide to return to Averidan—now?"

"How will you go?" A faint smile twitched at Sandcomber's broad lips, and he smoothed his fluffy beard. "Has your Crown recovered itself, or will the Cayds have altered their minds about you? Sooner or later my tongue will get me into trouble again, and I shall be obliged to leave. Wait until then."

I realized that locks and manacles were unnecessary. Rriphirrizē itself was our cage. "I could speed that day," I said, nettled by his tone into recklessness. "If I'm so careless as to repeat a few of the conversations we've had atravel. Some of them would, I'm sure, crisp your Governor's hair."

With another mournful sigh Sandcomber rejoined, "We have been friends so long, it is a shame to resort to mutual threats. I could, for instance, mention to our wise men the existence and powers of the Crystal Crown, which I had honorably promised Xalan's uncle the late Master Magus I would not do, and so ensure your enforced residence here while they examine the fragments . . . No, I should prefer to regard you with amity, as before, and have you so regard me." Tentatively, he held out a large dark hand, low and to one side so that if I spurned it he could pretend it had not been offered.

The gentle threat made me writhe in frustration. The word "slavery" would not be mentioned among these word-precise folk, but that did not alter the fact of it. I did not doubt that resistance would lead only to further embarrassment. I thought with irrelevant yearning of our travels, when almost all problems could be resolved by either waving a sword at them or sailing away. Now I fell back upon prudence and patience. It was no longer in my power to force the issue. And as for Sandcomber's claim that he had done the best he could for both himself and us—I had my doubts about the Rria, but not him. If we quarreled with Sandcomber, we would be slaves indeed. Slowly I reached out and clasped his hand in my own. "My health had recovered itself," I announced with a straight face. "When do language lessons start?"

CHAPTER 8

A Querulous Serenity

As Sandcomber had predicted, the "parties" ceased, either from his influence, or because everyone who would pay for the privilege of staring at us had already done so. The general populace was instead granted the privilege to goggle at the leopard. Ensconced in a larger cage set in a private courtyard, Fleabite's spirits remained poor. She would hide her golden head from her visitors, who would offer food and make clicking noises to get her to look up. Sticks or stones were strictly forbidden.

We had leisure to explore the house and tour the city. Out friends' tales had built up in our heads a town of great sophistication and glory. The real Rriphirrizē now seemed both simple to the point of crudity, and convolute. We spoke so little Rriat that when Sandcomber could not accompany us, we moved in a sort of sphere of incomprehension.

Groups of brilliantly-tattooed women sliced hib-roots and spread them out on racks to dry. But what happened to the roots after—brewed into beer, ground into flour, or fed to wyverns—we could not discover, though the ladies tried to tell us. But the hot damp smell of the hib, the high strange songs the women sang, brimmed with a knowledge not of words. So the fish must feel when, after their brief youth in the rivers of Averidan, they swim out to sea: another world, full of new things to see and know, flowed around us.

Another district we enjoyed without understanding was the street of the tattooers. There are complicated rules and customs in Rriphirrizē regulating the color, size and intricacy of one's decorations. Tattooing is not begun until a Rria is nearly full-grown, lest his further girth or height distort the patterns. Since we did not know any of the rules, our enjoyment was quite simple. We spent an entire morning watching an artist slowly engrave a pattern of curling purple on the dark shoulders of a young man. The artist traced the general design in with milky-pale ink, and then pricked the pattern out in its full complexity with the finest of bone needles. The purple dye powder was delicately massaged in, inch by inch, with a padded rubbing stick. With gestures, the tattooer indicated the open spaces in the design would be filled in later, with pale green.

Both artist and subject were highly flattered by our interest, and if we had not fought shy the tattooer would have given us a free sample of his work, on arm or leg. "It's not a Shan custom," I explained politely; but of course the fellow understood nothing.

And in a courtyard behind the woodworkers' district we found a marvel—a statue twice as tall as a man. Wood is the favorite Rria medium, everything from houses to clothing to dyestuff being somehow made of it. This statue, representing a squatting and grossly distorted figure, was obviously the epitome of Rria art. Three or four big beams were mitered and glued into a suitably large block. The image wore a high square headdress such as I had never seen before. It was pierced like lace and towered above the image's bent neck. The artisans were just putting the final touches on the gleaming and eye-piercing paint. The supreme complexity of the design—blue and green curlicues, pale red and yellow squares with rounded corners and flowery centers, and wavy stripes in three or four other hues—made the figure seem very aristocratic and grand, even to our foreign eyes. Again, the purpose of this statue was beyond our understanding; we had not seen similar works anywhere else.

Sandcomber was often busy now with his own affairs, so that except at language lessons we seldom saw him. I quite understood, especially in view of his long absence. Even when there was a chance to ply him with our many questions, though, he was curiously restrained. The occasional foreigner in Averidan is always sucked into Viridese life. I should have expected to feel helpless in Rriphirrizē, instruments rather than masters of our fate.

The first barrier to be surmounted was language. I had rather expected to be forbidden to learn Rriat. But it seemed the attractions of our stories overmastered any worries about our sullying Rria society. The Governor placed every convenience before us, in our lessons. A Viridese will rarely learn another language, preferring to scrape by with crabbed translation scrolls on the rare occasions when foreigners have something to say worth hearing. But Sandcomber had many exciting ideas about learning and teaching tongues.

During the cool of the early mornings we watched slow, elaborate mimes enacted by carved wooden puppets. The art is one we do not have in Averidan. Behind a flimsy lath-and-cloth stage, the manipulators stood on either side out of sight. Thin, almost invisible black rods moved the puppets this way and that. A narrator would declaim a simple sentence, and while we repeated it as best we could the puppets would dramatize its meaning.

In this way we picked up such useful sentences as, "I find your methods of wyvern training offensive," and "There is never a hinge repairer when you need one." My favorite, which I learned off by heart so that I could astound passersby in crowded streets with it, was "The intricacy of a good toe-pattern is a constant delight to the initiate." By the time puzzled listeners had finished examining the foot-tattoos of everyone present, we had usually moved on.

During all of these activities we were guided and attended by young men and women who, with Shan thinking, we referred to as aides to the Governor. In

the Rria fashion, though, they all had special names
that referred to their attendance upon us. By now I
had enough Rriat to recognize that their name "hus"
was similar to "ahus," Sandcomber's name for Four
Circles, Spine of Red, and the others. But since I
never heard it in any other context, I did not learn
what the word meant.

Our afternoons were spent differently. We sat in the
vividly-patterned main room, and answered the questions of learned men. There were more of these than I
would have thought possible for a town Rriphirrizē's
size, all with their area of passionate interest. "A lot
of overactive livers here," as Xalan acutely assessed
them. "Like magi," he added, with less accuracy, since
these scholars put their learning to no practical use
that I ever saw. Such single-minded energy bored me;
I spent a good deal of time staring out at the steep
green flank of Iphalar mountain that rose behind the
house. Paths wound up the slope, with a scattering of
huts clinging to the cliffs, and I promised myself I
would explore them.

Our mastery of the language was still unequal to
subtle talk so Sandcomber translated back and forth.
"Oh, Wizard, tell us of magery," the first scholar
asked in Rriat the first day. When Sandcomber had
turned the question into Viridese, Xalan took a sip of
atye and leaned confidently back in his chair.

"Let me know if I go too fast," he said happily.
"My apprentice lessons aren't far behind me: Magery
is broadly defined as all the ways man may impose his
designs upon nature . . ."

As he half-closed his eyes to better recite the old
lessons, I watched the dozen Rria listeners who sat on
the floor. Those with an interest in the question stared
at Xalan with the beady intensity of hens at feeding
time. They sat cross-legged on the floor as Sandcomber
translated and scribbled notes madly upon long strips
of fine-woven cloth. The strips were pleated for convenience in storing, and sometimes in their haste to keep
up, two scholars would grab either end of the same

strip. Then there would be a brief argument in hissed undertones before new strips were snatched from the stacks before them.

While Xalan droned on about the division of all existence into earth, air, fire and water, I looked over the scholars' shoulders to get a glimpse of their writing. Reed pens frantically scrawled what looked like bird tracks in strong-smelling purple ink which soaked quickly into the unsized fabric. Not all the scholars were so intensely involved. One of them who was not taking notes let me try his pen. He immediately took the opportunity to murmur in simple Rriat, "Can you write, oh, Once-King?"

I dipped the reed pen too deep in the little gourd of ink, and made blots. "Apologies," I said in my bad Rriat. "Yes, I can write." But I felt he did not believe me, since I could not show any skill. Before I could marshal any more vocabulary, Sandcomber interrupted in Viridese.

"Please don't demonstrate anything just yet," he asked me. I nearly retorted by asking whether they were paying by the hour or the question, but didn't.

Since the order of the questions was set by precedence—or possibly by bid—the inquiries rambled terribly. Over the course of several weeks we moved from magery to fashion, sketching memorable robes for our hosts' edification. The Rria tailors insisted on trying to reproduce them, with indifferent success since tree-fiber cloth was so different from linen or silk. Also, our faulty sketches left a good deal to be desired. But the Rria were so hugely delighted when we wore then, we felt bound to continue, however uncomfortable and hot the garments were.

We also discoursed on cooking—this took several sessions—road construction, and how the wax for our writing tablets was prepared. This last was of interest because bees were unknown here. Alas, none of us knew anything about bees or wax. Melayne hardly ever wrote anything; Xalan was a town-crow from youth, and my family had never kept hives. Magi however notoriously dislike exhibiting even minor ignorance. So Xalan made something up out of his vivid imagination, and the scholars went away happy. "As long as they don't go and try that tablet-coating recipe!" I rebuked him.

"We're perfectly safe," Xalan blithely assured me. "Where would they get the wax?" Xalan was by far the most popular of us among the Rria, since he could work wonders. Only the most elementary and mundane aspects of geomancy, like building houses so that they don't fall down, or digging drains, and suchlike pedestrian things, had been developed here. Tricks like walking on air, or making sand creep about, enthralled the Rria. Several of them even undertook to learn magery, and Xalan demonstrated the elementary exercises he had begun with over and over. But no one made the slightest progress, and Xalan had to conclude magery was strictly Viridese art. "Either that, or I'm a vile teacher," he said.

My turn came to shine when the inquiries turned to government and politics. Since I did not in any way want to bring up the Crystal Crown, I spoke of Averidan's recent wars—the Ieor campaign and the Caydish conflict. The recounting of these happenings of the last several years enthralled our hosts for days.

Characteristically, the peaceable Rria maintain excellent relations with their simpler neighbors but have a vast appetite for tales of turmoil. Even the Governor took time those afternoons to listen, and the scholars scratched reams of notes until the sweat fairly rolled off their dark foreheads. Such a craving for vicarious experience struck us as almost pathetic. The rigid ways of Rriphirrizē that sheltered its inhabitants so well could be downright tedious. With all our flaws, at least the Shan have the courage to live their lives with both hands. "Have a war of your own," Xalan proposed. "For educational purposes only." But Sandcomber, scandalized, refused to even translate this.

Our intensive tutoring in Rriat slowly had the desired effect. In a month or so we could stammer in quite understandable Rriat, and comprehend almost everything addressed to us as long as it was not spoken too fast.

In this way I found the path up the mountainside one morning—by asking directions. I began to climb congratulating myself on my mastery of tongues. The path was narrow but well-kept, the rock cut into steps at the curves and the low juicy vegetation frequently cleared away. The climb to the smoky peak was far too stiff for a mere morning's ramble, particularly under Rriphirrizē's grilling Sun. But I ambled content enough along the slope just above the town.

The view was superb. Rriphirrizē's golden roofs crowded close together below, and ample green banks clothed either fork of the river. The lush feather tree-tops beyond looked like league upon league of rumpled green carpeting. A shimmering strip of whiteness coiled like a snake's shed skin among the brilliant green—the river, cloaked under its morning haze.

I settled down on a stony outcrop to catch my breath and enjoy the prospect. It was still very early—I had left Melayne asleep, and my Rria escort had not come on duty yet. But already the city was astir as potters and craftsmen took full advantage of the fleeting morning cool. Boulirr on sparse-feathered leather wings flapped screaming overhead to their roosts, and in the distance some large ruddy-feathered reptile stood on its hind legs, rabbit-wise, to inspect me.

Then I looked again. The boulirr was larger, and more distant, than I had thought. As it began to approach across the slope, climbing over the rocks, I noticed that it rose taller on its back legs than a tall man. Uneasily, I tried to remember hearing of large dangerous beasts in the area, but could not. Then, with a final readjustment of perception, I realized it was no boulirr, but human, a man with a long full beard. Mats of thick ruddy hair hung over the neck and furred the arms and legs and torso. A leather apron and crude sandals of sinew and wood were the only emblems of humanity. I stared fascinated as the tall stooping figure approached, never having seen such a one before. Surely he was not a Rria. Lost in pondering the propriety of asking whether he was cross-bred between animal and man—and if so, what kind of animal—I started when he spoke.

"Rush eve thee," he said, in tones so thick and slurred I leaned forward.

"It's a nice day," I had to reply at last.

From under the mat of curls deep-set eyes glittered at me. A hand the size of a small ham indicated the thick chest. "Rush eve thee," he repeated.

"Oh, I see!" I exclaimed, enlightened. "You say you're *rousivē.*' Which is Rriat for "guest"; I should have recognized the word because our hosts used it for us all the time. "So, of what race or folk are you?"

I had instinctively put the question in Viridese, but when he stared mutely at me realized our only common language was Rriat. Considering our mutually feeble grip on the tongue, I might have contented myself with staring back. But I persisted, saying in slow and ungrammatical Rriat, "I come from there." And I waved in a general northerly direction. "My name Liras."

My new acquaintance grunted, and pointed south. He waved his hands palm up, in a rising circular motion, until I grasped the idea of a very high country. Then he indicated his own chest again. "Hwe," he dubbed himself; I was sure this was no Rriat nickname but his real one, just as I had instinctively used mine.

The mutual repudiation was a bond. I made room for him on the stone and we conversed, or tried to, for nearly an hour. I do not think of myself as unduly bright. But compared with Hwe I was a mental giant. We gradually fell into a pattern of his struggling to understand and answer my questions, rather than the reverse.

I learned that Hwe came a long journey by his standards, though whether it was a month or a year in duration I could not make out. His homeland was cold, poor, and sparsely settled, and the Rria's tales of their town's glory—I wondered if Sandcomber had been one of them—had moved him to accompany them here. He had lived with the Rria for a long time—again, the actual period he could not convey.

What I really wanted to ask, of course, was beyond my ability to voice, and I had to glean answers from what went unsaid. Was he happy here? From the lonely glance of the deep-set eyes I doubted it. He was the only one of his kind in the land. When I recalled my original intent to leave Melayne and Xalan behind, I shivered. Henceforward I resolved to value my friends more. Had the Rria questioned him as enthusiastically as they did us? Surely, or how could Hwe have learned Rriat? Then had they tired of him? Did he often wander the mountain alone? A new, and not very flattering, light was cast on our mutual hosts. Would we be so sought after and honored in another month's time?

With surprise I noticed the Sun had climbed quite high. I rose hastily, and pointed downhill. "Come and meet my wife," I invited, thinking that the Rria's reaction might also be interesting.

But Hwe shook his head. "Iffle air ne want," he growled.

My ear had grown so accustomed to his accent it took a mere moment now to understand. "What do you mean, Iphalar doesn't want you to?" I asked in Viridese without thinking, and then more laboriously added, "Say again," in Rriat.

He pointed uphill at the peak. "Iphalar," he repeated earnestly, and I remembered the mountain was a god here.

"Surely you, a sojourner in this realm, don't worship the local deity," I said in Viridese. But my skill was not sufficient to render this into Rriat that Hwe could grasp. In the end I left Hwe on the hill as he wished. When I had descended some way, I turned and waved. Once again Hwe looked scarcely human, until he raised a hairy hand in reply.

I went in, eager to tell the others of my encounter. But Xalan was busy demonstrating house-alignment to an avid group of Rria, and Melayne was nowhere to be found. "She took the baby to town," Xalan called to me over the white-haired heads clustered around him, and then continued lecturing, "This window is placed wrongly in the room. If we assume the current of force flows this way . . ."

By our lights Rriphirrizē is quite crime-free; a town that can impose exile for asking awkward questions has a flourishing social conscience. But I worried anyway until Melayne came back, accompanied by the usual Rria handmaiden. Hot and happy, she plumped the baby onto my knee and said, "Look what I got!"

I glanced at the tanned bare arm she held out, and said, "Very pretty, dearest. What's it made of, enamel?"

The wide tight bracelet was patterned in blue lozenges and green bars. "No, it's much better than that," Melayne said with pride. "It's permanent jewelry—a tattoo!"

I grabbed her wrist and stared. "It's what? Melayne, how could you! You heard me say such things aren't done in Averidan!"

"You're getting excited about nothing," she countered with some astonishment. "It's just one, that's all. I'm not intending to have patterns done all over."

She could not comprehend my disgust—indeed I hardly understood it myself. The quarrel that followed was our first major disagreement in years. I insisted she try to scrub the tattoo off, and Melayne refused in her most mulish tone: "Try and make me!"

I was tempted, but did not truly dare. By this time Xalan and Sandcomber had come in, and I appealed to them. "She can't do this, can she? The Viridese don't indulge in tattoos."

Glancing at Melayne for permission, Xalan prodded her wrist. "I don't think soap will help, Liras," he remarked. "But no one at home will think it's anything but a bracelet."

"I am certain soap will have no effect whatever,"

Sandcomber added. "And how is tattooing different from trimming one's nails or shearing one's hair? All are alterations of the natural state."

As usual a cogent retort escaped me. I could only implore Melayne to acquire no more patterns, and after infinite trouble extracted her sullen promise. "But I'm only indulging your whims from the kindness of my heart," she said, crushingly. "You'd better appreciate it!"

To my frustration Xalan and Sandcomber also agreed that my objections were slightly unreasonable. I was so vexed I could hardly swallow any supper. Nor could I sleep well that night, because Melayne curled up all elbows and knees, and would not snuggle next to me.

She forgave me the next morning with a hearty kiss; Caydish tempests blow over swiftly. But as I sat on the floor and entertained Tarys while Melayne prepared her bath, the colored band round my wife's wrist seemed to mark her: the first insignia of the growing influence of Rriphirrizē. We were three Shan, alone in this foreign place, and Melayne, who had so thoroughly adapted herself to us, was now the most susceptible.

To identify the problem, however, did not bring me any nearer to its solution. I looked into my daughter's bright eyes; Tarys might well grow up calling herself a Rria. She gurgled at me, baring toothless pink gums.

Then with a perfunctory tap on the door Sandcomber burst in. "My friend, are you at leisure to come for a walk?"

The suppressed emotion with which he delivered the urgent invitation recalled Sandcomber's excitement on arriving home. Melayne bent to take the wriggling baby from my lap and said, "I can easily bathe her alone, Liras." So I put on one of my stiff pseudo-Viridese robes and allowed Sandcomber to sweep me downstairs and around to the public entrance. He said nothing, and I was too busy looking about to question him.

I had never been in the front wing of the house where the Governor conducted his official business.

The atmosphere was familiar, though the place was on a smaller scale than my own Palace. Clerks filed cloth records away, folded neatly like bed-linens, on shelves. Pottery tallies of produce or livestock were stored by years or seasons in compartmented boxes—though the honest Rria did not seal the boxes against tampering, as we did at home. The corridor reeked of the rather pungent purple ink; after copying, the squiggly-patterned records had to be hung to dry, laundry-wise, before folding.

"Now," Sandcomber intoned in my ear, quite startling me. "No one will remark us speaking Viridese together here, whereas if we climbed the hill, or descended to sit on a river rock, any who saw us would smell trouble." He ducked under a sagging drying line.

"Trouble?" I followed him pushing past damp lengths of hanging cloth. "Are you in trouble again?"

A bench set against the cool plaster wall was heaped with dried and folded cloths waiting to be put away. Sandcomber unceremoniously transferred one stack to the floor and took the cleared space, gesturing for me to sit beside him. The stink of ink-vapors formed an almost visible shield around us.

"It was quite unintentional," he said in a low tone. "I had been reading aloud, at a party of some patrons, from the draft of my latest, most monumental work: *Journals of a Scholar's Travels Over Sea.*"

"What scholar?" I asked, confused.

"I myself, of course—it is my account of and commentaries upon these five years' journeyings." He broke off to cough apologetically. "My discussion was of the Viridese historical record system, chronicles as opposed to plaiv, neither truly truth but together reflecting an almost agglutinated reality."

I coughed too. The enveloping miasma of the ink was becoming truly abominable. "If you continue to hedge much longer, we'll neither of us ever smell properly again."

"Well—having heard so much my friends were greatly

excited, and acquitted themselves quite wittily upon the subject of Shan self-deceptions."

Although no one could be more aware of our mental quirks, I felt peevish at the thought of their amusement. "I've often wished to understand Rriat better," I said sourly. "I'd get more out of your humor."

"I used to be so dispassionate," Sandcomber went on sadly, passing over my comment. "Now I fear my long association with you has warped my thinking somewhat, and not for the better. I felt just as you do—so much so that I detoured briefly from my text to remark that we Rria are not so superior either, in the area of intellectual honesty."

"That was handsome of you," I said, touched by his loyalty.

"It was foolhardy, and after only one moon at home too. I went on to supply a few examples—which," and he coughed again, "you will feel no interest in. The upshot was that the news trickled back to the Governor's ear, and my name fell into imminent peril of being altered once more."

"Exile again?" I grinned at him. "You would come back, like a counterfeit coin. Your Governor should take up lapidation instead. We have a proverb that problems buried under a load of rocks don't return. Perhaps we could offer to demonstrate it for him."

Sandcomber's return smile was somewhat frail. "I can comfort myself that you yourself have been rolled in enough Rria thought for some to stick," he said. "You would not have spoken so when we first met, eh? To progress—I could not bear the prospect of leaving home again so soon, and was forced to offer the Governor a price of my forgiveness."

"A bribe, we'd call it—another example of dishonesty for you."

"There was dishonesty on both sides," Sandcomber confessed, hanging his fluffy white head. "I told him, my dear Liras, about the Crystal Crown."

Another good-humored remark froze in my throat. "You what?"

"I suppose I haven't violated the *letter* of my promise to the old Magus," Sandcomber argued, more to himself than me. "I merely mentioned you had in your luggage the fragments, of a mysterious and unheard-of substance, of a Shan national relic. The Governor was of course thrilled to the core, and instantly sent for the scholars and you. So you see why I had to lure you from your quarters, to warn you. No doubt the page is interrupting your good Lady in her work even now."

I had leaped to my feet, but nearly got tangled in a drying line, and sat down again. "Thank the One, bathing the baby takes time!" I burst out. "Melayne will stop them from searching my bags, and simply taking it!"

"Oh, that's not at all the sort of dishonesty we're subject to," Sandcomber said, wounded. "You could quite easily refuse to show or discuss the Crown at all, and no further questions, even, would be asked, for a while anyway—"

He broke off, and with a silencing gesture ducked under the hanging cloths on his side. No sooner had he done so, than a little page parted the drying records at my elbow and said in Rriat, "Come, please? The Governor wishes to speak to Once-King."

There was nothing for it but to obey. I rose and casually glanced back; Sandcomber's dark face, framed in damp hangings, seemed to express sympathy and urge fortitude.

CHAPTER 9

An Englightening Ascent

The large empty room I was shown into disconcerted me. The Shan King's governmental role by tradition involves people. I therefore expected the Governor to be installed in a grand chair, surrounded like a sea rock by the deferential ebb and flow of underlings. Instead he sat at a plain wooden table which to my eye would not have looked out of place in a kitchen. It held nothing but a gourd of ink, a rack of reed pens, and a little covered dish of the white paste used for correcting mistakes. Documents waited to be read in a folded stack at his elbow, beside the inevitable flask of atye. Framed in the wide low window was the mighty green slope of Iphalar mountain.

"Be seated," he said in resonant Rriat. I took the only other chair, beside the table, resolving to keep my wits about me. The Governor began with great candor. "I spoke just now to our friend Traveler." I nodded; this was Sandcomber's current Rriat name. "And he happened to mention a valuable and sacred antiquity you have brought with you."

Here he paused to pour us some atye, and I felt his assessing eye. Carefully, I did not react to his interpretation. Instead I said, as Sandcomber had suggested, "I do not wish to speak of it at all." With a happy inspiration I added, "Our customs forbid it completely, else I should be pleased to oblige you."

"Can we at least see the relic? I understand it was smashed; perhaps we can help repair it."

Taking a sip of atye I congratulated myself on finding an impregnable position. "Quite against custom."

"Perhaps you could tell us about these trammeling beliefs," the Governor said, a little desperately.

I beamed serenely upon him. "Impossible. You, who head so devout a folk, will quite understand when I say that my people would abhor any discussion."

"Well, as to that—" the Governor slowly twiddled his cane beaker between big hands. His expression grew confiding, and he stretched his dark eyes wider, "The peace of Rriphirrizē is in my care. One may liken it to keeping your young leopard. On the one hand there was disruptions and disturbances, mostly small boys to be shut out by a stout gate. And on the other, there are the bars, to close the creature in. Now, me—when I find a Rria who disturbs us, he is simply named exile."

He gave me a sly half-smile, looking to see whether or not I knew Sandcomber's history, and I nodded to show I did. "And the bars, oh, Governor?"

"Ah!" He leaned back in his chair and gazed musingly out the window. "Let us say that I do not rely blindly upon our sentinels to keep the mountain from exploding. That is merely a natural phenomenon."

This gentle confidence did not shock me, as it might have once. I felt very old now in the management of power. Certainly I had not been forced by political expediency to enact rites I myself no longer believed in. Perhaps I was only lucky. My reply was as cynical as any of Sandcomber's could be: "Yet to keep your people believing, you ape piety. Well, so must I. The relic, as you call it, is bound up in our worship of the Sun. If I discussed it, I should never be respected in Averidan again."

Faced with such intransigence a Cayd would have exploded and a Viridese became icy. But I dealt with a Rria. The Governor returned my smile with scarcely any effort. His fingers interlaced around the beaker and gripped it hard. "Perhaps you do not clearly grasp your position, oh, Once-King," he said. "You may, after all, never return to your far home. The glory of Rriphirrizē may woo you away, to make your home with us."

All of a sudden his words sank in. I stared dumbfounded into his dark cordial face surmounting the brilliantly tattooed chest. It was as if I had seen and carried a beautifully embroidered scabbard, and only now found it hid an envenomed blade. No naked threats would ever be passed, I realized. But the swaddlings of courtesy and hospitality did not make the hidden steel any less sharp.

"While you are settled here, you need feel no scruple about shedding your former bonds," the Governor was saying. "I look forward to hearing all about your artifact very soon." Perceiving that some idea had struck me, he radiated encouragement and reassurance. "Think about it, discuss it in your own tongue with—" And here he used his other name for Sandcomber, the variant of the "ahus" that had also applied to our four traveling companions and our daily attendants.

The meaning of the word penetrated at last. "Keeper," I translated, flabbergasted. "We aren't captives, nor even slaves, but pets!"

The room with its gaudy colors whirled, and how I took my leave remains foggy. I found myself running out into the sunny courtyard, with only one coherent idea dominating my mind—that the Crystal Crown was in peril. By hook or by crook, using whatever weapons came to hand, the Governor intended to get it. And not even to exploit its power, as Xerlanthor had, or to become true King of Averidan, like King Mor—the Governor was impelled by a mere lust to collect a thrilling and exotic toy. Such a despicable end for so wonderful a treasure was unendurable. Even in pieces, the Crown was my responsibility. Obscurely, I felt more tender of its dignity than my own.

I glanced about sharply as I made for the stair to our rooms. As usual, the big rambling building was full of Rria—solid elders solemnly debating policy, scholars fussing over their records, and youths running on errands. Any one of them might accost me, with a glib request to view the "artifact."

Upstairs Melayne had bathed and dressed the baby, and was just settling down to nurse her. The moment she saw me she said, "The Rria were here looking for you."

"I don't doubt it. I've spoken to the Governor already."

Her clever small hands, so competent with needle-knife or bow, carefully adjusted the baby's sun-cap without disturbing the infant's meal. The Rria were obviously very sure of me, else Melayne would show more anxiety. "And what did he have to say?"

"I'll tell you later." I rummaged through our baggage. With a grunt of triumph I dragged the Crown out in its box. Not until then did I realize what I meant to do. What was left of the Crown should be forever mine, totally untouched by foreign hands. Rather than allow it to fall into the Governor's hands, I would destroy it.

But here a new difficulty arose—to grind the crystal into powder was probably beyond my power. The Cayds, strong men all, had tried and failed. Here I had access to neither tools nor equipment for destruction. Hurriedly I left, giving my wife a deliberately vague excuse. Sandcomber might have been optimistic when he claimed that the Rria were above barefaced robbery.

I emerged, blinking in the hot morning glare that filled the little courtyard. In her cage the young leopard did not bother to look up as I trotted past. When I was safe outside the gate, the solution came to me. The plaiv tell that Shan Xao-lan the first Magus forged the Crystal Crown in fire. Doubtless the Cayds had already tried to melt it in an ordinary metal-working forge. According to Xalan, however, here in Rriphirrizē dwelt a hotter flame yet, on top of Iphalar mountain. I knew little about volcanoes, but once dropped in, the precious crystal fragments could surely never be recov-

ered. If I told the Rria their god had claimed the
Crown, all argument would cease. And the Governor
would scarcely be in a position to object!

Quickly I turned and began to climb up the path,
before anyone appeared to "escort" me. Preoccupied
with my own thoughts, my surprise when Hwe waved
at me was considerable. He had apparently been sitting on a rock beside the path above. Had he been a
Rria, I would have lied about my errand, but this furry
primitive was harmless. Also, it occurred to me he
must know all the mountain trails. I labored up to him
and said in panting Rriat, "I'm going up the mountain,
Hwe. Would you like to come too?"

He nodded, without surprise and without comment,
and fell in behind me. The day starts early in Rriphirrizē; though so much had happened, it was only midmorning. I set a brisk pace until the day's increasing
heat grew too oppressive. Looking back, the Iwa was
nothing but a squiggle of silver ribbon, and the town a
gilded toy. But ahead, the main bulk of the mountain
still remained, the zig-zag thread of road dwindling
rapidly into invisibility above. It was daunting to see
how far we had yet to go. "How far is it?"

Units of any sort were not Hwe's strong point, but
after a while I gathered that his gestures toward the
east meant the journey would take a full day at least.
Gloomily I hitched my sash a little tighter, and wished
I had given my impulsive expedition better planning.
There was no prospect of lunch, supper, or even—
since at best the return downhill would take till next
morning—breakfast.

I had, however, underestimated Hwe's forethought.
When we stopped for a rest he passed me his leather
wallet. Inside were several tough flat slabs of Rriat
bread. We divided one and chewed in contented silence. It tasted not a little of rough-cured leather, but
I licked up every crumb, knowing the other slices must
be saved for later.

By midafternoon we were high enough to enjoy the
cool, moist upper air. Knobbly twigless trees resem-

bling gigantic mosses leaned over the turns of the path so that we went in and out of green tunnels. Hwe's long hairy legs seemed thewed with copper cable, but my calves and thighs began to ache. The inexorable upward grade was more grueling than roads that go up and down, and life in Rriphirrizē had not fostered the maintenance of leg muscle. My shoes, badly modeled upon Shan footwear, chafed so badly I finally abandoned them under a bush. On the paved path bare feet were not uncomfortable.

The road tacked back and forth, higher and higher, green and slick with moss. Sometimes when it curved, I could look beyond into steep mountain valleys, clothed in greenery and apparently uninhabited. How there could be such empty lands so close to a bustling and populous town was incomprehensible to me. In Averidan every village sits in the center of a wide cultivated belt.

At the close of the day we found ourselves so high the view made me dizzy. In every direction but one the land swooped down and away. The river was almost invisible, its valley no wider than my palm. To the south and east the riotous forests resembled the nap of a beautifully clipped green velvet; on the distant northern marches were fields of yellow-green that might have been anything. We had climbed high enough to get a close view of other peaks to the north and west. They rose higher than Iphalar mountain, their snowy tips the sole embassy of winter in this southern clime.

The peak ahead was only a bowshot or so away. The bare gray rock rose in a rough circular rampart, like the crown of a molar. Steamy smoke billowed up from one side. The actual top of the mountain, and the source of the smoke, was invisible from here. Then I noticed the roughly-smoothed terrace cut into the mountainside, furnished with a few simple benches made of slabs supported on rocks. A cold and gritty wind plucked at our clothes and hair. We had arrived.

"This is it?" I asked Hwe. "Is this where the Rria worship their god?"

Hwe shook his head. "Iffle air," he said, pointing up the hill.

"Then why are we halting?"

Hwe tried to explain until his craggy face turned dull red, but I extracted only a few words—"fire," and "rocks," and "warm."

Finally I asked, with some curiosity, "Will the Rria be angry if I climb a little higher and look?" When I gathered they would not, I had Hwe sit down on a bench, and turned to hurry up the final slope. The swift tropical evening was almost upon us; a veil of twilight was draping this whole face of the mountain, and the last mellow rays of daylight gilded the western sky ahead. Even a self-professed hero need not explore a fire-mountain in the dark.

The last ascent looked to be solid rock, but underfoot revealed itself to be loosely-packed pebbles and light dust. I slid back one step for every two I took, and when the slope grew steeper had to tuck my box under my arm to free my hands. In this way I noticed the pebbles were mostly pumice, and also learned why only Iphalar lacked a snowy cap. The stones were ever so slightly warm, a tiny heat that was only noticeable in the cool air of the heights. Sunk deep in the dust my bare feet were toasty warm.

The phenomenon so diverted me I hardly realized its significance. As I neared the top the wind shifted and wafted smoke in my direction. I choked, coughed, and slid back several steps. The sulfur-laden steam reeked of rotten eggs. After some experimentation, however, I found it possible to go on by holding a piece of cloth torn from my wide sleeve over my nose.

I squinted up at the rim to see how much farther it was, and nearly tumbled backward in surprise and horror. A monstrous head was peering over the rim at me! And at intervals around the stony verge other heads stuck up, grotesquely shaped and the size of boulders.

I sprawled in the dust, shivering in spite of its warmth. As if I had not had trouble enough with gods in Averidan, I now had to meddle with Rria ones! Then it occurred to me that none of the heads had moved. Bellying a little higher, I stared sharply at the nearest one. Gaudy paint had peeled from its tall headdress, and its carven face did not even face me. Smiling at my own foolishness, I stood up and began to climb again. These must be Rriphirrizē's vaunted guardians. The ornate and garish statue we had seen below must be one of many, set up around the caldera to protect the town.

Very carefully I stuck my head up over the rim, and gazed in awe. The top of the mountain was hollow. The caldera below was nearly three hundred feet across, a huge rocky dish that held, puddled in the bottom, multicolored liquid fire gently steaming with sulfur. A slow and stately boiling motion kept the pool in constant motion, and after some while I realized the glowing stuff was indeed molten rock, just as Xalan had said. It upwelled from some deep interior source, white-hot like metal in the forge, and slowly cooled and congealed, from white to incandescent yellow, and then to ruddy orange, before darkening to red and then solidifying into black stone. Every now and then one of the solid bits of crust would break off and float slowly off into the fiery eddy, like foam on boiling jam.

Perhaps half a hundred squatting statues stared unwinking into this furnace, grimacing or glaring. They were spaced evenly only around the rim nearest the town. Many were old and peeling, and one or two were so battered by heat and weather they were mere lumps of wood.

For excellent reasons no path from lip to bowl existed; whatever rites the Rria indulged in when they installed a statue were probably conducted from below, where Hwe waited. Quickly, before my nerve failed me, I slid between two images and down the inner slope. The cup of the crater penned in both heat and vapor. The ashy powder raised by my descent made my eyes water. When I reached bottom I sneezed, wiped my sweaty brow, and squinted in the ruddy smoke-filled glare. "Xalan will be sorry he didn't come," I said aloud. The pent-up heat under the rock struck painfully up underfoot, and I regretted abandoning my shoes. I decided not to explore, as Xalan would have insisted on doing, but instead shook out the box. The fragments of the Crystal Crown fell to the ground.

In the hot orange light the chunks of crystal looked like rough-cut gemstone. What a sad end, for such a mighty talisman! With a sigh of regret for all the lost opportunities and powers, I stooped and picked up the biggest chunk to toss it into the fire-pool.

Although we talk of the Crystal Crown as powered by its wearer, it is really much more simple. Warmth, living or otherwise, is the key to its workings. In the moments that fragment had rested on the rock, it had absorbed an unbelievable amount of heat. With a yelp I dropped it, and stuck my scorched fingers into my mouth.

The piece of crystal bounced onto one of its fellows. To my astonishment it stuck there, one on top of the other, the way a comfit sticks to the other pieces on the sweet-tray. I could scarcely believe what followed: the two chunks melted into each other. And the united fragment now a semimolten blob, seemed to ooze itself over to join the third. In an eyeblink the Crystal Crown was whole again, though resembling nothing more than an upended bowl of milk jelly. "It's a miracle!" I exclaimed. Thinking only that the thing might liquefy further and seep away into the rock I again bent and picked it up.

There are proverbs about those stupid enough to touch hot metal twice. Too late, they all surged into my head. But to my amazement my hands were not burned. Hotter and more alive than it had been since its forging, the Crystal Crown *moved*. It clung to my fingers like candy, and its hot crystalline substance crawled between my palms. No sensible person would consider for a moment the thought of wearing such a double handful of living molten glass. So how I found myself seriously entertaining the idea was a mystery. Perhaps the sudden living beauty of the thing, seductive as an uncut cake, dared me to try. Or perhaps for the first time in earnest, I stepped out of fear into freedom. The action was no longer suicide but adventure.

As the Crown touched my head there was a fleeting instant of painful heat and light. But almost immediately I passed into a new state: not precisely without volition, since I assented to what my body did, but not an everyday frame of mind either. The inhabitants of the Deadlands, they say, know nothing, not even that they are dead. I had been dead, all these months since Uwuna, and hadn't known it. Now I could know it, because I was alive again. Life, heady as plum brandy, rushed down to my very fingertips and drew back my parching lips in a smile of rapture. In all our uneasy grapplings for supremacy this, I realized, was what the Crown and I had been fumbling for—a poised unity, an unenforced peace.

Preoccupied with this triumph, I did not notice my body turning toward the pool of fire until the heat pressed like a fiery hand on my chest and face. My bare feet, however, cleverly stepped over steaming cracks and around hot crumbly slabs of newly-birthed stone. It was disconcerting to feel no pain underfoot. My hair began to singe, and the skin over my cheeks felt taut and overcooked, before we stopped on a spur of fairly solid rock. The restless lava ahead fumed so bright and hot I had to half-close my eyes.

For a long time nothing happened. Even the thick roiling throb of liquid rock slowed, as if the earth's hot blood had calmed somewhat. Then a convulsion shook the fiery surface. A large bubble slowly swelled up from the surface, gathered smaller bubbles into itself, and at last exploded in a shower of attendant

sparks. The usual vapors swirled up, and within it
something not at all usual: a human figure. It had
legs and arms and a head, but these were superficial.
Fleetingly I recalled the Governor's foolish phrase, "A
merely natural phenomenon." Deeper than thought,
my blood and bones thrummed with the knowledge
they had no kinship with this being; even dogs and
cats and boulirr are not so foreign, for they at least are
natural, the children of Ennelith. This figure was
archnatural. It was made of flickering white-hot flame,
and about the size of a child's doll. Though it did not
look to be more than a few feet away, a vast distance
seemed to flow between it and me.

Surely this was Iphalar, god of Rriphirrizē. The
memory of the cheerful skepticisms I had learned
from Sandcomber made me sweat. And how dared the
Governor be so utterly wrong about this object of Rria
veneration? A foolish sense of outrage swept through
me, at his inefficiency and obtuseness. I could not
have hailed the deity of myself. But the god spoke
first: "Liras-ven Tsormelezok, Shan King."

If fire itself found words, it would have spoken
so—a remote rushing voice, with a crackle and hiss in
it. At the sound, a heady, almost delightful terror
filled me. Here at last was the appropriate and proper
place for fear, and here in its rightful place the emotion was no burden or obstacle, but merely due appre-
ciation. Only a fool would not have been afraid. Alone,
I could not have dared so much as to look up. But
with a rush of relief I knew I was not alone. On my
brow the Crystal Crown fairly glowed with supporting
power. I could lean on it the way a magus leans on his
wand, or the way a baby holds on to furniture in
attempting to walk. So I found myself saying, "Lord
Iphalar."

The conversation was particularly eerie because of
the long intervals of silence that punctuated it, as if
the words had to travel a long way. At every iteration
the shock struck no less freshly, turning blood to water
all over again. If one listened to that voice for a year

one should not grow accustomed. A timeless moment
slid by before the god replied. "In this land I am
named Iphalar. But you have called me otherwise.
See, though you have abjured my service, and for-
sworn your kingly oaths, and fled from me, yet I have
sought you out."

It took some time for this to completely sink in;
when it did, my skin chilled and crawled, the volcanic
heat notwithstanding. These past few months I had
thought not at all of the estrangement between the
god and me—deliberately covering over the wound,
layer upon crusty layer, until I no longer felt it. And
all these leagues the deity had pursued and lured, as
the patient fisherman plays the fish into his net. Trapped
at last, the scabs torn off, I clutched at my old grievance. "We trusted you, and what was the result? War
and starvation and sack and death! Are you not a god?
How did you come to allow this?"

Aghast, I heard these bold words tripping off my
tongue. The Crown might suddenly pulse with heat
and cook my brains, or the lava pool might spit a gob
of molten rock at me. But as I waited for the deity's
slow answer, I felt no real fear. The huge and intoxi-
cating dread that filled me made such merely mortal
ones look small.

The answer came not as argument but the simplest
statement of fact. "The Shan are my children," the
unearthly voice of molten gold said. "Would you use
your daughter so?"

Vividly the memory rushed back to me, of the vi-
sion I had, once of the deity's raw, unwatered love for
us. When the Viridese boast of being Children of the
Sun, we usually mean that the Shan have the best of
natural circumstance, soil and weather; after traveling
across the world I felt I could attest to the truth of
that. An emotional tie would not be anyone's first
thought. Yet the god appeared to mean exactly that.
We were his family, and as a Viridese will sweat and
connive (and sometimes, regrettably, cheat and steal)
for his relatives, so he cared for us. My bitterness

struck me as outgrown and threadbare, like a garment worn too long. Having made a stand, though, I felt bound to defend it; besides, the question was entirely valid. "But we have suffered, terribly," I said. "Why?"

Small but dreadful, the glowing figure did not move when it spoke. "Two reasons are there, an old and a new. Slowly over many years Averidan has moved away from me. And as I am fixed, the realm drifted out from under my protection."

"We didn't mean to," I said, but under my breath, because my own heart again rebuked me. The Viridese had all these millennia maintained the vaguest and most offhanded worship possible. The Sun had not been a demanding god because we ourselves wanted him that way. In the face of this awful entity, so terrible and lovely one could not look steadily at it, our folly appeared incredible. "And what is the new reason?" I asked at last.

"There are wills that thwart my own—for a while."

"You are a god, you could have made the Cayds go away," I argued.

"I compel no one." I remembered the god had said something similar before. "And the being that sets itself against me is not in Cayd but in E-Basu."

"I don't believe it," I said stubbornly. My own boldness amazed me; the Crown's support must make this independence possible. "I never heard of the country."

"It is a city on the eastern shore of the Tiyalene Sea. The Rria know it well. If they bring you there, so that you may see and understand, will you believe?"

This incredible proposal did not strike me at all as one likely to be embraced by the Rria. So it seemed safe to concede, "If they do, and I see there these reasons, we shall be friends again."

The words sounded very rude. But to my relief the deity paid my tone no attention. "We shall converse again, and often. For now the Crystal Crown is as it was meant to be—the medium for our dealings, and once again the Shan King shall be its master. Now—rise, and give me your hand."

Bemused, I stood up. The lava glowed white-hot, and the crater was filled with a glare like a smeltery. Near the edge the rock looked soft yet brittle, very bad footing. But the god's power warded me from the heat. It was distinctly uncomfortable, but no more than that, as I walked to the very brink and stuck my right hand out over the abyss.

The glowing-white doll-sized figure reached toward me. As I have said, though it looked small, I was sure this was illusion. And now my instinct was proved correct. Just as a man seems to get larger as he walks closer, so the divine hand extending toward me got bigger, with infinite slowness, as if the distance were very great.

It grew and grew, and with a sudden final correction of perspective I realized the god must be huge. By the time it reached me, his hand could easily cup Iphalar mountain from crown to root. I covered my eyes as if that would hide me. But I could see better than ever; the Crystal Crown still did its work. A childish terror swept over me—that the world could not hold anything so big, and might burst like a bubble. The rock under my feet trembled. An ominous rush and thunder of hot displaced air buffeted around me. If I were the first mortal the deity had so honored, perhaps he did not realize how frail we were.

But I had forgotten the old plaiv about the deity's epiphany to Viris, ancestress of all the Shan. The softly firm touch against my palm could have been a girl's cheek, almost cool in comparison with the scorching air. In a stupor of happy relief I exclaimed, "Then it was true!" And thinking to better see the god face to face, without any intermediary, I lifted the Crown up off my brow.

The experience was more than I bargained for. Of themselves my eyelids clenched tight against the raw white light. A bellowing uprush of gas and heat from the fire-pool tumbled me backward even as I clapped the Crown back on. But I took no hurt and had no time to be frightened. Confidence filled me and left no room for minor frettings.

I found myself sliding on my back headfirst down the mountainside; the deity had obviously brought me up and out of the crater. Fortunately the ashy soil was fine and free of large rocks, and my tunic was woven of stout stuff. I careened to a dusty halt against some wiry bushes, and sat up. Hwe galloped downhill toward me with huge raking strides. "Come, come!" he urged, and hauled me to my feet.

"What's the hurry," I panted in Rriat, trotting along as fast as I could around the hill in his wake. My hair was full of grit and ash, and I wanted to sit down to catch my breath. But his anxiety was understandable. Night had fallen some time ago, and against it the mountain top glowed with sullen orange fire. Even as I watched a shower of white sparks shot up. The tinder-dry wood of the statues ignited in little puffs of smoky flame as thick fingers of yellow lava touched them.

When we came to the stone platform and benches, I noted with pleasure that Hwe had built a small fire. "Let's eat something," I proposed, but to my annoyance he did not even pause to tidily extinguish it. Instead we turned and began to race headlong down the hill, not keeping to the switchbacks of the path but sliding straight down, sometimes on our backsides. Whenever I showed signs of slackening, Hwe gestured me frantically on.

The fiery glow from above lit the valley like eerie sunshine. At intervals I could see the town below, glittering like a toy, and strange batlike creatures awing above it. These last resolved themselves into wyverns. With prodigious leaps a small flock of perhaps eight of them were scaling the mountain toward us. Even Hwe's bronze-thewed limbs seemed weary now, and with rescue nearly at hand we tottered downhill at a more reasonable pace.

In a clamor of harsh cries the wyverns swooped down upon us. They were extremely restive, shrieking and bouncing like fleas, and their three or four Rriat riders had to cling for dear life. "Come on, quickly!" the rider of the leader shouted.

I made for a riderless wyvern, keeping a wary eye on the claws of its wings, which, whenever the creature touched ground, would violently and briefly dig into the earth for balance. Someone inexperienced might easily find himself impaled on a talon three feet long. I wished I had seen someone mount one of the creatures before this.

But the lead rider called to me, "No, no! You must ride with one of us!" And I saw that Hwe was clambering on behind another Rria. So I came as close as I dared to the leader—a handsome yellow and black creature—and with a tight rein and a stranglehold round the bare neck its rider held it still for me to mount. I did so very awkwardly, darting under the threshing wings and dodging the huge fidgety legs.

The instant I was firmly seated, the Rria released the choke collar. With an ear-splitting yelp the wyvern bounded into the air, wings flailing. My stomach lurched down. Because of the mountain's slope, we looked to be soaring at least a league into the air. I clutched convulsively at my companion's colorful arms as my bottom began to part company with the wyvern's back. "It takes practice to stay on," he yelled back at me over the wyvern's hoarse panting and the buffet of its wings. I had to agree.

With startling suddenness the noisy straining and flapping stopped. I was sure the beast had expired from the strain. But no—its leathery wings were now spread out stiffly, cupping the air, and we glided smooth as silk and faster than a horse can run. The wind sang past our ears like water. "A nice long 'slide,' from this height," the Rria was able to remark in a normal tone. "You're lucky we saw your signal fire. You guests must be crazed, loitering about in Iphalar when our sentinels have so much to do!" He jerked a thumb over his shoulder. Careful to maintain my grip, I turned.

The mountaintop smoked like a chimney, the gases forming a dark pall in the sky that was luridly lit from below by the restless lava. Things were plainly coming to some kind of crisis. As we made landfall with a thump, the crater gave several preliminary burps of sulfur and then belched fire. A warehouse full of fireworks could not have made a more impressive roar— not very loud, but making both earth and air quake. Glowing like liquid metal in the forge, the lava overflowed and trickled downhill. However, the spill was confined to one side and the town below did not appear to be in danger. White and yellow, shimmering with heat, the secret stuff of the earth oozed very slowly down to the north, darkening and solidifying as it went. Trees or plants in its path ignited in little explosions of flame, and a hot sulfurous wind beat down upon us.

The Rria clucked at his mount, and it gathered itself to leap again. "Warm air is good for sliding," he yelled to me. "We'll be home in no time."

And truly our weary climb was retraced in only a few more mighty bounds. The wyvern needed no guidance but steered toward the meadows across the ford north of town. Its subordinates bounded along behind at their own rates, spread out like an hysterical and partially plucked flock of hens.

Throngs of people milled along the riverbanks and in the meadows. When I pointed them out, the Rria said, "Didn't you feel the earthquake? Everyone came away, lest the town should fall down." I began to apologize for the disturbance; my interview with the deity had caused all this. But before the words left my tongue, I felt the gentlest tickle just behind and above my eyes. A tidy and coherent fact—that no one below would be found to have suffered so much as a scratch from the volcano's convulsions—was deposited into my head. No intrusive voice or presence broke into the privacy of my thoughts; it dropped into my awareness with only a faint noise to draw attention to itself, like a walnut falling into an empty jar. The arguments of separate voices were quite past; the Crown was mine at last. I could not resist repeating my information aloud to the Rria, who cast an uneasy glance over his tattooed shoulder at me and said, "I'm sure our guardians can be relied upon—we've put enough work into them!"

"Suppose they've burnt away in all this eruption?" I could not resist asking.

But my rescuer grew very ruffled. "We'll make more!" he said stoutly.

When we arrived, the wyvern consented to stand for me to dismount. The moment I got off, the creature bounded away across the grass; the others fretted so to follow their leader that the other riders were hard put to descend. People surged around us, commenting on our folly and calling for news.

A small firm hand seized my shoulder from behind. "Look at you!" Melayne cried in Viridese. "What did you do, tussle with a charcoal-burner in a trash heap?"

I looked down at myself in genuine surprise. What with the baking heat and my tumble downhill, my skin had taken on a look of filthy leather. A number of scrapes and singes were only just starting to hurt, and my clothes were grimed black. With mounting outrage Melayne examined my face. "You've burnt off your eyelashes and eyebrows," she accused. Clouds of gray ash flew in puffs out of my tunic as she dusted it with vigorous sharp blows. Then with a gasp she exclaimed, "The Crown! However did you stick the bits together again?"

I took off the Crown, and blinked to discover neither internals nor externals altered at all. No longer was I dragged willy-nilly back and forth between reality and the realm beneath. That realm, it came to me, was bad for mortals; another of the proper roles of the Crown was as a sort of fire-tongs, enabling one to work with a dangerous element without getting too close. The organization, the dovetailing efficiency of its functions made it positively a pleasure to wear the thing. I set it back on my head—it kept Melayne from raking ashes out of my hair—and replied, "The god did it, it was a miracle."

"The Sun?" She spoke without surprise. "But it's just come night time. Or do you mean what's-his-name, the Rria's god?"

"They are the same," I said, awed anew at the thought. "Do you realize, the One has chased me around the world?"

Such matters meant little to my practical wife. "A *considerate* deity wouldn't have let you risk your neck like this," she grumbled. "A really nice god is more polite."

It was simpler not to reply to this remarkable complaint. I had almost forgotten how absorbing it was to "read" people, it had been so long. It was like kindling a lamp in a dark treasure-room. The contents of every heart around me lay open ready for inspection, needing only a slight effort on my part to yield up what was hidden. The danger of being sucked too deep into the tide of emotion was gone. I took Melayne's arm and let her lead me back toward town, absently saying, "Would you like to go back to Averidan soon?"

"By sea?"

I did not really need the Crown to see that Melayne would never consent to do that. So I suggested, "We could travel by way of Tiyalor and Cayd; I understand the Rria have dealings with E-Basu on the Tiyalene."

Immediately she said, "Certainly, then—let me know when you want to start packing." I glanced sideways at her, slightly surprised at the easy victory. The god must be anxious indeed to get me back; I was not sure whether to be flattered or alarmed. He plainly had no need to crudely compel people. By manipulating circumstance and character he could get them to do nearly anything.

What had troubled me most about invasion and exile, aside from the obvious inconveniences, had been

the loss of order and control. The confidence that
someone was in authority, untrustworthy or not, was
tremendously and unreasonably cheering and calming.
All the Rria were crowding down to cross the ford and
return home. In the press I saw Xalan, balancing the
baby on his red shoulder, and Sandcomber bulking
above them. I resolved to enjoy the situation as much
as possible, and hailed them in Viridese. "Look, I had
a miracle."

Between the lappets of his imitation magus cap
Xalan's eyes seemed to bulge. "The Crystal Crown,"
he breathed. "Viris bless us all! Who repaired it for
you, was it a Rria?"

"It was the god on the mountain." I took the sleeping baby from Xalan and cocked an eye at Sandcomber.
"My skeptical friend, not only have I proved you
wrong, but I find our deities are the same. His name
here is Iphalar."

Sandcomber's white eyebrows were in motion, first
up, in surprise, and then down, the better to assess me
from under them. "What is his name in Averidan
then?" he instantly retorted. "If you don't have an
appellation, you can have no label, no communication, no handle by which to touch a person."

I paused, waiting in vain for the Crown to drop
some neat return argument into my head for me to
pass along. All I got was the sense that the Crown was
not made to augment the wearer's intelligence. When
it came to swift back-chat I was on my own. Fortunately Xalan, though a little tipsy, had been quick to
step in. "You don't know his name here either—calling
the god Iphalar after his place of residence is like
naming a fish 'river.' And there *is* the Crystal Crown,
in working order again. Someone repaired it—why not
the god, who decreed its construction in the first place?"

"I haven't heard that plaiv," Melayne said. She
gave her wide skirts a hitch and began to teeter from
stone to stone across the ford. I followed, carefully
clutching the baby.

"I have, and found belief difficult." Sandcomber

wallowed splashing beside us, ignoring the stones as if land and water were one. "Why would a deity want such an object made?"

"I know why," I announced. "So that he could use it to talk to the Shan King." My words rather stifled further comment, so I added, "By the way, Xalan, you win our wager."

"Our wager?" He blinked, and then grinned. "Oh, you mean about being abandoned! Then I get off being Master Magus?"

Indeed, at the moment he did not much resemble a proper Master of the Arts Magian, with his dark hair unshorn and the merry glint in his eye. His Rria version of a red robe hung in stiff creases from his arms, so that it looked as if he slept in it. But now we were returning to Averidan I would need an alert Master Magus to hand, willing and prepared to help reconquer the country. So I replied, "You can take a breathing spell awhile, as I promised. But when we start home, I will call upon you as Magus again. And you will obey me."

Xalan gave me a startled glance, but I saw he would acquiesce. Watching the emotions of those around me was like peeping into several pots cooking away on the stove. Melayne's mild interest and Xalan's surprise were less absorbing than Sandcomber's seething mind, so much more capable than my own. A Shan King doesn't need intelligence, or the ability to win battles or get things done, if he can draw on those who can. As Sandcomber concluded, with some dismay, that this would set Rriphirrizē by the ears, I forestalled him by saying, "I will speak to the Governor about it."

Xalan, who had thrilled the crowd by bounding across the river in one wyvern-like leap, cheerily pointed out, "If Liras has the ear of Iphalar, he could take over the rule of Rriphirrizē if he liked, couldn't he? If you boast of being directed by the god."

"Not so loud, even in Viridese!" Sandcomber pleaded, though the people were beginning to thin out as we climbed the hill.

I had to laugh out loud. It was true; I, who yesterday was powerless in Rriphirrizē, could now do anything. The temptation was easy to resist. If nothing else, the increasingly weary weight of Tarys in my arms reminded me that power had its responsibilities too. "To resemble King Mor wouldn't be very pleasant. The idea is to rule Averidan, not Rriphirrizē. I want to return by way of E-Basu."

"This is a new plan of yours," Sandcomber said, beginning to flag under successive surprises.

"Not mine," I said, and bit back a smile as Sandcomber glanced apprehensively at the Crown.

CHAPTER 10

An Enforced Departure

In my years of kingship I had often been frightened, annoyed, or disagreeably surprised by the Crown. It was a new experience next morning to don it with relish. Like a man whose sight has been restored, I sat in the courtyard and simply absorbed information, observing and drinking up more than could ever be said in words.

A good deal was going on today. The Rria were mightily disturbed and puzzled by the volcano's antics. After all, their elaborate sentinels were supposed to forestall this sort of disturbance. Some claimed the images had quite failed, while others insisted that since the town survived intact, they had functioned as well as anyone could expect. Nearly every woodworker and paint-grinder in Rriphirrizē dropped by, to be assigned a part in the carving and adorning of more statues to replace those burned.

Naturally the news of my presence soon spread, especially in view of my dogmatic secrecy yesterday. The Governor sent for me before noon. In the large audience room I was not surprised to find a dozen scholars, palpitating and honing their pens, and Sandcomber, looking rather frayed. The scholars dashed up to me with little cries of excited joy, and I took the opportunity to condole in Viridese with Sandcomber. "It must be hard, to be our friend as well as theirs."

"Your sympathy is new," he observed, staring. There was not opportunity, and it would not have been prudent, to tell him I had just sifted his heart thoroughly, and satisfied myself of his basic honesty. As I skimmed the characters of the noisy scholars around me, I saw that Sandcomber alone, of all the Rria, really questioned everything. No wonder he frequently upset his countrymen.

When the Governor entered, the uproar died down somewhat. He signaled for atye to be poured all around, and said, "Is this the valuable and sacred antiquity that was not to be sullied by foreign eyes?"

"Yes," I replied amiably, also in Rriat. "I decided you might view the Crystal Crown, since with it I learned some news."

"A crystal crown!" "Is it really crystal? Of what sort?" "How was it faceted, do your folk often carve gems?" "What rites surround it?" "Are such items common in your land?" "Take it off, that we may examine it!"

I raised a hand to stem this torrent of enthusiasm. "I have only one thing to tell you about the Crystal Crown. It was designed to allow the Shan King to consult with our national deity—you are aware that we Viridese revere the Sun. Last night I did so, and learned that he is identical with your deity, the one on Iphalar mountain." The quiet was complete; jaws were dropping and eyebrows were rising. It would have been unkind, to tell the Governor he had been quite wrong. Quickly I rattled through my conclusions. "The god informed me we are to go to E-Basu. He also said you Rria know where the city is and how to get there. Since our god is yours, I feel sure you will be happy to oblige."

The god, being so set on it, would contrive to get us there no matter what I said. So I had not bothered to use any but the baldest and bluntest of words. It was a little trying, therefore, when no miracle happened; instead the Governor broke the ponderous silence by slowly saying, "I find this most difficult to believe." It sounded as if he referred to going to E-Basu. But I saw his real belief—that I had met no one at all, but had mysteriously contrived to repair the Crown by myself.

Sandcomber nervously picked up the theme, speaking in Rriat so swift that without the Crown I should never have understood him. "I feel it most unlikely that two such different folk, severed by such distances by land and sea, should worship the same deity. To find two exactly identical pebbles on the riverbank would be as probable. And there are really no visible points of congruity. It is not easy to confuse the solar orb with our mountain. The Shan maintain an ornate marble Temple in their chief city, in which sacrifices are daily burnt and wishes often made. Not at all similar are our beautiful and vigilant images on the mountain—"

He might have gone on forever had I not interrupted. "Why don't you just go ask Iphalar, however you do that, and see what he says?"

I looked sharply into the Governor's heart as I said this, anxious to learn how the Rria did it. To my annoyance he was giving my question only a fraction of his attention. The bulk of his interest, like nearly everyone else's, was fixed upon my interesting artifact. "I will do so," he said. "But first, may we examine your Crown?"

I sighed. "It's against custom. But—" Plain as paint I could see that they were going to be stubborn about this. Having ascertained that Sandcomber had been right about the Rria and theft, though, I could think of no more genuine arguments against it. So with only a little reluctance I lifted the Crown off and set it on the low table.

The scholars positively lunged forward, the way seagulls will dart to scoop up a broken clam before it can bounce twice. As I stepped politely back, Sandcomber remarked in Viridese, "Another novelty; I recall Shan Kings are not ordinarily so casual."

I shrugged. "It is more mine now than ever. Besides, this entire business is in the nature of an experiment. I want to see how badly the god wants me—"

I broke off in alarm. Though without the Crown my understanding of the tongue was lessened, through the volleys of excited Rriat I caught the drift of the talk. Sharply I called in that tongue, "Do not put it on your head!"

The scholar who held the Crown looked a little sheepish, but the others bayed, "Why not?" "Is it custom again?" "Who knows if perhaps your god will not talk to us, too? Think, to consult a foreign deity!"

"I don't know why," I admitted, with less certainty. "But I'm sure it would be unlucky. We have a saying that the Crown has only one living wearer. I should hate to test that."

"Now that I doubt is no more than tripe," Sandcomber said, slipping into his jolly skepticism again. "Surely the proverb must mean that there is only one King in Averidan at a time. And even that is not always so, as witnessed by the recent political convulsions there . . ."

His voice trailed off. Alarmed, I looked round again. The scholar, emboldened by Sandcomber's reasoning, was just setting the Crown on his head. I leaped to my feet, upsetting my untouched beaker of atye, certain that something would happen, though not what. Such a situation would never have occurred in Averidan, where the Crown commands a healthy respect.

The Crown began to glow. The unfortunate Rria's eyes rolled back white in his head as the cool white radiance suffused his dark flesh. In an eye-blink the light waxed to an intolerable glare, like a forge fully stoked. As everyone shouted or screamed, I dashed around the table, but already the crystal was too hot to touch. A stomach-turning odor of burnt hair and flesh filled the room. The dead man slumped forward, and when his head touched the tabletop the spilled atye flared up instantly.

Not being men of action the other scholars stampeded. Some bolted out the door while others, less sensible, leaned from the windows howling for help.

I retreated only as far as the corner. The Governor

stood his ground with me. "It's your artifact!" he shouted in my ear. "Can you tame it?"

"The fire first," I yelled back. "Else the entire building may catch." I stripped off my tunic. Sandcomber quickly followed my example, scooping up an armload of writing cloth to beat out the flames. The liquor burned brisk and bright but not dangerously hot, so our task was easy. The house had never been imperiled; only the polish on the tabletop was ruined.

I had to nerve myself to touch the dead scholar. The searing white light had died away, but the Crown still felt hot. "A fire-tool would be helpful," I said, gulping. "Tongs or a poker, or even a stick." The Governor jerked his head at Sandcomber, who silently fetched a green cane. With this and a thick pad of writing cloth I pried the Crystal Crown off the lolling head.

Summoned by the commotion, some Rria in the corridor outside were calling questions. Leaving the Governor to calm them and conduct tidying operations, I pushed through the crowd with the Crown bundled under my arm.

Before I reached the stair, Sandcomber caught me up. "It might not be wise to loiter about," he shakily commended me, and in unspoken agreement we made for the open air, hot as a steamed spice bun in the noon sunshine.

This time I did not make the mistake of waiting for my courage to evaporate. By the time we came to the river's edge, the Crown was cool. I knelt on a flat rock and held it under the rushing green water. Chilly as the snows that fed it, the torrent scoured away all remnants of the morning's calamity. "I blame myself, somewhat," Sandcomber said in Viridese. "My disbelief encouraged the poor fellow unduly. But who could have guessed such a gruesome—" He broke off with a gasp. "Are you mad?"

Flicking the last drops off I said, "Didn't I say that the Crown has only one living wearer? Well, I am that one—I hope." This last escaped before I could catch the words back. Before anything more could be said I quickly clapped the Crown onto my head. With haste Sandcomber stepped away to a more removed rock, plainly looking for me to burst into flame. But nothing whatever happened, good or bad. I had forgotten that warmth was essential to the Crown's workings. I sat down on the rock again and resigned myself to wait until the river-water's chill passed off. "Wasn't it about here that we first made landfall in Rriphirrizē? Did they ever drag the river for my vest?"

His gaze was still wary but Sandcomber edged close enough to answer, "I believe so, but without profit."

Belatedly, I realized I could tell this was not completely true, and sighed with relief. Dismissing the question for now, I turned my full attention within, to test the Crown's promised powers of communication. In one respect Sandcomber had been right—a name would have been useful. Instead I addressed my query aloud to the air: "Was it necessary to roast him? You could perfectly well have simply scorched his hair. Getting away now will be ten times more difficult."

My eyes had been fixed on the chuckling, foam-flecked water. The god spoke from a restlessly shifting patch of glare where the sunshine reflected as from a mirror. "Should your sword be blunted because you loan it to a fool who cuts himself? The Crystal Crown is of its very nature perilous."

It was one thing to suspect this, and another to have it confirmed by divine authority. Forlornly I suggested, "But the Crown is no danger to me, is it?"

"Had I not caused it to shatter, in Uwuna, you surely would not have survived," was the answer.

Faced with the identical predicament, when I first became Shan King, I had resorted to all sorts of evasions before resolving to learn courage. That battle had been totally won. I could accept the perils of the Crown as one of the risks of life, and move on to my other request. "Please tell the Governor you want us in E-Basu; I don't think he believes me."

"I will surely do so," said the blinding glitter on the silver skin of the river, and the audience was over. I was so delighted at the ease of the interview that hardly a cutting comment came to mind, when I found that Sandcomber had crept back to town and returned with an audience to view my abstracted state.

For some days I waited for the god to prod his Rria worshippers. The time was pleasantly diverted by the antics the Rria went through whenever I appeared in public. The circumstances surrounding the sudden demise of the foolhardy scholar had by the Governor's order been kept secret. But I could have told him that such commands are never completely effective. Sometimes the tale had it that I had knifed the fellow for offending against Shan custom; other people said the Governor had ordered it lest the Crown make the fellow a rival. Since there are no customs of execution in Rriphirrizē, all criminals and malcontents being renamed exile, the death excited intense feeling. Some folk even suggested we should be exiled too, as troublemakers; to my disappointment this idea did not catch on.

"If we must leave, why don't we just walk away?" Xalan argued. "There are no bars or locks or manacles to prevent it. 'Escape,' indeed!"

"You would rather stay," I said, answering the intent behind his words. "Poor little Fleabite is falling into the same state—cage-bound."

"I am not," Xalan said, flushing. "We've only just arrived, and the journey back is sure to be long and tiresome. Besides, my question is good. Just look at us now, for instance." He waved one red-clad arm at the river valley and sky, the other being weighted with a coil of rope. "No attendants or 'keepers,' even, now that they're scared of you."

"Bonds don't have to be forged of bronze. We can't sneak off if we bring Melayne and the baby. Any travel will call for planning and provisons. And furthermore—" I shifted my burden from one arm to the other; the grappling hooks in their sack were massively heavy. "The god greatly desires me to get to

E-Basu. So I might as well hold out for a dignified departure and a comfortable journey."

Xalan's expression remained blandly innocent, but I wore the Crown and so could tell he was dubious. I dropped my sack, which made a resounding clank. "I got the idea for this when I came here last week."

"When Sandcomber said you were talking to yourself?"

Ignoring this I continued, "You remember these flat gray rocks—this is where we first arrived."

"Ah, and we're going to drag the riverbed for your vest? The Rria said they did it already."

I nodded. "They didn't. Money, in a sense, is power. As long as we didn't have any, we could get only what the Rria gave us. And what would you guess the answer would be, if I asked them to give us, oh, one of those boats?"

Xalan accepted one of the big three-pronged hooks and began to tie it to the rope. "So we're fishing for proof of their lie?"

"No, we'll be devious, the way a Viridese should. We'll simply find the money and spend it on equipment for our journey," I grinned. "The Rria don't really lie, you know. They just omit facts here and there. We'll do the same."

Xalan shook his head but said no more. My only doubt was whether the hooks were heavy enough; I had borrowed them from a Rria farmer without telling him why I wanted them. But they were solid drop-cast brass and sank quickly below the sparkling green surface. It was, of course, impossible not to get wet, and though the sunshine was hot, the chilly water filled our shoes and dragged at the coarse cloth of our sleeves. We made a dozen fruitless drags before clawing up a sodden clump of wadded linen. "Here's half of it, anyway," I said, laying the dripping rags out. "Try again." At last we dredged up nearly the entire garment, so far as we could judge.

Xalan sighed at this final proof, and reluctantly conceded I had been right. "I thought they were our friends."

"The Rria? According to their lights, they are."
Some of the vest's contents were lost forever. But
after slashing the dripping cloth into shreds, I had
salvaged a good pocketful of pearls and twenty slips of
gold, and was disposed to be generous. "We must
simply help them to be the sort of friends we want."

I found fishing for one specific fact, even with an
obedient Crown, a humbling experience. Emotions
and mental timber I could "read" with ease. But to
penetrate beyond the surface babble of sensation and
reaction, and reach the buried storehouses of knowledge, was as frustrating as digging in water. The Rria I
probed persisted in thinking about their family and
friends, or the annoying blight that had fallen on some
hib fields, or the niceties of wyvern-training. They
never mulled over the available facts about E-Basu, or
the best ways to travel there. I borrowed an embroidered map of Rriphirrizē and surrounding lands, and
saw that E-Basu was not even on the way home. A
land journey to Averidan would be vastly shortened
by going east of the Tiyalene directly into Tiyalor and
Cayd.

Only one useful tidbit came my way. The stray
thought of a clerk warned me that journeys to E-Basu
were a fairly rare occurrence. In six weeks some Rria
were leaving to make the long trek there during the
cool season; the next visit receded into a misty gray
future in the back of the clerk's skull. Fretfully I sifted
the fellow's mind for reasons, details—why so infre-
quent, were the journeys unbearably hard? But the
clerk's attention, distracted by another's question, did
not return to the subject.

Armed with the knowledge that time was of the
essence, I saw the Governor again. I had not spoken
to him since the scholar's death. His wide dark face
wore a look that was quite harried; Rriphirrizē was
not accustomed to guests who meddled so airily with
the state cult. With the correct Rria promptness I
came directly to the point. "Did you consult Iphalar?
What did he say?"

I had run him to earth in the large garish parlor, site of that first party. This time I felt no anxiety. The Governor set his large jaw into a stubborn line. "We have many things to consult Iphalar about, oh, Once-King. Your query was not of the first importance."

I doubted this, but the Crystal Crown, knifing through to the truth, showed me that indeed the question had not yet been put. "When will you find the time, then?"

I put the question in a patient and mild tone, all the while keeping a close watch on his feelings and thoughts. "The press of affairs will not lessen until spring," the Governor began, matching my mildness with generous details.

I ignored all this surface pother, and looked for the real reason. Since it was heavy on the Governor's mind, I had no difficulty. The Rria would never find leisure to confirm the god's instructions because the Governor could not afford it. We ahus were a lesser order, the named rather than the namers. With surprise I saw the Governor's own name might even be endangered if he tamely acquiesced to guests, or even appeared to do so—as a house-builder might suffer, if he consulted the convenience of the mice and swallows that would live in a house, instead of its human residents.

Though it was presumably vital from the god's viewpoint, I bore the Governor no malice and felt our departure was a silly incident upon which to wreck his career. I had resolved to be very wary in my dealings with the Sun. "If you got word from Iphalar, you could push all the blame onto him," I suggested, cutting the mellifluous excuses off.

The Governor shot me an irritated glance. "Must you wear the artifact all the time? It makes everyone uneasy."

Disconcerted by his perception I lost my train of thought. Though the Crown lent insight, to influence minds and events calls for plain hard work: conniving, manipulating, persuading. Had my heart been set on E-Basu, I might have undertaken the labor. Instead I took a pinch of my own advice and tossed the problem into the deity's lap. "No doubt Iphalar has his own ways of expressing his wishes to you," I said, rising from my seat. "I will leave it to him to change your mind."

Melayne was outside on the main stair, Tarys in her arms. The baby was old enough now to have a mind of her own, and what Tarys enjoyed was looking at things. Both Melayne and I spent a good deal of time holding her near the wall patterns, while the baby examined them, softly babbling all the while. Anything was better than a screaming fit, but it was more than a little dull for the adult involved. Personally, I looked anxiously forward to the day when Tarys could sit or stand on her own to look at things.

I was in two minds about the Rria attitude, but only voiced one to Melayne as she slowly carried the rapt infant down the stair. "E-Basu isn't on our way home anyway," I said after summarizing our talk. "I will consult Sandcomber about the possibility of striking directly across on our own for Cayd."

Melayne rocked the baby from side to side, saying, "How should my infant like to meet her aunts and uncles and cousins?" I hushed her, to listen. A sudden commotion of voices filled the street outside. Melayne stared up the central well of the staircase, which in this hot climate was open to the sky. "Look at the funny color the clouds have gone," she chirped to the baby. "Is it going to rain on my darling? Let's go out and see."

Disturbed, I led the way. The double wooden doors to the street were almost blocked by the people outside. Chattering in swift and agitated Rriat, clambering higher through the steep streets for a better view, barging onto their balconies until the flimsy structures were in imminent danger of collapse—apparently the entire population of Rriphirrizē was out, staring and pointing at the sky. Leaving Melayne standing on the threshold I pushed through the crowd and looked too.

A shadow was nibbling away at the noonday Sun.

Already a third of the orb was darkened. The magnificent blue of the Rria sky grew faded and wan, like the cheeks of a blighted flower. Uncanny shadows chased each other through the colorless air as I hurried back to Melayne.

"An eclipse," I said, drawing her in.

I made to shut the door but she protested. "I've never seen an eclipse! What are you nervous about, are they dangerous?"

"No, not exactly." I lifted Tarys to my shoulder. "The dark of the eclipse is considered unlucky in Averidan, that's all. Besides, the crush out there isn't very safe."

"Then let's go up to a window," she countered, and not having more protests to hand, I followed her back up the stair.

Before we had gone far, though, the curtain to the first floor was flung aside. The strange new dimness made it hard to recognize Sandcomber. Catching sight of us he shouted in Rriat, "Are you, Once-King, responsible for this?"

Magnified by the stair-shaft, his voice woke echoes through all the levels of the house. A tall red cap showed around the door jamb behind him. "I told you it's a natural celestial phenomenon," Xalan said in mildly reproving Viridese. "Eclipses happen often. The herognomers could tell you the why of it, better than me."

"And the pirolurges?" Coming closer, I saw the unnatural twilight was not entirely to blame. Sandcomber was in fear, terrified as he had not been by threats from unruly barons or the turmoils of Viridese war.

"Pirolurges can manipulate fire and all that burns, that's true," Xalan said, interlacing long fingers around his wand. "But believe me when I assure you the Crystal Crown confers no such power. It works outside our more conventional skills. The limits of magery have been well-mapped over the ages, ever since the first Magus began the pursuit of the Arts Magian. As his latest successor—"

Sandcomber did not seem to hear this erudite little lecture. He put out a shaky hand to seize my sleeve. Seeing that he had not the nerve to drag me forward, I obliged him by stepping smartly into the room. Without strong light the wall colors looked ghastly. The low wide windows were further dimmed by solid Rria torsos jammed within the frames, as those worthies followed the progress of the eclipse. The balcony was likewise crammed full. The Governor sat in his low chair where I had left him minutes ago. His head was in his hands, but as Sandcomber shepherded me closer he looked up, revealing a haggard, almost gray countenance. Without preamble he demanded hoarsely, "Do you know when the eclipse started?"

Xalan began to reply, but the Governor cut him off with a curt word and stared at me. I had seen a partial eclipse once before in childhood, and now could recall only the blood-curdling tales Zofal had tormented me with during the eerie darkness. At the time the twilight had seemed to last a month, but surely memory played me false. I hazarded a guess. "An hour ago?"

Both large hands slapped the arms of his chair as the Governor jerked upright, trembling with the fear of one who has created an instrument of policy only to have it come alive. Irrelevantly, I wondered if Shan Xao-lan had felt the same way when he made the Crystal Crown. In a faint voice Sandcomber said, "That makes it even worse, if he didn't know."

Without troubling to answer this, the Governor said to me, "It began the moment you said you would let Iphalar convince us."

Someone must have been on the balcony listening to our talk—probably Sandcomber himself. We had been using Rriat; now Xalan said in Viridese, "Coincidence, I'm certain of it. How does one say 'coincidence' in Rriat?"

I didn't know, and Sandcomber plainly had no intention of translating. So I said, "Surely that was a happenstance. If we Shan, who as Sandcomber points out are so often enslaved by superstitious tripe, think that, then you Rria ought to be well assured the phenomenon is merely natural."

Sandcomber gave a little cackle of hysterical laughter. "Here's a reversal, if you like. Have we spent too much time in each other's company, or are attitudes more contagious than we like to think?"

No lamps were lit, so the room was gloomy. "Even if it is natural, why did it happen just now?" The Governor ran his fingers through his damp white hair, and spoke for the first time with a note of real faith in his voice. "There must be something in it. What shall we do to placate the god?"

At the window Xalan had captured a sunbeam in his cupped hands, casting a circle onto the floorboards. "It has a big bite out of it too," Melayne marveled.

"Suppose you think about it for a little time longer," Xalan said cheerfully to the Governor. "The eclipse—a partial one—is passing off, and afterward you'll not feel so glum."

The Governor eyed both him and me with distrust, as one does a wild animal. "Perhaps we'd be safer if you did leave," he said. "And E-Basu is suitably far away . . ."

I hardly heard our dismissal, or Xalan explaining to Melayne as we climbed the stair how eclipses are caused by the disobedient moon-cat asserting her independence by occluding the Sun her master. The Rria collapse was incredible; who but a god could have contrived such a ploy? Devious in conception though not perhaps in execution, it was very typically Shan. I wondered if all the occurrences of life were like that—carefully planned threads of inconsequential circumstance and chance events, cunningly woven and overlaid until one was enshrouded, enwebbed by divine intentions. Of course we were not safe on the road to E-Basu yet. Perhaps the people of Rriphirrizē would object to our leaving?

But everything fell into place with unnerving ease. In the first shock of the eclipse the Governor had not thought to keep his convictions to himself, and anyway

Sandcomber's shouted words had been heard by everyone in the house. Our professed Sun worship took on a new and ominous significance. Though the scholars pumped me energetically on how one may cause an eclipse, the ordinary Rria did not want their placid lives disrupted. Trouble was an affliction of foreign realms, and if a guest persisted in pursuing it, better he should do so elsewhere.

About a week after the eclipse I found myself one morning trudging north out of town in company with Xalan, very excited, and Sandcomber, still quite subdued. On this journey I had no intention of handing myself and my folk totally over to another. My insistence on viewing, and if possible mastering, our mode of transport irritated the Governor, but he did not dare say so.

Beyond the ford the shallow northern fork of the river was fringed by the usual odd trees. Once past this belt the land changed. A yellow-green turf, not grass but grasslike, rolled to the sky line. It was not smooth, but puffy, like a pan of risen rolls. Our feet sank in past the ankle, as if we walked on quilts. Every step kicked up insectlike, thumb-sized boulirr that whined high above our heads in a cloud of metallic green and gold with occasional twinkles of scarlet. "We could fry them in fat, like grasshoppers," Xalan suggested.

"They are food for wyverns," said Sandcomber, "if you care to fight them for some." And indeed we soon saw in the distance a band of the bad-tempered creatures swooping along, threshing up dozens of fat insects with each flapping bound before snapping them up in their thick toothy bills.

After the wyverns, it was odd to climb a slight rise and discover in the dip beyond a quite ordinary herd of commonplace oxen—the first we had seen since leaving home. In his exuberance Xalan almost embraced the beasts like a brother. They were not of the piebald thick-horned Viridese breed, but lean as rails, with smooth brown hides and cream-colored noses and bellies. Under the charge of half a dozen Rria herd-boys the cattle seemed entirely tame, bowing broad meek heads to let us scratch between their curved short horns. "Why don't you use them to work the fields as we do in Averidan," I asked, "or for meat and milk the way the Cayds do?"

Shading his eyes against the sunshine Sandcomber inspected the herd. "The beasts are not ours. They came from E-Basu, drawing loads of ligat-wood and other Basuan goods."

I knew that ligat-wood—or more exactly, an extract from its ashes—played an important role in the preparations of certain paints and dye. Xalan said, "And then you send them all back? You should rather keep a few cows for breeding, and so build up a herd."

"We have tried several times," Sandcomber said. "Cattle do not thrive here; after a few years they invariably sicken and die. Even these are not as they were. You will see." Sandcomber had strenuously refused to accompany us if I brought the Crown. So I could not now view the truth of this unlikely report. But he was continuing, "There will be wagons aplenty returning, with room for all three of you."

Here I was able to respond with a previously-gleaned kernel of information. "What about the wyverns? At least one of us should learn to ride them."

Sandcomber's glance was so sudden and uneasy I knew he had been enjoined not to mention this. "Oh, that would not be possible. None of the wyverns you have seen, the commonly-held flocks, are going. A high-bred private one has been named to go, and the flyers already purchased in."

A wyvern flock is so costly that, except for those maintained by the town as a whole, an owner customarily sold off shares in it, as a shipowner might divide among several investors both the costs and profits of a large vessel. So I said, "I will myself buy in. You can introduce me to the owner today."

"Glorious, I want to come too!" Xalan whooped, adding on a more sober note, "Then I can rescue you when you're thrown off."

"Reconsider," Sandcomber begged. "Wyverns are not as donkeys or even horses. The taming of them is a sport, a danger, costing more than money. Suppose you were maimed by one, or fell, as Xalan rightly fears, and broke a limb? No learned assistance would be closer than E-Basu."

I gave him a confident grin. "You would agree that the god intends for me to get there, yes? Then, knowing no disaster will befall, why should I not employ an interesting way to go?"

"Interesting, pah!" Sandcomber muttered, but said no more.

Of course, it was not quite so simple to purchase the right to fly with the wyvern flock. The elderly Rria who owned it was utterly devoted to them. My offer that afternoon of a handful of Viridese pearls sorely tempted him, but he stood firm. "If you have no affinity for my spirited darlings, you shall never make a good wyvern flyer, and no wealth should buy you a place." He agreed however to let me try my hand at it, I, for my part, stipulating that I should wear the Crown. I felt I might want to communicate with the deity in a hurry.

This second expedition to the wyvern fields quickly took on some trying aspects. To begin with, the old Rria was lame, having broken his hip once in a wyvern fall. He had to be drawn there in a little two-wheeled cart by half a dozen servants. Their progress down the narrow stepped streets was slow, noisy, and not very safe for the old gentleman. Trailing behind came the eldest son, who named himself 'Vernflyer as was appropriate for a wyvern fancier. He was to be the rider of the flock leader for the coming journey. Much as I wished, I was unable to discuss it with him. He spent every moment either fruitlessly begging his father to hold on tighter to the rail, or cursing the clumsy management of the servants whenever the cart took an overly exuberant jounce down a step. All I could do was admire his flying outfit, an elegant yet protective white cloth jerkin and leggings reinforced with strips of cane—an intricate and obviously costly costume.

Attracted by the noise, other Rria with nothing to
do joined the procession. While I negotiated with the
old Rria, Xalan had been sent up the hill to get the
Crown, and had taken the opportunity to tell Melayne
all about my idea. The baby being asleep after her
midday feeding, Melayne insisted on coming too and
was now full of advice, as ill-informed as it was well-
meaning. "If you feel yourself getting nauseous from
the movement, get off instantly. And empty your sleeves
and pockets, you only have one handkerchief left as it
is. You should have worn your boots, I'm sure the
nails in them would give you better footing."

"*I'm* sure the wyvern in question would disapprove
very much," Xalan laughed. The Rria members of the
party had as usual brought their flasks, so he was
flushed and not at all disposed to take things seriously.

On impulse I said, "After we leave Rriphirrizē will
be the time to wean you from the atye."

Startled, Xalan paused with a flask in hand. "Whyever
for, will liquor be in short supply?"

I brushed golden dust out of the harsh stuff of my
wide sleeves. "You've noticed that atye doesn't intoxi-
cate our hosts at all?"

"I've noticed, and envied."

We were speaking in Viridese, but I lowered my
voice. "You may be sure they know it well. Not that
atye is deliberately used to enslave—but they never
mention you have to be brought up to drink it like
water."

With a heartfelt sigh Xalan stoppered the flask again.
"All right. So fetters don't have to be made of bronze."
Here a bold and silly Rria maiden interrupted to ask
me, with much giggling and nudging from a bevy of
young friends, whether the Crown kept my head unduly warm. So the rest of Xalan's complaint was lost.

Once out of town and across the ford again our party
became less frenetic. A well-worn path led east of the
cattle-herd's pasture to brilliantly yellow-green meadows that positively boiled with wyverns. 'Vernflyer led
us to his flock. I had wondered how such energetic

mounts could ever be restrained—neither tethers nor fences would suffice. I now saw the patriarch of the flock was wearing a light jacket, giving the creature with its red and yellow plumage a very Rria appearance. The garment, nothing more than two short sleeves connected by a band across the back, was stitched all over with pockets of varying shape and size. It seemed the cloth prevented the wyvern from building up sufficient momentum to soar. Meanwhile, by inserting wood or metal weights into the pockets, the judicious flock manager could force a patriarch to build up the strength of his wings, and so climb better.

Father and son instantly began to debate the current weight distribution, 'Vernflyer defending his arrangements while the old Rria pointed out numerous errors and omissions in terms too technical for us to understand, all the while picking out new weights from a big cloth bag. The wyvern put an end to the discussion with a skull-piercing scream of impatience.

It grudgingly consented to stand while the harness was put on, though I noticed 'Vernflyer kept a cautious eye on the spear-sharp beak with its two downpointing teeth, and the deadly clawed feet. But once the two bands were snug around the bare neck and hulking shoulders, the patriarch began to bounce like a cricket, and several Rria had to cling to the straps, dodging beak and claws, until 'Vernflyer climbed on. Though its wings were still trammeled, the beast immediately tried to fly. If anything, its flaps and screams and struggle delayed the moment of liberation. 'Vernflyer had his work cut out to drag first one, and then the other sleeve free.

Then the patriarch jumped! One mighty push of the huge hind legs sent it soaring high above our heads. Augmented by furious flapping, the wyvern mounted to become a mere red and yellow blot against the unclouded zenith. The two dozen hens and youngsters of the flock, discovering their lord suddenly gone, fell into a paroxysm of emulation, and leaped into the air with deafening hoots of excitement.

Meanwhile the patriarch began its slide down from the heights. Once the entire flock was away, it became possible to talk and think again in the relative quiet. "I liked your horses better," said Melayne. "You'll never get *me* to ride a wyvern."

"They don't seem very intelligent," I admitted, but of course did not repeat this to the proud owner of the flock. Instead I discussed with him what points the fanciers bred for. This flock was among the elite of the breed, noticeably more vigorous and spirited than the humbler wyverns I had seen before. Sweet tempers and common sense were not especially prized. The Rria favor strength, size and, typically, brilliant plumage.

It hardly seemed possible that a single man could force the rapidly-receding flock back, but 'Vernflyer slowly contrived to do it, guiding his mount in successively shrinking circles. Finally the red and yellow leader halted, panting hoarsely, a short distance from us. The flock came to rest too, only an occasionally wyvern hopping as if the turf beneath its claws were red-hot. The old Rria cried to me, 'Quickly now, while they rest! Try the white one!"

Startled, I hurried forward. Other Rria flyers, either shareholders or friends, dashed up to help exercise the flock. There was only one white wyvern, the color not being vivid enough of Rria tastes, and even it had a green and blue head. The creature fixed me with a peevish yellow eye but made no protest as the servants swiftly fastened on the straps.

It occurred to me that no one had discussed how an "affinity" with a wyvern was established. I did not dare hesitate but as soon as the buckles were tightened hauled myself up the bony flank, imitating 'Vernflyer's easy motion as best I could. My shoes slipped on the coarse webbing, and the irritated wyvern began to fidget almost before I straddled it. The hard-muscled shoulders were so much wider than a horse's back, I could not grip with my knees. I adjusted the Crown on my brow but for once it quite failed me; I could "read" nothing at all from my mount.

From the corner of my eye I saw a red and yellow bulk soar up and up. Just in time I curled my fingers under the edge of the webbing. My wyvern bounded up with a jerk that nearly unseated me. Every straining downstroke of the huge wings dragged us higher, and I stared fixedly at the birdy head bobbing on the bare neck just beyond my knees. The creature seemed frantic to catch up to its leader. We achieved an incredible height before the wyvern relaxed into its slide, coasting down to bounce briefly on earth before repeating the whole performance.

I had thought wyverns habitually take a few smaller leaps before starting on a high one again, but no. Without respite, the earth below surged and ebbed, and the skies revolved dizzily around us. With every impact the wyvern's spine met my tailbone.

Our little jaunt could not have lasted very long. With a final breathless thump the wyvern slammed into the ground. It leaped no more, but instead gave vent to its emotions by screaming like a pig under the butcher's knife. Hastily, before it should change its mind, I slid off.

To my fuzzy astonishment the people crowded around with words of praise, and the old Rria leaned over the cart-rail to seize my hand in hearty congratulation. "A very spirited exhibition, very spirited indeed! I can see you possess the audacious temperament of a true flyer. Why, I didn't see you use the choke once! Very few maiden flyers are so bold!"

"The choke-collar?" I had quite forgotten it; of course a choke is the only way to slow a wyvern at all. If I had used mine, the creature would not have cut such a tearaway course. But a slow safe ride is not at all admired in Rriphirrizē. Though I was beginning to doubt the wisdom of my decision, this chance was too good to let pass. "So, we have a bargain?"

"Yes, yes—you have the right temper. Fast and high, fast and high!" The old man chortled in recollection of the reckless slides of his youth.

Xalan pushed through to my side, Melayne speechless for once in his wake, and announced, "I change my mind. Oxen for me, please. In a tone of new respect he added, "I don't see how you do it!"

With what I hoped was not too wan smile I said, "You can see that I've been working on being a hero."

Our departure for E-Basu was a day of great excitement in Rriphirrizē. The importance of the dangerous triannual journey, added to the novelty of our departure, ensured that no work was done and no order kept.

Generous to the last, the Governor supplied us with all the equipment and provisioning we were likely to need. He had been resigned when I declined the Rria offer of a flying outfit in a Shan style. Instead I patronized 'Vernflyer's tailor, who had been delighted to make me a properly sensible suit in green cloth, with only the necessary modifications: a sword belt, and a back pouch for the Crown. The effect was not unlike Viridese lamellar armor.

On the last morning Sandcomber came to help us tie up our bundles. Now we were leaving, I found myself reluctant to bid him farewell; our acquaintance dated back even before my accession. "When next you get yourself into the fire, come visit again," I invited. "You could always go farther from Averidan, north and east to the Tsorish Isles."

Interested, he sat back on his heels. "Where some of your forefathers hail from? Is there much commerce between the realms?"

"Well, no," I had to say. "In fact I've never heard of anyone who's gone there, have you, Xalan? But it must be possible, if the sea-reavers did it."

"You don't seem to worry about taking over the country again," Xalan observed, pulling a knot tight with his teeth.

"Yes, I should hate to call and find you deceased, Liras," Sandcomber said earnestly.

"So should I! Don't worry, I will be Shan King and everything will be as it was."

Sandcomber shook his head doubtfully. "I say to you now, my friend, as I did once—one cannot go back."

There was no lack of willing hands to carry our luggage to the ford, beyond which the wagons and oxen waited. While Xalan looked under the beds and behind doors for forgotten items, I fretted, "Where's Melayne? She promised to be back in time." She had taken the baby, and what little that remained of our money, on a last shopping trip.

"She might be getting a final tattoo," Xalan suggested mischievously, and I scowled at him.

For the last time we descended the stair. Melayne was not outside, but perhaps half the town was, the other half having already gone down to the river. Fathers held their children up for a final glimpse of the guests, and everyone grinned and waved. Though we knew their enthusiasm was fickle, it touched us all the same. I patted babies and children while Xalan, daringly, offered kisses to the unmarried maidens, who giggled incessantly under the operation. Trapped in his own doorway, the Governor shouted at people to move on and let us by.

As the press began to lessen, I said, "Wait. We've forgot something." Ducking back into the courtyard I cautiously lifted the door of Fleabite's cage. After so many months of imprisonment the unhappy leopard seemed to have given up hope. Her spotted gold fur was dull and thin, and the golden slit-eyes stared at nothing. The cage stank of old food and cat droppings. The Rria had tired quickly of their pet; I was ashamed not to have insisted on better care for her. "Want to go back to Averidan?" I said softly, but received only a blink in reply. Sandcomber looked in at the gate to see what I was at, and shutting the door I called, "Help me carry this cage."

"You're robbing the town of all its monuments," he grumbled but did not refuse to help. The weight of the wooden structure nearly bent us double, but once outside there were plenty of helping hands to which we relinquished the burden.

Melayne still had not returned, and I reluctantly let the Rria conduct us down the narrow ways and across the ford. To my great relief she was waiting on the farther shore. Or, more exactly she was supervising the loading of our luggage into a wagon. "Watch the baby dearest, please, while I find a good place for these diapers?" And with this casual greeting she handed me Tarys.

Resigned, I swung Tarys to my shoulder. The dozen wagons were drawn up in a row, two teams of oxen already yoked to each. The wainwrights of Rriphirrizē probably worked in the building trade when the wagon business flagged, for the vehicles greatly resembled wheeled Rria houses: lumbering and square, equipped with doors, windows and steps. Several were actually fitted out as miniature houses, complete with sleeping spaces, little roof terraces, cookstoves, and all the necessities of life. Most of the convoy, though, carried merely cargo—dyes, atye, bark-cloth and other trade goods. Each wagon was painted in the vivid Rria style, so that they glowed bravely in the brassy morning light. It was strange to recall my naive surprise when first I had seen such a vehicle—Sandcomber had been driving one, painted in precisely such a riot of color, when I met him. These wagons looked quite ordinary now.

Most of the crowd was gathered round the dozen wagoners and three flyers; apparently someone about to depart for foreign parts was nearly as diverting as someone recently returned. At the fringe of the press a lean hairy figure towered over the brightly tattooed folk. "Hwe," I greeted him. The sad eyes smiled a bit at the sight of my daughter, and impulsively I said, "You come too." It was not clear whether he understood me, but Hwe made no objection when I led him to our wagon and pushed him within.

Our baggage loaded, Fleabite's cage was hoisted to our wagon roof. Before our wyvern escort bounded up to make all conversation impossible, we made our farewells to our many Rria friends. The Governor meanwhile ceremoniously handed over some cloth records of previous journeys to E-Basu to Baldspot, the eldest driver. Then he spoke a few words. These were of the blandest and most well-omened sort, wishing safe travel, a pleasant sojourn in E-Basu, and so on. Busy watching the flock approach, I did not even prick up my ears when he concluded, "And keep well our guests so that they may come to their homeland."

The thunder of sparse-feathered wings forced the Governor to end his remarks. The wyverns' discordant cries made the air tremble as I handed the baby up to Melayne on the terrace of our wagon. Xalan drew a final round of approval by lifting to the driving seat. I just had time to exchange a final handclasp with Sandcomber, before running to my impatient mount. Baldspot clambered up to his place on the foremost wagon and made his whip crack half a dozen times in quick succession, like an exploding firework. As we on wyvern-back bounded away, the wagons, infinitely slow in comparison to us, began to move. A cloud of what looked like dust, but was really insects, slowly rose up behind, blotting out the Rria's waving hands and smiling faces. The noise of the wyverns drowned out their farewells.

CHAPTER 11

A Genuine Pseudonym

The ideal beast of burden might be a cross between wyvern and ox. As it was, the two halves of our expedition had to divide a catalogue of advantages between them: speed, the ability to carry burdens, ease of management, comfort. On my wyvern I could ride to E-Basu in perhaps six weeks, providing I was willing to carry no cargo and eschew both food and sleep. To plod there, the oxen would take as many months.

For the flyers that first day's work was minimal, since everyone knew the destination—a creek-fed pond barely a league and a half from town. In the wake of their big red-and-yellow leader the wyverns hurtled there in no time. Upon arrival, all four of us had to dismount and help 'Vernflyer wrestle the restraining jacket onto the patriarch.

That done, I thought we were more or less at leisure. But 'Vernflyer began trimming the tender tips from the bushes edging the stream, while without instruction the others set about cutting turfs for the evening's fuel. Unwilling to be the only idler, I took out my knife and came to 'Vernflyer's assistance. That worthy seemed startled but with a brusque nod allowed me to help peel the tougher bark from the stalks. When we had gathered and prepared quite a heap, I ventured to break the silence by asking, "How do you cook these?"

He stared at me. "The wyverns digest the greens

better raw," he said at last. I smiled weakly, pretending to have known all along, but from then on became more casual about the peeling.

A first hint of twilight was beginning to soften the blue sky dome before the wagons appeared. Glad to stretch my legs, I walked out to meet them, hoisting myself up the side of our wagon to hug Melayne and the baby. The brief southern evening was well-advanced by the time the oxen were unspanned. The Rria laid a large fire of turves, which burned well enough though with gouts of heavy black smoke. Our encampment ordered itself into a pattern that would soon be quite familiar: the wagons drawn up in two rows with tailgates pointing in, the fire roaring in the middle, wyverns quarreling over their greenstuff to one side while the oxen grazed on the other.

That first evening, though, all was new and strange. The night sky seemed larger here than in Rriphirrizē or even Averidan. The local boulirr chattered and hooted dismally from the dark just beyond our firelight. We sat shyly on the steps of our wagon while supper was ladled from the common pot: roots and meat boiled together. Even under the best circumstances the Rria do not cook as a Viridese would define the term. Under travel conditions the fare was downright tedious. As I scraped my plate, I meditatively eyed Xalan's red-clad back, and toyed with the idea of naming him camp cook. It would be a highly undignified role for any magus, let alone the Master Magus. But after all Xalan already changed diapers—what was one more menial but necessary duty?

I put the idea away for later consideration, and climbed up the four steps into the wagon. Its interior seemed very crowded. Of course the little chamber was fitted with bunks, cupboards, a staircase-ladder to the roof, and every other comfort a Rria needs to make life endurable away from Rriphirrizē. But the square of floor was further heaped with boxes and bags. Not wishing to strike a light, I sat down on a roll of something and fumbled awkwardly over one shoulder for the Crown in my back-pocket.

Undeterred by the dark or the thin wood of the wagon-walls I looked over those outside. As I had expected, Xalan and Melayne, being the harmless members of our party, got on better without me. Leaning over Melayne's arm the cooing baby was harvesting hearts the way a crow steals grapes, and diplomatic Xalan was complimenting 'Vernflyer on the health and strength of the wyvern flock.

None of the Rria had wanted to leave home—an unwelcome but unsurprising discovery. No member of the party had been to E-Basu before or had any experience of travel. "Folly," I grumbled to myself; the Rria who had gone before had naturally refused to leave home again. Foreign travel is merely odd in Averidan, not a vexing civic duty. My Viridese soldiers had been less depressed, when I had led them out to war.

I read 'Vernflyer for some time before discovering he suspected, rightly, that I did not love wyverns as a part-owner ought. My stated intention of going on from E-Basu was also a grievance, since that necessarily involved forsaking the creatures. Himself, 'Vernflyer would not have left his flock for any consideration. I sighed; there was nothing to be done about this except to pamper my wyvern.

Absorbed in these observations I did not at first notice the arrival of a new knowledge in my head. The recollection was forced upon me, of the Governor's parting words. We guests still had keepers. If I meant to deal with that, I was informed, the time was now. It no longer mattered that I had sought privacy so that the notorious Crown should not upset the Rria. Rising, I pushed the door open and descended into the light of the fire.

The heat of the day was already gone from the air. But the coolness that fell upon the camp at the sight of me was of another sort. Only Melayne seemed indifferent to it, and came up to thrust the baby into my arms. "I held her all day, now it's your turn," she announced. "I have an idea about my hair." Her beautiful red-brown tresses had grown somewhat over the past months, and she now began to comb it into Caydish braids again.

I frowned, then realized Tarys was, if anything, an asset. One cannot appear threatening while dandling an infant. I tucked her like a bolster under my elbow and took up a central position near the fire. "My regrets if you have a rite or custom to reveal a new name," I announced to the company in general. "But I am now going to rename myself and my friends." Pointing with my free hand I continued, "She is properly the Lady of Averidan, he is the Master Magus—remind me, Xalan, to call you Magister now—and I am the Shan King."

The Rria muttered uneasily among themselves, and looked from each other to the Crown on my brow. On the farther side of the fire Xalan raised a black eyebrow but made no comment. "I never liked 'Red Hair,' " was Melayne's placid remark.

When it seemed no one else would speak, 'Vernflyer said, "The Governor has the authority to give you new names."

"He isn't here," I returned. "Do you not ordinarily name and rename yourselves?" Of course this was precisely the issue; by claiming the prerogative of defining myself, I was no longer a foreign novelty but an equal.

This sort of thing did not interest 'Vernflyer much, not being related to the care or flying of wyverns, and he might have subsided had the others not nudged him on. "Only we Rria are namers," he insisted at last. "The appellations you choose will not be used by us."

Their attitude was annoying, but I did not show it. "That is your difficulty," I said with dignity, and turned to withdraw into our wagon again. Before I could mount the step, though, the green-and-blue striped door opened. And there stood Hwe, whom I had completely forgotten. He must have just awoke from a nap, for he yawned hugely and knuckled one eye so hard the hairy eyebrow above rasped audibly against the hairy wrist.

A clamor of dismayed and angry exclamations rose. "Look, it's Furpiece!" "Did he stow away?" "No, the Shan King—I mean, Once-King—stole him from town. . ."

Melayne stared too. "Do you tell me that thing was in our wagon all this time? Is it tame?"

I shook my head at this. "You've been living in Rriphirrizē too long," I rebuked her. "He's quite human, and his name is Hwe." I shot a glance at the Rria to see if they noticed I used Hwe's proper name.

This new surprise completely diverted our hosts' ire, and in the subsequent debate over whether to go on, or return to Rriphirrizē and bring Hwe back, all questions about naming were forgotten. Tarys had fallen asleep, hanging head down over my arm like a plump bat. The Rria seemed well set to argue into the night, so I led the way to bed, well pleased with my evening's work. Only Xalan touched on any significant anxiety, and that in an undertone: "With an extra belly—and such a big one too—I hope we don't run short of provisions!"

Early next morning several innovations were found in our wagon. The first was that Hwe had adopted us, and, being far too tall for a bunk had disposed himself to sleep in the center of the floor. By pure bad luck Melayne made this discovery by treading on his foot; her yelp of surprise jerked Xalan and me, to say nothing of Hwe, out of sound slumber, and made the baby howl.

In Averidan communal sleeping chambers are for peasants. The nobles build houses so that even married couples have separate bedrooms, the better to facilitate family tiffs. I rubbed the sleep from my eyes, very irritated indeed to have to cope with all these personalities right away. In the bunk below, Xalan sat up and cracked his head on the wooden base of my bed, so hard that I felt the impact through the straw mattress beneath me. He sagged back, groaning loudly, while the baby yelled and Melayne demanded, "Is this person going to be a fixture? Why can't he sleep outside? I don't want Tarys to get a flea or something."

I pried myself out of the bunk, legs and back aching from yesterday's wyvern-riding. "If you would nurse the baby, she might go back to sleep," I said crossly. With a disdainful sniff Melayne lay down again with Tarys in her arm. I drew the sheet over them and then turned to Xalan. As might have been expected he was more startled than hurt. "You aren't even bleeding," I accused.

"I'm probably concussed," he moaned, hugging his pillow over the damaged part. "My skull is probably broken. Call the bonesetters."

During this interval Hwe had prudently retreated up the little ladder to the roof. Taking advantage of the relative privacy I climbed into my clothes. "Are all these bags our luggage? There would be more room if they were put away."

Melayne peeped over the edge of the sheet. "Whisper, she's dropping off," she hissed. "Those are presents from the shopkeepers of Rriphirrizē."

"Presents? You're supposed to *pay* for things!"

"Why should I," my wife yawned, "if they will give? Your money is in my belt-purse there." She snuggled back under the covers. It was difficult to argue in whispers, and anyway Rriphirrizē was behind us. So I let the matter drop.

That day was the first of many, all alike, of our journey north across the plains. The wagons trundled in single file so slowly that one could easily keep up by walking. The wyverns leaped and slid, guiding the caravan around gullies or outcrops, and scouting for streams or ponds to camp beside. There were no roads and no towns. We met nobody. We might have been the only people in the world, from horizon to undulating green horizon. The autumn season, by Shan reckoning, slid into winter, and yet without varying its sunny clarity the weather grew slowly warmer. We crept along under the great searing blue sky dome but never managed to creep out from the exact center.

At first there was not much for us on wyvern-back to do, since the wagons set such a leisurely pace. To spare the fragile wings and legs of our mounts, we took it in turns to ride with the wagons. The contrast, between tearing speed and slow plodding, jerking leaps and creaking wheels, was very pleasant. I wore the Crystal Crown nearly every waking moment now, and noticed a parallel in my own circumstances. In Averidan my power had been like riding a wyvern—frequently uncontrolled and always tumultuous. Now it was set right and I could progress, though slowly, learning and building on what I learned.

When he realized that any moments of idleness would surely be filled by undignified menial chores, Xalan discovered a renewed zeal for magian study. "No geomant has ever been here, or will again, I suppose," he pointed out, and with the aid of his long black wand began tracking the earth currents. For lack of parchment or wax, for the scholars had successfully begged him for the writing tablets, he recorded his results on cloth. Preliminary sketch lines were made with charcoal, but the final delineations had to be embroidered on with colored thread. The resulting map looked like a tablecloth after a family of unwashed charcoal burners had gobbled an enthusiastic meal. Xalan alone could decipher it. "Well, I've never used a needle before," he defended, sucking a grimy and well-pricked forefinger. "The charcoal will wash out."

In the monotony of those weeks every occurrence became a landmark: our first encounter with the shrikes, for instance. The tiny creeks or shallow muddy ponds we camped by did not encourage swimming, and proper baths are not the custom among the Rria anyway. We Shan had long since become resigned to washcloths and basins. Hwe, however, would not even have this. To our horror he eschewed washing completely—inarguably a sign of barbarity in Averidan. Melayne particularly deplored it. "He smells!" she complained one glorious clear morning.

"She wasn't so fastidious when we wed," I said to Xalan, but in a tactful undertone. "Haven't I been a civilizing influence?"

Xalan wrung out his washcloth and draped it on the door-handle to dry. "Then get your influence cracking on Hwe. I hold with Melayne—we have to sleep in the same wagon!"

Just then the subject of our talk shambled into sight carrying a brimming bucket. Hwe displayed a touching enthusiasm for being helpful, but what with language difficulties and his size and clumsiness he did best with simple tasks. The pond, no bigger than a large puddle, lay in the marshy bottom of a small dell. It was entirely unremarkable when a flock of small birds rose from the reeds beyond.

Melayne knotted the baby's diaper. "And why has he adopted *you*, Liras? The Rria found him, didn't they?"

"They tired of him," I said; we were speaking in Viridese so I could be frank. "I think he knows it—" A sudden shrill clatter drowned my words, a noise like a thousand chickens being killed. Just beyond the wagons Hwe bellowed at the top of his lungs and fell flat. A whirlwind of pigeon-sized birds assailed him, pecking and tearing at his long ruddy hair. For an instant we could only stare. But Baldspot pushed past us, armed with his whip. Yelling and flailing he attacked the birds. Xalan caught up his wand, I my sword, and we ran to help.

But already the creatures were swirling away into the bright morning air, shrieking with glee. Wisps of ruddy hair drifted down the breeze. Hwe wept like a child as we examined his hurts. The tufts had taken some skin along when they were dragged out, and his broad hands had been pecked. "At least he had the wit to hold them over his eyes," said Baldspot.

Xalan bent to pick up a stunned bird. It was, of course, a boulirr, white and green and yellow, the hooked beak further armed with wicked teeth. "Did they disapprove of his haircut, or what?"

"Stupid creatures, they thought he was a boulirr. They usually attack anything feathered, pluck it bare and blind it to prevent escape."

"And then tear the victim to pieces for dinner," I finished for him. It came to me that the minimal Rria fashions were rooted in common sense, if the vicious birds took clothing for feathers. "What about the oxen?"

"You flyers will have some work now," he said with melancholy satisfaction.

With some pushes and many encouraging words we urged Hwe to his feet and led him into camp. No one knew how to begin dressing wounds on a furry hide, so Melayne reluctantly took charge. "I've bandaged sheep and goats," she said. "Do you think he'll balk if I say that bathing is part of the treatment?"

"Try it!" I turned to Baldspot. "What do you call these bloodthirsty boulirr?"

He gave me a rather sour glance. "You're the namer now, what should you call them?" So I named them shrikes, after the aggressive insect-hunters we have at home.

We were considerably more cautious after this episode. Melayne watched the baby like a hawk during the day when the shrikes liked to hunt. A full-grown wyvern was too big to be threatened, but a younger one, too small to be ridden, was mobbed one evening. The patriarch bounded screaming to the rescue, and we humans also, but the shrikes were so numerous the young wyvern was plucked nearly nude in an instant. Defeathered, it could not keep up with the flock. His face was drawn with pain as 'Vernflyer performed the grim necessity the following morning, and cut the creature's throat. "Shall we bury or burn the carcass, and so deprive the shrikes?" Xalan suggested.

"Not worthwhile, there are so many," 'Vernflyer returned. The red-and-yellow patriarch seemed to dimly grasp what was going on, and hooted until our heads rang at the sight of the shrikes fluttering down to feed. When 'Vernflyer made to put on the harness the patriarch lashed out with a razor-taloned foot, and we all had to help strap the bands on. As the wagons pulled away, the shrikes drifted down like snowflakes, cloaking the little wyvern's body in white and gold with flecks of green.

Formerly as benign as a well-stuffed quilt, the endless gentle yellow-green swells of the plain became perilous. During daylight hours a vigilant cloud of shrikes was almost always visible somewhere. They could soar up and then swoop down with the speed of a falling axe. A prompt and vigorous defense could drive them off, and here the wyverns were invaluable. When an ox was mobbed, 'Vernflyer would send the entire flock bounding down. Their big wings and thick gooselike beaks swatted shrikes out of the air; the wyverns swallowed the fallen and stunned whole, like oysters. We got fewer exhilarating long slides ahead now, with the grassy earth falling away behind. Instead, we mostly circled the slow-moving wagons.

I had been letting Fleabite out to run of an evening, and with bits of meat slowly made friends with her. About this time it occurred to me that a large cat was just the defense against birds. The next morning when I swung open the cage door, the leopard gave me a startled golden look before bounding out. "Let her follow the wagons," I told Melayne and Baldspot.

That evening Melayne proudly showed me four shrike carcasses. "The leopard caught six, but ate the other two," she reported. "They were just ganging up on an ox."

"Very good!" I applauded, and the Rria agreed. Any ally against the shrikes was welcome.

Xalan shot me a suspicious look. "Did you expect the beast to be so useful, when you made us bring her from Rriphirrizē?"

"Of course not." Lounging sated and self-satisfied under a wagon, Fleabite did not condescend to look up when Baldspot offered her a chunk of flat bread.

"She deserves a new name," 'Vernflyer suggested. "Those spots don't look like flea bites any more."

I grinned. "There's only one name for any cat of

mine." I took the bread from Baldspot. "Here, Sahai, this is good for you." Even when I laid the crust by her nose, Sahai only yawned. Boldly, I stroked the flat skull between her tufted ears. Sahai slowly closed her eyes in pleasure.

"Now be careful, dearest," Melayne begged. "The creature isn't tame."

In spite of our vigilance and Sahai's help we lost several oxen. Having neither hands nor wings for defence, their eyes were dreadfully vulnerable. The Rria had had the forethought to bring a dozen extra beasts. They were dubious when I proposed cutting out the best bits of beef from the dead cattle, but, when I volunteered Xalan as cook, gave way. Xalan insisted that I help and advise; we were both shocked to discover that eating, though it is an art, is quite a different art from cookery. Even after an hour of tinkering with the seasonings, our attempt at stewed beef was barely edible. Fortunately most of our diners were not critical. But Melayne, who in Averidan eats only the best, said judiciously, "Onions would taste better than those roots."

"There aren't any to be had," I said peevishly.

The wyverns hated their new duties. Their furious nature was, as the old Rria had said, to leap high and far, never lingering. To be forced to return again and again to nearly the same spot raveled their short tempers. It grew to be an unpleasant adventure every morning to put on the harnesses, and freeing the big patriarch's wings took every available hand. Once at liberty the entire flock would sometimes storm away and leave us secondary flyers lamenting, until 'Vernflyer could force the leader to stand and let us mount our beasts.

Inevitably the morning came when vigilance lapsed. While loosening one sleeve Baldspot broke off to sneeze. In that moment the patriarch lashed out a big yellow foot, catching him on the thigh. Baldspot toppled, but with a supreme effort choked down his yell of pain, lest the wyvern should become yet more ner-

vous. In a tense silence filled only with raucous hoots
we dragged him well clear.

"It can't be too bad, the talon didn't pierce your
skin," said one driver.

"Don't be a fool," Baldspot panted through set
teeth. When the cook gingerly felt the limb over,
Baldspot almost fainted. His thigh was broken.

I waited for the first babble of dismayed comment
to pass before pushing forward. "I'll heal it for you,
shall I?"

Again there was silence, during which the Rria's
intense thoughts were almost visible: Everyone knew I
claimed to talk to Iphalar. Everyone had seen the
eclipse. I might well be able to do as I said. The
Crystal Crown softly gleamed in a very convincing way
on my head. And if I failed, no harm would be done
to poor Baldspot. Most of the Rria present therefore
concluded there was nothing to lose, and the cook
edged over to give me his place. Only one fellow
muttered a minority opinion, "Bad enough to leave
home—did the Governor have to send a zany with us
as well?"

I knelt down. In Averidan healings had been my
specialty. I laid a hand on his thigh, where a swelling
lump was already starting to distort the swirling orange and blue tattoos. Scarcely any effort was needed
to knit the broken bone back together, as if I brimmed
with such overwhelming power that it trickled casually
out from my fingertips. Baldspot's sweaty clenched
face sagged into astonishment. He sat up, exclaiming,
"What did you do?"

Helpfully, Xalan said, "It's not perfect—the bruise
will take the usual time to go down."

No one heeded him. Instead the Rria surged around
Baldspot, urging him to his feet, stroking the still-
swollen limb, exclaiming and gesturing with their dark
hands. Without thinking about it they gave both of us
a wide berth. Xalan muttered, "Please, don't heap us
with thanks!"

"Don't fret about it, Magister," I said, turning back

to the wagons. I liked to be liked, and had worked to please. Now I saw that ordinary human fellowship was closing itself off to me. One pays a price for power. I had spent years trying to evade that payment; now, a little sadly, I accepted that seeing what others cannot, walking in the realm beneath, has to be done alone.

Then, trotting to catch up, Xalan said, "Oh, well. At least they don't immediately go into fits and yell 'witch!' like the Cayds did."

"Yes, that was always tiresome." His matter-of-fact cheer made me feel better. "Do you ever feel disturbed by the things I do?"

"Frequently," Xalan said grinning, and then added, "But then I'm Viridese. I expect the Shan King to do gusty, romantic deeds."

The realization struck me so forcibly I said it aloud. "You think of the Shan King as a resident of the realm beneath!"

"The what?" Xalan raised a black eyebrow.

"An idea of mine," I said with a smile, and turned the talk to dinner.

CHAPTER 12

A Minor Prodigy

Very gradually over the weeks the climate grew hotter, the country drier. The wyverns soared out early to search for the coming evening's water, so that if there were none within a day's march, we could fill a few water casks before departing. The rolling yellow-green turf faded to lemon yellow, then grew sparse and scrubby so that cutting greens for the wyverns became a chore. Without crossing any clear border we were journeying from plain into desert. It was obvious that this same journey, in full summer, would be impossible.

The morning came when the wyverns found no water ahead at all. At the height of our slide I could see only a few tufts of growth struggling among the sandy gravel wastes north and west, to where a shimmering glare of heat veiled the utmost horizon. 'Vernflyer brought the flock back to camp, and to my surprise began unharnessing the wyverns and jacketing the patriarch. "The books warn we'll need all day to prepare for this leg of the trip," he explained.

The water of yesterday was a small cloudy pond surrounded by mud cracked dry. Every cask and container we possessed was filled with its unappealing water. Then the wyverns drank, by scooping up mouthfuls and letting them trickle down their throats, and then the cattle. I called Sahai to drink, but she refused and curled herself disdainfully on a wagon roof. By then the pond was much smaller, trampled and thick with mud, and day was almost over. Every spear of greenstuff within walking distance had been plucked and stored away to supplement the oxen's usual fare of sliced roots. We ate our evening meal in a distracted spirit, brooding on the trials to come.

As ever, the next day dawned bright and clear. "If I were a herognomer, I could tell you when it rains here," said Xalan longingly.

"I can—I asked Baldspot," Melayne said. The Rria had discovered that the journals of previous expeditions were not very helpful in practical matters. In Melayne they found an old hand at the care and management of cattle, and now they consulted her often. "It rains in the spring only, rather like Averidan."

Xalan gloomily surveyed the arid landscape. "I only wish it *looked* more like Averidan."

Never had the disparity between the two parts of the expedition been more maddening. By giving the wyverns their heads, we could cross this dry belt in two or three days. But without food and water the wyverns could not survive even that brief time. Unable to carry provisions for themselves, the swifter boulirr were chained to the oxen. So everyone had to suffer through the longer journey.

The first day was not too bad, the only aggravation being the lack of washing-water. The following morning, though, the wyverns took a violent prejudice against the barrel their water was stored in, apparently taking it for some peculiarly vile trap. We actually had to force each stupid creature's head down into the opening to touch the water before the wyvern would drink. The screaming and wasteful splashing that accompanied the operation was unbelievable.

That evening the big patriarch turned up his beak at the hib-root and greenstuff 'Vernflyer offered, and dealt him a sharp beak-blow that would have cracked his ribs except for his protective flying outfit. "You'd think the creatures wanted to die," I incautiously said, and regretted my words immediately when 'Vernflyer shot me an outraged glare.

"They're finicky eaters, that's all," he snarled, wiping a dark hand over his dust-streaked face.

In the cool before the dawn the wyverns bounded off on the day's search. 'Vernflyer led us on a zigzag course covering as much ground to the northeast as possible, while on our following beasts we peered through the glare and dust, straining our eyes for any telltale luxuriance of greenery. Because we did not give up until well after midday, camp had already been made when we returned, very late. "It must have been a drier season than usual last year," Baldspot surmised when he heard our bad news. "We can just do it, I hope—if those bad-tempered creatures of yours don't spill any more water."

"What about those sponges you call cattle?" 'Vernflyer demanded. "Cut back on their share!"

The quarrel was so silly none of us joined in. Instead we concentrated grimly on pushing the head of the smallest wyvern into the water barrel. The idiotic boulirr flapped and struggled, its claws scraping over the barrel staves and its desperate yells echoing oddly inside. "The less the oxen drink, the slower their progress," Baldspot retorted.

'Vernflyer drew in a breath to reply. But the wyvern took advantage of his inattention to kick out furiously with its sinewy legs. The ugly head popped free and the thick beak tipped the barrel right over.

"Oh, no! Hold on, it's breaking away!" The water splashed over our feet and was gone. In a unity of disgust we let the wyvern flap crossly over to join its fellows, and looked at each other in dismay.

'Vernflyer scuffed his shoe through the wet gravel that marked the disaster. "I don't suppose there is a wizardry to raise up spilt water," he said tentatively to Xalan.

Xalan rubbed his mustache with a dirty finger. "A hydromant might have that skill," he said regretfully. "Or if I'd known you were going to spill it, I might have treated the earth to repel the water."

There was a moment of silence. Then I realized everyone was carefully not looking at me. "I'll think over the problem," I said.

Back in camp I asked to see Xalan's earth current chart. He shook the cloth out onto the sand with a brisk snap, saying, "I haven't washed out the charcoal these past few days."

"I can see that." The lower half of the coarse white fabric was so heavily smudged with black that the crazy straggle of colored embroidery was hard to see. Crouched at the edge I touched it with my fingertips, to keep the charcoal off my hands. "Do any of these lines have anything to do with water?"

Of Xalan's explanation I understood not a syllable; they use their own terms in the art Magian. "You're trying to say the answer is no," I hazarded.

"Not precisely. There is a very complex relationship between earth currents and water-bearing strata. The magus Xaclis expressed it in a controversial equation—"

"All right, all right! Where are we now on this thing?"

Xalan pored on hands and knees for some time over the dirty half of cloth before saying, "Ah! Here—I've been marking our progress with a big thorn, but it's fallen out."

The hole where the thorn had been was near the center of the breadth; Xalan had allowed plenty of fabric for future notations. I sat back on my haunches and relaxed, putting a hand up to my brow. I could supply an answer only if the deity gave one and passed it to me through the Crown. If he wanted me to get to E-Basu, he would have to do something. After some moments I found my gaze returning again and again to a certain spot on the map, a fairly clean one not far north of the thorn hole. Reaching over I put my finger on it, and felt a faint thrill of knowledge. "Here, mark this place. No, not with that disgusting charcoal, use thread—I want to be able to find it tomorrow."

Xalan unwound a bit of green thread from the needle stuck in one hem. "Why, what's there?"

"Water, I hope. It's a little east of our search path today."

He took two stitches to make a clumsy cross, and

then tied the thread off in a crude knot before giving me a searching glance. "The Rria won't be happy if you're wrong."

I yawned, displaying a confidence I did not entirely feel. "Neither will I. I'm tired of being dirty. Do you suppose dinner is ready yet?"

I did not realize until after the meal that Xalan would have to come with us on the wyverns. Only he could read his map, and use earth currents to identify the marked spot. Furthermore, he would have to ride double with 'Vernflyer to lead the flock. Neither Xalan nor 'Vernflyer nor his red-and-yellow mount were pleased with the prospect. For my part I routed out two shovels and a pry-bar the next morning, and tied them together to carry. "You mean it's not a pond or brook?" Xalan exclaimed.

"I hope so, but suppose it's an underground water-course there instead? We may have to scratch around a bit."

"The terrain isn't right for underground rivers," Xalan said darkly, and tucked the folded map under his arm.

A morning sufficed for the wyverns to reach the spot. The trip was more than long enough for Xalan—I could tell, even from my following wyvern, by the way his cloth map flapped despairingly with every jerking leap. When 'Vernflyer drew the patriarch to a halt, Xalan appeared to fall off and lie prone. The other wyverns hopped like peas on a hot shovel, and I coaxed mine to stand only with difficulty. "I'm seasick," Xalan moaned in greeting.

"Is that all?" I said, relieved. "You can't be; we're hundreds of leagues from the sea."

All around us the arid plains stretched empty away, baked a pale biscuit brown under the merciless Sun. From his seat high on the wyvern's neck 'Vernflyer called, "I see no water!"

"Is this the exact spot on your map?" I demanded.

Xalan sat up. "You can't tell?"

"I had an insight, but only on the map. That's why I needed you."

"A highly unusual way to divine water." Unslinging his long black wand he paced over the sandy soil, feeling for the area's distinctive pattern of earth currents. "This is as close as I can come. The scale on my map is fairly large."

Shouting, I told 'Vernflyer we would have to dig, and that he must guide the wagons here. The journey would be rather longer than a usual day's trek; I could tell he wanted to point out we had to find water by the time they arrived. But an impatient wyvern is a poor platform for argument. 'Vernflyer had little choice but to wave a signal at one of the other flyers, and after the fellow dismounted, start off on the return trip.

"I arranged with Bodkin here to lend a hand with the shoveling," I said. "You, Magister, will help by geomantically loosening the soil."

I had selected Bodkin—whose nickname I never learned the provenance of—solely for the breadth of his red-tattooed shoulders. Tracing a rough circle in the earth with the pry-bar I handed him a shovel. Between us, we soon scraped out a layer of loose sand and gravel. The rock and earth beneath was solid as a floor. Xalan sighed. "I want to go home, where I'll have plenty of magian underlings to delegate these tiring jobs to." With a circular stirring gesture of the black wand he broke up the tight-packed soil.

"You didn't even need to touch it," Bodkin marveled.

"Suppose water is quite close to the surface." Xalan frowned into the hole as we threw the loosened dirt out. "Perhaps it would be easier to use a small 'quake."

We climbed out to let him stab at the bottom of the hole with the butt of his wand. At the impact the earth quivered and split, leaving a large crack. I probed it anxiously with the pry-bar. It went down only a foot or two. "Dry," I reported. "We'll have to do it the slow way."

It rapidly became grilling hot at the bottom of our excavation. The shoveling, and the tedium of climbing in and out of the deepening hole, might have been more bearable if we had not all labored under crushing doubts. How had I allowed myself, once again, to gamble on the trustworthiness of that god? Would I never learn? And pausing to wipe the sweat and dust from my face, I noticed Xalan consulting his grubby map once again.

Most disheartening of all, though, was Bodkin. His strength of arm did not translate into strength of spirit, and as the hole became deeper and wider he poured out an unrelenting stream of complaint, criticism, and questions. "At least, if you must use wizardries, let them be reliable . . . My shovel isn't sharp enough . . . Why did I not think to carry more than one water-bottle? I can inform you why. Because you were supposed to be leading us to water . . . We should have more diggers, an awning for shade, a pick . . . Can't your magics break up the earth a little deeper?"

By late afternoon everyone was exhausted. The hole was six feet deep and sloped to keep the sides from falling in. Its bottom was as perfectly dry and hot as the inside of a bake-oven. Thoroughly discouraged, we gave it up by common consent and lay down in the scant shade of a nearby dip in the plain. "We should have dug down here," Bodkin remarked. "Water flows to low places."

I blew on a broken blister in my palm, and brooded about hitting Bodkin on the head with the pry-bar. But my soul sickened at the thought of touching a tool again; the pleasure would not address the main issue anyway. In a pale tired voice Xalan said, "The wagons will be arriving soon. What shall we do?"

I didn't know. "I begin to think it doesn't really do people any *good* to deal with gods," I said with vague irrelevance. "Surely the troubles involved far outweigh any benefits you gain."

Bodkin knuckled his shoulder muscles and groaned gently. "We Rria have always suspected you were mad."

When we heard the distant creak of wagon wheels, I had Xalan go and meet the arrivals. He did not at all wish to carry the burden of explanation alone, but I

insisted. "You're the smooth talker, not I." Bodkin
went along too, to give his own version. I alone remained lying on my back, watching the pale purple
cloak of twilight slowly unfold from the cloudless eastern horizon. The rage I would have felt once had
given way to weary self-contempt. The deity had all
the weapons, but did I have to lift my chin to let him
cut my throat?

From the west came the flaps and panting of the
wyvern flock. Xalan would soon have to repeat his
account. The day was ending, but its heat still shimmered in the wind and soaked up from the earth. I
closed my eyes and listened to the shrill approaching
babble of angry comment and peevish lamentation.
The most draining aspect of being Shan King was this
perpetual turmoil. Wars and sieges, battles and es-
capes, travel and plots—one never had a peaceful
moment to sit in the garden and relax.

Something damp hit my right eyelid. I opened my
eyes. A mass of thundercloud was rolling down from
the north faster than the swiftest horse. The wind blew
suddenly cool, and the first fat raindrops made circular
splash-marks on the dry earth.

"Xalan!" I leaped up and ran. "Xalan, use your
magery on our hole!" As I galloped up to them the
skies opened with a roar of thunder. I bellowed my
idea into Xalan's ear and he nodded. Through the
downpour we made our way to our excavation. Xalan
paced around it, muttering a formula to render the
porous soil briefly impervious. He turned to shout, "I
can't maintain it long, we had better start bailing."

The Rria were already dragging out the barrels and
casks. Bowls and cups were set out, and dirty laundry
laid out on the wagon-roofs. Sahai fled with a yowl
between the wheels of a wagon, and disgustedly shook
out each golden paw in turn. The wyverns bounded
wetly around their hobbled leader, shrieking gleefully
at every crack of lightning and kicking up mud and
wet gravel. Clothing was shed and shoes kicked off.
The rain slashed down so hard it made the skin tingle

delightfully. My hands were seized and I was whirled away in a happy impromptu dance by the jubilant wagoners.

The storm passed off as quickly as it had come. The winds pushed it south and west into the night. With some difficulty, for everything was wet, we lit a fire. While some bailed out the water pooled in our hole, others unspanned the oxen and prepared supper. Xalan walked around and around the pool with his wand poised as first the wyverns and then the oxen drank. By then the remaining fluid was muddy and trampled. I nodded, and Xalan let his wand fall. In a few moments the puddled rainwater leaked away, leaving only silt behind.

"So you deal in miracles?" 'Vernflyer said, very respectfully.

Without answering Xalan staggered past, his soaked garments drooping around him. I said, "If you consult those journals, I'll wager you find we are coming into a region of small sudden rainstorms." Ungraciously, all things considered, I added, "It wasn't quite a miracle—just a little practical joke."

CHAPTER 13

A Startling Resident

In the weeks that followed we often saw sudden local-
ized storms, though we were not often lucky enough
to catch one. From a distance the abrupt torrent looked
as if a gigantic sky-pitcher of water were pouring out
onto the earth. When the winds set from the north, it
blew rather cold, a brief ambassador from the winter
that still locked the northern lands. The Rria would
shiver and complain at the slightest chill. Pools and
creeks became common again, and the vegetation altered. I examined the thin wiry stuff and found it was
grass, a genuine grass rather than the pillowy yellow-
green plants that pass for it in the south. The discovery was somehow tremedously moving. "We're going
home!" I waved a handful of the stalks at Melayne.

She rubbed the stuff between her palms. "The oxen
will pull better on this," she announced with satisfaction. "I'm certain Rria hay tastes odd to them."

Certainly the draft animals began to thrive on their
new diet. Their brown hides grew sleek, and the lean
flanks beneath plumped out in spite of the work. The
oxen had been placid so long we were taken unaware
when, fueled by the better food, they wandered far
from camp one night. We had to track them on wyvern-
back and drive them back to the wagons. Thereafter,
we set Hwe to watch them at night.

In a peculiar reversal of the normal order, the blaz-
ing summer of our journey seemed to unwind into
spring. The air blew cooler and cooler, and yet a

228

fresher green crept into the wide grasslands. And the land began to change. The little creeks and rivulets which threaded every which way across the plain felt it first. Instead of losing themselves in ponds or sloughs they commenced running north and east, joining together into quite respectable streams. Now when the cattle snuffed the north wind, they grew livelier than ever. In the evenings they milled around in a sort of lumbering romp, bellowing and clicking their short horns together. "They scent their home," Melayne said, turning her face to the roaring wind. "Ah! And so do I. I never thought I should see Cayd again."

Visiting one's relatives is a highlight of Viridese life, so Xalan very properly asked, "Why, is Liras so strict a husband he would forbid a visit to your kin?"

Melayne gave him a pitying glance. "We were going to conquer Averidan," she reminded him. "*They* would visit *me*."

One night it even froze; the grass the next day was crisp and white underfoot and the cold air pinched the sleep from our faces. For us Shan it was a delight, after so much broiling heat, and from pure happiness Hwe capered clumsily about like a drunken bear. But I felt sorry for the Rria. Having never known frost until now, this sudden cold snap tormented them. They dressed in every garment available and, since these amounted to very little, rolled themselves in all their bedding. Then they huddled shivering by the central fire and moaned.

Nothing we could say could persuade them to get moving. Finally, clever Xalan said, "Do you know, I think the wyverns are cold too?"

"I don't hear any shrieking or bouncing," I agreed gravely. "In this weather they'll need a lot of food to keep warm. I rather doubt that you and I alone can gather enough, Xalan."

"Oh, why did I ever consent to leave Rriphirrizē?" 'Vernflyer groaned, dragging himself to his feet. "Why didn't these accursed journals warn us to bring more clothing?" At least he had a flying outfit. Baldspot

ordinarily wore nothing but a loincloth and a short
white jacket. Now the straw mat wrapped around his
torso and legs barely strained the wind. While I helped
with the wyverns, Melayne and Xalan took it in turns
to assure him and the other drivers that E-Basu was
surely full of spinners, weavers, tailors and seamstresses
who could bundle them in warm clothing.

At last, on a day of high driving cloud, we topped a
low rolling hill and saw the sea. The Tiyalene Sea we
called it, though the Rria used their own name. It was
hard to believe it was landlocked, that we stood hundreds of leagues from the true ocean. The thin blue
shadows of wind-driven cloud scudded across an expanse of silvery water that stretched far north and
east. A deep belt of brighter green fringed the curving
shore. "Reeds and marsh," 'Vernflyer decided, after
consulting the journals, and set us on a northerly
course well clear of them.

We watched eagerly now for signs of human habitation and E-Basu. In the evenings the shivering Baldspot
read aloud from some earlier Rria traveler's account:
"A city smaller than Rriphirrizē, and infinitely less
fair, being built over the flat lake shore. The people
pretend to a civility which, in comparison to their
ruder neighbors to the north, is indeed considerable,
but not truly of the same ilk as ours . . ."

"It's all very well, loving your home," I muttered to
Xalan in Viridese. "But to hear everything compared—
unfavorably—to Rriphirrizē?"

Xalan whispered back, "Imagine what Sandcomber's
tales of Averidan must be like." I winced at the thought.

Despite its blatant bias the journal was interesting.
E-Basu's foundation appeared to be unknowable. In
'Vernflyer's great-grandfather's day the humble fishers
and herders of the district had gone to the shore to cut
reeds. And there beyond the reed-beds, where only
placid waters had murmured before, was a city, all of
red-brown stone.

"There must have been some movement in the
earth," Xalan guessed. "Or else the lake shore shifted

somewhat. It sounds more wondrous if one doesn't mention that. I'd wager the stones were low, little more than foundations, to be covered by water like that."

"Well, it does say here the Basuans built wooden walls onto the ancient stones." Baldspot smoothed another breadth of cloth record over his knee, and tucked the blanket more snugly around his neck. "On that beginning they've erected quite a bustling town. They do more than fishing and herding now; the town is a center for trade in all the wealth of forest and plain."

"A notable achievement for such an upstart place," 'Vernflyer said condescendingly. "Of course Rriphirrizē is far older, twenty generations at least."

I bit back a smile. The Shan hold that Averidan has been a realm for ten thousand years. The expression of blank innocence spread like milk over Xalan's face too.

We journeyed up the green lake shore for ten days without coming across so much as a sheep-trail. The Rria began to worry, folding and refolding their maps and journals, until Melayne pointed out the long low banks that crisscrossed the grassland. We had thought them some quirk of the local landforms, but she said, "They're pasture boundaries. Only in Cayd we would top the turf ridges with posts and rails. A little bump like those wouldn't fence in a Caydish cow."

Upon examination the nearest ridge did indeed yield up some rotted fence-post stumps, nearly hidden in the tangle of grass roots. "Not very well kept up," Bodkin said judiciously. "We Rria would be more conscientious."

What Bodkin disparaged I felt bound to defend. "Why bother with maintenance, since there's no livestock?" We climbed up the three-foot bank to survey the surrounding fields. The tireless winds made the lush new grasses bow and sway, but no beasts could be seen. "Perhaps there was some sickness among the cattle, or maybe this is merely a summer grazing ground."

The following day we came across a road. It was overgrown and grassy, as if not used often. Only from wyvern-back was the faint track threading away north readily visible. Overgrown or not, the wagons made better progress on it, and that evening we congratulated ourselves on tomorrow's conclusion to our journey. "Our last camp," 'Vernflyer gloated. "Now my faithful wyverns can rest properly."

"This was ever so much nicer than our sea-trip," Melayne said to me. "Wagons are the civilized way to travel. And I shouldn't mind wagering that E-Basu is a pleasanter town than, say, Uwuna."

"Wasn't that a scary place," Xalan said in a sleepy reminiscence. "Shall we start for home right off, or rest awhile?"

I yawned; the cozy crackle of the fire was soporific as neat brandy. "We've all spring to get there." On the roof of a wagon opposite Sahai yawned too, with a gleam of terrible white teeth, before carefully folding her paws together. Tiny golden flames reflected from her slitted yellow eyes.

Not until the next day did our confidence falter. The journals had warned 'Vernflyer that the crowded streets were unsuitable for wyverns. The flock was therefore left in a field; we flyers climbed onto the wagon-roofs. By noon, E-Basu had crept into view over the swells of the plain: thatched peaked roofs and mud-daubed chimneys. Xalan and I set up a cheer, until Baldspot pointed out the clear blue sky above the town. "No smoke from those chimneys," he noted.

"Make these beasts move," 'Vernflyer shouted impatiently from a farther wagon. "We'll never fathom this, sitting here!"

We saw other roads now, wide double-rutted tracks worn into the earth by wheeled traffic, and narrow foot-trails. All were weedy and disused. The wagon-wheels groaned in their axles, and the oxen's broad feet kept up a steady thudding rhythm. Melayne hummed a Caydish lullaby to Tarys at the breast, and the wind sighed through the grasses. Underlying and overarching all these noises, however, was the silence. Not a voice or a tool or a beast did we hear, from the town before us.

The Basuans did not build as the Rria. The town proper still brooded ahead, but houses and farmsteads began to appear beside the road. At the first of these Baldspot halted his wagon. "Shall someone go in and ask for news?" he called back to 'Vernflyer.

As 'Vernflyer slid to earth and came forward, I saw he had the journals bundled under his arm. "A good thought," he said. "It says here the population of E-Basu is a hundred score households. Perhaps they've all gone to a festival on the other side of town."

No one moved, and after a moment it was borne in on me that I was that "someone." "Your sword, that you handle so well, might be helpful," 'Vernflyer said, appeasingly.

As I climbed down, Melayne hugged the baby and scowled over the roof-rail at me. "Suppose it's plague?"

"I'm sure it's not." The deity would certainly warn me off, through the Crown on my head, if that were so.

"Well, if there's anything dead inside, don't touch it."

I promised to be careful, and drawing my sword approached the fence. This was a rickety affair, obviously meant only to keep children and poultry off the high road. The lath gate sagged open on one leathern hinge. The wooden house had a peaked roof from which the reed thatching was raveling away. I padded up the path to the door, and rapped politely with my sword-hilt. There was no answer; I pushed the door open and went in.

The wind mourned through some unchinked crack as I explored the single dim room within. Clothing, livestock, food, tools—all had been either taken or looted away. Only the larger bits of furniture were left, a dusty bedstead and an empty wood-box. The ashes in the fireplace were dark and crusted. "A winter's rains have fallen down that chimney," I reported when I returned to the wagons.

"I wish you hadn't brought up the subject of plague," Baldspot said unhappily to Melayne.

'Vernflyer, who had been vainly skimming the journals, now threw them down and said, "Let's leave the wagons here and go into town on foot. It's not far, and we can explore better."

Everyone agreed to this. During my absence, though, Melayne had laid the sleeping baby down in our wagon. "After the battle I had, getting her to sleep, I'm not raking her out again. I'll stay behind, and perhaps peel some vegetables."

This seemed safe enough, especially when I told Sahai to stay behind too. We trudged down the road, peering nervously round every shed or outhouse we passed. It was hard not to imagine people peeping out from the empty windows behind our backs. Surprisingly, the way went over the marsh, in a wooden causeway that had not yet begun to rot. When the marsh gave way to water, we had arrived. As Baldspot had recounted, E-Basu was built over the sea.

The wooden streets were laid over pilings of ancient red stone. A vaguely repellent smell of sodden wood and water-borne trash rose up from between the creaking planks. The houses were tall and broad but placed haphazardly, ordered, we supposed, only by the availability of sound stone foundations. The lack of visible order, and the sly chuckle of wavelets beneath our feet, seemed to underline the town's desolation. "I don't think there's a soul here," 'Vernflyer said in hushed tones. "Where has everyone gone?"

"The Governor will be vexed, if there's no one here to take our goods," was Bodkin's comment.

"Perhaps there are provisions, foodstuffs left behind?" Xalan suggested.

No one cared to be left when I opened a door at random, so we explored the building in a body. It was different from the first, and not only because of the eerily echoing stair linking the four stories, or the glimpses of placid water one caught from the upper windows. Clothes hung limp on hooks, dusty cups sat on the tables, a cooking pot hung near the cold hearth, though when I lifted the lid I found only cobwebs. "If the town was conquered, everyone slain by some foe, and that first house looted, why is this one spared?" Thoughtfully I set the lid back. "And if everyone moved away, why did no one pack up the goods here?"

"Don't touch that," Baldspot begged. "Perhaps the residents here died of disease, and those outside town then gathered up their belongings and fled."

"All this water isn't sanitary," 'Vernflyer agreed.

Though the Rria felt the cold keenly, scavenging the household goods did not appeal to them. We trooped back downstairs, trying not to let our feet clatter, and into the street. "Let's go back to the wagons," Bodkin said in a nervous squeak.

"There must have been a government here," Xalan countered, more sensibly. "A king or a viceroy or a lord. We must find his house, and then search it for written records."

"A sensible idea," 'Vernflyer admitted. So we went on, deeper into the town, farther out over the murmuring water. On the wooden ways our footsteps made an echoing rumble, like distant thunder. Behind us the Sun sank toward evening, so our search would necessarily be short. I was secretly glad of it, and could tell my companions shared the feeling. E-Basu was no more unpopulated than the plain. But its emptiness weighed absurdly heavy on the heart; by comparison the wilderness we had crossed had been a holiday, shrikes, drought and all.

No one knew what an official Basuan building might look like. We glanced into the doors of the houses we passed, and down every side street, hoping to see a meeting-square or market-place.

At last we came to the farthest edge of the town. In every direction stretched blue water, fading to gray in the long shadow of the stone pilings. A single building

stood on the verge here. Other reddish stone foundations were visible beyond, extending just beneath the
water's rippled surface. Some of the Rria peered into
the depths, and the rest of us waited impatiently while
Bodkin trotted up to the final door and pushed it
open.

His whinny of surprise made everyone jump. Framed
in the doorway was a woman. Even in that first instant
of shock her sex was obvious—she was stark naked.
"Apologies," Bodkin gurgled, bug-eyed, and began a
shuffling retreat. "Continue with your bath, I beg.
We'll call again—"

The feeble words were cut off by an animal shriek
that froze us all. In a streak of pale skin the woman
leaped upon Bodkin and bore him to the ground.
'Vernflyer began some shocked exclamation, as the
woman twined hands like knotted ropes around Bodkin's neck. With the gesture like one breaking the wax
seal off a wine bottle, she twisted his head off.

It was the sort of impossible action that occurs only
in nightmare; people need tools to decapitate anything
bigger than a chicken. But this was no dream. Bodkin's arms and legs gave a single convulsive jerk, and
his blood spurted out of the broken vessels, pooling on
the planks before dripping through into the lake below.

Even as Bodkin died, I fell into a curious state. Any
Viridese will boast of having two minds, and this was
not the first time the Crystal Crown had thrown me
into a true experience of it. But now I had some
measure of control, moving at will from the surface of
things to the perils below. One part of me watched as
the Rria did, nerveless and unmoving with the same
shock. The other, larger bit was skittering like the
wyverns through a thunderstorm, whirling and bounding in a frenzy of excitement through a downpour of
knowledge, a flow so torrential most of it was lost to
me.

The external eye saw a young woman, pale-skinned
and fair in the way of most western barbarians. But
the true and inner eye showed me quite a different

sight. Poor Bodkin's lifeblood dripped not from fingers, but claws, three and three on short bandy arms. The human image hung like a puppet from a flexible stalk that sprouted from the top of a small round head. That, and a body longer than its width, was all I could discern, because the creature was lapped in roll upon roll of its own skin, greenish-white and slightly iridescent like turning meat. Even the head with its dangling lure was hooded in sagging folds, as if the thing had once been much fatter.

"Much more well fed!" I exclaimed, and with a rush my two halves surged together again. Things which had moved very slowly while I was "beneath" suddenly assumed their normal pace. Hwe, who had all this time trailed tamely behind, turned with a hoarse scream, and ran. Before anyone could follow his excellent example, the monster's short arms shot out, fast as a toad's tongue. The claws locked around another Rria's leg. "Run! Everybody, run!" I yelled, and drew my sword.

But when I made to run forward, a crushing fact fell on my consciousness, impeding my limbs like setting clay. This was not the way to attack the enemy, and now was not the time. "What do you mean, this isn't the way?" I demanded aloud, and reached up to give the Crown a rap. "Isn't this the way to use the other realm?"

I rapidly realized, though, that now was not the time to argue with the deity either. The creature had used the moment to rend the Rria into several gruesome pieces. It was intelligent enough to kill as many as possible first, before settling down to eat. With a sidewise slithery motion, holding out the illusory human image temptingly before it, it approached me through the gathering twilight.

The instant I turned to retreat, the treacly restraints vanished from my legs. I galloped down the deserted streets, the fear I had forgotten until now chilling the sweat on my face. The others had lingered for me, and turned as I came up to them, so that we tore out of E-Basu together.

The following morning, snug in our camp, the entire adventure seemed dreadful but unreal, like a bad dream by daylight. The unwarlike Rria were quite ready to assume they had erred somehow in searching the town. When I heard them over their breakfast, debating how big a gift would suffice to demonstrate their regret, I hurried down barefoot and unbuttoned from our wagon to set them aright.

When I told of the flabby creature, though, everyone looked incredulous. "Do you mean the thing is visible only to one wearing the Crystal Crown?" Xalan asked. "That's quite a rare weakness. How convenient, that we have a Shan King on hand."

The Rria even drink atye at breakfast, and of course tea was now a mere memory. Grumpily, I sipped at a cup of hot water and said, "That's ridiculous. Anyone can learn to see the under-realm, it's beneath everything. Without the Crown it's just more dangerous, that's all."

"But we saw a woman," 'Vernflyer objected. "Undoubtedly." He accepted a platter of hot flat bread from the cook, and cast a nervous glance at Melayne. Propriety had forced us to edit the details of yesterday's encounter a little.

"That was only the bit on this side." I tried to share a little of the torrent of knowledge that had rushed over me. "The thing can work in both realms at once. It keeps most of itself safe over there, and only extends the necessary portions of its body here, to where we can see."

"I don't know what you're talking about," Baldspot said bluntly. "The fact is that we have to summer somewhere. We can't set out for Rriphirrizē again until after the hot season. We must placate this woman, or creature, if we mean to stay."

Xalan crammed a wedge of bread whole into his mouth, and swallowed it down with amazing speed.

"You could always come on farther, to Averidan," he offered. "I calculate it can't be more than a hundred-some leagues distant."

"Through mountains and barbaric nations," 'Vern-flyer said. "And then we'd have to wait while the Shan King here reconquers his country . . . thank you, but no!"

"Cayd is not a barbaric nation," Melayne retorted. "But I wouldn't vouch for the Tiyalor or the Basuans." She set Tarys onto her fat feet. The baby teetered dangerously, and overbalanced as she snatched for a piece of bread from Xalan's hand. Both he and Melayne, and all the Rria, applauded vigorously and pronounced her the cleverest baby in the world.

Doggedly, I tried to keep the discussion to the point. "You can't bribe this monster with presents, it would be folly—like trying to bribe a fire with dry straw. Bodkin and Kneediamond are already gone. More will die, I promise you, if we don't take the greatest care—"

"Did you say that Bodkin was dead?" Melayne interrupted. "Look!"

Up the overgrown road trotted a familiar form. The red bar-and-dot patterns around the broad shoulders bunched and shifted as he waved. "I'm back!" Bodkin called.

"Wait!" I commanded, and those who had risen to greet him sat unwillingly back.

Hwe began to whimper. 'Vernflyer shut his mouth, which had dropped open in surprise, with a snap. "We saw him die, saw her tear his head off!"

"Wait," I repeated, "and let me look." The Crystal Crown was still in its bag in the wagon; I had not ventured into the other realm in a long time, without its help and support. But a quick glance was all I needed. "That's not Bodkin. It's the lure. The creature is just behind, waiting."

Melayne scooped up Tarys and bundled her so quickly into Xalan's arms that he dropped his third wedge of bread. "Keep her safe," she ordered. "Lift if you have to, and leave us, but keep her safe."

The baby wriggled, crowing, to tug on his mustache. Xalan winced and glanced helplessly at me. "Perhaps Liras would rather I helped fight the monster?"

Absently I shook my head. Of course I had to battle this creature. But would the Crystal Crown be a help or a hindrance? Its assistance yesterday had not been encouraging. As I ducked into the wagon for my sword, though, I decided any help might prove welcome. A being that had depopulated E-Basu must be proof against mere swordsmanship.

Outside, though, one of the flyers was unable to restrain himself. "Bodkin, what happened?" I heard him call. "How did you escape?" Throwing down the sack, I set the Crown on my head and ran back out.

The others still sat where I had left them, watching fascinated as the foolish Rria hurried to grasp the false Bodkin's hands. I sprinted to catch up, cursing the Rria trustfulness and trying to concentrate on the real monster, beneath, rather than its representative. The creature had filled out some; like a partially-filled sausage skin, the limp white belly showed a faint outline of yesterday's meal. On either side of the round head two globular eyes, gleaming like gray egg yolks, kept watch as the Rria drew near. Before I could close with the thing, it struck. The six claws shot forward to spear the Rria through. With an easy practiced motion the creature flicked the dying man over its shoulder. In an eye-blink the arms were in front again, claws unburdened and ready to receive me.

At this inconvenient moment a knowledge again dropped into my consciousness, plain as a pebble among a dish of peas. "The feat cannot be done this way."

Sharply I retorted, "I do not welcome discouraging, nay-saying distractions! Make only helpful contributions!"

From habit I had said this aloud, and was considerably startled when the monster spoke in reply. Manipulating the false Bodkin's mouth it said, "Deathless am I, hero."

It used Rria, rather than whatever language the

Basuans spoke, so I answered in that tongue, "There's a first time for everything." Then I aimed a slash at one bulging eye.

To my horror the eye shot straight out at me, balanced on a long retracting stalk like a snail's. Instinctively recoiling from the touch of the shining organ, I was knocked sprawling by the Bodkin-lure, flung on the end of its ligament by a jerk of the monster's head.

I twisted from under the daggerlike claws just in time, astonished. The virtue of the other realm, at least for a Shan hero, is its role as a thumb on the scales in a crisis. But the gusty and romantic chances I had relied on were not sliding toward me. When I rolled to my feet, my boots slipped on the trail of shining ooze the monster had laid down as it passed. Beyond the lightning swipe of the claws I glimpsed an ancient malice in the oysterlike eyes as they swayed on their stalks. Older than I, and at home in that realm, the creature was already tipping the scales—toward itself.

The thing was uphill now, between me and the camp. I hoped my companions had had the sense to flee. I staggered to my feet again and silently marshaled the powers of the Crown, to wrench the flow of luck away. Running forward, I pretended to slip again. Three claws instantly slashed down, but my sword was held ready above me. The keen slicing-edge met hardly any resistance as it shored through the bandy arm.

The monster screamed, a dreadful whistling inhuman sound. The wounded stump, from which a thick whitish fluid slowly dripped, retreated into the folds of the body. Even the eyes shrank suddenly back, as if realizing their peril. Only the lure, the false Bodkin, covered the creature's rather ponderous retreat up the road. The jerking, flailing form battered aimlessly at me while the still-smiling lips screamed shrill nonsense syllables. When I realized the monster's sluggish pace was the speediest in its power, I made a looping run to the right, to reach the wagons first.

But my involvement on the physical level had lessened my concentration elsewhere. All of a sudden the
oxen, who had been grazing in the field beside the
road, raised their heads. Frisking and bellowing in a
sudden surge of high spirits, they lumbered across the
road toward the pond. Unable to either turn the stam-
pede or pass through it, I was forced to race around
the herd.

My detour gave the monster just enough time to
ripple its pale body up to the nearest wagon—our own,
as it happened. To my surprise it oozed right up the
three steps, up over the door, and on to the roof
before pausing. Draped over the gaudy wagon, like a
huge limp slab of squid laid out to dry in the Sun,
surely could not be a good offensive position. I racked
my brains to think whether any of our goods in the
wagon were irreplaceable. My best move might be to
seize a brand from the nearby campfire and torch the
vehicle—incinerate the creature on the spot.

Then my heart seemed to stop beating. Something
was moving inside the wagon, rattling at the door and
then flinging open the single window. Framed within
its narrow compass I could just glimpse Melayne's
annoyed face. "Did you kill it, Liras?" she called.
"The door is stuck—"

She broke off with a shriek. A large quivery eye
extended on its stalk had nearly hit her on the forehead. "Climb out the window, Melayne, quick!" I
shouted, almost dancing in my anxiety. But before she
could even begin to squeeze through, a triple-clawed
foot reached down and seized the shutter, plucking it
casually off its hinges. "No, Melayne! Go back, stay
inside! Keep away from those claws!"

The battered lure hung gruesomely in midair, like
something on a fishhook. It bobbed up and down as the
monster used its lips to say, "This one within is precious to you." I could not speak, but in any case there
was no denying it. The monster seemed to sag with
satisfaction, spreading the limp pale folds of its body
over as much of the wagon as possible. "I hunger," it

continued, gloatingly. "Go. Tomorrow by sunset bring me one of your men, and I may not eat this one."

"You will release her then?"

"Probably not," was the only, chilling, reply. When I made no move to depart, the claws picked threateningly at the window frame.

Crushed, I retreated farther up the road. My head was whirling. Even trading another life for hers would not save Melayne. Should I be so pliant as to bring a replacement meal tomorrow evening, the creature had as good as promised to repeat the entire performance, demand yet another victim the day after. No doubt, after consuming everybody foolish enough to volunteer, it would eat Melayne anyway.

In a sudden reversion to the old impotent rage I snatched the Crown off my head. "How dare you let this sort of thing happen?" Of course I could receive no reply. Nor did I get the chance to put the Crown back on and thrash the matter out with the perfidious god. Around the bend of the road, in the shadow of an outhouse, waited the rest of our party. Fresh anger swept through me at the sight of the Rria's tremulous faces, and Xalan's pale look of condolence. "How did you come to let her go back?" I roared.

The Rria murmured and shuffled in sympathy, and Xalan held Tarys before him like a shield. "Melayne insisted the baby had to have some diapers," he explained unhappily. "We couldn't stop her, and she promised to be quick."

'Vernflyer gave my shoulder a tentative pat. "The Lady was a stubborn woman, my friend. But you must not lose heart, your daughter has only you now—"

Their words suddenly sank in, and I jerked away. "She's not dead yet!"

"She's not?"

I took hold of myself. The whining baby leaned across Xalan's arm toward me, holding out her hands. Sitting down I put her in my lap and breathing deeply said, "Let me explain."

When I had done so there was a silence, broken

only by Tarys' whimpers of hunger. "Then what are we going to do?" Baldspot said at last.

"We must kill the thing." I glanced around. 'Vernflyer seemed dazed, while the other Rria looked openly at me. "Do you wish me to direct the enterprise?"

Everyone nodded except 'Vernflyer, who said in a hollow tone, "I never should have left Rriphirrizē. Other lands are a midden compared to it. Yes, I suppose you are the only one able to manage our plight now, Shan King. What must we do?"

Tarys had sucked in vain at each of her own fingers and toes in turn, and was now fretfully grinding her first tiny tooth into my knee. Thoughtfully I said, "We must first feed the baby." There was of course no milk to be had for leagues; even our draft animals included no cows. The Rria's loincloths and little jackets had no pockets, but Xalan and I turned out our own. 'Vernflyer explored the pouches of his flying suit and produced the only edible item among fifteen men, an aborigine, and a baby—a rind of old bread.

When Tarys grudgingly consented to gnaw on this, I apportioned the other priorities. I sent most of the Rria to the shore to find food. "It's probably late for eggs, but you could fish, or snare birds, or gather freshwater mussels." Burdened with the baby and Hwe, Xalan would accompany this party, as the only person familiar with northern wildlife. 'Vernflyer and several others began walking back to the wyverns' pasture. Two Rria under the direction of Baldspot would conceal themselves to keep watch on the creature—a safe enough undertaking, I was careful to point out, since the monster had to guard Melayne, and it was readily visible now it was not hunting. We would meet again by sundown at that first deserted farmhouse, on the edge of town.

Xalan tried to slide his wand out of its back sling while balancing Tarys, and had to give over. "What are you going to do, while we're all drudging away?" he demanded, harassed.

My smile was somewhat bitter. "I'm going to find a quiet nook somewhere, and lie down."

Xalan opened his mouth to comment, looked at the Crown under my arm, and closed it again. I took the baby and hugged her while Xalan arranged himself; the tiny solid body held a wonderful sweet warmth. "She smells so good," I said softly.

Xalan snorted. "Not for long. The Lady has more sense than any of us. All her diapers are in that wagon."

CHAPTER 14

A Deferred Submission

When everyone had gone, I set off due west across the fields, away from the lake and the camp. The land was treeless, but where men settle they plant them, and a few pastures away were three small apple trees. No Basuan had survived, to pick the fruit. The few apples that still clung to the boughs had been stunted and wormy at best, for want of culling and pruning. I kicked the rotted windfalls away and sat with my back against the trunk before putting the Crown on.

It was nearly noon; freckles of sunshine the color of gold coins flicked and danced across my outstretched legs, clad in faded green cloth striped with reinforcing slats. Sahai ambled up from her morning constitutional, yawned, and insinuated her lean body into a thicket of grass nearby. In the dappled light her spotted hide could scarcely be seen. Deliberately, joint by joint, I relaxed, letting the anxiety and terror and anger of the morning drift from my open hands, using what I had learned in the months since my climb up Iphalar. Only then did I say, "This is a point I will not accept argument upon: Melayne must be rescued."

The reflecting sunshine made Sahai's slit-eyes look like discs of heated copper. From them the god said, "I will do so. Will you for your part fulfill your promise?"

"What promise?" I said, a little alarmed.

"Have I not brought you to E-Basu?"

"Oh, that one!" A sense of justice, or perhaps only

the manners my mother had whacked into me, forced
me to say, "Every time we needed help you lent it.
You have never failed me. I take back all those accu-
sations. They weren't fair." Then, as my mind flew
back to the current predicament, I said, "Is that thing,
that pale monster, root to all our troubles?"

"Yes. Ixfel arose shortly before your accession and
began to devastate E-Basu."

"Ixfel! I thought Ixfel was no more than a plaiv—"
But who should know better than I, that things one
hears of only in tales sometime take on reality? A
being who could eat three people a day must have
terrorized E-Basu. When Ixfel proved impossible to
kill, only one alternative remained for the Basuans: to
move. On the other side of the sea populous Tiyalor, I
knew, had suffered political turmoil for some time.
They, in turn, must have retorted upon Cayd, yet
farther east. And now I remembered that the Cayds
had invaded us because the Tiyalor had overrun them.
"It's going to be a lot of work, to undo all this," I
could not help remarking.

"Some evils cannot wholly be mended," the god
answered; the truth of this sank into my chest like an
arrow-shot. "Ixfel cannot be humbled by mortal
strength."

Dismayed, I sat up so sharply that Sahai blinked.
"But Melayne—how then can she be saved?"

The divine presence shifted effortlessly to a glittering pinpoint of mica between my heels. "My power
will help you do it."

I thought this over. "A greater power than you have
put into the Crown?"

"Yes. You must give yourself over to me completely, that I may act through you."

A final twinge of doubt assailed me: that this was
what the god had been working toward for years,
manipulating men and events—to get me. But there is
never total proof of anyone's benevolence, god or
man; at some point one must trust. Without thinking I
said, "What is your name, god of Averidan? Is it a
secret, or may I know it?"

The tireless wind tousled the boughs above me, setting the thousand circles of light to dancing. "My name is *Thausra*. Remember it, and when you come to the City again, tell it to the rhetors and chroniclers and priestesses, that the Shan my children may know it also."

All of a sudden my heart was absurdly light, the blood bubbling merrily in my veins. In the teeth of so many pressing things to fret about, I cast off worry. I leaned back against the friendly tree and said, "Do, *Thausra*, as you will."

I almost expected some stunning, unimaginable rush of nameless energy, such as the one that overwhelmed me when I first put on the Crown. But all I felt now was warmth, a pleasant coziness that enfolded me from head to toe like a quilt on a cold night. And like the quilt, I knew I could throw it off at any time. But I did not, for I allowed it to take me. My eyes, which had been idly wandering skyward, fixed on the shriveled brown knobs of fruit in the branches above. With interest but no understanding I listened to words of authority rolling off my tongue.

Then my skin was prickling with chill. The power had come and gone, leaving me empty. "What happened?" I almost wailed.

"This was a small test of power," *Thausra* replied. "Assail Ixfel at the wagons tonight, and I will move through you to ensure the victory."

With that the audience was over. Rising to my feet I paused, astonished. What had happened to the miserable little apples? Between the leaves clustered perfect specimens of the orcharder's skill—apples red-yellow and perfect, the size of two fists clenched together. I reached up and plucked one. The magi can cast a glamor to alter appearance. But when I bit into the apple, it was sound and sweet, dead-ripe and better than any the Palace garden could offer. Nibbling, I moved around the tree. Only a dozen apples had been changed; the rest of the boughs bore ordinary fruit, decayed or dried, nibbled by insects or pecked by birds.

I picked all the preternaturally perfect apples and stowed them in my capacious jacket pockets. By then the afternoon was nearly spent. Years ago in my first and only conversation with the magus Xerlanthor, he had told me the Crown's power was over living things. As I walked to our meeting place, I reflected he must have been a genius after all.

It was not far to the appointed house, where 'Vernflyer had already seen to clearing the hearth and kindling a fire. I set the apples on the mantlepiece as my contribution to supper, and went out to help with the wyverns.

The other groups straggled up together, noisy in their triumph and relief. Xalan handed Tarys to me with a weary sigh. "She's hungry," he announced. "Do you think she would eat fish?"

"No." I surveyed their meager catch strung on a reed. "I suppose the really big fish swim farther out. What a pity you only got six."

"Try fishing sometime, without hooks, lines, or nets." Xalan laid himself flat on the dusty floor and covered his face with his hat. "My left arm has stretched three inches longer than the right, from the weight of that infant. Thank Viris I will never be a parent!"

Tarys squirmed wetly in my arms, quite smelly and sodden, not pleasant to hold. I untied her diaper and let her toddle about in nothing but a shirt—"There are no carpets for her to puddle on." Then I peeled an apple and let her gnaw it.

By then the fish were roasted. Eating them without plates, implements or handkerchiefs was a grubby business. This first course was followed by apples, which the Rria had never eaten before. Only Xalan was knowledgeable enough to raise an eyebrow at their perfection, but he was too hungry to ask questions.

Supper had been so scanty that I received only gloomy nods of agreement when I proposed, "We'll go defeat that creature as soon as it's fully dark."

"And then let's have another meal," Xalan added eagerly.

I passed over this and asked, "What has Ixfel been doing?" Receiving only blank stares I hastily explained, "The name of the monster is Ixfel."

It was wonderful how this announcement cheered the Rria. "Well, if you can *name* it—" "It'll be snugger sleeping in our own bunks, this floor has drafts." "I've a net in my wagon, we'll go back tomorrow and fish properly."

Baldspot, who had been trying to make himself heard, waved the others to silence. "Before you get too giddy, hear our news. That creature is eating our oxen." Imperiously he bore down on the others' dismayed exclamations. "It's using that lure on the end of its nose to call up the cattle by twos and threes."

"And *eating* them? How many?"

"About six so far." It was incredible; even tigers take a day or so to devour a carcass. "If we don't stop this quickly, we'll lose them all. And then we'll be trapped here, never to return to Rriphirrizē."

"Nonsense, there are other oxen in the world," Xalan said comfortingly. "It wouldn't delay you more than a year or so."

But this supreme threat filled the Rria with an anxiety scarcely understandable to outlanders. 'Vernflyer actually wrung his calloused hands. "Look, the twilight is fading," he noted in a quivering voice. "Quickly, tell us your plan, Shan King."

The strategy I had developed was simple, leaving plenty of room for *Thausra* to act. Ixfel had never seen wyverns before. One could be sure of this, since the last Rria visitors had found E-Basu thriving and well-populated. Their speed and numbers would match well against Ixfel's sluggish progress and short reach. Though the wyverns would not instinctively fight, as they did against the shrikes, those mighty legs and powerful talons could still be deadly—and Ixfel had no hide or armor for protection.

Guided by 'Vernflyer on the big patriarch, the flock would inflict as much damage as possible. If Ixfel could be slain, all to the good—otherwise they could gradually chivvy the monster away from the wagon. Xalan and I, as the only armed members of the party, would release Melayne. The other Rria would unblock the wheels of one of the heaviest-laden wagons. A sluglike creature like Ixfel, with no bones or carapace, could be cut into several chunks by speeding wagon-wheels.

I explained all this carefully to the Rria. They were unenthusiastic, Baldspot protesting the risk to the wagons while 'Vernflyer grumbled that his pets were too fastidious to soil their nails on a slug. Another flyer said, "But what about your precious baby here? I volunteer to stay and watch her."

Everyone looked put out, that they had not thought of it first. The flyer lifted Tarys to his knee and chucked her chin. The baby gave him a winsome grin, and urinated on his leg. After this I got less dissent, though Xalan did make a final effort: "What do gardeners do about slugs? Is there an idea there?"

"We salt them, or hack at them with trowels," I said. "For Ixfel it would take about a wagon-load of salt."

"Which we haven't got," Xalan conceded sadly.

The stars gave just enough light for us to see the road, a pale streak curving gently down the hill. On its dusty surface our feet made no sound. 'Vernflyer would not bring the wyverns round until we had time to get into position, so the night's little noises briefly reigned alone—chirping crickets, the flick and buzz of midges in the reeds down near the lake, the sough of wind through leaf and stem. With infinite care we tiptoed down to the first wagon in the row, and peered between its wheels.

An eerie scene spread before us. Glittering trails of slime crossed and recrossed the open area between the two rows of wagons. It puzzled me, that Ixfel had dared to leave Melayne unguarded, until I craned my neck to glimpse our wagon. It was sealed more soundly than a corked brandy-bottle, by thick slime. The wagon was buried in a layer of gleaming jelly perhaps six inches deep, spread like a horrid blanket over the entire vehicle. I prayed that Melayne had not suffocated beneath it.

Then, from beyond her prison, Ixfel rippled into view, and we had to smother our gasps. The loose white folds were gone. Sleek and fat, Ixfel's body was nearly as high as the wagon-seat in the middle, though it tapered at each end to a less daunting girth. We cringed as the pallid head with its two eyestalks reared up to survey the camp. The wound I had inflicted this morning was already healing. From the stump of the arm, smaller than ever now in comparison to Ixfel's regained bulk, grew a new undersized set of triple claws.

Ixfel swung its lure forward into position. Not surprisingly, it now resembled an ox. The simulacrum shook its ears engagingly, and mooed in a most pathetic and lonely tone. The cattle were grazing on the slope between the road and the marshy lake shore. Some had already raised their broad heads to gaze at this puzzling new ox.

Then a new sound began to swell among the small night noises: the flap and rattle of straining wings, hoarse panting, and irregular thumps of landing wyverns. As the flock swept up, the flyers, as I had instructed, yelled insults and nonsense, to confuse our foe. Unwilling to be outdone, the wyverns themselves also shrieked, until the lake-valley rang with discordant echo. 'Vernflyer expertly controlled his mount's slide so that the huge beast landed square on Ixfel's spotted back. The wyverns' racket was momentarily drowned out by Ixfel's piercing whistle of pain. "Now's our time," I whispered, giving Baldspot a nudge.

As the Rria nervously crept off toward the chosen wagon I drew my sword. Xalan and I ran behind the line of wagons to the end. Our wagon looked as if it were englobed in molten glass. "Well, what are you waiting for? Lift up there and start clearing the roof trap. I'll hold off Ixfel."

Xalan poked at the jellylike mess with the tip of his

wand. "I'm just trying to decide which would be worse—to stand barefoot in the glop, or to lose a shoe in it."

I could have swatted him. He must have seen this in my face, though; without further talk he bounded lightly to the wagon roof and set about scraping the slime away. I stood near the wagon's side and watched the pale mass of the monster writhing and lashing out. The wyverns were circling and leaping overhead, just out of Ixfel's reach. We had chosen the roof-door rather than the main one, because it was less noticeable. But it would not take the monster long to realize what was going on.

"This isn't going to be quick," Xalan panted. "The stuff oozes—look!" He dragged up a double handful. The slime clung to itself, the consistency of fresh egg white.

"Scrape it down toward the edge of the roof," I said, watching the monster. I froze as one swiveling eyestalk pointed my way. Directing everyone's role in the battle, guarding against Ixfel's attack, and waiting for *Thausra* to make his move—all of this raveled the nerves. When something tapped me on the shoulder, I almost bit my tongue. Then I turned to look. "Melayne!"

"Keep your voice down!" She threw herself into my arms. "Where is Tarys, how is she?"

"Very hungry, and missing you." I tucked her head under my chin, weak with relief. "However did you get out?"

"Oh, that dreadful thing sealed the door and window. So I used the poker to pry up a floorboard."

There was no time to compliment her ability and acumen. I leaned closer to the wagon and hissed, "Xalan!"

In the darkness I could see the gleam of his smile. "You've got her! Viris be thanked—" The smile vanished like a snuffed candle, and he cried, "Quick! Your hand!"

We whirled. The tiny head of Ixfel loomed above us, both eyes glaring balefully from their stalks, the arms outstretched to grasp and rend. I hugged Melayne hard to my chest with my right arm, and held up my left. Xalan seized it and lifted. With dreadful slowness we rose up into the night sky. Melayne and I stared past our toes at Ixfel's reaching arms not three feet below. "Higher!" I shouted. "Can't you go higher?"

"No, I can't," Xalan panted. "The two of you are beyond my strength." Instead he drifted very slowly over the open space between the two rows of wagons. Ixfel twisted to follow, slinging the false ox around on the end of its ligament. The wyverns whirled past, screaming and driving the air in great gusts around us. When the lure flicked past our dangling legs, Melayne moaned with fear. I still held my sword in my right fist, but could not use it without dropping her.

"Stay aloft just a moment more," I begged Xalan, and then shifting to Rriat shouted, "Now! and get a good running start!"

The wagon at the top of the hill began to move. As it trundled backward faster and faster down the road, I could see the dim forms of the Rria and Hwe behind it, pushing for dear life on the box and tongue. They gave over too soon, of course, letting the wagon continue downhill on its own momentum alone. Ixfel tried to ooze out of the way, but too late. With a tremendous crash the wagon hit the monster broadside on.

In a flutter of red sleeves Xalan dropped suddenly to earth, gasping. Melayne and I fell sprawling in the trampled, slime-matted grass. To my disappointment, Ixfel had grown too fat to be run over. The wagon ground to a halt with one wheel pinning Ixfel's tail only, near the narrow tip.

Still, the opportunity was not to be missed. I staggered to my feet and ran to attack. However, Ixfel must have been stunned by the impact. Instead of facing me, it began to climb up the side of the wagon, thinking perhaps that it was Melayne's prison.

Then, with the suddenness of a descending wave, *Thausra* swept me aside and took over. As the warmth enfolded me I heard myself call, "Everyone! Push!"

Scared but sensing a crisis, my friends obeyed, lifting the wagon-tongue and heaving the wagon forward again. The wheel jounced over Ixfel's tail, and then the vehicle, still with Ixfel draped over it, began to roll freely down the road. The power rose in me like a consuming fever, passing through my flesh like the flow of lava on Iphalar mountain. And the pale length of Ixfel glowed paler and brighter yet. All of a sudden the monster was burning, blue flames leaping up as if the very flesh of the slug-body had been doused in oil. In an instant the wooden wagon-body caught too. After the mild starlight, the fiery glare made us blink. The entire mass of flame was still rolling, down the hill toward E-Basu.

For a moment no one had a comment to make. At last Xalan said, in a hushed tone, "Not even the pirolurges do that."

Cold and a little sick with reaction I made no answer. 'Vernflyer was already bounding on his wyvern down to the lake shore, to see what would happen. When we made to follow, Melayne announced, "I must go to the baby. You can manage from here, dearest?" I nodded and leaned to accept her kiss. Hwe was deputed to go back with her. We made our way down the road. It curved enough so that the wagon could never reach the town proper. Instead it rammed a cluster of outbuildings and store-sheds at the first bend of the road. After the long autumn and winter they were dry as tinder, and ignited in a blossom of yellow fire. Choking in his mount 'Vernflyer yelled, "Should we try to douse it?"

With an effort I brought myself back to the mundane. "Not worth the trouble," I called. In the midst of the conflagration Ixfel could be seen—unmoving, but a good pyre would make its end sure. No other buildings abutted the fire, and the area was surrounded on two sides by marsh. Besides, through the Crown came the certainty that all was finished. Suddenly I was swaying with exhaustion, nearly asleep on my feet. The day, so full of incident, must have lasted a year. "Let's go home and go to bed," I said.

The others had to help me back up the hill. I lay down on the grass between two wagons and fell asleep instantly, confident that no one would touch the Crown beside me. Later I learned that while the cook prepared a late supper, Melayne returned with the baby, and forced the rest of the company to clean off our wagon so that she could get the baby a diaper. Scraping the ooze off with sticks completely spoiled everyone's appetite except Xalan's.

The spring season was not quite over, it being merely early Ynnep by Xalan's reckoning. There was plenty of time to make the last leg of our journey, around the Tiyalene Sea and down the pass to Averidan, before Mid Summer Day. The Shan year begins then, and it would be the fifth anniversary of my accession. In the interest of stories to come, I felt that I ought to settle everything by then. And the Rria pleaded with us to stay a while. They had counted on passing the summer as guests in a populous town, and leaving before winter well provisioned with a load of Basuan goods. Nor could we well leave, since there were no oxen to spare, and no market to buy more in. So I agreed, adding, "Don't throw away your trade goods yet. Ixfel can't have eaten everybody. When we're settled here, we'll search the area about."

The idea of camping, however briefly, in the echoing town, with the lonely lap and murmur of wavelets and the mournful wind carrying a phantom presence of the recent residents, was a disquieting one. Nor could the livestock live on the lake. By unanimous consent we settled into a humbler house outside town: "Sod and thatch roofs aren't as grand, but oh! so much more comfortable," Baldspot confided. "And warm!"

We explored the town systematically. The fleeing Basuans had abandoned much that would prove useful over the coming hot season. Meanwhile the spring breeze was still sharp enough so that the Rria gratefully donned woolen leggings, thick tunics, heavy cloaks, and winter boots, only slightly moth-eaten. Having defeated Ixfel, we felt we had earned anything we could salvage from the town. With their vivid tattooing covered in clothes I almost had to relearn my friends' faces. "You'll *stew*," Melayne told them. She herself, with her northern blood, regarded the climate as ideal for human habitation.

'Vernflyer searched, with increasing discouragement, for the trade goods they had hoped to carry back to Rriphirrizē. "It says right here, that the Basuans had it all waiting together in a warehouse," he said, brandishing a journal.

"Perhaps they were too busy battling Ixfel to dig roots or amass hides," Xalan offered.

I was more anxious to find food, both for now and for traveling later. Nothing perishable in the way of provisions was left, but in a storehouse we discovered stone bins of grain. "Oats," Xalan said in disgust. "At least the last time we starved, we did it on barley gruel." All these western realms raise oats, so Melayne undertook to prepare us some. Xalan and I ate with some trepidation, for we had had trouble before with spoilt grain. The thick porridge was edible—sufficient to sustain life, though one could say little more in its favor.

To supplement it I set the Rria to hunting and fishing, this last with the help of a leaky punt we found in the reeds. We smoked or dried all we did not eat or feed to the animals—the wyverns spurned the red meat we gave to Sahai, but enjoyed gulping small fish down whole.

When all this activity was well established, 'Vernflyer and I went to Tiyalor. The wyverns made short work of the trip, and in this good weather we need carry only our own food. Early the third day out we sighted Seaside, the country's only town. As its name indicated, the capital of Tiyalor was built on the shore, just where the mountains enclosed the sea. To the northeast the peaks seemed to crowd down to the very edge of the blue water, bending near to admire the

last snow of the season on their heads. The gap where
the river ran through to Cayd was invisible. A cool
tang of pines and spring air blew up across the unruf-
fled sea.

Seaside itself was a sad contrast to its lovely setting.
The royal line had been wiped out some years ago,
during Tiyalor's wars against Cayd and Averidan, so
no strong government had kept up the town. And in
their conquest the Basuans had apparently used fire.
The melancholy settlement remaining was made up of
rickety wooden buildings, and narrow muddy streets
stinking of sewage. Burned scars showed on the sagging sod roofs. In every open space in town, and in a
wide ragged fringe around it, were tents and lean-tos
and miserable shelters woven of reeds.

Confronted with the prospect of settling here, the
leader of the Basuans should jump at the chance to
return to E-Basu. Or so I thought. Like all the western folk, the Basuans esteem physical courage; when
Ixfel arose, nearly all the lords and nobles had gone
out one by one, in order of precedence, to give it
battle. Even I could hardly conceive of a worse battle
plan, considering the foe.

The current lord of Seaside was the first Basuan
leader too sensible to go be eaten. In E-Basu this was
accounted cowardice, and meant that his sovereignty
was unsteady indeed. The skinny barefoot children
directed us to a large burnt-over area. Crews of laborers were dragging rubble aside and sorting over the
debris for usable stone, metal or timber. The Lord was
busy directing operations, and greeted our news with
distracted disbelief. "Slew the demon, did you?" he
snapped. "Over there with that beam, it's roof-length.
The thing probably threw you back, as too small to
eat."

Like most barbaric nobles the Lord was very tall,
though because he was thin and balding as well, he
resembled a worried vulture. But I was used to jibes
of that sort. The brief exchange gave me the chance to
read him thoroughly, for I wore the Crown under my

hood. Having been driven into inglorious retreat, and venting their shame on the Tiyalor, the Lord could never lead his people back. The mere announcement— that a troupe of wandering travelers had done what Basuan warriors could not, that the costly invasion of Tiyalor was for naught, that everyone could pack up and go home again—would spell his political destruction.

Still, I could not let it rest there. If the Basuans stayed in Seaside, the Tiyalor would retain Cayd—and Averidan should never be rid of her conquerors. So I said, "Do you love this sty then, that you cleave to it in preference to the roofs of your fathers? In E-Basu now there is nothing to fear."

This last word, particularly, was imprudent. I had meant to be bracing; a Rria would have smiled, and a Shan obliquely returned the insult. The Lord of the Basuans merely drew a knife. "We fear nothing," he said evenly. Now, will you leave with your gizzard or without it?"

For convenience in flying, my sword was strapped to my back. As I reached for it, though, 'Vernflyer plucked at my arm. "It's hopeless," he said in Rriat. "We're here to trade goods, not wounds!" So I gave way.

Livestock were so scarce in Seaside there was no marketplace for them. By questioning the children we found the one Basuan with oxen to sell. 'Vernflyer had to promise nearly the entire shipment of Rria trade goods in exchange for a dozen skinny beasts. He ground his teeth audibly at the hard bargain. "We shall go back with nothing, just empty wagons."

"At the least, you'll get back," I pointed out. "They're costly, because the Basuans may have to eat them."

Donkeys, not being reckoned edible, were somewhat cheaper. I paid for six with the last of Zaryas' pearls and gold. We made arrangements to return for the beasts, and went home calling ourselves fortunate.

There was time now to spend with my family. I taught Tarys all the Viridese children's rhymes I could remember, and spoke to her in that tongue so that her

ear would grow accustomed to it—Melayne sang only
Caydish lullabies. She was more than a year old now,
beginning to really talk, and for a while I worried that
her polygot life would make her completely dumb.
But Tarys sorted out the language perfectly, babbling
a Viridese word or two to me, calling for her mother
in Caydish, addressing the Rria in their tongue, and
grunting at Hwe. "Now, if only I could remember that
one Uwunan swear word I picked up," Xalan said,
"she could have a toehold in no less than five languages!"

Though the others inquired several times, I made no
plans about reconquering Averidan. "You always complained I was a worrier," I said to Melayne when she
took me to task about it one evening.

The baby had almost doubled in height, and long
since outgrown all her Viridese clothes. Melayne was
sewing her a little coat out of an old Basuan cloak.
"It's not that deity my brother Mor has vowed to kill,"
she retorted. She tightened her stitches with short
vehement motions. "I'd feel better if you were guarded
by a god with more practical common sense. You have
no soldiers, hardly a copper-piece in money, and exactly one sword. What are you going to do—walk up
to the Palace and ask Mor to move over?"

I lay on my back on the rough board floor. Tarys
perched on my chest, bouncing and yelling as she
played at wyverns. "I may well do just that," I said
equably. "With the Crown I have every right to do so.
Thausra will supply the power. We're all in the plaiv
now, wife. We had better resign ourselves to some
lurid happenings."

It seemed only prudent, though, to keep my title
and Crown secret until we actually crossed into
Averidan. The Shan King was no more than distant
legend in E-Basu. But the Tiyalor might not have
forgotten the Viridese role in past wars, and any Cayds
we met would doubtless try to kill me immediately.

After a few weeks, when the Rria had become as
comfortable as any Rria might ever be expected to feel
away from home, we started preparing for our final

journey. I chose a route south around the sea, rather than back to the north and on into Tiyalor. Considering the Lord of Seaside's chancy temper, I did not care to take my family into his reach. Also, Melayne knew the roads of eastern Cayd.

After all we had endured together it was hard to bid the Rria farewell. They planned to linger in E-Basu three months, until the autumn equinox. Having made them my responsibility, I worried. "Are you sure you wouldn't rather summer in Averidan?" I asked 'Vern-flyer anxiously. "It's a pleasant place, well worth seeing. Shall you truly reach Rriphirrizē safely?"

"We'll certainly be hungry," he predicted dispiritedly. "I wish you could stay with us. We'll need your luck."

"I can't, but I'll mention your plight to *Thausra*, or Iphalar as your folk say."

More practically, Xalan suggested, "Eat your oxen slowly as you go. You won't need them to make any more return trips, and the wagons are nearly empty anyway." Then he blinked. "What an un-Viridese bit of advice, slaughtering draft-oxen is one of the things we despise the Cayds for."

Impelled by mild guilt, I helped Baldspot lay out a schedule to cull the beasts efficiently, and listed hints on butchery and cooking. I also divided the hoarded stores with such a generous hand that Melayne protested. "I know it's only a week or so to Cayd," she wailed, "but we'll have to eat more than once on the way!"

"That's right, think of the baby," Xalan urged. He hefted the single sack of oats I had set out to bring, and grimaced. "The donkeys alone can eat this in a week. Suppose there's nobody left in Cayd to beg from?"

I grinned at him. "You simply don't want to risk missing a meal. I tell you that if it comes to it, the fish will leap out of the sea into our pockets, just like in the plaiv."

"Can't the tale then be one of glorious feasts served up by comely maidens?" he grumbled.

At the last we were all in tears, Xalan wiping his nose on his sleeve, 'Vernflyer embracing me till my ribs hurt, the baby clinging wailing to their dark hands as the Rria followed along beside our prodding donkeys. They halted on a ridge, waving, and from the valley we turned to wave back. Not until then did I notice that Hwe had not fallen back with them. His brown hairy skin shaggier than ever, Hwe strode along at the bridle of the last donkey as if that were his assigned place.

Confused, I drew my beast to a halt. The donkeys following behind stopped too, and began resignedly to tear up mouthfuls of summer grass. "What, did you forget something?" Melayne asked, and then, noticing Hwe, cried, "Oh, no—not another pet to feed! Sahai at least hunts game!"

Letting the lead rope drop I went back. "I had meant to send you back to Rriphirrizē, Hwe. From there Sandcomber can return you to your homeland."

Hwe looked at me mournfully from under his shaggy brow. "Iffle-air," he said in his thick Rriat. Wearing the Crown I immediately understood. We were kin; in his own way Hwe also followed the One, lured by desires almost beyond his understanding to far realms and strange altars. I trudged back to my donkey and dragged at the rope bridle again.

"The Rria will search for him," Melayne objected.

Xalan warned, "We'll run out of food."

"*Thausra* wishes it," I said, quashing all argument.

CHAPTER 15

A Retraced Road

The weather was almost perfect for traveling. The north wind felt merely refreshing and brisk, and the ground was dry except in the very deepest draws and dells. Under the cloud-tumbled, wind-roaring sky we made our slow way south around the sea. Several days northeast along the farther shore, and we sighted a different country. The rolling grasslands still extended as far as we could see. But the horizon, north and east, was now prickled with spears of deeper green. "Can you scent their air?" Melayne cried. "Once among the pines, and we're in Cayd!"

We watched for signs of humanity, but western Cayd has never supported a big population. Sparse and scrubby at first, the pines quickly thronged close around us. The perpetually soughing wind sounded quite different through their needles, and deprived of the Sun's guidance we lost our line of travel several times. The main road, when we came to it, was not encouraging— merely a trail thrugh the forest, paved with pine mast and slippery moss. Eagerly Melayne turned her mount east, whacking the donkey until it broke into a brief, reluctant trot. "Surely tomorrow we'll arrive in Lanach. Do you suppose any of my brothers still reigns there?"

"I should be very surprised," I called to her, but I doubted she heard. Though I had explained to her in detail the upheavals in Cayd, Melayne could not really visualize any change there.

We ate the very last of our grain that night, dividing

it between the donkeys and ourselves. Confused perhaps by the forest, Sahai had for the first time failed to bring us some game. Xalan shook the final bits of chaff from the bag and growled, "Here we are, the Shan King, a princess of Cayd, and the Master Magus of Averidan, partnering our supper with the beasts of burden. Thank Viris, there are no witnesses to our humiliation except Hwe."

The next day I noticed something familiar in the landscape. The ground was steep and rough, with an occasional small mountain meadow wedged in among the stands of pine. To the north beyond the tall straight trunks the pallid spring sunshine dropped into emptiness—a gorge or deep valley. "Melayne," I called. "Where are we?"

She looked about, frowning. "It can't be far to—"

"Ieor!" Xalan whooped, delighted to arrive in familiar parts at last. "Perhaps there's still a settlement near the dam!"

The chance of this, though not very great, could not be passed by. Leaving the road we pushed through the trees to the lip of the gorge. The ground fell steep and rocky to the green rushing river below. Xalan and I got our bearings immediately. "Two more bends downstream," I told Melayne, "and you can view the site of my very first battle."

She sniffed. "I just hope that Xerlanthor is really dead. Suppose he's still lurking about?"

"I would know," I said, with slightly less confidence; it was a daunting thought, and the forest instantly looked more ominous and brooding. "I wish you wouldn't have such ideas."

But nothing leaped out of the undergrowth as we picked our way downriver. Women are not warriors in Cayd, so this was Melayne's first sight of the dam which had, among other things, prompted our union. She stared at the massive stonework, a young mountain now tumbled and broken, so that the river rushed boiling and foaming through. Then she looked at me with new respect. "And you destroyed this yourself!"

"We magi did the real work, with earthquakes," Xalan put in. "And look—is that a goat? I can smell those cutlets now!"

The object of Xalan's interest was evidently a half-wild stray from the flocks that once were pastured here. Though Melayne wheedled it in Caydish, we could not approach the goat at all. It danced away down the meadow in a very maddening way just out of reach, forcing us to run through the slippery sparse grass. In the end Melayne had to bring the beast down with an arrow, as if it had been a deer. We laid the head downhill to let the carcass drain, and sat on some rocks to catch our breath. "Look how we've progressed," I congratulated Xalan. "The last time we were here, if I had told you to cut a goat's throat, you would have turned green."

"If you like to call this progress." Xalan rubbed at the grime and drying blood on his hands. "Me, I wouldn't object to a wash."

So we rose and began to pick our way down the rubble-strewn slope to the river. Just below was a mound of rotting and burned wreckage: all that remained of the dam's guard-tower. Hwe squatted among the ruins, scratching busily at the mud. When he saw me he called and waved.

"What have you found?" I stepped carefully along the slick half-charred logs. On the broad leathery palm Hwe held out a pebble, rather smaller than a pea.

"Inedible," Xalan said, disappointed. "A jewel?"

"Not quite." With Hwe's permission I took the lump and buffed it with the hem of my cloak. "Look—do you recognize that white?"

The Crystal Crown is cut and faceted, but Xalan identified this pellet immediately. "It's that bit of what-did-he-call-it, phlogiston, that Xerlanthor had. A bit of the Crown itself!"

"It's the one bit of crystal that definitely isn't," I corrected him, and passed the lump back to Hwe.

Xalan yelped in protest. "Is that safe? Think of the damage an unscrupulous person can wreak with it!"

"It's safe—does Hwe look like a new Xerlanthor?" We watched as he wrapped the pellet up in a scrap of leather, before stowing it carefully into the amulet-bag around his hairy neck. His care was the more wonderful, because Hwe surely did not understand a fifth of what we said.

The pack animals could not share our goat stew, roast goat, or goat cutlet. Since the grazing was thin, the poor donkeys declined. It was a relief to breast the final ridge, and see Lanach's thatched roofs on the slopes below.

Melayne wished to go down immediately, but I took precautions. Xalan and Hwe were left in charge of the baby and animals well outside of town. After so many vicissitudes our clothing no longer smacked of any particular country, and I wore a deep hood to hide both my race and the Crystal Crown on my head. "We must barter for grain for the animals."

"If any kinsman of mine is home, I'll invite you to dinner," Melayne promised. "Just think, we've never been in Cayd together."

"Melayne," I said for the tenth time, "surely things have changed."

Indeed they had. The town had never had walls, sieges being too tedious a warfare for Caydish taste. So the Tiyalor had overrun Lanach with ease. Great black scars were all that remained of many houses. All westerners are fair, so to me the populace did not look much different. But Melayne, trembling, said, "They're all foreigners. I don't recognize anybody. Where are my people? My family?"

At her insistence we peeped in at the gate of the King's house. In the yard a gang of Tiyalor archers quarreled over their target practice. I stared at the tall gate-post a moment too long; when Melayne followed my gaze she began to sob. A dozen skulls, mostly pecked clean now, had been nailed to the cross-piece above. The faces were unrecognizable, long gone.

Mercifully, it seemed to be a major market day, so two strangers were not remarkable in the small town.

In the marketplace I traded our Rriat goods for provisions, while Melayne wept into her cloak. "Something wrong with your woman?" the grain-seller asked in Tiyalene.

My Caydish is poor, and the tongue only partially resembles Tiyalene. So I replied as briefly as possible, "Gave her a beating this morning." The answer was unremarkable in Cayd, but I hurried away before more questions could be put.

We made camp several valleys over, lest our fire be seen from town. Our Rriat goods were rarities in Lanach, and my aggressive trading got us plenty of supplies. I had bought milk, cheese, grain, and even a skin of sour Caydish ale. But though this was her native fare, Melayne's appetite was poor. "Everyone's dead, my brothers, my sisters," she mourned. "I'm the last Cayd left."

"I'll wager you anything you like, that most of your family's still alive," Xalan tried to console her. "I can even tell you where they are right now—I don't need my mirror."

Melayne blew her nose. "Where?"

He laughed across the fire at me. "They're all at Liras' table, sitting down to a glorious banquet of ten courses, feisty as bears in the spring."

"Oh!" Melayne turned to me. "And you have to defeat my brothers to get Averidan back! Will you be very careful, Liras? Don't hurt them!"

Xalan laughed out loud at this, thumping his heels on the pine needles carpeting our camp. I solemnly continued trotting the baby on my knee. "It's inconvenient sometimes when you embrace Shan sensibilities, Melayne. I remember distinctly a few years ago, when you urged me to kill them all."

"Well, you should have, then," she retorted. "It would have saved trouble. I wouldn't have had to change my mind. You can do anything; look what you've accomplished already."

Her confidence was alarming. "We'll see when we get there," I promised helplessly, as Xalan dissolved into laughter again.

The next day we descended the Tambours. I feared
the narrow pass would be guarded or even blocked, in
these disturbed times. But the only opponents we met
were the wind, and the thunder of the rejoicing waterfall. As we came round the final cliff and saw Averidan
spread out below us, the tears stood in my eyes. It was
almost summer, and in its honor the trees had put on
their full leafy green. The curve of the falling water
glinted silver, its roar drowning all conversation. Behind me Xalan wiped his eyes on his hand, our handkerchiefs having long since been lost. We might have
stood there for hours in a welter of sentiment if
Melayne, encumbered with an impatient child at the
rear, had not given the donkeys a jab so that they
jostled us.

As we crossed the bridge, I was prey to strange
emotions. There at the edge of the forest—a forest of
trees I could name!—were the huts of the Tambours
garrison, seemingly untouched by the years. There
was no soldier in sight, just like the last time I had
come this way. The Cayds were getting slack, I reflected; even if the entire realm was upside-down, this
strategic point should be strongly held. If I myself had
been so prudent, Averidan might never have been
conquered.

As I went up to the first hut, Melayne anxiously
called, "Don't start re-invading the country alone,
dearest. If the garrison is Caydish, I can talk them
around."

Drawing my sword I kicked the door open. And just
as before, my brother Zofal-ven stared indignantly
back at me from his bath. I had boasted of being in
the story, but this congruence made my ears ring and
my head swim. In Averidan *Thausra*'s power was
supreme.

His bathwater steamed gently in the cold draft from
the open door. In unsteady tones Zofal said, "Come
in and shut the door, Liras-ven. It is you, isn't it?
Ought you wear the Crown so casually?"

I flung my arms around him, forgetting my sword so

that in the excitement I nearly slashed his leg open.
"You're supposed to be dead, Zofal-ven!"

"So are you! Or lost—it's been more than a year!
Where have you been?"

Interrupting each other, tumbling over our words,
we talked as Zofal climbed out of the tub and dressed.
That Zofal in the confusion of siege and sack had been
unable to get word to me was not perhaps surprising.
He had contrived to reach Mother in her lair on the
coast, and within the year quarreled irretrievably with
her over the management of the Shan armed resistance. "That's you all over—tactful!" I commented.

"This western district is where the real work is."
Zofal flicked his wet hair back, with the familiar gesture I had never thought to see again. "The Cayds are
unsteady in the City, will never take the coastal
regions—but here in the forests they're truly settling
in. I suppose it's only a little less barbaric than their
homeland—"

Again the door was flung open. Melayne stood, bow
in hand, ready to rescue me. Recognizing my brother,
she relaxed her grasp on the arrow, but continued to
eye him without much warmth. "Cayd is not barbaric," she snapped. "Or it wasn't, before the Tiyalor
moved in."

Zofal had the grace to blush. "Hallo, sister-in-law,
you've cut your hair. Where do you keep your knives
now?"

Before the conversation could get too jagged I said,
"Zofal hasn't been introduced to his niece, poor fellow!"

In the grove outside Tarys was running wild, squeal-
ing and toddling after squirrels until the wood echoed.
In nominal charge, Xalan sat cross-legged on a stump
and stared raptly into his mirror. "I never thought I'd
enjoy scrying," he excused himself.

The noise soon attracted Zofal's troops, who I assumed had just driven off the Caydish garrison. They
were a mere dozen, clad in well-worn green and brown
and armed with a motley collection of Viridese and
Caydish weaponry. My surprise at Zofal's successes

vanished when his captain came up to report—a woman, strong and lithe as braided copper cable. Only the warrior Sisters could do so well here. She stared suspiciously at Melayne's red hair. "Is that a prisoner, General?"

"No, she's my wife," I cut in quickly, before Melayne could take umbrage, and threw back my hood.

"The Shan King!" "At last!" "The Crystal Crown returns to Averidan!" The little band cheered and shouted their excitement, and embraced each other, the Shan King being too respected to get clapped on the back.

I took advantage of the tumult to remark, " 'General,' eh? I don't remember giving you that rank."

"I needed it to run this campaign," Zofal replied, quite unabashed. "I knew when you came back you'd confirm it."

That distracted me from the sharp comment he merited. "You expected me?"

He gave me the old irritated glance, as if galled by a younger brother's stupidity. "Why, surely—there must be fifty versions of it, in the plaiv."

Before I could pursue the matter, we were interrupted by the whir of the grindstone. All Viridese garrisons have one, to hone spears and swords on, and someone had set this one going beside the well. "We had better sharpen our weapons," the Sister was advising. "Now His Majesty is back, there'll be no more toying with the foe."

"You mean you haven't already slaughtered the garrison?" I asked Zofal.

"The Cayds *will* all go out together, to hunt or pillage the nearby settlements," Zofal explained. "We time our raids for then, and make a good show of driving the cooks and sweepers and so on out of the camp and into the forest. Of course they're all Shan," he added.

"And then you clean out the Cayds' larder?"

"Pretty poor food they stock too," one forester grumbled. "Our kin in the villages hide all the choice provender—they never think that we, their brethren, live off what the Cayds steal too."

The complexity and contradictions of this chain of thievery made me dizzy. "The battle will be in earnest now," the Sister said with relish. "We'll hide in the woods and cut the Cayds down as they return."

Hastily I said, "It would be better to go on as before, at least for a while. We can't kill every Cayd in Averidan."

Only Zofal had the face to ask the natural question, "Why not? Isn't that why you came back?"

I could hardly say that my wife had begged me not to. Instead I said, "To attack your enemy's littlest toe is a waste of time. One must slash at the vitals. I want to arrive at the City soon, with as little fuss as possible."

I had forgotten how pleasant being an absolute monarch could be. Everyone acquiesced instantly, and a few minutes sufficed to ransack the huts. I noticed that the food was conveniently packed for travel, and that a "stolen" pair of leggings were cut to Shan proportions and not for a tall Cayd. The various contenders for western Averidan seemed to have struck a quite comfortable balance.

Evening shadows were gathering fast as we followed Zofal to his base. It was cleverly sited on a sandy island about a league downstream. As we crossed the swift Mhesan on a log raft, the mild midsummer twilight lay blue and clear on the water. "This is the most beautiful land in the world," I sighed. "We've always said it, but now I can affirm that it's true."

"Too lovely to hand over to foreigners." When Zofal leaned forward to see my face better, the raft lurched alarmingly. "The country's gone to pot while you've been away, Liras-ven. At first we were deliberately helping things slide—to annoy the Cayds, you understand. But now—" He shook his head. "Some of Mother's tricks, especially, are crazy."

"There's such a thing as cutting off your nose to spite your face," I conceded.

"Here." A bit of stamped metal glittered in his palm.

Taking the copper coin, I rubbed it between my fingers and then bit it. "It doesn't feel quite right, but then I've been away awhile."

"Mother set some goldsmiths to adulterating the currency—we did need the money. Now there are coiners in every village. Soon they'll be stamping the coppers out of old shoe leather; the coins won't be worth much more."

Money, both in theory and practice, has always fascinated Zofal. Passing the coin back, I dismissed his worry unthinkingly: "Now I'm back, all will be as it was."

To avoid Caydish notice we spent all the following day resting in Zofal's hideaway, and did not set out again till nightfall. A full night's hike brought us to Mhee. I had almost forgotten that early in the war the town had been surrounded and torched. Thus it was doubly shocking to see the charred husk of the once-prosperous town. Only stone piers were left to show where the many bridges had spanned the river. King Mor's viceroy showed little interest in rebuilding, and without warehouses and shops and guildhalls, Mhee's thriving commerce had withered.

At my accession the town had been the fourth largest in Averidan, after the capital and Ennelith-Ral and Mishbil. Now there were scarcely enough inhabitants in Mhee to fill a big village. Those townfolk up and about in the dawn horrified me. An old woman's face, all scarred with the marks of fire, a child with one leg setting up his begging-pitch for the day—everyone seemed lame or unsound. "Did no one survive whole?" I asked, aching with pity.

"All the sound fighters have joined us, in the forests or the cliffs," Zofal reminded me.

But I could take little consolation in this. Leaving the others to hire a barge for our trip downstream, I handed Xalan my cloak and hood and climbed onto a fire-blackened stone bollard. "I am the Shan King," I announced simply. "The power is in me to heal."

"What if the Caydish garrison sees you?" Xalan

hissed, but I ignored him. The bargeworkers and rivermen stood and stared, disconcerted. No one in earshot doubted my identity, for the Crystal Crown is the sole badge of the ruler of Averidan. The tales of my return, fanciful as they must have been, had prepared my way. But custom does dictate that the Shan King keep aloof, reserving any arcane powers for high use. Instinctively now I knew this was wrong, that tradition had once again done the Shan a disservice. Crooking a finger I said, "You, messir—in the brown tunic."

This man plainly had been a spearman in my army. He saluted me, awkwardly because of his twisted shoulder. The broken collarbone had not been set properly. With a touch I drew the mishealed bone straight again. Astonished, the fellow waved his arms around like a mill wheel before crying, "My powers in your service, Your Majesty!"

Things grew confused after this. Workers called the news to their fellows, and folk ran to fetch friends and relatives. In a twinkling the shabby waterfront filled with both anxious wounded and excited spectators. Zofal and Xalan wormed with great difficulty back and forth through the press, to drag our baggage from the pack animals to the barge.

Once before I had healed people until I collapsed. But now the Crown was tamed, I expected to feel no fatigue. Nevertheless after the first hour the strain began to mount. I paid it no notice for as long as I could and then, a little desperately, said, "*Thausra?* My god, I need more strength."

I sat down on a baulk of lumber and waited for the surge of hot power to restore me. Chattering and calling for my attention, the people crowded so close that I had to gasp for breath. Then the words rang in both the inner and outer ear: "Learn to think with your head, not your heart!" And Melayne thrust her way to my side, angry as a shaken beehive. "You don't have the sense of a chicken, and after traveling all night too! Xalan, how dare you let him sneak off to perform tricks, like a tamed bear! And you, brother-in-law, don't lounge about! Help him up. Get us on that barge before they suck him dry!"

Under the lash of her tongue everyone leaped to obey. The townspeople fell back, grumbling dangerously until they recognized Melayne as my wife. I was bundled over the barge's rear rail. A narrow avenue opened in the crowd so that the baby, closely followed by Hwe, could toddle down to her mother. When shouting failed, Xalan had to go back and actually drive Sahai aboard. Dockworkers untied our craft and pushed it out into the current. Rallying somewhat, I sat up to wave at the people. "Bring the rest of your casualties down to the City after I retake it," I called in farewell.

This final bit of *chun-hei* infuriated Melayne. "That Crown has addled your brains!" she began. Before she could really elaborate on the theme, however, the barge began to sway and slide forward. The boatmen stabbed their poles vigorously into the water, and leaned against them until the ripples foamed past. Melayne collapsed onto the nearest bench, and groaned in misery. Sahai, crouched beneath, looked equally unhappy.

Selecting another empty place, I lay down too, and took my cloak back from Xalan. "Don't let Tarys fall overboard," I adjured him, and fell asleep almost before I could draw the garment up.

I woke late in the afternoon. My head was perfectly clear, perhaps because I had slept in the Crown. It would not do to get used to the sensation, since I was certain Melayne would never allow the Crown into our bed. But now I put my feet up on the rail, to watch the canals and fields slide by, and consider *Thausra*'s advice. Though Melayne had echoed it, I knew the god's voice. My promise had been supremely unpractical. To repair every damaged body in Averidan might be within my power—but only by neglecting every other royal duty.

Impracticality, however, has its appeal in Averidan.

If anything, that was our real inheritance from our divine forefather, this appetite for wildly romantic events. Having dark hair and eyes, like Viris, or being able to trace one's genealogy, Sandcomber had rightly called tripe. I pitied my usurper; a stolid suspicious Cayd without a vestige of *chun-hei* must find Averidan a heavy burden.

My cogitations were interrupted by Zofal-ven, who came to lean on the rail before me. "The captain says we'll arrive at the City's river-gate very soon, Liras-ven. What are your plans? Will you take a boat to Cliffhole and join up with Mother?"

Though I had no strategies, I was able to immediately say, "No. We'll go up to the Palace this evening, and call on King Mor."

"And just ask him to step aside for you?" I could see Zofal swallowing more incredulous questions. "All right. I can see you've changed, learned to work wonders. But—well, is it fair to risk Melayne and the baby like that?"

I had to laugh at the way dismay struggled with respect in his voice. "I could have them wait for me in the lower City—but no," I corrected myself. Though I had no plan, *Thausra* did; my every suggestion was either accepted or instantly rejected, as if each was measured against some master strategy. "I'll need Melayne to get past any Caydish guards. They won't recognize me unless King Mor has been warned. And surely we've outstripped rumor—only magic mirrors could pass the news fast enough."

Zofal gave me a startled look. "You haven't heard—no, how could you? King Mor decided the Order of Magi were witches."

"I remember the word," I said, bracing myself. "They think I'm one, you know . . . Was every magus in Averidan put to the sword?"

"Not as many as you fear," he hastened to reassure me. "Don't look so grim! It seems the old Master Magus had some sort of warning before he died—oh, you know that? Well, many magi stripped off their red robes and paid visits to kinfolk, or took a trip to the provinces.''

I sighed with relief, glancing over my shoulder to where Xalan lay on the deck snoring. Apart from the calamity to Averidan, to discover himself the only remaining practitioner of magery would have crushed my lighthearted friend.

By this time our destination was visible in the east. The scarp of the upper City reared up so high its white buildings still glowed briefly in the day's last light. The lower town was already in evening, here and there showing a cheerful golden speck of lamplight. The glamor of sunset painted over the scars of war, any marks of the seasons gone by; it was as if I had never left the City at all. Then, stunned, I noticed that the Temple Dome no longer glowed gold. The barbarians had stripped off the gilding.

"Low bridge!" the captain called, and himself stepped off the rear deck. With alarming speed the barge slid down toward the many-arched bridge over Mhesan. But the barge-men had done this before; with casual skill the steersman guided the craft under the high central arch. For a long moment we could see stonework skimming by overhead and the water's chatter echoed hollowly in our ears. Then we were safe out again, with the sea gulls above crying sarcastic comment on our feat.

Our vessel tied up at the river harbor pier, among half a hundred other barges. I noticed most of them were battered or half-derelict. Mhee's decline had dragged the river-trade down as well. But the taverns and cookshops and wine-sellers were doing good business, as busy and well-lit as ever. "Ah!" Xalan lifted a big bundle to his shoulder, tucked a bulging sack under the other arm, and took hold of a pack with the free hand. "I haven't had a decent meal in almost a year and a half—think of it and shudder! And before that we were besieged, and ate horse soup and dog-tail stew. I know a tavern nearby that does redfish-with-four-spices."

"Sounds good." Zofal also staggered under many pieces of luggage. "Perhaps we can leave your baggage there—spare ourselves the trouble of hauling it up the hill until we know what your welcome will be."

"Eat!" Tarys squealed, wriggling down from Melayne's grasp.

Lest I be recognized too soon, I had removed the Crystal Crown and was carrying it rolled in a sack under my arm. "Later," I felt bound to say. "I want to get to the Palace quickly, before word spreads."

This was greeted with blatant barefaced mutiny. "Wine," Xalan tempted me ruthlessly. "When did we last sip a decent Viridese wine? Do you remember that last drop of plum brandy? Utterly wasted—rubbed onto a leech, as I recall."

"Don't mention those things now!" Melayne was pale and drawn but reviving quickly. "I would feel better, dearest, with something in my stomach to settle it."

"You're not carrying very much, Liras," Zofal threatened. "I'll do your porter duty. But you have to feed me!"

"Eat," Tarys whimpered insistently, clinging to my knees. So I gave in. Xalan led us through the City gates and down the narrow streets. The distinctive atmosphere of this harbor district filled our noses, a smell, compounded of donkey manure, fish offal, wine lees, and salt water, that visitors often complain of. Incense could not have been sweeter. We halted before a combined tavern and cookshop.

The cookshop counter in front served those who bought their food to eat at home. The tavern behind was crowded to the doorsills with narrow trestle tables and benches scarred from many a rowdy drinking-party. The heat of fragrant cooking and many bodies rolled into our faces as we passed within. But the intense silence of the customers, the silence of discriminating diners concentrating on their food, boded well. A hired shed received our baggage, and a few coppers in the taverner's hand got us a table at the back, out of casual view.

Viridese cookshops specialize, each dealing in only one or two suppers. We all sighed with happiness when a huge platter of stewed redfish was set in the middle of the table. The pink chunks of fish had been browned to a crusty perfection before stewing, and the glorious thick sauce was a marvel. With this came boiled barley, little trays of pickles, sweet red wine— all the proper accompaniments of a decent Shan repast. Xalan and I, particularly, were weak with joy. In a moment the platter was scraped clean, divided among us. Zofal signaled for more, and when the second serving was as rapidly eaten, yet more.

"That feels better." Xalan even smiled indulgently at Hwe, who was swabbing the last drops of sauce up from the platter with one leathery forefinger. "Who's still peckish?"

"Three helpings of redfish are enough." Zofal patted his mouth fastidiously with a silk handkerchief. "Let's try their other dish instead."

When the deep earthenware bowl was set down, we all leaned forward to look and sniff. "This is something odd," I said, dipping with the ladle. "Is it a proper viand?"

"It's lamb," Zofal said, taking the spoon and helping himself generously. "Of course it's a viand, and very good, too. The Cayds brought all their sheep with them, and Shan cooks are bold."

"We've eaten so many marginal meats already," Xalan made excuse, and held out his dish.

My scruple evaporated after the first spoonful. One usually finds pork cooked thus, baked on a bed of onions, garlic, and cabbage and topped with crumbled barley-cake. But lamb was even tastier. When it was gone, I sat back with an intense feeling of inner satisfaction. "When everything settles down, I'll have my cooks start serving lamb. There must be lots of ways to eat it."

"Invite me," Zofal encouraged. "You don't care for your kin properly, Liras—"

He stopped, wide-eyed, and Melayne pulled her

straw hat down over her brow. Past the counter crowded
half a dozen Caydish axemen. Barbaric copper rings
glittered in their ears, and their axes bore the patina of
long use. Their worn leather armor seemed to strain to
cover the big shoulders, and their red or fair braids
gleamed incongruously in the lamplight. Feeling stealth-
ily under my cloak for the hilt of my sword, I tensed to
meet their first rush; good cooks should be defended.

But to my surprise the soldiers seemed to harbor no
designs of looting or killing. They sat up to a table
quite like civilized people, with only a little jostling
underneath to accommodate their longer legs, and,
when the baked lamb was served, ate with manners
not even as ungracious as Hwe's. The Shan customers
stared a bit but were not long distracted from their
own plates, showing this was a fairly frequent haunt
for the invaders.

"They may well recognize Melayne or me," I said
quietly, and pointed toward the back door. As the
others stole out, I murmured to Zofal, "I haven't any
money."

He loosened his belt-purse and glared at me. "I'm
always paying, little brother. As far as the family
advantage goes, you are a loss!"

In the narrow yard we paused only to untie Sahai
who, I had decided, would not understand cookshops.
After such a meal, the steep winding road to the
Upper gates taxed everyone. Tarys refused to even try
to walk, and we had to take turns carrying her. Though
the night air was cool, and the breeze coming off the
harbor, I sweated under the double load of a bellyful
and a stout toddler. "What if the gates are closed
early?" Xalan panted.

"Then you can work off your supper by lifting us
over the wall."

However, the huge bronze doors still stood ajar.
The Caydish guards at the Main Gate below had
scarcely been visible, gaming or drinking in their guard-
house. Those in charge of the Upper Gate were more
alert. As arranged, Melayne went forward alone while

we searched the gutter and path for rocks. Taking off her hat she called in Caydish, "Is my brother Mor at home this evening!"

Startled and uneasy, the guards came out of the massive gateway to question her. "It's the princess Melayne!" "Did you stab the Witch-King in bed, then?" "Where have you been, princess? The king said you were whisked off by enchantment."

"How would half a brick do?" I whispered to Xalan.

"Well enough," he said, drawing out his wand. "But don't throw them all at once."

I tossed my two missiles up as high as I could, making no attempt to aim them. "Now don't clout Melayne, or she'll take it out of your skin."

"I've done this before!" he replied crossly. The control of falling earth or rock is an elementary geomantic exercise; no Viridese would have been lured from the shelter of the gateway so readily. With a slight gesture of his black stone wand, Xalan directed my half-brick to land square on a Cayd's head. He sagged like a falling tree. Before the second rock hit, Zofal lobbed a few more. Soldiers crumpled all around Melayne, who herself stood untouched like a single daisy in a mowed lawn.

Only when all the rocks were gone did I see the one Cayd wearing a helmet. It was a much-dented Viridese one, probably loot, and instead of a solid thump the chunk of brick made a resounding clang when it struck. Slightly dazed, the soldier flicked out his sword. "Faithless whore!" he yelled.

Melayne was too indignant to draw her own needle-knives. "Did you hear that, husband? what he called me?"

"Shocking," I agreed, interposing my own wide sword between them. "Allow me to rebuke him." The really experienced veterans were too grand to stand guard duty. I grinned confidently at this unfortunate young Cayd. "The Witch-King has returned," I told him in Caydish. "Drop your sword, and I'll allow you to run."

"You ought to dice his liver," Melayne grumbled, still in a huff. Perhaps the threat of her dudgeon, added to fear of me, was too much. My foe wilted, letting his sword fall to the ground, and galloped down the hill so fast his blond braids streamed out behind him.

Leaving the fallen guards lying we went in and wrenched the geared wheels around to shut and lock the gates. The moonless dark was dimly pierced only here and there, by lamplit windows. King Mor had evidently ended the old custom of lighting every inch of both Palace and Temple at night. But both Xalan and I could pace the turns of the way with our eyes shut. When we paused to change over the baby, Zofal tiptoed up to a shuttered window. His head showed black against the mellow light leaking through, and I saw him beckon. I stepped softly up, and he whispered, "Listen."

The wall was plastered so thick I had to stoop near to catch the speaker within. ". . . and after the dragon, the river, and after the rain of fire, the gushing ice. . ."

"A rhetor reciting a plaiv," I murmured, losing interest, but my brother gestured for me to listen again.

". . . only when all these trials had been made, could the Shan King turn his steps toward Averidan again." I closed my mouth before Zofal could see it sagging open. For a moment the old eerie feeling came trickling coldly down my spine again. Then I remembered I was a resident of the realm beneath now, and smiled.

"I want to put the baby to sleep," Melayne hissed from behind us, so we went back.

CHAPTER 16

An Anticipated Return

Xalan lifted over the garden gate and let us in. We
trod carefully along the walks toward the Palace. Sahai
padded hungrily off into the gardens, flicking her tail.
The paths were not raked and trimmed to their old
perfection, and every flower bed I passed seemed to
cry out for care. But it was pitch dark, and there were
more pressing matters to hand. Pausing on the gloomy
terrace, I put on the Crystal Crown and surveyed the
triple-arched windows. With its help, finding the one I
wanted was easy. "There," I pointed. "King Mor is
in the large salon."

Zofal had been growing more and more nervous.
"And you still don't have any ruse. You're just going
to open the window and say, 'I'm back'? You've been
listening to too many stories about yourself!"

"Have I?" At the indicated window I pried up the
latch with my dagger. The curtains beyond were
unlooped, contrary to former practice, so that no one
inside saw me. With my sword I swept the drape
aside, and stepped in.

Without my commanding it, the Crown flared with
white light, bleaching the colors from the wall-paintings,
blanching into flat masks the faces of those within. It
was pleasantly reassuring, to see *Thausra* in control. I
opened my mouth to deliver some dramatic announcement. Then I suddenly recognized the screwed-up face
nearest me. "Siril-ven, you poor girl!" I exclaimed,
idiotically. "How have you been?"

My elder sister shielded her eyes from the glare. "Oh, dear—it must be Liras-ven. Can you damp that thing down a bit?"

I did so, and the countenances sprang back to life. Siril looked exactly as she had two years ago. War and siege, widowhood and an enforced second marriage, conquest and chaos, had all passed her over without rumpling a strand of her dark high-piled hair or disarranging the droop of her trailing robe.

The hulking blond bearded Cayd beside her was surely her new spouse, Prince Musenor. I nearly laughed out loud at the sight of him, tricked out in the fullest of full Viridese court dress. His bushy blond beard oddly topped the long silk robes of a delicate purple-blue, and full sleeves trailing two yards long prevented him from unsheathing a sapphire-encrusted sword that surely was a mere ornament. Trammeled with sash, handkerchief, and elegant jewelry, the Prince looked as unhappily incongruous as a leopard in shoes. At least the garments fitted his bulk; I felt I recognized Siril's taste.

In the grandest silver-gilt chair sat King Mor himself. Only by his seat and his gold circlet did I recognize him. Even to my eye the man looked seriously ill, his face gray and wasted into a hundred haggard lines, the red-gold hair faded. He stared at me without recognition as I slowly walked up the long room toward him. The pompous words deserted me. Quite kindly I said, "I don't wish to inconvenience you, but I've come back to reclaim my kingdom."

King Mor's sunken mouth worked. "The Witch-King!" he cried thinly.

"The Shan King," I corrected. "The Shan, you have probably found, are ruled only by the wearer of the Crystal Crown—"

The inner door was flung open. I had completely forgotten the ten stalwart warriors whose duty was to guard King Mor from supernatural attack; his words had been a summons, not a salutation. Fortunately I had not sheathed my sword. Ducking and parrying a hail of axe-strokes, I backed against a pillar on the far side of the room to guard my rear.

All around, underneath yet present, that other side surrounded the battle—not precisely tamed, the realm beneath would never be that, but as safe as it would ever be. I could count on it, as I could Sahai, to be frequently helpful as long as I took care. The power made me faster than my foes, who were in any case reluctant to close after all the lurid tales they had heard of me. Distracting one with a feint, I kicked him in the crotch, then slashed another's arm as he raised his axe to chop at me.

To defeat them all, armed as I was with supernatural advantage, was grim but necessary. I went about it with clinical professionalism, controlled and calm, riding the power as one would a spirited horse. Vaguely I was aware of the others coming in from the terrace, the vociferous reunion of various siblings. Behind me Melayne commanded, "Now you stop that, before someone gets hurt!"

I took her to be addressing my opponents, since she used Caydish; the last axe-man thought so too, and glanced doubtfully round. I cut him down, and took a deep breath. The chamberlain, attracted by the noise, hovered nervously in the doorway. I flicked a finger at the floor. "Have these removed."

Zofal stood nearby, fidgeting with his own sword. "I did think about helping you, but Xalan and Melayne said better not," he said. "Where did you learn to do that?"

Before I could find an answer, Melayne hurried up to tug at my sleeve. "Liras, come! Mor has fainted or something."

Quick to bow to a rising sun, the chamberlain had run to fetch some porters, and now stood ready with a towel and some plum brandy. Wiping my hands and blade, I followed Melayne. At the other end of the room King Mor had been eased from his seat to lie on the mosaic floor. Musenor squatted near his head, inexpertly feeling at his half-brother's face and throat.

Melayne knelt and pressed one limp hand between her own. "Can you heal him, dearest?" she pleaded.

I sighed. "Once you called Mor a snake. Is it a prudent thing for me to do, truly, to repair my usurper?"

Melayne's stare held only outrage. "He's my brother!"

"I shouldn't quarrel about it," Xalan put in. He bent to press an ear against Mor's brocaded chest. "There's no heartbeat."

Trembling, Melayne accepted a handkerchief from Siril but did not weep; it was entirely true that Mor had been everyone's least favorite brother. Musenor sat back with a stunned, almost lost expression on his craggy face. "He was ailing, we all knew that," he rumbled in Caydish deep in his chest. "And he wouldn't see the herbals, for fear of poison. But he shouldn't have just quit like that."

He shot me a suspicious blue-eyed glance; my reputation for arcane skills was unquenchable. Xalan did not help matters by remarking, "Do you know, I think you frightened him to death?"

I resorted to Sandcomber's favorite disparagement. "Tripe!" Briskly, I took charge. "His demise is very sad. What is the Caydish rite—burial? Let King Mor be sent to the Deadlands decently, in accordance with all the customs of his race."

"Musenor can see it done right," Siril suggested.

I agreed, and passed on to other details. "I wish to see the Lord Chamberlain, if any still holds that office."

"Your Majesty's former Lord Chamberlain was killed in the sack," the salon chamberlain timidly informed me. "That late—er, King Mor never appointed a successor. But his deputy has been performing the duties . . ."

"He will do." When that worthy arrived, I ordered the royal chambers cleared, and whoever was in the Lady's old rooms to be moved out too. "My first desire, and that of my companions here also, is for a long bath."

Xalan sighed in anticipation. "We haven't had a decent bath since we left," he explained.

"How can you still be *alive?*" Siril recoiled so violently she bumped into Hwe, who stared solemnly down at her as she shuddered away. "This one probably has vermin!"

I ignored all this fuss, inquiring after government officials. A discouraging number had fled or been deposed or executed. During all this adult business, Tarys had happily busied herself tearing the stuffing out of a pillow. Now, bored, she set up a howl. "And find me the nearest children's nurse, immediately," I interrupted myself to add.

"I'm sure Siril will share hers with you for a while," Zofal remarked, with a touch of malice.

I could only gape as Siril called in a nurse who carried a fat little boy. The infant was less than four months old, with one black tuft standing up on his soft head. He was so solidly porky that only big Musenor could have been his sire. "He can sit and creep already," Siril announced with boundless pride, and at her gesture the nurse carefully balanced the infant on his broad diapered bottom. "Goris-lat, can you greet your uncle?"

My new nephew stared mutely up at me. "Sister, my heartiest congratulations!" I said, beaming. Tarys looked at this younger rival, and, taking up the half-gutted pillow, bowled little Goris head over heels.

The thrashing of ten Caydish warriors was not so ear-splitting as Siril's yell of fury. "If your ill-mannered brat has hurt my darling, I'll never speak to you again!" She scooped the screaming baby up.

"Small loss," Melayne bristled, gathering up Tarys in her turn. Siril turned upon her, snarling like a leopardess. I intervened before the Viridese-Cayd truce could disintegrate. A new nurse, for Tarys' very own, was sent for. Siril took the shrieking Goris away to nurse him into quiescence. Melayne went to bathe Tarys and herself—"Find me some baby clothing," she flung at the poor chamberlain in passing—and I gave Xalan leave to return to his magian tower and do likewise.

"It's a compliment to me, I know," Xalan replied

with a smile. "But I haven't your moral suasion, Liras. To go in the dark through a Palace full of magi-killing Cayds, merely to bathe and sleep is beyond me. Perhaps you could come with me tomorrow, and help clear out the invaders from my rooms."

Put that way it sounded only sensible. "And I suppose your objections would be the same, Zofal, to taking charge of the Palace guard this evening?"

"You're the one with the knack for triumphing unexpectedly against ridiculous odds," Zofal agreed. "In fact, I'd prefer to camp in your antechamber tonight."

Xalan endorsed this, adding, "And use your bath too."

"Oh, very well—if you'll wash Hwe as well. Go." Musenor and I were left to look at each other over King Mor's stiffening body. I poured out two cups of brandy and passed him one. "Come, out on the terrace."

The stars reigned undisputed in an unclouded sky; the moon, in its last quarter, would not rise until very late. Though it was well past midnight many windows in the Palace were still bright; my return had doubtless banished sleep for a while. In silence we paced along the marble terrace to where it ended in an overlook. The cliff dropped steeply beyond; far below Averidan's fields and canals were just visible as a texture in the starlight. Only the Mhesan returned the light, glimmering gently like a sleek black snake. I sipped my brandy, totally at peace.

Musenor spoke first, in Viridese this time, accented but otherwise very fair. Siril must drill him. "You have no fear, then, that we will rush upon you and slay you in your sleep."

It was a statement, not a question. "Nor do I fear," I said, "that you will shove me over the balustrade here . . . If this were Cayd, and Mor newly dead, would you not be king?"

"I am named Mor's heir." The massive silk-clad shoulders shrugged. "But this is Averidan."

"You seem to have grasped our customs admirably. We returned to Averidan through Tiyalor and Cayd. I am prepared to accept that your people cannot return there."

Musenor's anger exploded out like wine from a dropped bottle. I braced myself for an attack, but then realized his rage was not aimed at me. It was the Tiyalor who had driven Cayd to invade us, pressed Musenor and his folk out of their homes. How bitter that retreat must have tasted, to the proud Cayds! Had it not been for the Crown on my head, though, I never would have known it, for Musenor's deep voice remained even. "Do you hold then with your mother's party, that we must be exterminated from Averidan, like a plague of invading rats?"

I frowned. "Well, I shall if you push me to it. Mother is a fearfully strong-willed woman. But I am Shan King. If I call upon all Viridese to lay down their arms, and accept you Cayds as immigrants, she is bound to obey—in theory," I felt bound to add, for I could not actually envision Mother doing any such thing.

Musenor turned to stare at me, though it was too dark for him to see much, and shifted to Caydish. "Do I hear you right? You wish us to settle down in Averidan under your rule?"

There was no point in being annoyingly precise, and explaining that no one actually wished it. "I see no other answer," I said. "You don't wish to rule the country yourself, do you?"

"No," Musenor said slowly, as if the idea had just come home to him. "I'm tired, we're all tired, of plowing uphill." Long ago Melayne had warned me that kindliness in Cayd is reckoned to be weak. A long sojourn in Averidan had somewhat softened Musenor's suspicious nature, and now he only said, "I don't see what you runts will get out of it."

"I have reasons but will not discuss them with you," I said loftily, and drained my cup. The lift of the brandy was passing, and I thought with sleepy pleasure of my bath. "Think it over, discuss it with the other Cayds, and tell me your intentions tomorrow. I am going to bed."

I had my sleep out, and took a second bath; that of the night before I had been too sleepy to enjoy enough. No sooner had I wallowed into the steaming herb-scented water, than Melayne came in. She eyed me appraisingly. "Do you know, we haven't been alone together in weeks?" So I made room for her beside me; there was plenty of space in the square sunken bath. What with that, and breakfast, and the difficulty of finding decent robes—my own were, of course, long gone, and the old Master of Wardrobe had been executed by King Mor in a fit of pique—the Shan King was not presentable until after noon.

In the daylight the scars of Mor's occupation were distressingly plain. Even the walls of my bedchamber bore marks of conflict—the plaster scraped and scored by the axes of Mor's guards, when they had leaned, bored, against the walls in the dark. Many new hangings and carpets muffled the windows and floors, relics of Caydish preparations for a hard western winter that would never come here. And the sight of my gardens outside made me wring my hands. A large herd of wiry Caydish cattle browsed on the weeds and hay that flourished where my lawn used to be. The sight must have greatly cheered Mor every morning, cattle being wealth in Cayd. But I ground my teeth to keep from instantly shouting for the Palace butchers.

I put the Crown on and these small annoyances gave way to larger burdens. First and most important was to settle with Musenor. I ensured Melayne would be busy by giving her charge over repairs and restorations in our suites. When I went to the grand audience chamber, though, I found it was now a dining-mess for Caydish officers. In the end I held court on the terrace, ordering a throne and then the presence of the prince. My purple klimflowers, neglected and unpruned, straggled above in an untidy canopy. Cows crowded up, blinking placidly in the sunshine, to scratch their sides against the marble balustrade. "Start a list of things to be done," I told Zofal, "and put those cattle first."

They lumbered off, shaking their horns warningly, when Sahai idled up. Her bulging sides and sleepy good nature showed that she had killed her own supper somewhere in the grounds, and she consented to sprawl at my feet to have her golden chin rubbed.

When Musenor appeared, I felt a prickle of alarm. He and the four or five Caydish elders with him wore not Shan robes, but Caydish battle-dress, of hairy wool and leather studded with bits of copper. The Crown showed me their counsels were divided. Now I was the handicapped one, in my long royal-green robe with its trailing triple sleeves. Of course Xalan and Zofal and Hwe were to hand, and Viridese courtiers and clerks hovered nearby. But I doubted they could kill the Cayds quickly, and if it came to killing, speed would be essential—before reinforcements could be called, or word spread.

Carefully I maintained an unworried countenance as Musenor spoke. "We won't give up our ways," he said bluntly, "and we want some say in how Averidan is run."

Time, I knew, would ameliorate his first point, so I addressed the second. "You're aware that the Shan King's rule is absolute. Of course, I frequently consult my friends and family, and there are various collegiums and councils to give me advice."

The Cayds consulted in whispers; Musenor had seen enough now of Viridese bureaucracy to know that appointment to any official organization was a sentence to crushing boredom. One demanded, "What surety have we, that you won't slay us all someday when the fancy takes you?"

"My wife would be very angry if I did that," I said solemnly. A flicker of contempt crossed some faces—in Cayd women are not highly regarded—but those advisors who had wed Shan wives nodded. "Likewise, if you Cayds assassinate me, Siril-ven Tsormelezok will

have something to say to Prince Musenor, here." The
prince seemed to shudder at the thought.

Someone had another idea. "Let the prince's son be
named the heir, with the prince to rule as his regent if
he succeeds before manhood."

In Cayd this would be a major diplomatic trophy.
Through little Goris, Musenor would stand second in
the kingdom. "But I have no say in choosing my
sucessor," I explained. "The Collegium of Counselors
will do that after I die. Suppose I name you, prince, to
that Collegium. Then when the time comes you'll be
in a good position. I don't doubt you'll outlive me."

This was a handsome offer. "But how is this choosing done?" demanded the canniest Cayd.

I blinked. "I don't know," I had to admit. "Magister?"

Through some devious contrivance Xalan had acquired a set of magus robes, of the deep red silk
proper to the Master Magus of Averidan. They even
fit him exactly. He shook his head, reluctant to concede even minor ignorance. "I wasn't Magus, and so
of the Collegium, when they chose Your Majesty.
Shall I convene them, and introduce the prince?"

"Do so," I said, watching Musenor.

Slowly he nodded consent. We looked at each other
for a moment, letting the novel flavor of amity settle
onto our tongues. Then Musenor's glance fell on Sahai.
"Limaot guard! Is that a leopard?"

"Her name is Sahai, the same as my other cat," I
said.

The Cayds muttered uneasily at this. "You are a
witch, aren't you?" Musenor asked warily.

"I am not a necromant," I returned, knowing this
was their real fear. "I am the Son of the Sun. If the
powers in my care are malign, I will surely meet a
speedy and bad end. If that happens, please choose
my successor with more care."

The Cayds withdrew, still not entirely happy but on
the whole resigned to my rule. "Do you really mean to
die young, Liras-ven?" Zofal asked anxiously. "Mother

arrives from Cliffhole this evening, and she'd be furious to hear it."

"I'll live as long as I can," I promised. "Bring her to supper tonight, after I see the Collegium. We'll have a family reunion."

Though this first hurdle was safely past, I faced many more that day. Zofal had naively wished for things to be as they were. If only it could have been so simple. For the good of the realm some things had to be restored as quickly as possible—the Order of Magi, for instance. While laborers dug out the hidden magic scrolls and records in his cellar, Xalan sent word to every town and village calling the magi back out of hiding. But many aspects of Viridese life would have to be weighed and entirely recast, to fairly accommodate both races.

Pondering, I strolled across to the Temple of the Sun. Memory plays one false; when I last saw the sanctuary it had been sacked, the priestesses slain and the sacred fire doused. But that one terrible glimpse dissolved away in a hundred recollections of the Temple peaceful and well-tended, the worshipers filing in and out to make wishes and bring offerings. I half-expected the place to be as it had been: the unchanging heart of the realm. The shock was considerable when I came past the columned entrance to the outer court, and met face to face with a bull.

"More cattle!" I cried, angry. My orderly timidly pulled me to one side, and the bull, stolidly chewing cud, ambled out at the head of his cows. These beasts were not of Caydish stock, but barrel-bellied and long-horned, the Viridese draft-animals bred to pull ploughs and turn water-wheels. Their progress was rather slow, but I understood when the last few cattle meandered through. The City townspeople were acting as cow-herds, unskillfully urging the herd along with shouts and hand-clapping.

As I stepped in the courtyard rang with cheers. "Averidan!" "The Son of the Sun!" The news must have flown through the City in mere hours. Today was a holiday, the day un-numbered and of no month allotted to preparations for tomorrow: Mid Summer Day. So everyone was at leisure. My throat ached with unshed tears, and I fumbled frantically in my sleeve for a handkerchief; a Viridese noble is never without one but today seemed to be my exception. A bold person in the crowd held one out. When I was seen to take it, people began pressing closer, nearer than etiquette allows, but I forbade my attendants to push back. Slowly, shuffling through stableyard litter and cow dung, I progressed in to the sanctuary.

All signs of its dishonorable use as a cattle shed were rapidly vanishing under brooms and scrubbing brushes. The muck and straw had been swept out, the marble floor rinsed clean. Only the domed ceiling above remained denuded of its gold, shadowy and unfamiliar without the gleam of firelight. People had climbed the hill, reclaiming the great circular chamber almost instinctively, first of all. Their devotion had been less, before the Cayds came.

The noise of the last cleaning work gradually died down. A young woman edged through the crowd into my view, and hesitated in an agony of shyness until others nudged her forward. "You are the last of the Priestesses of the Sun," I surmised.

"Yes, Your Majesty." She bobbed a half-curtsy. "I had gone into the Upper City to order the sacrifice, that day . . ."

With the Crown's aid I assessed her. In memory of Viris our foremother, who we are told gave birth to Shan Vir-yan at the age of forty-two, Sun Priestesses aer usually women in their prime. This one, the most junior two years ago, had naturally performed the humbler duties. She did not look like a priestess now, barefoot and dressed like a vegetable seller. But I saw she was sensible and pious, not yet wise but possessing the seeds of wisdom. "I name you then the first Priestess of the Sun. Gather to the service of the god other good women, and maintain his worship as of old."

"My powers in your service, Your Majesty," she whispered.

Palpable as a tap on the shoulder I felt the presence of the One, reminding me. "The god has told me his name," I said shakily, with a sudden foreknowledge of what was to come. "Henceforward we must call him by it: *Thausra*."

There was a shocked pause, then a hum of whispered comment. The god's new Priestess diffidently voiced the inevitable, unanswerable reply: "We have never done so before. And the flames, the holy presence—we have no sacred fire."

The divine presence mounted up hotly in my chest, squeezing my breath and ringing in my ears. Yet I could control it to some extent, as one may a restive steed, hold it in until the time. "Bring fuel," I said tensely. "Wood, charcoal, tinder."

As they did so, I approached the altar, fixing my mind on the task of setting my feet one after the other. The roundel of granite was cold, but the black left by ten thousand years of fire could never be scoured away. A final sweep of a drying-rag, and then the wood and tinder were piled up by many hands. Someone passed the Priestess his flints to spark the first flame, but I gestured them away.

My flesh burned so warm I felt lightheaded, as with fever. "*Thausra*," I breathed, groaning. And as the god burst through, my voice repeated in a shout, "*Thausra!*"

The clustering shadows in the curve of the dome scattered like bats as the power arrowed through me into the stacked tinder. White light spouted from its center. In an instant the heap was alight and burning furiously. Swaying with the reaction I hardly heard the sigh and murmur of wonder from watchers all around. "I will speak to you of these matters later," I said to the new Priestess.

My spirit quite failed me when, emerging into the sunny central plaza, I found a host of Viridese casualties, the wounded and halt and lame. Many of these had just arrived from Mhee, and set up a cry for me to fulfill my promise.

In despair I leaned against a column, limper than an old dishcloth. The people were asking the impossible. Melayne had been right.

Then, very gently, the god spoke again through my mouth. I let the words emerge. "Bring Hwe," I heard myself command, and an attendant hurried to obey.

This second divine hint at last penetrated; I had to admire *Thausra's* management. Hwe shambled up, his shaggy brown head towering above those of my subjects, who gaped and pointed at this freak. In Rriat I told him, "Watch now what I do."

Selecting a man with a shriveled, tendon-cut leg, I reunited the hamstring with a touch. Then, smoothing away someone else's livid scar, I said, "Now you try."

The Shan disapprove of strangers on principle, but my endorsement made Hwe acceptable. The next in line, an old lady whose one thigh had set shorter than the other, did no more than watch sharply as Hwe put out a leathery hand. The bone straightened and strengthened, just as I might have made it. Hwe's deepset eyes lit up. "I can do!" he said in his thick Rriat.

"Do you know why?" I asked curiously, and he nodded, point at the amulet-bag hanging round his neck. "Keep it safe," I approved.

Stepping back, I called three of my courtiers forward. "Attend Hwe as he heals the wounded. See that he has food and rest, and whatever he may wish."

"But Your Majesty! Can he make his own needs known?" asked one, appalled.

"Not in the least," I smiled. "The lack makes him the best possible deputy for me. You shall have to exert your imaginations and intelligence."

It was late afternoon, already high time to meet with the Collegium. I hurried along the corridors, where the glass-polishers and lamp-fillers busily prepared the lamps for nightfall, and scattered suggestions and orders as they came to me. "Let all the officials of the Royal Mint wait upon my coming tomorrow . . . Surely all these crude draperies are unnecessary, could they be cut up into horse blankets? Oh, and have some stables cleared out, Zofal-ven will surely make a trip to the marshes and bring back his horses very soon . . ."

In the antechamber Prince Musenor waited, with not a very good grace, for me to call him in. The inner chamber where the Collegium sat was opulent with mosaic and carved wooden chairs, but not large, the Counselors being only the seven masters and mistresses of the ancient Shan orders. And only five had been able to answer Xalan's summons in time. "We must get the magi and their mirrors working again," Xalan grumbled.

I hardly heard him, as a slim figure in brown linen rose from her chair. "Silverhand!" Until this moment I had assumed the Commander was dead. Now I realized I had foolishly underestimated her courage. Though it is not prudent to touch a Sister of Mir-hel uninvited, I swept round the table and embraced my rescuer.

Commander Silverhand's smile warmed her keen face, incongruously sweet as ever. "I want to hear all about your triumph over Mor!" she said, squeezing my shoulders eagerly. "You've heard our saying, that to win without a battle takes supreme skill."

"Well, as to that—Xalan?" I made an inviting gesture.

Quickly he opened the council. "Honored ladies, esteemed sirs, I am Xalan the Master Magus. His Majesty had directed me to lay before the Collegium a proposed settlement with the Cayds."

As I had expected, my Counselors were not enthusiastic. "But we must kill them all," Silverhand said, as if stating some basic truth. "They've preyed upon us, now we must wipe them off Averidan's fair countenance, and put things right."

"Yes!" "Let them go back home, or die."

I held up a quieting hand. "The Master Magus here and I came through Tiyalor and Cayd to Averidan. It is my opinion that the Cayds cannot go back."

Xalan smoothed his mustache thoughtfully. "I wish

it weren't so, but it is," he confirmed. "As for killing them all—we're about two years late on that. If we couldn't do it then, with a strong Sisterhood and a full-strength Army, is it even possible now?"

"But I don't wish to live with them." The new Sun Priestess spoke up in trembling tones. "The Cayds are barbarians. I saw the Temple sanctuary, that terrible day it was sacked. You can't imagine it."

"I too was there," I put in gently. "And I say to you all, that this is the only way remaining to us. It won't be nearly as bad as you dread. Don't the stories say that, invaders or immigrants, everyone who lives in Averidan eventually becomes Shan?"

"Plaiv," the old Lord Chronicler sniffed.

"There is nothing the Cayds can offer us," the Mistress Herbal insisted. "I want things as they were."

"Oh, but that wouldn't be *entirely* desirable," Xalan said quickly. "Think of all the things we'd have to give up—lamb and veal and beef. And butter, and cream. Draft-oxen are pretty poor eating, but the Cayds know how to raise toothsome livestock. Has anyone visited the riverside cookshops? There's the place to sample some treats . . ."

The entire discussion, diverted by clever Xalan, turned down culinary byways. I let them run on a while, only interrupting when the Mistress Herbal tangled herself in a complicated recipe involving that delectable new substance, butter. "Prince Musenor waits outside. Let us call him in to take his seat on the Collegium."

The Lord Chronicler, accustomed to taking the long view, asked, "Do you mean to create a Caydish seat, then? Forever expand the Collegium from seven to eight?"

It did not take me much thought to respond. "No—this is a sole exception; Musenor shall not hand the seat to his heirs, or designate a sucessor either. He will outlive me, and so get to help choose the next Shan King, which is all he wants. And when he dies, you will be seven again."

"Maybe I'll hasten that day with a knife," Silverhand said, but without heat.

"Oh, but wait—before he comes in." I looked round the table. The gentle midsummer twilight filled the room, but no servant could enter to light the lamps while the Collegium sat. "He will ask this, so tell me as well—how is the Shan King chosen?"

So terrible had these past years been, that few here had been present when I was selected, out of all Averidan, to be Shan King. The Priestess of Ennelith, her aging face placid between the blue sidepieces of her headdress, smiled at me. "From the genealogies we choose out the names of young men, and from them those of decent life."

"And then?"

Silverhand laughed softly at my eager interest, but the Priestess remained grave. "We use a pin—I believe, five years ago, it was one of these." She indicated one of the long bronze pins that held her headdress. "The Priestess of the Sun has the privilege of pricking out on the scrolls the one name. Of course," she added, "we invoke the Sun, and Ennelith, to guide the pin to one of true honor."

"Then it's *random?*" It took me a moment to recover from this blow to my self-importance. When one came to think about it, though, it was obvious that anyone would do. The Crystal Crown is the continuity of Averidan, the sole channel through which transforming power flows. Rightly had *Thausra* told me, that its power was to change living things. At last I said, "Were I you, I'd tell Prince Musenor only that last part. Let him hear about the pin a few years from now."

Leaving them, under Xalan's tactful direction, to become acquainted with their new colleague, I hurried to dress for supper. In these few hours the long-frustrated royal robemakers had created a garment of supreme elegance, all liquid green silk under stiffer emerald satin. Yards of trailing sleeve, lined and interlined with tints of green made swift motion impossible.

Decent Shan jewelry would take some days to craft, and my wardrobe attendants deplored the cruder Caydish gems, not quite holding their noses over King Mor's caskets. So by former standards I left their hands quite under-dressed.

It felt very odd all the same, to walk with silk sliding over my legs, and I discovered I had nearly forgotten the trick of keeping my sleeves out from under my feet. Only one incident delayed me, when as I passed an open door someone cried, "There he is!"

The chamberlain tried unsuccessfully to shut the door, but Zaryas of Mishbil imperiously thrust him aside. In a swish of green and white sleeves she bowed low before me, her narrow face smiling all over. "It's unceremonious but I have to say it—I told you so," she declared, smugly.

I had to grin too, and dented etiquette further by taking her old dry hand in both of mine. "I see the Cayds didn't catch you! Did they sack Mishbil after all?"

"Ah! they never got so far. Though I did entertain several belligerent Caydish envoys, and oiled them all over with meek promises. They were saving us for when the coastal resistance was scotched." She dismissed all these politics with a gesture. "I've brought you a welcome-present."

"Your presents always delight me." I was surprised, though, when I saw three guardsmen of Mishbil inside. They surrounded a richly-dressed Viridese, hunched up in misery on the tile floor.

"Not as perfect a gift as I'd like," Zaryas frowned. "I think he's Bochas-hel, that rhetor who sold the City out during the siege. But he says he's not. You'll have to find someone who knew him then."

"Not so." I smiled as she glanced sideways at the restored Crown on my head. I cast my eye over her captive, and read him to the core. "Yes, it is he."

At the sound of my voice Bochas slewed round, ashen. "No! my name is Sarnet, I'm a rhetor from the north—"

"Truly?" He faltered, and I had to smile. "No one can lie to the Shan King."

Rhetors are nothing if not glib. "Then, I meant no harm, I didn't think that—"

I cut off the rattle of words with a gesture. "Is Execution Rock still extant? Good. Have my men see to his lapidation, princess. If you have it tomorrow morning, plenty of people can participate."

My tardiness had given the family plenty of time to coalesce into two opposing camps, an atmosphere so homelike and comfortable that I paused in the doorway to enjoy it. The two children were for once playing amiably together, Tarys busily collecting the cushions and pillows into a heap while little Goris hailed each contribution by patting it. Melayne and Siril-ven sulked at either end of the room. Beautifully dressed, poor Musenor sat between, trying to conciliate wife and sister with a series of uncomfortable remarks: "Don't you think, Melayne, that Goris has a look of our royal father? Especially the hands, already he has a grip of bronze . . . Wife, I don't like to see you scowl. You've been fretting about your younger brother for years, and now he's back you're gloomy . . . I like your bracelet there, Melayne, is it of metal?"

"Where is Mother?" I interrupted.

"Changing out of her traveling robes," Siril said. "You have to talk to her, Liras-ven. She's getting far too cozy with those pirates at Cliffhole, and neglecting us. Do you know, she even refused to meet Musenor here?"

"Well, it was only reasonable while she was working to overthrow Mor and me," Musenor said, with resignation. "I wouldn't have cared to meet her then, either—it might have been awkward."

His sensible explanation passed right over Siril's head. "And she hasn't seen my darling Goris!"

"She's seen Tarys," Melayne put in silkily. "I remember her saying the baby was the loveliest infant— even prettier than her own, when they were born."

Siril, who is unutterably vain, glared at her. "I'm so

glad I bore a boy," she snapped. "My spouse wished for one."

"Did you really now, Musenor," I broke in, in great haste. "Do you plan to train the boy up to the use of arms? Caydish mode, or Viridese style?" With my brother-in-law's help, I forcibly held the talk to neutral subjects until Mother entered on Zofal-ven's arm.

Running a revolution suited my formidable mother; since I saw her last, she had resorted to hair-dye again, so her high-piled tresses were black and glossy as ever. Delicately painted, her face looked like that of a much younger woman, even when I leaned close to kiss her. Much was explained, when my pirate friend Pol followed her in; the shoredwellers have a well-known fascination with strong women. Only her shoulder bones still felt fragile under my embracing arm. "You haven't been eating properly," I said, swallowing tears.

"Neither have you!" Her slim hands patted my cheek possessively. "But that scar's almost gone. You are as weather-beaten as a fisherman, Liras-ven! And how is your poor hand?"

"Perfectly usable, I never need those two fingers. You must greet Tarys and Melayne—Tarys-yan, do you remember your grandmother?"

Tarys plainly did not, and showed it by flailing her arms and legs when Mother tried to hold her. "How big she's grown," Mother marveled, doting. "And you still nurse her, my dear daughter-in-law?"

"Yes, mother-in-law," Melayne said. She dipped her trailing sleeves and long hems, all the color of buttercup blooms, into a low dutiful curtsey. I was proud of her; no Viridese could do better.

Screaming her fury, Tarys squirmed free. "Here is a much more mannerly baby, dear Mother," Siril said. "Your first grandson!" She thrust little Goris forward.

Mother did not quite recoil, but folded her arms firmly inside her sleeves. Beneath the paint her face was hard as wood. "I dreamed of poor Dasan-hel the

other night, daughter. I'm certain it's because he had
no proper funeral."

This mention of Siril's first husband was a slight that
even Musenor could hardly miss. His embarrassed flush
was plainly visible under the fair Caydish skin. Pol
rolled his eyes eloquently, but did not dare interfere.
Siril bit her lip and hugged her baby. I clapped my
hands for the chamberlain. "Food," I ordered; no one
in Averidan talks seriously while eating, so there would
be a respite.

Still, the meal was so tense I could scarcely enjoy it,
and after three courses sent for Xalan. My Master
Magus obligingly left his own table and, sitting at the
farther end of mine, chatted amiably with Musenor
and Siril about the weather. Meanwhile at our end
Zofal and I talked distractedly to Pol about the horses,
and thought hard. Mother must be made to unbend.

Everyone felt better when the meal was over, and
we rose. Zofal seated Mother on a couch and began to
extol the sweetness of Viridese family unity, a subject
with very little evidence to bolster it. Melayne took
advantage of the bustle to murmur, "I'm weaning
Tarys tomorrow."

It was a surprising decision to make at a supper-
party. "You are?"

"Yes—and come to my chambers tonight. We're
starting on your son immediately."

I sighed but knew better than to argue. As I had
expected, Zofal's argument had quickly become graveled for lack of examples. He gave me a grateful look
when I came up. "Do you remember, Mother, the last
time we dined together so, and walked out on the
terrace? Come take a stroll with me now."

I put her hand on my arm and curbed my longer
stride to match hers. "My joints still ache somewhat,"
she sighed. "It's all that damp coastal air."

"You must come back inland sometimes now, and
visit," I said. "Siril still retains the old house and its
lands."

She bridled a little at the mention of Siril, and then

sighed again. "I do not understand that girl. To wed a murdering Cayd, the killer of her own spouse!"

"But Mother, I wed one too." I patted her hand. "She had no choice at all, and you know it. Besides, she's done her best to tame the prince. Look at his clothes."

I could not suppress a snort of laughter, and after a moment Mother sniggered too. "He looks like a clown—far too grand for his station. Of course he's trying to compete with you, dear. Siril should choose him a more restrained wardrobe-master."

The night was mild and clear. Above, the stars sparkled like the very best sequined beading on a black silk sky-dome. Mellow lamplight poured onto the pavement from every triple-arched window, so that we trod in and out of pools of gold. I had put off the Crown, knowing it would make my family nervous. This battle could not be fought with that weapon. Reflecting on my words, I spoke slowly. "A wise man told me once that one can never go back. Nothing we do can really restore Averidan to what it was. Even if I could, I would not. When Shan Vir-yan had the Crystal Crown made to ensure Averidan's existence always, he didn't exclude growth. We have to go forward to meet life."

"You mean, we have to cozy up to our conquerors." But Mother's voice was a little less resentful. We turned, and began to stroll back. "You always were ridiculously afflicted as a child with the most toplofty ideas. You almost make me wish you were right."

"*Chun-hei*, I have found, is the most important quality in a Shan King." The children had followed us out. Tarys toddled up to wrestle ferociously with my robed legs, and little Goris followed, crawling as Siril had boasted. "I wouldn't ask you to clasp Musenor to your heart. But you'd be sorry, later, to have snubbed little Goris-lat here. He has a look of you."

I spoke this blatant lie with complete gravity, counting on the fact that the child's features were so fat he might grow up to resemble anybody. Tarys yelled with

jealous fury when I lifted the boy and held him out.
With a final sigh Mother took the child. "Viris love
him, but he's heavy."

This was not the moment to suggest that Goris
inherited his father's build. "Well-fed," I said. I swung
Tarys to my shoulder and stood aside so Mother could
go back in. The lamplight poured past us, making the
children rub their eyes. Inside, my family stared open-
mouthed at the reversal I had managed to bring about.

"He does have black hair," Mother noted, pleased.